"Keep your se[illegible] ear made her jump. "They're innocent enough."

"How do you know?" She wished she'd bitten her tongue. The last thing she wanted was to spend time on the schoolhouse steps for all the town to see, engaged in a soul-searching conversation with Grey North, but she could not tear herself away without hearing his answer.

"It's in your clear green eyes and your rosy, kissable mouth." He leaned forward, so close she was afraid he meant to put the "kissable" comment to the test . . .

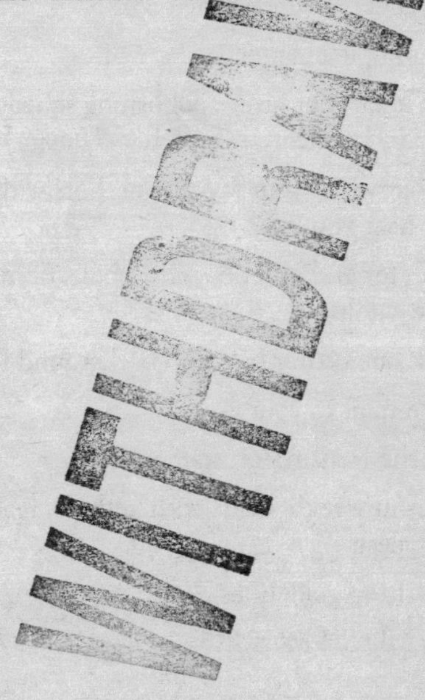

Her One And Only

ALICE VALDAL

ZEBRA BOOKS
Kensington Publishing Corp.
www.kensingtonbooks.com

ZEBRA BOOKS are published by

Kensington Publishing Corp.
850 Third Avenue
New York, NY 10022

ISBN: 0-8217-7837-4

First Printing: July 2006
10 9 8 7 6 5 4 3 2 1

Printed in the United States of America

With thanks to my editor,
Hilary Sares,
for her wise insights,
her encouragement
and her willingness to guide a neophyte
through the mysteries of the publishing world.

Chapter One

Emma Douglas stood alone on the schoolhouse steps, watching the bride and groom drive away in their brand new buggy. The other guests had gone inside, out of the November chill, but she lingered a little longer, watching the lifeless leaves scudding along the empty street, studying the frost-blackened corn stalks in the vicar's garden. She shivered and glanced once more toward the disappearing buggy. *Lucky Lottie. She'd a second chance for happiness.*

Her eyes misted. The soul-deep love she'd glimpsed between Sean and Lottie as they'd exchanged their marriage vows was the stuff of dreams. She straightened her shoulders and turned back to the schoolroom. She'd lost the time for dreams.

"Lovely party, Miss Douglas." Rev. Acheson shook her hand before departing.

"More than she deserves," Thelma Black huffed, making Emma wonder why she'd been so eager to usurp the hostess's position behind the teapot. Before she could ask the question, Thelma pushed past her and sprinted down the steps in pursuit of Prospect's most eligible bachelor. "Oh, Mr. North!"

"Are you sure you don't want me to stay and help you clean up?" Sadie Gardener, laden down with hampers of empty teacups and cake plates lingered in the open doorway after all the other guests had departed. Her husband, Abner, waited impatiently beside his horses, casting an anxious eye at the lowering sky. "I hate to leave you with all this mess."

"Nonsense." Emma was brisk and cheerful. "I'll have it all set to rights in no time. You get on home." She took one of the hampers from Sadie's hand and carried it out to the wagon. "Hurry home now. You want to get ahead of the weather." She waved them off, then hurried inside, closing the door on the November wind. Alone, she surveyed the empty schoolhouse.

The pupils' desks had been pushed aside and a long table set up under the windows along one wall. Cake crumbs and dirt from mud-caked boots littered the floor. Beside the potbellied stove debris from the firewood awaited a broom and a dustpan. The water bucket was empty. All that remained of the festivities was a large message of congratulations to Sean and Lottie written on the blackboard at the front of the room.

She firmed her lips and reached for the broom. A draft of cold air circled her ankles. "Want some help?" Grey North, broad shouldered, blonde, and handsome, ambled in through the unlocked door, his cheeks ruddy with cold, his blue eyes alight with vitality. His curly brimmed hat set at a jaunty angle, his coat casually unbuttoned to reveal a finely tailored waistcoat, he filled the room with his presence.

Emma stiffened and stepped behind the teacher's desk, centered on a raised platform at the front of the room. "I can manage alone, thank you." She didn't like Grey North. He made her nervous. Though he spoke with the precise tones of an English public school, he was careless in his dress and much too casual in his manners. As a proper, spinster schoolmarm it behooved her to keep him at a distance, but he seemed impervious to her cool attitude. She'd tried to hide behind a wall of reserve, but he blew through her careful life like a strong wind.

"Don't go all starchy on me, Emma. I'm not one of your pupils." He grinned at her, completely unabashed by her tart tones. "It seems to me you could use a hand." His glance took in the rows of desks still shuffled against one wall.

"Mr. North!" She would not permit him to call her by her first name. Her father . . . She closed her mouth on the angry words. Her father could no more defend her honor than he could his own.

"Grey, please."

"I beg your pardon?" She blinked rapidly, trying to clear her memory of the sight of her beloved, distinguished father sprawled on the expensive Axminster carpet of his private study, a pistol in his hand and a pool of blood beneath his head.

"Call me Grey," her impudent visitor repeated. "We're on the frontier now, Emma. There's no room here for the nonsensical formalities of San Francisco's upper crust or London's stuffy hostesses."

"What do you know of formalities?" She shot a haughty glance at his mud-caked boots and carelessly knotted tie.

"A damn sight more than I care to," he muttered, and for a moment she saw a blazing anger behind the bland smile. He covered it so quickly she might have imagined it, but just for an instant she believed she had seen the real Grey North. Despite herself, she couldn't help wondering what had brought that flash of wrath to a face that seemed always to smile and keep its secrets.

She gripped the broom more tightly and closed her mind to such foolish imaginings. She neither knew nor cared where Grey North had come from. She only wished he would get out of her schoolhouse and let her get on with things. "If you don't mind, I've work to do." She stepped away from her desk to ply her broom on the schoolhouse floor only to scuttle back to the safety of her rostrum when he plucked the whisk from her hands.

"Really, Mr. North," she primmed her mouth to its most school teacherish, "I wish you would go. It's not proper for us to be here alone." Even standing on the platform she was only at eye level with him, a fact that allowed her to see his teasing twinkle all too clearly. She wished she could squelch him as easily as she did her impudent pupils. Unfortunately, a hard stare and a sharp word had no effect whatsoever on Grey North.

"Then you'd better hurry up and finish tidying the place," he said, "'cause I'm not leaving until you do." He swept vigorously, raising more dust than he cleared, then opened the schoolhouse door and brushed the dirt outside. She'd have to do it over again, properly, and sweep the front steps besides.

"If I go and get some firewood, can you manage to clean the blackboard by yourself?" His mocking smile was designed to infuriate. "I'll move the desks after I've filled the wood box."

She knew he was goading her, trying to make her rise to his bait, but she couldn't halt the angry flush that stained her cheeks. She sought refuge in a haughty silence but Grey was undaunted. The silence between them stretched long and loud as he waited for her reply. She wouldn't put it past him to remain stock still in the center of the room until nightfall and beyond if she refused to give her assent. "Yes, fine," she snapped and picked up the brush to clean the blackboard, pointedly turning her back on him.

"Good." He left her then, bent on his errand.

The minute he was out the door she rushed from behind her desk, intending to lock him outside, but his mocking voice floated back to her as she shot the bolt. "If you don't unbolt the door, I'll stay out here in the street and shout at you until all the citizens of Prospect come running to see what the fuss is about."

She had no doubt he'd make good on his threat and reluctantly undid the lock. But she wasn't taking orders from Grey North. She grasped the first set of desks and shoved, sending them sliding into place with quick, efficient movements. The next set followed the first and then another, until all five rows were restored to their places, ready for her twenty pupils at nine o'clock on Monday morning. She dusted off her hands and regarded the alignment of the desks critically, then used her hip to nudge the back row a fraction to the left.

"And what would the good ladies of Frisco say to that maneuver?" She whirled about to discover Grey, his arms full of wood and his blue eyes full of frank appraisal, regarding her from the doorway.

She blushed a furious red and wished she *had* locked the door. At least he'd have made a fool of himself as well as of her if he'd been seen shouting in the street.

He sauntered toward her, as tall and proud as a lord, despite the ungainly load of firewood in his arms. She couldn't imagine any of her beaux at home performing such a menial task with such careless insouciance. Certainly not Parnell Wilde. Her mind shied away from the thought. Parnell with his dark elegance, graceful carriage, and immaculate tailoring was as far from this hard-bodied, powerful blond giant as San Francisco was from Prospect.

Grey dropped the wood into the box beside the stove, then strode to the front of the room to erase the last of the chalked messages on the blackboard. "Now, why couldn't you have done that and left the heavy lifting to me?" He turned; his eyes challenging her, a lazy smile playing about his lips. "I thought you ladies," he made the word sound like an insult, "didn't stoop to hard labor."

Furious with his insolent manner she forgot about her embarrassment and let her temper run free. "Mr. North, I did not ask you to come here. I did not ask you to perform my work. I did not ask your opinion of my character or my background. You are rude, insulting, insinuating, and impertinent. I have endeavored to be polite, but you are apparently too thickheaded to recognize when a lady wishes to avoid your attentions, so I will tell you outright. I don't like you, Mr. North. I want you to leave me alone."

There was a moment of stunned silence while she congratulated herself on having put him in his place. Oddly, she was no longer blushing, although such an unladylike outburst should have left her covered with embarrassment. Instead, she felt wondrously free and powerful. Using plain words instead of honeyed hints was delightfully refreshing. Then he threw back his head and laughed, his amusement issuing from his throat in rich, genuine mirth. Her self-satisfaction wilted like an alpine flower before the frost, but her anger flared as brightly as the fire that filled the stove. She picked up a small stick of wood from the wood box and hurled it across the room at her tormentor, catching him smartly on the shin.

Horrified with her behavior she would have apologized, but he laughed even harder. "Ah, Emma," he gasped between guffaws, stooping to rub his injured leg, "you're wonderful, with a temper to match that fiery hair of yours. You'd have been wasted in some namby-pamby drawing room down south. Welcome to the frontier, my dear. I love a woman of spirit." He shoved his hands in his pockets and rocked back on his heels, studying her with a thoughtful gaze. "I understand you've just refused your third marriage proposal."

"Fourth." She corrected him without thinking, then blushed when amusement lit his face. "Not that it's any of your business."

"Sit down, Emma." He perched on the edge of a pupil's desk, bracing himself with one foot, and crossed his arms over his chest. "I've a proposition for you. No, wait." He held up his hand to still the angry words that hovered on her tongue. "Nothing indecent. I believe, since you have refused *four*"—he emphasized the word—"proposals, that you have no interest in marriage. Right?"

She glowered at him, refusing to reply to such a presumptuous question.

"Do you know your eyes turn green when you're angry?" he remarked in a conversational tone. "They're very green just now." He grinned and swung one foot, the action emphasizing the length of his legs.

Emma jerked her gaze away and stared pointedly at the clock over his shoulder.

"Taking refuge in silence?" He shrugged. "Maybe it's just as well, gives me a chance to lay out my entire argument without interruption." He cleared his throat and launched into what sounded to Emma like a rehearsed speech. "Since you've no interest in marriage and no more have I, my proposition, Miss Douglas, is that we form a mutual protection league. I'll pay court to you and you'll smile at me and bat your lashes, both of us fully aware that we are only playing a game. The result of our charade will be to fend off unwanted suitors for you and remove me from the sights of predatory females."

Her eyes widened in shock and she plopped into the nearest seat with a gasp. "That's preposterous."

"Why?"

"It's dishonest."

"Not if you and I agree to the terms beforehand."

She opened her mouth to argue, then closed it again without speaking. Even though she wanted to reject the whole idea, she found herself actually considering his proposal. The stream of would-be suitors who accosted her on every occasion was tiresome. Necessity had forced her into school teaching, but it had also given her an independence she valued. Grey was quite right to assume she had no interest in marriage. She cocked her head and studied his face. He was handsome, in a square-jawed sort of way, even if his manners left something to be desired. "I'd have thought you could discourage Thelma Black without my assistance." She couldn't resist the gibe.

"Ah," he nodded with satisfaction, "you've noticed. I'm flattered."

"Don't be," she snapped. "It didn't take any particular attention to note Miss Black's interest in you."

"I stand rebuked." He pushed himself off the desk and swept her a courtly bow, but a less contrite face she'd never seen. "Now, what do you say? Shall we make a bargain?"

"I'll think about it." She stood up and went to fetch her outdoor clothes, but he was there before her.

"Come on, firebrand." He held her coat for her. "I'll walk you home."

"You will not."

"Shall I follow you, then?" His eyes sparked with mischief. "Like the prince consort, two paces behind Her Majesty?"

She wouldn't put it past him to do just that, making her a laughingstock for the whole town. She scowled and thrust her arms into her coat, then stepped quickly away from him. "I've just recalled that my contract requires that I teach Sunday school and observe an eight-o'clock curfew and not entertain gentlemen callers. I fear I cannot accept your proposition, Mr. North."

"Your contract hasn't discouraged other suitors," he pointed out with calm logic. "Now, put on your hat and let's go." He stood solid and unyielding before her. "We'll discuss it further on the way."

She glowered at him and wished she could best him on at least one point, but in the end came to the conclusion that if Grey North intended to see her safely home, he would not be dissuaded. Obnoxious, pigheaded, irritating . . . She set her hat on her head, stabbed a long pin through the unadorned felt, and yanked on her gloves. She marched past him and out the door, then turned to face him, hands on her hips, and made one last attempt to assert herself. "I haven't yet agreed to your subterfuge, Mr. North, and I don't need an escort. It's perfectly safe for me to walk to my boardinghouse alone. I do it every day of the week." She turned the key in the schoolhouse door and tested the lock with a hard shove.

"It was safe yesterday, and it may be safe today—or maybe not."

"Why not?" His mysterious manner goaded her into asking the question.

"We all have a past, Emma. Yours may have caught up to you."

"I don't know what you mean." She attempted an

offhand comment, but her lips felt stiff and her heart thudded hard against her ribs.

"There's a chap over at the hotel, says he's from San Francisco. Been asking about an Abigail Douglas." He caught her arm and steadied her as she stumbled on the boardwalk. "Hold on. You all right?"

"Yes, yes, of course." She hated the breathless quality of her voice and strove to cover her confusion. "It was just an uneven plank in the boardwalk. I've noticed it before."

"I'll have it repaired."

She shot him a quick glance and saw that he was entirely sincere. Much as he irritated her, Grey North was a man to be reckoned with. His hotel, the Rockingham, was prosperous and popular, hosting not only miners coming into town to spend their earnings, but visiting dignitaries from the provincial capital in Victoria, wealthy tourists traveling the territory, and businessmen looking for new opportunities. He was a member of the Prospect Mining Association, a kind of informal town council, and, she suddenly recalled with chagrin, one of the school trustees. He well knew the terms of her contract.

"This man at your hotel," she said as they paced along the street, "did he say anything else?" She hated having to ask but couldn't help herself. She'd made no secret of her California roots when she'd come to Prospect, but that was all. She'd divulged nothing of her past, including her reasons for leaving San Francisco.

"Can't say as he did." He pushed open the gate in her landlady's fence and waited while she walked through. "Seemed a secretive sort of chap." He halted at the steps to the house and fixed her with a compelling gaze. "Anything you want to tell me, Emma? I'm ready to stand your friend."

For a moment she hesitated, then shook her head. "No." Her voice was soft but determined. "Thank you for your escort, sir." She held out her hand to him.

"It has been my pleasure, Miss Douglas." He bowed low, doffing his hat and practically sweeping the walkway with it in a mockery of polite manners. But when he raised his eyes to hers the laughter died, replaced with an icy blue intensity. "Take care, Emma. I told the man at the hotel I'd never heard of an *Abigail* Douglas, but he's staying on another three days. I'll be here in the morning."

She nodded briefly, then without another word turned on her heel and fled.

"Oh, Miss Douglas, there you are." Mrs. Royston's penetrating voice assailed her ears the moment she stepped inside. "You're very late."

She gripped her hands together hard and turned to present a calm countenance to her landlady. Mrs. Royston was a widow with a large house and an even larger inquisitiveness about the schoolmarm who rented her second bedroom. Of all the hardships Emma had endured since coming to Prospect, the lack of personal privacy was the most difficult to bear. Secretly she longed to have a house of her own, but such a wish was foolish. In spite of existing on the edge of the wilderness, Prospect was very strict about the proprieties. Victorian decorum prevailed even in this remote outpost of the British Empire. Young women did not live alone.

"Miss Douglas?"

"Yes," she said coolly, schooling her features to betray none of the agitation that churned inside her, "there was considerable work to do putting the schoolroom in order following the wedding reception. I hope I didn't worry you with my tardiness."

"Well," Mrs. Royston seemed taken aback by the suggestion that she should be concerned for her boarder, but she recovered quickly, "of course I feel a certain responsibility for a young lady such as yourself, alone and unchaperoned."

But not enough to stay at the schoolhouse and sweep the floor. Emma's thoughts were waspish, but the words she spoke were bland and conciliatory. "You're quite right, Mrs. Royston." She made to move past her hostess and mount the stairs to her room.

"Oh, you're not going up already, are you?" Mrs. Royston's avid features loomed in front of her. "Do come into the parlor and have a cup of tea with me. We've not had a chance to discuss that outlandish dress Crazy Lottie—I should say Mrs. O'Connor now—wore for a wedding in November. Yellow silk, for heaven's sake. And her with a ten-year-old son already." She led the way into her front parlor and Emma had no choice but to follow. "A woman like that should have been content with a plain black suit and a quick word in the minister's study. Mind, when my Henry passed on, I didn't come out of mourning for five years."

Mrs. Royston bustled about the ornate room, straightening a lace doily on the sofa back and seating herself on a low chair, the tea things laid out on a small table in front of her. She poured tea into a fine china cup and passed it to Emma along with a plate of sweets. "Do sit down, Miss Douglas. Yellow silk, indeed!"

"As I understand it, Mrs. O'Connor has been a widow for ten years." Emma felt compelled to defend the new bride. Lottie's son, Michael, was one of her pupils, and from what she knew his mother had endured much hardship and sorrow. It wasn't for the likes of Mrs. Royston to begrudge her her happiness now. Besides, Emma had her own particular reasons for discouraging gossip.

"Widow, my foot." Mrs. Royston bit into a cake with relish. "Crazy Lottie was never married. Young Michael is a b—"

"Mrs. Royston, please! Such language is offensive."

"Well," Mrs. Royston conceded, "I guess now that there's so many ladies in town I'll have to remember my drawing room manners. Not like the old days. We pioneer women were a lot tougher than today's misses."

"I believe Mrs. O'Connor was one of you."

Mrs. Royston looked thoughtful for a moment and the gleam of spite faded from her eye. "Yes," she nodded slowly and took another bite of cake, "yes, she was. It was more than ten years ago. Times were harder then, but she seemed eager for adventure. She was just a green girl, but after she made her mistake she gritted it out and made a life for herself. Young Michael has never been hungry or cold." She swallowed the last of her cake and dusted the crumbs from her fingers. "You're right, Miss Douglas, Lottie has earned her place. Besides," she said with a demure glance, "Jed Barclay from the Mercantile sets great store by her, and Jed's no fool."

"I'm sure you're right." Emma set down her empty cake plate and stood up. She would have gone to her room but, once again, Mrs. Royston forestalled her.

"Tell me about your pupils, Miss Douglas. Is that Smith girl learning anything or just avoiding her chores by going to school?" And so it went. Mrs. Royston asking questions about various families with children in school and Emma doing her best not to add spice to the pot of gossip her landlady kept constantly on the boil.

At the same time as she fended off Mrs. Royston's curiosity, Emma brooded about the visitor at the Rockingham.

Who had come looking for her? The police? The bank? Her head began to ache from thinking so hard. When Mrs. Royston finally stopped to draw a breath, she made her escape. "Thank you for the tea, Mrs. Royston. If you don't mind, I believe I will go and rest for a time before supper."

"Before you go, Miss Douglas," Bella Royston had on her sly look, "there was a gentleman here earlier today asking after you." She cocked her head to one side, her beady eyes giving her the look of a curious blackbird. "A Mr. Jergens? Said he was a friend of your family?"

Emma sat down abruptly, all the air escaping her lungs in a sudden burst of warring emotions. Everett Jergens must be the man staying at Grey North's hotel. Everett was her staunchest supporter, a longtime friend of her father's, the only one to stand by her when Matt Douglas died. He was also the man who could have her arrested.

"You all right, Miss Douglas? You look kind of pale."

"I'm just a little surprised," Emma said, fanning herself with her hand. *A little surprised?* That had to be the understatement of all time.

"Seems to me you'd best be watching your step, Miss Douglas. A gentleman from the States asking after you and Grey North walking you home? Prospect expects its school teacher to be above reproach."

"There has been nothing untoward in my behavior, Mrs. Royston." Anger stiffened Emma's backbone and she rose swiftly to her feet. "It is not my fault. . . ." She bit off what she had intended to say. She would not give her landlady the pleasure of speculating about her and Grey North.

"I'm sure it's not, dear." Mrs. Royston effused sympathy. "Why don't you tell me all about it? Perhaps I can help."

"That won't be necessary." This time Emma succeeded

in removing herself from the room. At the foot of the stairs she turned. "Thank you for the tea, Mrs. Royston. I'll see you at suppertime."

"What do you want me to say if that Jergens fellow calls again?"

Emma closed her eyes and silently implored her Maker for courage. "You may tell him I am in," she replied, and fled up the stairs before Mrs. Royston could find another excuse to detain her.

Alone in her room she removed her hat and placed it on the hatstand on her bureau, folded her gloves neatly into the top drawer, and flopped backward onto the bed with a fine disregard for ladylike posture. She stared at the ceiling while her thoughts whirled through her brain like the images in a kaleidoscope. Everett Jergens standing by her at her mother's grave. Everett teaching a ten-year-old Emma to ride, leading her pony around the paddock while her father watched from the top rail of the fence. Everett and her father watching her with indulgent admiration as she'd set off for her first debutante ball. Everett's worried countenance in the days leading up to her father's suicide, when the two men had held long consultations behind the heavy oak door of Matt Douglas's study. Finally, with tears in her eyes, she remembered Everett Jergens standing steadfastly beside her while the police pronounced her father dead by his own hand.

In their own self-interest, the bank had suppressed word of her father's embezzling but they'd confiscated all his accounts. Very soon after, old friends no longer came to call. With Everett's help, she'd sold everything she owned and turned that money over to the bank as well. Her loyal friend had then offered her a home. Yet, despite Everett Jergens's protection, she couldn't face the whispers and the sneers of people she had used to count as friends. Even Parnell Wilde, her fiancé, had turned cold and distant. When she'd offered him his freedom, he'd taken his ring and bolted like a rat leaving a ship. It was the final ignominy. She'd run away, taking the money from Everett's desk to purchase her passage. She'd left a note, promising to return it, but she never had. No matter her intentions, she was no better than a common thief.

And now Everett was here, in Prospect, and Grey North thought she needed protection. It was too ridiculous. She got up and poured cold water from the ewer into a basin and splashed some on her face. She was no longer the girl who'd run away from her problems. She had grown up in the last two years. It was time to face up to the consequences of her actions. She owed Everett more than money.

She couldn't go calling at the hotel this late at night. Even if she could have escaped Mrs. Royston's watchful eye, she daren't risk her job. She would have to find a way to see him tomorrow. Firm in her resolve to right at least one wrong, she tidied her hair, pasted a smile on her face, and went downstairs to have dinner with her landlady.

"Oh, look! He's here!" Mrs. Royston turned from peering through the lace curtains in her front window. "Hurry, Miss Douglas. He's waiting right there in the street."

"Thank you, Mrs. Royston." Emma checked her appearance in the hall mirror one last time, trying to pretend that she wasn't torn between apprehension and an eager desire to see her old friend. Satisfied that her hat was straight and her coat neatly buttoned, she sailed out the front door, head high, back straight, acutely conscious of Mrs. Royston's eager eye at the window.

"Good morning, Emma." Grey's mocking tones drove the smile from her face and the lightness from her feet.

"What are you doing here?" She stopped dead and looked up and down the short street, seeking the burly form of Everett Jergens. Apart from Grey North, the road was empty.

"Keeping my promise."

"Mr. North," she practically huffed with exasperation, "what can I do to persuade you I neither need nor want your escort?"

He appeared to consider her question for a moment, then shook his head and offered her his arm. "Can't think of a thing."

Emma ground her teeth and turned smartly away, setting off for the schoolhouse at a brisk pace. Grey sauntered by her side, his long legs easily keeping pace with her while she nearly panted in her efforts to outdistance him. "What's in the package?" He indicated the flat parcel wrapped in brown paper that she carried under her arm.

"A photograph," she answered shortly. "Since the school trustees saw fit to hire a photographer to take a school picture, I've had nothing but trouble over it. The white children are so excited they won't pay attention to their lessons. The Indian children are so frightened they won't come inside. I've brought this photo to show them what it is and to assure them they won't die if a man takes their picture."

"And how will your picture persuade them of that?"

"I'm in the photo," she snapped, "and as they can see, I'm not dead."

"Very enterprising." They walked a few more steps in silence before Grey asked, "Want to hear about my American visitor?"

"I already know about him." She felt a rush of satisfaction in finally having surprised Grey North. "His name's Everett Jergens and I would be delighted to meet with him."

"Is that a fact?"

"Yes. Your chivalry has been entirely wasted on me, Mr. North. Everett Jergens is an old friend." They had reached the steps of the schoolhouse and she shot up them grateful for the first time since she'd taken the position that the school trustees required her to arrive at least thirty minutes before the pupils. She needed the time to build up the fire and bring in water from the well and, this morning, to compose herself after her encounter with Grey North. She unlocked the schoolhouse and hurried inside, rubbing her hands together against the chill.

Without taking off her coat or hat, she went to the stove and opened the firebox, pushing in a handful of shavings and a piece of cedar. She struck a match and set it to the kindling, waited a moment until the wood caught, then added a larger stick, closed the door and adjusted the dampers, pleased to see the fire drawing well instead of filling the room with smoke as it often did.

The sound of clapping made her spin around. Grey lounged against the door, a bucket of water at his feet and a mocking smile on his mouth. "Well done, Emma. You've finally got the knack of that stove. No clouds of black smoke billowing from the schoolhouse windows this morning."

"Mr. North," Emma took her place behind the teacher's desk, appreciating the advantage of the raised platform. She was considered tall for a woman, but she got a crick in her neck talking to Grey North.

"Grey." The twinkle in his eyes invited her to laugh with him but she resisted.

"Mr. North," she repeated sternly, "it is my understanding that you have built a hotel and have developed a very successful business. It is my further understanding that you are in the process of expanding that hotel and have taken an interest in Prospect's fledgling newspaper. With all that to occupy you, I would have thought my small affairs would be of no concern."

"But I find you endlessly fascinating, Emma Douglas." He raised his eyebrows. "I take it Douglas is your correct name?"

"It is," she muttered tight-lipped, "and so is Emma."

"So your deception is only a small one." He studied her thoughtfully. "Does that make it less dishonest, Emma?"

"Don't you dare!" Fury caught her by the throat, sending her voice soaring into the higher octaves. She had always prided herself on her honesty. It was a trait inspired and encouraged by her father. "People entrust me with their money, Abby," he would say. "We must be extra vigilant. No whisper must touch our family name." She steeled herself against the pain in her heart. He couldn't have stolen the money, and yet his note acknowledged his guilt. She gripped her hands tightly together, trying to reconcile the police version of events with the man she knew.

"Relax, Emma. I don't hold it against you." Grey's laconic tones broke into her thoughts. "There's not a soul in the territory doesn't have some secret he'd just as soon leave back home."

"And what's yours?" She uttered the rude challenge without thinking.

Grey's brows lifted in admiration. "Well done, Emma. You should speak your mind more often." The clatter of boots on the steps announced the arrival of her first pupils. "I'll be off now."

"You didn't answer my question."

"And I don't intend to," he grinned at her, "but feel free to ask again. It will give us something to talk about while we carry on our supposed courtship." He handed the bucket of water to the tallest boy coming in the door. "Put that in its place, son." He touched the brim of his hat to Emma and finally left the schoolhouse.

The children shuffled into their seats and waited with puzzled expressions as she removed her hat, coat and gloves, then rang the bell a good five minutes after school should have begun. She clapped her hands and the children rose to their feet to sing an off-key rendition of "God Save the Queen." Emma read a passage of Scripture, and they all recited the Lord's Prayer. "Take out your spelling assignments." The day had begun.

Through the arithmetic, reading, and social studies lessons, she attempted to maintain a calm demeanor but couldn't resist frequent peeks out the window to see if Grey North was wandering down the street or if Everett Jergens waited outside. To add to her agitation, her pupils all seemed particularly troublesome and obtuse this dull November Monday. No matter how often she explained the difference between "lay" and "lie" to Bessie Smith, the girl just stared at her with cowlike stupidity. What was the use? At thirteen Bessie was making eyes at Tommy Watson. By the time she turned sixteen the girl would be married and well on her way to producing a brood of dull children destined to frustrate the next unfortunate woman to accept the post of schoolmarm in Prospect.

"Miss, Miss, Miss!"

"What is it, James?" she answered shortly, after Bessie's

brother's repeated importunities penetrated her miasma of gloom.

"It's quittin' time, Miss. Ain't you gonna ring the bell? I got chores at home."

"Don't say 'ain't,'" she replied automatically, then gave up and called the class to attention. "Put away your work everyone. Stand, please." The children scrambled to their feet, clattering the desktops and slamming the fold-up seats. "You will leave in an orderly fashion, one row at a time, beginning with the front row. Class dismissed." She rang the handbell on her desk. "Don't run," she shouted as the smallest of her pupils made a dash for the door. Her words went unheeded, and in less than a minute the schoolroom was empty, leaving her with the task of cleaning the boards, sweeping the floor, and trying uselessly to scrub the ink stains from several of the desks.

"Why ever did I become a school teacher?" she muttered aloud, then jumped a foot in the air when a deep voice replied from the back of the room.

"I've asked myself the same question."

"Uncle Everett!" She dropped the scrub bucket and launched herself at the burly gentleman blocking the door. Fatherly arms closed about her and for the first time in over two years she felt comfort and love. "Oh, Uncle Everett, it's so good to see you." She inhaled his familiar soap and tobacco scent. Then she took a step backward to gaze up at his kindly face and caught her breath on a gasp of dismay. He looked old and gaunt, his face furrowed with deep lines, his skin pallid and waxy. "Uncle Everett, are you ill?"

"No, child, just old and tired." He smiled with just a hint of reproof. "It's a long way from San Francisco to Prospect, and in the middle of winter."

"I'm sorry. I should have written. I meant to. I wanted to pay back the money I took from you, too, but I was so ashamed." She dropped her gaze and brushed at the chalk dust she'd smeared on his heavy coat. "I've been foolish and thoughtless. Please forgive me."

"Abigail," he admonished, catching her fingers and pulling her into another bear hug, "or is it Emma? I heard you're using your middle name now."

"I . . . Yes, I wanted to make a clean break. Start over. I thought a new name would help. Abigail reminded me of so much. It's also why I never wrote." She ducked her head, hoping that her honorary uncle had a large enough reserve of compassion to forgive her.

"I understand." He pushed her a little away from him and studied her up-turned face soberly.

"I have the money." She rushed to make amends. "I can pay you back."

"Don't be silly." He tapped a finger against her chin. "I didn't come after you for the money." He took a deep breath and let it out in a long sigh. "There has been a development."

"Tell me." The hope that refused to die surged in her breast. Eager questions trembled on her lips, but another look at Everett's somber face stilled her tongue.

"We have a great deal to discuss, Emma. Let me treat you to tea at the hotel. I'll tell you everything I know."

She looked back at the less than spotless schoolroom, prepared to explain that she had chores to do before leaving, but her spirit rebelled. Today she was fed up with chalk and scrub brushes. Tomorrow she'd be a good and proper schoolmarm, but today, just for a brief hour, she wanted to be cosseted and indulged and made to feel precious.

"Why not?" She burned her bridges. "I'll just dampen down the fire and we can go."

She hurried into her coat and hat, then picked up her family photo, once again carefully wrapped in brown paper and tied with a string, and tucked it under her arm. Then she stepped outside with Everett, just in time to catch the season's first flakes of snow. Prospect's long winter had begun. She shivered and pulled her coat tightly about her, regretting the furs she'd sold for the cash they would bring to clear her father's debt.

They walked the few blocks to Grey North's hotel and were shown into the fancy dining room. She hesitated for a moment, but the room's lace-curtained windows and polished plank floors were as decorous as Mrs. Royston's front parlor. Once seated, she glanced hastily about the room and breathed a sigh of relief when she didn't find Grey North. She'd considered asking Everett to take her to some other establishment, but the Gold Nugget, the only other hotel in town, was no place for a woman, even when accompanied by a respectable gentleman.

While they waited for the tea to be brought, Everett described his journey north and Emma fidgeted, wishing he would tell her what had brought him so far away from home.

When their meal arrived, Emma poured the tea from a fine china pot and passed a plate of delicate sandwiches to Everett. "Now then," she said, unable to bear the suspense any longer, "tell me what's happened."

"There've been questions raised at the bank," Everett explained, thoughtfully turning his teacup around and around in his hands. "There has been another irregularity. The bank has hired an investigator. Matt's case may be reopened."

"I can't believe he was a thief." Emma shook her head

as the old arguments played over and over in her mind. "Maybe he was threatened or tricked or . . ." She sighed and put her half-eaten egg sandwich back on the plate, her appetite gone.

"You may be right."

She looked up in sudden hope. "You've found new evidence?"

"No, and not for lack of trying, let me assure you." He shook his head slowly from side to side. "The ledger sheets are still missing. . . ." He pursed his lips and regarded her from under bushy eyebrows. "I wish he'd confided in me. There must have been something I could have done. To take his own life . . ." He shook his head again.

"So, why have you come now?" Emma swallowed hard against the tears that clogged her throat. Losing her father had been bad enough, but to have his name besmirched and his reputation shredded made her sorrow ten times worse.

"There was a break-in at your father's office. Of course, his papers had all been taken away by the police, so it could be that the intrusion was totally unrelated to the case, but it raised some suspicions. Especially when the thief trashed the place but didn't appear to take anything."

"When did it happen?"

"The day after you ran away."

She blushed and lowered her eyes.

"Abby . . . Emma"—he reached across the table to clasp her hand—"I've loved you like a daughter since the day you were born. Your father was my closest friend, and I'd have married your mother myself if Matt hadn't beat me to it. Do you think I'd just let you disappear?"

"How did you find me?"

"It wasn't difficult. I checked the passenger lists of all the ships leaving San Francisco that day. I traced you to Victoria. Then I relied on the Canadian obsession with keeping official records. Your name and position are neatly noted in the Department of Education's files at the provincial legislature. I haven't contacted you before because I believed you needed solitude and independence."

"And now?"

"Now"—Everett leaned back in his chair and steepled his fingers—"now, there has been another break-in, this time at what used to be your home. Again, the thief ransacked the place, even tearing up floorboards in the study, but as far as anyone can tell, nothing was taken."

"But why would you think that incident was connected to me? The house was sold before I left San Francisco."

"That's true." Everett thumbed his chin in thought. "But your home was sold with all the furnishings. I think someone knows something and is still hunting for those missing ledgers—and I believe he's desperate. You could be in danger, Emma. I want you to think. Is there anything you remember that might point us to those missing papers? Anything at all?"

She shook her head, misery sagging her shoulders. "I went over it so many times with the police and the bank inspectors." She knotted her hands tightly in her lap, unwilling to relive the darkest days of her life. "All I know is that Papa seemed particularly distracted for the last few weeks of his life. He spent nearly every evening shut up in his study. You know. You saw him." Everett nodded but said nothing so she went on with her reminiscences. "Even at dinner time he barely spoke. Parnell," her voice quavered, but she swallowed and pressed on, "Parnell came to call a few times and he talked with Papa, but even though I asked him, he could not discover what worried my father so deeply."

She fiddled with the teacup, then took a deep breath and asked the question that hovered at the back of her mind. "Have you seen Parnell?"

"I thought you broke off the engagement?"

"I did." She smoothed the gloves in her lap. "I just wondered if he'd found someone else."

"Good afternoon, Miss Douglas." Grey North stood by their table, his eyes dancing with mischief, reminding her that his formal manners were merely superficial. "I trust everything has been to your satisfaction."

"The tea was tepid." She wanted to wipe the smug look from his face.

"I'll speak to the kitchen at once." He snapped his fingers and a waiter appeared. "Bring Miss Douglas a fresh pot of tea, and be sure it's very hot."

"Right away, sir." The waiter hustled off to the kitchen and Emma felt mean. She sincerely hoped none of the staff was in trouble because of her personal quarrel with Grey North.

"A bit harsh, weren't you?" Everett fixed her with a puzzled frown when Grey had gone.

She squirmed under his censure. "Yes, I suppose. It's just that man." She jerked her chin toward Grey, still watching them from the doorway. "He rubs me the wrong way."

"Seems like a decent sort to me."

"I don't want to talk about Mr. North."

Everett turned a speculative eye upon her, but she refused to say anything more. She couldn't put her finger on why Grey irritated her. He just did.

While she struggled daily with her new life, one minute resenting the restrictions placed upon her, the next enjoying the independence of earning a salary, Grey seemed to embrace his life wholeheartedly. Where she chafed against the deprivations of frontier life, Grey met each challenge with humor and energy, transforming every trial into an opportunity. Just once she'd like to see him uncertain or troubled. She shook her head, angry with herself for wasting her time thinking about him. Since he made her uncomfortable, the best thing to do was put him out of her mind altogether.

She drank a second pot of tea that she didn't want, then allowed her honorary uncle to walk her home. At the foot of the path leading up to Mrs. Royston's front door she took her leave of him. "I won't ask you in," she explained with a wry smile. "I wouldn't wish to subject you to Mrs. Royston's catechism."

"Then I'll say good-bye, my dear." Everett kissed her cheek. "I'm off first thing in the morning. I won't write to you until I have news to report."

"Good-bye then, and thank you." Emma turned and walked slowly up the front walk, reluctant to face Mrs. Royston's nosy questions but resigned to the inevitable.

"Good evening, Miss Douglas." Her landlady must have been waiting just inside the sitting room door, for she exploded into the front hall the moment Emma stepped inside.

"Good evening, Mrs. Royston."

"You've missed your dinner."

"Thank you, Mrs. Royston, but I had a light supper at the Rockingham with Mr. Jergens." There was no point in trying to avoid the landlady's probing. Better to give her a few basic facts than let her imagination run riot.

"You went to the hotel?" Mrs. Royston's eyes fairly snapped with curiosity, her voice rising to a small shriek. "Really, Miss Douglas."

"There was nothing improper, Mrs. Royston. I've

known Mr. Jergens since I was a little girl, and the Rockingham is a very respectable establishment."

"But a hotel, Miss Douglas. A saloon!"

"We were not in the saloon." Emma felt her irritation rising and placed her foot on the bottom step, eager to seek her room before she could offend her landlady. Much as Mrs. Royston grated on her nerves, she would be hard-pressed to find another place in Prospect as comfortable and convenient. An imp of mischief made her add, "I believe your ladies' sewing circle might consider taking tea in the dining room of the Rockingham. No doubt, Mr. North would do everything possible to make you comfortable."

She fled up the stairs, smiling inwardly at the vision of Grey North surrounded by Bella Royston and her friends. Her smile broadened. She determined to find a way to make Grey North play host to the busiest bodies in Prospect. She pushed open the door to her bedroom and all mirth fled in the instant.

Chapter Two

"Oh no!" She put her hand to her mouth and gazed in horror at the shambles. The wardrobe stood open and empty, all her clothes dragged from its depths and tossed to the floor. Every drawer in the dresser had been pulled from its runners and upended, exposing her undergarments to immodest view. Her carefully starched blouses were crumpled and soiled. Even the bed had been ransacked, the sheets and quilts tumbled into a heap and the mattress shoved half off its frame.

She took a step into the room and spied the little traveling desk she'd brought with her from San Francisco overturned and vandalized; the sloped top torn from its hinges, the pigeon holes emptied. The tiny secret drawer where she'd saved pretty buttons or beads as a child had been discovered and smashed. Her diary lay open on the floor, its pages stained with spilled ink.

She backed out of the room, the photo she still carried clutched to her bosom, her eyes fixed in dismay on the mayhem in her bedroom. "Mrs. Royston," she called, her voice little more than a quavering rasp. "Mrs. Royston," she tried again.

"Miss Douglas"—the landlady hustled up the steps—"are you ill?"

Mutely Emma gestured to the open door of her bedroom. Her landlady bustled forward, peered into the room, then fell back with her hand to her breast. "Merciful heavens!" She retreated from the chaos. "Rose!" she shrieked. "Rose!"

When the housemaid arrived panting at the top of the stairs, the landlady pointed a trembling finger toward the mess. "We've had an intruder, Rose. Run and fetch a constable."

The little housemaid spun about and clattered down the stairs. The front door slammed and Mrs. Royston collapsed on the stair, fanning herself with a handkerchief. "Imagine," she lamented, "a whole detachment of Mounted Police in the town and a poor widow isn't safe in her own house. It's a disgrace!" She leaned against the newel post, bewailing the insult to her home and her dignity.

Emma felt like crumpling to the floor and having hysterics herself but the din created by two shrieking women was too much to contemplate. Besides, the implications of the vandalism were far too worrisome to be cured with angry exclamations. "I think we'd best search through the rest of the house," she said.

"Oh, I couldn't," Mrs. Royston waved her handkerchief even more wildly. "I couldn't bear to see my things tumbled about like that." She jerked her chin toward Emma's room then covered her eyes, apparently overcome by the disorder.

Cold dread gripped Emma's heart as she considered that this was not a random housebreaking. Could the mayhem in her room be related to the break-ins Everett had reported? Had she been victim of a personal attack? But that was ridiculous. Besides Everett, no one from the city knew she was in Prospect, and, besides, she had nothing worth stealing. The vandalism in her room couldn't be connected with events in San Francisco. More likely it was a simple case of theft and the burglar had been interrupted before he could ransack the rest of the house. "Has anyplace else in the house been disturbed?" Emma joined her landlady on the top step.

"The parlor is in perfect order," Mrs. Royston huffed.

"Have you been in your bedroom recently?"

"No. Oh, Miss Douglas," Mrs. Royston dropped her haughty tone and clutched the lace at her throat, "do you suppose he stole my cameo? That pin was one of the last gifts Henry gave me." As always when she mentioned her late husband her eyes grew damp. "Oh, I can't bear it. Not my cameo."

"Oh, no." Emma scrambled to her feet, oblivious to her landlady's cry for sympathy. The mention of Mrs. Royston's cameo sent her rushing into the chaos of her room, the photo still clutched in her hand, to gaze frantically at the empty drawers of her dressing table. In a kind of daze she laid the photo on the bureau, then got down on her knees to pick through the mixture of gloves and ribbons and hairpins scattered on the floor. When she spied the pearl earrings that had belonged to her mother she scooped them into her hand, cradled them against her cheek, and silently thanked God that she'd been spared one more heartache. She returned to the top of the stairs. "At least he didn't steal these." She opened her hand to show Mrs. Royston the precious mementos.

Bucking up her courage, she placed her hand under her landlady's elbow and urged her to her feet. "Come. We'll check your room together."

"No, no." Mrs. Royston shook her off, then lowered her voice to a harsh whisper. "What if he's still here?"

"Don't frighten yourself," Emma said sharply, trying to cover the dread that knotted in her stomach. "Even if he'd been here when I found that . . ." She waved at the shambles in her room, searching for the word to describe it, then gave up. "When I found that and called you, he'd have been out a window or down the back stairs in a wink. Come. You'll feel better if you know the truth."

"Not without the policeman." Bella Royston wouldn't budge.

"Then let's go downstairs and wait." She placed an arm about her landlady's waist and helped her totter to the bottom of the stairs and into the front hall.

"What's keeping them?" Mrs. Royston twitched the curtains impatiently, but it was far too dark outside to see up the street.

"I'm sure they'll only be a moment." Emma tried to contain her own impatience. "Ah, that must be them." She sighed with relief as a commotion on the front step announced the arrival of the law.

She hurried to open the door to Rose and a stalwart young man in a scarlet tunic. "Evening, miss." The Mountie tipped his hat. "Understand you've had a bit of bother."

"It's more than a 'bit of bother'!" Mrs. Royston surged forward, apparently recovering her mettle now that the police had arrived. "My house has been invaded, young man. Miss Douglas's room has been ransacked, and who knows what other crimes have been perpetrated on my property. We're frightened to death! I don't know how I'll ever sleep in this house again. It's a great deal more than a 'bit of bother'!"

"Yes, ma'am. The young lady told me." The constable appeared unmoved by Mrs. Royston's outburst. "Now, if you ladies would like to wait in there"—he pointed to the parlor—"I'll just have a look around."

"You think he's still here?" The landlady's eyes grew as round as saucers.

"Unlikely, ma'am, but it pays to be careful." The constable moved quietly up the stairs. Emma took Mrs. Royston into the parlor and waited, her ears straining as she listened to the sound of the officer's boots as he entered each of the upstairs rooms.

"I ain't staying here no more," Rose declared, while her mistress rocked back and forth in her armchair, declaring over and over again that she didn't know what the world was coming to.

"Don't be silly, Rose," Emma said in her best schoolmarm voice. She wished she had the courage to tell Bella Royston to be quiet, too. Her landlady's lamentations made it difficult for her to follow the progress of the policeman, but at last she heard him come down the backstairs, through the kitchen, the pantry, and the dining room. He returned to the parlor, a puzzled frown marring his young face.

"Well!" Mrs. Royston shot to her feet. "Did you catch him? Did you get my cameo pin back?"

"You didn't report a stolen pin, Mrs. Royston," the constable replied. "Are you sure it's missing?"

"He's been in my room. Of course it's missing. It's the best piece I have."

"Excuse me, ma'am," the officer said, "there is evidence of a search in only one room of the house. I would say the intruder came in through the kitchen window, there's a dirty boot mark on the sill, and Miss Douglas's room has been completely turned over, but there doesn't appear to have been any damage elsewhere in the house."

"There wasn't?" Mrs. Royston looked first relieved and then affronted. "Well," she huffed, "what kind of a thief would go through Miss Douglas's things and not mine?"

The constable's lips twitched. If Emma hadn't been so upset she would have shared his amusement, but his report on his investigation only confirmed in her mind that someone had come after her deliberately.

"Were you at home all day, ma'am?" The constable took a small notebook from his pocket.

"No. I paid a call on Mrs. Clark in the early afternoon and then stopped at the Mercantile on my way home." Mrs. Royston simpered a little. "Jed Barclay remarked at the wedding that he admired my cakes, so I took him a piece of the one I baked this morning." She smiled smugly. "He liked that one, too."

"And what about you? Rose, is it?"

"Yes, sir." The girl's bottom lip came out at a belligerent angle. "I was here. Mrs. Royston wanted me to do the ironing and to scrub the kitchen floor."

"You never left the house?"

"Well, only to gather the eggs," Rose blushed.

"And when was that?"

"I don't know, after Mrs. Royston went out, I guess."

"Rose, were you flirting with that Murphy boy over the back fence?" Bella Royston shook an accusing finger at the housemaid.

"I wasn't flirting." Rose scowled and dug her toe into the hooked rug. "Charlie was out gathering their eggs, too, and we just talked a little, about whose hens were laying the best . . . and things."

"So you were outside for maybe ten minutes?" the constable asked.

"If she was talking to Charlie Murphy it was more likely half an hour." Mrs. Royston's voice rose in complaint. "So that's it, then. While you were off making sheep's eyes at that ne'er-do-well of a neighbor of mine, a criminal was inside my house."

"It's hardly Rose's fault," Emma said quietly. "I'm sure you wouldn't have gone calling on Jed Barclay if you'd had the slightest suspicion someone would break into your lodger's room." She paused a moment to let her landlady digest what she'd said, then continued, "The only person at fault here is the miscreant who invaded our home."

"Well said, Miss." The officer smiled approvingly at her and put away his notebook and pencil. "Now if you'd come with me, Miss, I'd like you to go through your belongings and tell me what's missing. If you can," he added hastily as Emma felt the blood drain from her face.

"Yes, of course," she said faintly, and turned to lead the way out of the parlor, steeling herself to face the devastation that awaited her at the top of the stairs.

"I'm sorry, Miss. It's an awful mess, I know, but if you could just have another look. If something's missing, it'll make it much easier for us to identify the scoundrel."

"I understand." Emma went slowly into the room and began sorting out her tumbled belongings while the officer waited politely at the door. When she picked up an armful of her underthings, he blushed bright red and studiously turned his back.

"Just tell me what's missing, Miss."

After a half hour of methodically turning over the mess, Emma was forced to conclude she could find nothing missing. "I haven't much jewelry," she explained to the officer, "and none of it seems to be gone. I don't keep any cash in my room. I really cannot think what anyone hoped to find here."

"Seems he wanted something pretty bad. You got any deeds or gold maps, anything like that?"

"No." Emma shook her head, but another quiver of suspicion shot down her spine. "I'm only a schoolmarm, officer. I've no secret goldmine."

"Well then, I'll just file a report of trespass and vandalism," the constable said. "We'll make inquiries, but there's not much to go on." He went down the stairs, the heels of his boots striking the bare wood of the steps with a steady thud. Emma followed in his wake. "Good night, Miss," he said at the doorway. Then tipped his hat once more and departed, leaving the three women to stare at each other and try to think what to do next.

"I ain't staying in this house," Rose repeated her protest.

"Don't be silly, Rose," Mrs. Royston scolded. "Whatever he wanted, the thief has been and gone. He won't be back."

"How do you know?" Rose looked mutinous.

"The police have been here, haven't they? He'll be scared to come back now."

"I ain't staying."

"And where do you propose to go, girl?" Bella Royston's frayed nerves made her shrill. "Your family lives way out by Barrel Creek. You can't go there in the middle of the night."

Emma touched her fingers to the pulse throbbing at her temple and wondered if there was anything that could make this evening worse. "Perhaps Rose would feel better if she slept in my room tonight," she said, interrupting what was fast becoming a screeching match. "We could keep each other company."

"Well, Rose?" Mrs. Royston glowered at the sulking girl.

"I guess." Rose hung her head, still scowling, but apparently ready to settle for the small comfort of sharing a room.

"Good." Emma tried her best to sound confident. "Come along, then, and help me straighten up. We'll be finished in no time if we work together. Then we can move in your cot."

Mrs. Royston threw up her hands in disgust. "Do what you will. I've had far too much excitement for one night. I'll retire to my bed. Rose, place a warming pan between the sheets and bring me some hot water before you help Miss Douglas. I'm too shattered to be trusted near a fire tonight." The landlady tottered out of the room, clucking to herself and waving her handkerchief before her face as she went.

"Hurry along then, Rose." Emma nodded encouragement to the girl.

"I ain't going into that kitchen by myself."

Considering that she was the only one in the house who had suffered at the hands of their vandal, Emma's patience with both Rose and Mrs. Royston had worn very thin. Still, she bit down on the cross words that filled her mouth and tried to be understanding. "We'll go together." She reached out and grasped Rose by the wrist and dragged her through the downstairs rooms of the house. "Look here," she said, pulling the unwilling girl into the dining room and lighting the lamps. "There's no one here. The window is closed tight." She went through a similar routine in the kitchen and pantry, double-checking the window the police officer had suspected as a means of entrance to the house. "Now, then," she said as she filled the warming pan from the water reservoir on the wood stove, "take this to Mrs. Royston and stop being so foolish."

Something in her confident manner must have gotten through to Rose, for she made no further complaint but took the warming pan and clumped up the stairs, her heavy footfalls thumping up the back stairs and along the hallway until she finally entered Mrs. Royston's bedroom.

Emma took herself back through the downstairs rooms of the house, extinguishing lamps as she went. In the front hall she checked that the door was securely locked; then, knowing she could put off facing the task no longer, climbed the front stairs. She took a deep breath, opened the door of her room, and tried not to see the violence in the attack on her property, especially around the little writing desk. It was one of the few possessions she'd hung on to. Not a very practical one, but a treasure from her childhood. Something that represented a place and a time when she'd felt utterly secure. She knelt and picked through the jumble of items on the floor, collecting the splintered bits and trying to fit them together like a jigsaw puzzle, but it was a hopeless task. The wood was too badly damaged. The desk could never be repaired.

For the first time since she'd come to Prospect tears collected in her eyes and overflowed, falling onto the broken piece she held in her hands.

"That looks bad, Miss." Rose stood looking down at her. "Best let me throw it into the fire."

For a moment longer Emma clung to the shattered wood; then she sighed and got heavily to her feet. "Perhaps you're right." She blinked hard and turned away to set the pieces beside the door, ready to be carried down to the kitchen stove. "Let's get on with this, shall we?" She picked up the bedclothes and placed them on a chair. "We'll set the mattress squarely on the bed first."

For the next hour or more she straightened, arranged,

and picked up, concentrating on one task at a time, closing her mind to the larger questions of who and why. With Rose's help, she replaced the drawers in the bureau and returned their contents neatly into place. She hung her dresses in the wardrobe and collected her soiled garments for the laundry. The actual damage was less than she'd expected. Her summer hat was squashed beyond repair, but a torn ruffle on her nightgown could be mended. It would take more than a needle and thread to mend her peace of mind.

"Thank you, Rose," she said when the room had been set to rights. "Shall we set up your cot now?"

"Naw," Rose yawned hugely, "I guess not. I'm too beat."

"All right then, go to bed and I'll see you in the morning." The girl departed and Emma breathed a sigh of relief. She readied herself for bed, said her prayers, unwrapped the paper from the photograph of herself and her mother and father and set it carefully in its place on the bureau, then climbed beneath Mrs. Royston's thick quilt. Thank goodness she'd had the photo with her. She couldn't bear to think of rough hands seizing it and tossing it to the floor, perhaps breaking the glass or tearing the stiff paper. At least that was one thing to be grateful for.

She wished she could discuss it all with Everett Jergens, but there was no point in alarming him. He was setting off at first light for the three-day journey to the rail head at Gold City. Besides, she'd already trod close to the line by dining with him. She couldn't blatantly flout the terms of her contract by going alone, late at night, to visit him at his hotel. In her current circumstances, she needed a job, and schoolteacher was one of the few respectable occupations open to her. Somehow she didn't see herself as a dance hall girl in Grey

North's saloon. She blushed at the thought and pulled the covers tightly under her chin.

To say she didn't sleep well would be a gross understatement, Emma decided the next morning as she dragged her weary body from the warmth of her bed. All night long, the slightest sound, the snap of the stovepipe or the creak of a tree branch outside her window or a gust of wind against the shutters, all brought her wide awake and fearful, her heart pounding, eyes staring widely into the darkness, ears straining for a soft footfall or the snick of a door latch. It was almost a relief when morning came and she could give up the pretence of sleep. She dressed hastily, shivering with cold and nerves.

Downstairs she found Mrs. Royston and Rose huddled around the stove in the kitchen. "It's too cold to use the dining room this morning," her landlady said, dishing out bowls of porridge from a pot simmering atop the cookstove. "I hope you don't mind sitting at the kitchen table, Miss Douglas."

"Not at all," Emma replied, holding her hands out to the warmth of the fire.

"Did you sleep well?"

"Not really."

"I barely dozed off myself. Couldn't help thinking some scoundrel might come to murder me in my bed." Mrs. Royston set a bowl of porridge before Emma, then took her own seat. "It's times like these I miss my Henry." Her eyes misted and she swiped a handkerchief under her nose. "Still"—she stuffed the hankie into her apron pocket and dug her spoon into the steaming oatmeal—"mustn't let ourselves be downhearted. I daresay it was just a prank. Maybe one of your pupils had a grudge."

She looked hopefully to Emma for confirmation of this theory.

The same thought had occurred to Emma sometime after midnight, but it hadn't brought her the degree of comfort it seemed to hold for her landlady. It was horrid to think one of her pupils hated her so much. Despite her frequent irritation with them, she had come to care about the students entrusted to her.

"Rose, mind the toast!" Mrs. Royston scolded as black smoke curled up from the slices of bread Rose held on a rack over the open flame. Rose sniffled and turned the rack over, quickly burning the other side as well. "What's the matter with you, girl?"

"I want to go home."

"You're not still on about that, are you?" Mrs. Royston poured out two cups of dark coffee, setting one before Emma and the second by her own plate. "Goodness, girl, where would we be if everyone in Prospect gave up and went home the minute something unpleasant happened?"

"I want to go home." Rose could be as stubborn as the landlady. Emma hid a smile as she made a wager with herself on which of them would win this battle. She buttered a piece of burned toast and bit into it. The singed bread crumbled, leaving specks of black on the lap of her gray skirt. She put the toast aside. Losing Rose in the kitchen wouldn't be such a loss.

"I want to see my mother." The girl sniffed.

"Oh, very well!" Mrs. Royston exclaimed. "Go home if you must, and for heaven's sake, stop sniveling!" She pushed her own breakfast aside and glowered at the girl. "I'll expect you back by tomorrow evening. See you're here, or I'll take on someone else. There are plenty of girls from the mission school would be glad of your place." She pushed back her chair and went into the pantry, returning with a loaf of bread and a jar of home-made preserves. "You can take these to your mother. She'll need them if she's to feed you for an extra day."

Rose snatched up the food and scuttled from the room.

Emma blinked. She wasn't surprised Rose was going home, she'd bet on the girl to win that one, but Mrs. Royston's gift of food took her aback. "That was kind of you," she said.

Her landlady brushed aside the compliment. "It's her poor mother I feel sorry for, tied to a sick husband and with a new baby every other year. Rose isn't much of a housekeeper, but at least she's one less mouth for her mother to feed."

"Is that why you keep her on?" Emma rapidly reviewed her opinion of Mrs. Royston.

"That and to try to teach her to be of some use. Besides, she's company of a sort." She went to the sideboard and cut fresh slices of bread from the loaf, put them in the rack and toasted them to perfection over the coals in the stove. "What can be so hard about making toast?" she muttered. "I pity the man that marries that girl. You're lucky to be a school teacher, Miss Douglas. You've an independence most women can only dream of." She dropped heavily into her chair and sighed. "Of course, I wouldn't have traded my Henry for all the independence in the world."

Nor I my comfortable life, Emma thought. But having had independence thrust upon her by necessity, she'd discovered she had a taste for it. She wouldn't marry for the sake of marriage. If she'd wanted a "Mrs." by her name, she could have accepted any of the four proposals that had come her way in the past several months. Not that she had foresworn marriage, but she would only enter the wedded state for a love too powerful to resist.

"My Henry'd have gotten to the bottom of this." Mrs. Royston's lower lip trembled, and Emma hurried to turn the conversation to a less lugubrious subject.

"You know Rose's mother well?"

"Not very well," the landlady regained her composure, "but she and I arrived here as new brides fifteen years ago, before we had a church or a hotel or a schoolhouse or even a wagon road. That kind of experience creates a bond." She heaped more jam on her toast. "I was lucky with my Henry, he struck it rich on the Wild Horse Creek and bought this house in town. Rose's family took up a homestead, but they didn't know the first thing about farming. They've been living pretty well hand to mouth for years and it's going to get worse. Jed Barclay told me they lost half their herd last winter in the big blizzard." She got up and bustled about the kitchen, adding wood to the stove and setting the kettle to boil. The grandfather clock in the hall chimed the half hour. "You'd best be going if you don't want to be late for school."

"Oh my, yes." Emma hastily finished her breakfast. "Thank you, Mrs. Royston," she said, and for the first time since coming to Prospect meant it sincerely. Her landlady was inquisitive, sharp-tongued, and tiresome. She was also secretly kind, generous and lonely.

She collected her school things, dressed as warmly as she could, and set off in a thoughtful frame of mind. Her preoccupation was abruptly shattered when Grey North fell into step beside her.

She halted and glared at him, lifting her hand to shield her eyes from the brightness of the sun. Once again, she wished it wasn't necessary to tip her head so far back in order to look into his face. "I thought we'd had this discussion yesterday. I don't want an escort to school." She spun on her heel and marched down the street, her head high, her back rigid.

"Good morning to you, too, Emma. I'm well, thank you for asking. Yes, it is a delightful day. Quite a gift this late in the season. There is a chill in the air, however. We'll be having a serious snowfall before the week is over, I'll wager." He grinned at her in his maddening way, ambling carelessly along by her side.

She stuck her chin in the air and refused to notice him.

"Yes, Mr. North," he said in a high-pitched snooty voice, "I do believe we'll have snow any day now. By the way, are you going to help out with the Christmas concert at the school? I would certainly appreciate it."

Emma stopped dead, whirled, and glared at her tormentor. "I do not talk like that," she snapped, "and I never asked you to participate in the school concert."

"Not yet," Grey replied, "but you will."

"What makes you so sure?" If she refused to talk to him he would just carry on his annoying game of putting words in her mouth.

"You want to raise funds to buy a piano for the school. You know I'm the best fund-raiser in Prospect."

"I'm considering asking Mr. Barclay from the Mercantile."

"Nope. Jed'll be too busy playing Santa Claus."

"The Reverend Acheson."

"Nope. He's the Presbyterian minister. If he asks, the Anglicans won't donate, and if the vicar from the Anglican church asks, the Presbyterians won't give."

"Mr. Roberts."

"He's a government agent. People won't trust him with their money. I'm telling you, Emma, you need me if you want a piano for your schoolhouse. Same as you need me to fend off more undesirable suitors." He tipped his head sideways and peered under the brim of her hat. "What do you say? Shall we make a bargain?"

"I'll think about it." Emma mounted the steps to the schoolhouse, unlocked the door, and stepped inside, only to stumble back, colliding with Grey North. For a moment she was glad of the strong arms that surrounded her and held her tight.

"Emma? What's wrong?" Grey looked down into her face, his teasing vanished and real concern showed in his eyes.

"Look," she whispered and nodded toward the schoolroom. Just like her bedroom, the place had been ransacked. Student desks had been emptied, the teacher's desk dismantled and actually upended. Papers, chalk, books—all were strewn about, many of them damaged. "Not again."

With a muttered oath, Grey shut the door on the schoolhouse vandalism and turned Emma into his arms, holding her with a tenderness that penetrated even her distress. "What do you mean, 'not again'?"

"Last night, at my boarding house." She was too shocked to resent his questions. "My room was torn apart. And only my room." She looked at him in dismay.

Grey's eyes grew hard and wary. The arms that supported her tightened, no longer tender but their steely strength comforted her nonetheless. For a moment, she was tempted to give way, to rest her head on his shoulder and pour out all her fear, to place her troubles into his capable hands and let him look after her. The sound of children's voices approaching brought her to her senses and she attempted to push herself away. Immediately, he slackened his hold, but he did not let her go. "Careful, Emma. You've had a shock. Don't go falling down the steps and hurting yourself to boot."

His rough tone jolted her to action. Grey North

wanted to pretend to be smitten by her, but in a moment of crisis all he could say was that she was too stupid and clumsy to be allowed to stand alone. "I'm not about to faint." She glared at him, not attempting to hide the temper that flared in her eyes. At this rate, they'd have a hard time convincing Prospect they were sparking.

"That's my girl." He squeezed her shoulders once, then reached past her to open the door. "In that case, we'll go inside. You can tell me about last night's burglary while we assess the damage here."

"Fine." She scooted out of his reach and strode swiftly into the devastated schoolroom. The sight of the teacher's desk turned on its side and tumbled off its platform made her catch her breath, but she refused to quail while Grey's eyes were upon her. "We'd better send for the police."

"Did you report last night's incident to them?"

"Yes." She picked up a dictionary from the welter on the floor and smoothed its pages, using her hands on purpose to still their trembling. "Since nothing was stolen he put it down to vandalism and a pupil with a grudge."

"That's quite a grudge." Grey blew out a breath and put his hands in his pockets. He rocked back on his heels carefully assessing the ruined schoolroom. "Any idea who it might be?"

"No." Tears prickled her eyelids. She'd become a teacher in an act of desperation but she believed she was good at it. She cared about the future welfare of her students and was at pains to discover their special interests and encourage them to excel. Granted, Bessie Smith often grated on her nerves, but for the most part she liked her pupils and believed they held her in respect, if not affection. "There are the usual discipline problems," she admitted, "especially with all this fuss over a photograph. . . ." She broke off and her hands flew to her mouth. "Oh my goodness. The photograph! It's scheduled for this morning." She looked helplessly at the rubble that littered her schoolroom. "What will I tell the photographer?"

"Tell him it will make an interesting picture." Grey's eyes held their familiar twinkle, although she could still see a hard resolve behind the teasing.

"Help me clean this up," she cried, rushing about like a demented chicken, collecting books and papers and placing them on the skewed desks. "Look at this." She pointed to a pool of ink in front of the stove. "I'll never get that out."

"Calm down, Emma." Grey caught her hands, forcing her to stop her frantic attempts to tidy up. "The police should see this before you put it to order. There may be evidence they can discover to trace your persecutor."

"But what about the children? And the photographer?" She looked toward the door as though expecting that worthy to appear on the instant.

"The children can do some schoolyard chores and the photographer will take their picture outside."

"They can't do chores. They'll be wearing their best clothes."

"Then you can organize a spelling bee, on the front steps. It'll make a great picture."

"That's a good idea." She gazed at him in amazement. Whoever would have thought Grey North could come up with a reasonable and positive suggestion for a gaggle of schoolchildren. She would have expected him to suggest a poker game or some other equally unsuitable pastime.

"Don't look so surprised." Grey pretended offense. "I'm not an ogre, you know."

She was saved the need to reply by the arrival of the first of her pupils, Tommy Watson, with Bessie Smith panting hard at his heels. She hurried to the front of the school, stepping outside and pulling the door closed behind her. "Tommy," she said, "run to the fort and fetch a constable."

"Miss?" Tommy's jaw dropped open and he stared at her in bewilderment.

"Don't gawp." Her fearfulness over the break-in replaced by anger at the assault on her peace of mind and on the welfare of her students. "Hurry now. There has been a break-in at the school. We need a constable."

"Oh, Miss!" Bessie took the opportunity to roll her eyes back into her head and clutch at Tommy, a perfect imitation of the heroine in a melodrama that had been staged in Prospect last summer.

"Bessie! Behave yourself." Emma took the girl by the arm and sat her down on the bottom of the three steps leading up to the schoolhouse door and shoved her head down between her knees. "Breathe deeply," she said. "Hurry along, Tommy."

"Yes, Miss." Tommy took to his heels, dashing down the street and disappearing as he cut kitty-corner across the vicar's front yard.

Other children arrived and Emma had her hands full explaining the morning's problem and keeping them out of the school. "So, until the constable has come and had a look around," she concluded her explanation, "we're having school out here." She clapped her hands smartly to get their attention. "Line up in two teams. We'll have a spelling bee."

"But I'm cold," whined the smallest Smith girl.

The morning was frosty, and several of the poorer children looked pinched and shivery. Her own fingers and toes tingled, but there wasn't much she could do. She put on her most cheerful smile and placed the child in a shaft of sunlight. "There you go, Molly. You stand there and you won't be cold. Ronnie, I think there's room for you here, too." She guided the little boy in a too-thin jacket into the warmest place available. "Now, who can spell 'rocker'?"

For another ten minutes she kept the children occupied, even commissioning Grey to keep track of the successes and failures of each team. His presence proved a good distraction, but it also raised a level of curiosity that was sure to make her next meeting with the trustees difficult. "I can spell 'saloon'," Bessie Smith offered, gazing adoringly at Grey's handsome face.

"I'm sure you can," Emma said grimly, "but can you spell 'laundry'?"

Grey's lips twitched and he recorded a failure for Bessie's side. The opposing team was made of sterner stuff and Mabel Johnson scored a win for her team with the correct spelling. But the game was growing tedious. Emma kept glancing down the street, searching for Tommy and the constable. When she saw the flash of a scarlet tunic she breathed a sigh of relief, only to fall prey to more misgivings as the children gave up any semblance of order and careened down the schoolhouse steps to swarm the policeman.

"Can you spell 'hero worship'?" Grey whispered in her ear.

"Can you spell 'superfluous'?" she shot back, and then had to apologize. Grey North had been a thorn in her side for months but it was unfair to castigate him for this morning's work. "I beg your pardon." She kept her eyes firmly fixed on a spot some distance away over his left shoulder. "Your assistance this morning has been very helpful. However, now that the constable is here, we need detain you no longer."

"Oh, Emma. Too cruel. I liked you better when you were frightened, and don't look at me like that," he added, his eyes growing almost black as he saw the suspicion leap into her face. "I did not wreck the schoolhouse just to drive you into my arms."

She blushed. It was humiliating that he could read her so easily. "I really must speak with the constable," she said, and threaded her way through the crowd of children to address the same officer who had attended her the previous evening.

"Miss Douglas." The constable touched a finger to the brim of his hat. "What's all this about, then? Young Tommy just said I was to come quick." His gaze took in the children ranged along the schoolhouse steps and clustered around him, then moved to study Grey North standing in front of the closed door to the schoolroom. His eyes narrowed and he flexed his fists. "That fellow been bothering you?"

For an instant Emma was tempted. It would be so satisfying to see Grey North reprimanded by a uniformed policeman, but much as she would have enjoyed his discomfiture, her sense of honor made her reject the notion. Besides, there was a serious crime to be investigated. "There has been another break-in." She led the way to the top of the steps. "When I arrived this morning, I found this." Grey stepped aside and allowed her to open the door, giving the constable the full impact of the destruction to the schoolroom.

"Looks like the same person." The police officer offered the same conclusion Emma had reached on her own. "Question is why? Once we get that figured out, the rest should be easy. Was anything taken this time?"

"I've not had a chance to check." Emma indicated the schoolchildren crowding the doorway and exclaiming, some with glee and others with dismay, over the disorder inside. "It seems unlikely. There is nothing here of any value."

"Any personal items in your desk?" The constable waded through the scattered books and papers and bent to examine the upturned teacher's desk. "He seems to have spent most of his time turning this over."

"No, I keep the school register in the bottom drawer." She picked up the long, leather-bound ledger from the mess. "It's still here. There were some papers I was grading, a rough draft of the history test for the grade six class. Other than that, my desk holds chalk, pencils, a ruler, the strap," she winced as she said the word. She'd never used the strap on any of her pupils and it was her fervent wish that she never would. "A handkerchief and some pens and an inkwell," she completed her litany.

"What about that test?" The policeman directed an inquiring gaze over the assembled pupils. "Any of your grade six pupils steal it and make this mess to cover it up?"

"I doubt any of them care that much," she replied dryly, as her students shook their heads vigorously. Nevertheless, she spent five minutes sifting through the debris closest to her desk until she found the list of questions she had written. "It's right here." She held up the dirtied paper with a grimace. She'd have to redo it just in case.

"Excuse me." A querulous new voice joined the excited hum of the children. "I have an appointment?"

"Oh," Emma exclaimed, "the photographer." She rolled her eyes heavenward, then turned and did her duty as hostess. "I'm sorry"—she moved forward to greet a little man with a round tummy and enormous side-whiskers, who was almost completely hidden behind his tripod and camera—"but we've had some trouble here."

"I sure would like to take that picture this morning. I got other appointments."

"Yes, I understand." Emma began to feel flustered with so many demanding her attention and no one offering a particle of assistance. "We thought outside, on the school steps." She cast a furious glance at Grey North, still dogging her footsteps but doing nothing practical to help out, either with the police or the photographer or the children. "Mr. North here," she smiled with false sweetness at Grey, "will help you. Come along, children." She clapped her hands for attention, and then when the noise had quieted and all the children looked to her for direction, she explained the picture-taking scheme. "Outside now." She shooed them toward the open door. "I'll be out in a moment. As soon as the police officer is finished taking my report."

The children bustled outside, eager to see the strange contraption the photographer carried on his shoulder. All, that is, except a small knot of Indian children who clustered into a corner and refused to move. Their stubborn, silent faces warned Emma of more trouble to come.

"You're not still afraid, are you?" She left the constable to his investigations and came to crouch down before the huddled children. "You saw the picture I brought in yesterday?"

Six dark-haired heads nodded in unison.

"And you saw me in it?"

Again the heads nodded, but no one stirred from the corner.

"And you see I'm still here? Having your picture taken

won't make you disappear." She patted herself all over, demonstrating the substantial fact of her being. "Don't you want to have your picture taken with the others?"

Six pairs of somber eyes stared back at her. Six dark heads moved from side to side, but no one moved a foot. She stood up, straight and tall, and adopted her firmest tone. "Now, that's enough. You get out there with the others. Everyone can line up according to their height on the schoolhouse steps."

Six pairs of dark eyes regarded her solemnly and sorrowfully, but not one child stirred from his refuge in the corner.

"All right"—she threw up her hands in defeat—"we'll have the picture without you. It's too bad. The pictured record of the school will be incomplete, but I won't force you." She turned to leave but the constable stopped her.

"Could be there's your problem right there." He nodded toward the six silent children. "They didn't want to have their pictures taken and they took it out on you."

"I don't believe it," Emma defended her charges even though it seemed the only plausible excuse for the vandalism. "They're shy and superstitious. They're not vindictive."

"If you say so, Miss." The constable shook his head and put away his notebook and pencil. "Anyway, seems as if nothing was taken. Just like last night. I'll file another report, but I'll wager once this picture-taking is over you won't have any more troubles." He marched through the cluttered schoolroom and out the door, leaving Emma to wonder why she'd bothered to inform him in the first place. It seemed terrorizing a woman in Prospect didn't merit the same attention as cattle rustling or claim jumping.

Thoroughly upset, she followed him out the door,

leaving her six native pupils to wait miserably in their corner.

"Hey, Constable, wait a minute." Grey left off helping the photographer organize the students and loped after the policeman. He held a short, whispered conference with him, and then returned to the assembled group, his face wearing its habitual mocking smile. Looking sheepish, the policeman followed Grey inside. They emerged shortly thereafter with the six Indian children in tow.

"Okay, line up," Grey said while the photographer ducked behind his camera and pulled the black cloth over his head. The six children took their places on the steps with the others, with the Mountie in their midst. "You, too." Grey pointed Emma to an empty spot in the center of the back row.

She squeezed between her two tallest students and assumed her calmest, most teacher-like expression. The photographer snapped his picture; a flash of white light exploded from his magnesium tray and the older boys cheered.

"That's it." The photographer emerged from under the hood of his camera and packed up his equipment. "I'll deliver the picture tomorrow." He slung his tripod and flash pan over his shoulder; picked up the case, the camera, plates, and other equipment; and strode off toward the Gold Nugget Saloon. Some of the older boys ran after him, enthusiastically, demanding that he perform the magical feat again, while the little ones clamored to know when they could go inside.

"All right, children." Emma raised her voice to be heard over the hubbub. "Tommy, Michael, come back here. Everyone inside. We've work to do to set the schoolroom to rights."

She avoided looking at Grey North but cast a glance

down the street and received yet another shock to her overwrought nerves. A shadow slipping around the corner of the Gold Nugget Saloon seemed all too familiar. She whirled to stare hard at the now empty street corner. Was it? It couldn't be. She shook her head at her foolish imaginings. Everyone in a new town thought they saw old friends from a previous life. It was a common illusion and not surprising given all the shocks she'd endured in the past twenty-four hours. The slight figure she'd seen sliding into the Gold Nugget couldn't possibly be Parnell Wilde.

Chapter Three

"You look like you've seen a ghost." Grey studied her face with a quizzical lift of his brows. "Keeping secrets, Emma?"

She turned away, unwilling to meet his eye. He had no business asking her personal questions, but she felt uncomfortable telling him an outright lie. He was big and bold and brash and probably had a few secrets of his own, but she sensed a soul-deep honesty in him that made her ashamed. "As you said, we've all got them."

"Keep your secrets, Emma." His deep voice in her ear made her jump. "They're innocent enough."

"How do you know?" She wished she'd bitten her tongue. The last thing she wanted was to spend time on the schoolhouse steps for all the town to see, engaged in a soul-searching conversation with Grey North. She should be inside, organizing the cleanup of the school, keeping watch over her charges, teaching them their sums and their letters, but she could not tear herself away without hearing his answer.

"It's in your clear green eyes and your rosy, kissable mouth." He leaned forward, so close she was afraid he meant to put the "kissable" comment to the test. Recalled to a sense of propriety, she jumped back as though she'd been bitten by a mosquito.

"Mr. North!" Heat rushed to her cheeks at the same time a curious weakness attacked her knees. During the period of her engagement, she'd shared a few chaste kisses with Parnell, but he had never looked at her with such hungry eyes or said words like "kissable." And she had never felt her stomach clench with anticipation or her breath come in short gasps as though her corset were laced too tightly. Yet hearing the word "kissable" on Grey's lips had produced all those uncomfortable sensations. "You are out of line." She tried to speak sternly, but produced only a ragged whisper.

He drew back, his usual cheerful grin in place. "Interesting," he said, touching a finger to her hot cheeks. "'Bye, Emma. I'll walk you home after school." He turned and sauntered off, leaving her to try to restore order to her feelings, as well as to the schoolroom. She watched him out of sight, despising herself for doing so, then forced her watery knees to stiffen and walked into the classroom with what she hoped was a calm face.

Some of her twenty pupils stood against the walls looking frightened and unsure of themselves, while others had taken the opportunity to wage a spitball war. "All right, children"—she clapped her hands sharply and moved to the front of the room—"we've had a great deal of excitement this morning, but it's time to settle down. I want the schoolroom put in order by lunchtime. Grade ones, you can pick up all the papers. Grade twos, your job is to gather the books and put them where they belong. Grade threes . . ." She went on detailing tasks until every child was busy. While they worked she sorted through the mess of her own desk. Someone, Grey or the policeman, had set it upright and returned the drawers to their slots, but the contents were still spewed across the floor.

By the time she rang the noon bell, the schoolroom was reordered, the students were at their desks ready to begin their arithmetic lessons, and she was no closer to a solution of what had provoked the two attacks on her property. Even if they were connected to the events in San Francisco, she had nothing worth stealing. Nor had she succeeded in putting Grey North completely out of her thoughts. He'd promised—or was that threatened?—to walk her home. She bit into the deviled beef sandwich Mrs. Royston had packed for her lunch and wished her stomach didn't feel all aflutter.

"Miss, can we start on the Christmas concert?"

In Prospect, the annual Christmas concert was the highlight of the school year for the students and their parents, and woe betide the teacher who didn't ensure that each child was featured in the dialogues, drills, and musical numbers that preceded the appearance of Santa Claus. Emma glanced toward the big clock hanging by the side window. There were still two hours to go before she could ring the bell for the end of the day. *Why not?* She put down her pencil and abandoned the geography lesson she'd been preparing for the grade eights. The day had been a complete waste in terms of academic work. Might as well use the children's restlessness and excitement for good purpose.

"Very well." She closed the text book on her desk. "You may all draw some decorations for the windows."

"Can I cut out snowflakes instead?" Molly Smith stuck out her bottom lip.

"When can we sing carols?" Mabel Johnson whispered shyly.

"I'm not going in any stupid skit." Tommy Watson folded his arms across his chest and glowered at her.

"But who's going to play Mary?" Bessie's petulant tones set Emma's teeth on edge.

"I said you could draw decorations for the windows." She walked down the rows of desks, handing out sheets of colored paper. "Anyone who doesn't want to do that can write out the twelve times table on the board."

The complaining ceased and twenty heads bent over their desks. For a few moments at least, she would have peace. Peace in the classroom, at any rate. Inside, her thoughts and her feelings warred against each other with all the ferocity of mortal enemies. Was Parnell in town? Did she want him to be? Did Grey North really think her mouth was kissable?

She frowned and tried to force her mind to the tasks at hand. While the children worked on their drawings, she graded the papers stacked on her desk, checking spelling and grammar and neatness, but she could not banish the enigma that was Grey North from her thoughts, nor the fleeting shadow she'd glimpsed disappearing around the corner of the Gold Nugget Saloon. It couldn't be Parnell. Or could it? Everett had found her. Why not Parnell?

Because he didn't want to, she answered her own question. It was a lowering thought but one she could not dismiss. The sight of him hastening away from her house with her engagement ring clutched in his hand was not one she would soon forget. The next time she'd seen him in the street he'd turned his head and pretended not to notice her.

To be honest, his ready belief in her father's guilt had

hurt even more than the broken engagement. She'd regretted the life she would have had as his wife and her pride smarted under the sting of rejection, but her grief was for her father, not Parnell. Considering how easily their attachment had dissolved, Emma sometimes wondered if Parnell had only used her as a means of promotion at the bank. Her vanity rebelled at such musings, recalling the extravagant compliments he'd paid her, his pride at having her by his side. It couldn't have been all a pretence. It was the disgrace that had driven him away, not a lack of affection. Unbidden, a vision of Grey North's steady blue eyes swam into her imagination. Grey would never turn his back on a woman he loved. The conviction sprang full-blown and unfounded into her mind, but she knew with certainty that it was true.

"Miss? Miss . . ."

And if it was Parnell at the Gold Nugget, what should she do?

"Miss!"

"Yes." She jumped slightly, recalling herself to the schoolroom and the rows of pupils watching her with puzzled eyes. "What is it, Tommy?"

"The fire's gone out, Miss."

She walked to the stove and opened the firebox. Tommy was right. The last of the coals had extinguished, leaving only cooling ashes in the bottom of the grate. Now she'd have to start the fire all over again. As she looked at the cold grate and the empty wood box, a mood of defiance surged over her. She'd discovered an unexpected satisfaction in teaching, but she hated the servitude of being a schoolmarm.

She looked down at her plain blouse and dull gray skirt and grimaced. Her pupils had done well on their Department of Education exams last June. Couldn't they learn just as well from her if she wore bright clothes or went to parties or stayed up late at night? What did keeping the schoolhouse clean, tending the fire, and having no privacy whatsoever have to do with teaching the children of Prospect?

She looked at the clock and slammed shut the door on the cold stove. Today she proclaimed her independence. "Put your things away," she said. "We'll dismiss early." Her pupils were startled into immobility for all of ten seconds, then they downed pencils, slammed books, thrust their scribblers into their desks, and scrambled to stand at attention. "Bessie, clean the blackboards. Tommy and James, go and fetch an armful of wood for tomorrow. See if you can be done before the rest of us finish reciting the six times table." The three children with designated chores rushed to complete them, while the remaining class chanted, "six times one is six, six times two is twelve, six times three is eighteen . . ." Bessie had completed a hasty swipe at the blackboards by the time they reached six times ten, and James and Tommy dropped a small stack of wood beside the stove just as six times fourteen rang out amid giggles from the littler students.

"Class dismissed," Emma shouted above the excitement. At four minutes to four the schoolroom was empty. She pinned on her hat, caught up her gloves, and prepared to depart as well. The knowledge that she could escape Grey North's escort home leant wings to her feet. It was pleasing to know that, just for once, he would not get his own way.

As eagerly as the children, she tripped down the schoolhouse steps, whisked herself along the path, and turned smartly at the first corner of the street. Safely out of sight of the school, she paused and caught her breath, then walked the rest of the way home at a sedate and proper pace.

"Miss Douglas!" Bella Royston's voice hailed her from the back of the house the moment she arrived home. "Miss Douglas, I must warn you I've invited company for dinner this evening, so if you want a cup of tea, you'll have to have it in here. I can't leave the stove." Her landlady poked her head out from the kitchen at the back of the hall, a smudge of flour on one cheek, her sleeves rolled up, and her dress covered by an enormous apron.

It was all so homey and ordinary. The undercurrents of doubt and intrigue that had plagued her all day vanished. A genuine smile sprang to her lips. "I'd love a cup of tea. Just let me get out of my coat." She ran up the stairs, hesitated a moment outside her bedroom, took a deep breath, then pushed the door open and looked inside. Everything was as neat and orderly as she'd left it in the morning. She sighed in relief and stepped through the doorway. Quickly, she doffed her outdoor clothing, splashed cold water on her face, and returned downstairs. With a peaceful heart, she made her way to the cozy kitchen at the back of the house. Mrs. Royston set a big brown teapot in the center of the table and invited Emma to help herself.

"And pour one for me, too. I just have to finish whipping this cream."

"Must be a special guest." Emma sipped her tea and took in the dinner preparations. A high chocolate cake cooling on a rack in the open pantry made her mouth water. Fresh biscuits heaped on a plate in the middle of the table filled the room with their wonderful aroma, and when Mrs. Royston set aside the whipped cream to open the oven and baste a prime roast of beef, Emma knew she was in for a treat. Bella Royston, at her best, could produce a feast fit for a king.

"It's Jed Barclay." Her landlady turned a flushed face

toward Emma. "We got to talking at the Mercantile this morning, about cooking and such, and before I knew what was what, I'd invited him to dinner." Was it the heat from the stove or Jed Barclay that brought the rosy tinge to the landlady's cheeks? *Curiouser and curiouser,* Emma's thoughts echoed Lewis Carroll's Alice. She sipped her tea and smiled to herself. Dinner would be most entertaining.

"At least, he's one of my guests." Mrs. Royston continued talking as she gave a final whip to the cream. "I've invited the new vicar and his wife as well and, to even out the table"—her eyes sidled away from Emma's—"Grey North. I believe you know him quite well."

Emma's smile vanished and she set down her teacup with a sharp click. "Mr. North is one of the school trustees." She refused to acknowledge any other relationship.

"So he is." Mrs. Royston looked sly. "Maybe that explains it, although I don't see the other trustees escorting you to and from school."

"I walked home myself today." Emma tossed her head. "And that was after another break-in."

"Another!" Mrs. Royston dropped the whipping paddle. "Where?"

"At the school." Glad to turn the conversation from Grey North, Emma regaled Mrs. Royston for the next half hour with all the details of the latest crime in Prospect.

"What did that policeman say?" Her landlady plumped herself onto one of the kitchen chairs and reached for a second cup of revivifying tea.

"He thinks it was a student with a grudge, maybe one of the Indian children who didn't want his picture taken."

"Well, when you find out who it is, I hope you give him the strap." Mrs. Royston gave vent to her fear. "Busting up public property, frightening people in their own homes. It's disgraceful."

"Well, the photographer was there this morning and will be leaving town by the end of the week, so let's hope that's the end of it." Emma tried to sound convincing, but the policeman's theory didn't comfort her. Her Indian pupils were generally quiet and painfully shy. She just could not imagine one of them as a housebreaker.

"Is there anything I can do to help?" she asked, standing and gathering the tea things together to carry them to the sink.

"If you wouldn't mind laying the table." Mrs. Royston brushed the back of her arm over her perspiring brow. "Of all times for Rose to decide to go home . . ." She left the sentence unfinished but muttered something about "ungrateful" and "feckless" before she plunged her hands into the dishpan, immersing herself up to the elbows. "It's not your place, being a boarder," she apologized, "but I'd be most grateful."

"Of course." Emma felt a sudden empathy for her landlady. They were both single women in a harsh country. The least they could do was support each other. The lines between rich and poor, privileged and servant were inevitably blurred by the exigencies of life on the frontier. She went into the dining room and opened the drawers of the Welsh dresser to find silverware and china.

By the time the Reverend Allen, a tall man with stooped shoulders and an ingratiating air, and his mousy-haired wife arrived, the table was set with Mrs. Royston's best china and silverware, glowing in the light of two tall candles, while a kerosene lamp on the dresser illuminated the edges of the room. The dinner was ready and waiting in the warming oven of the cookstove. Mrs. Royston had dispensed with her apron, washed her face and smoothed her hair, ready to play the lady. Emma repressed a smile as her landlady strove to be a good hostess while peering anxiously toward the window for her other guests, or, as Emma suspected, one particular guest. When a second knock fell on the door, she practically flew down the hall to open it, leaving Emma to entertain the preacher and his prissy wife.

"Mr. Barclay." The usual shrill overtones of Bella Royston's voice had completely disappeared. She sounded gentle and gracious. "Do come in. And Mr. North."

Emma's smile disappeared.

The moment Grey North entered the parlor, his size and vitality dominated the room. His eyes sought out Emma at once and he shook his head slightly. "Ah, Miss Douglas, I'm glad to see you looking so well. I was afraid, when you dismissed classes early, that you had suffered some ill effects from the morning's disturbance." The words were smooth and polite, without a hint of impropriety, but the mocking gaze he turned upon her told her very well he hadn't the slightest doubt as to why she had locked up the schoolhouse and fled five minutes before the accustomed time.

"What disturbance?" asked Mrs. Allen.

In the ensuing retelling of the two break-ins and the policeman's speculation about a disgruntled student, Emma was able to school her features and turn bland and innocent eyes to Grey. Much to her chagrin, she couldn't help admiring the breadth of his shoulders, encased in a beautifully cut jacket. She bit her lip and deliberately turned her head.

"I saw the school picture late this afternoon," Grey remarked. "I thought it turned out very well."

"The children will be pleased." She wanted to end the conversation but couldn't help asking, "How did you and the Mountie persuade the Indian children to pose?"

"A bit of local knowledge, Miss Douglas. The natives

have a great trust in the scarlet tunic. If the constable was willing to have his picture taken, they knew it was safe."

"You have Indian children in the school?" Mrs. Allen's tone left no doubt as to her horrified opinion of such a situation.

"Mostly they go to the mission school as boarders," Emma explained, "but some parents prefer to keep their children at home, and they attend the public school." She turned back to Grey. "Do the trustees plan to hang the photograph in the school?"

"They've asked me to see to it. I'll come by tomorrow at four o'clock," he paused, his eyes alight with mischief, "if that is convenient, of course."

Emma knew very well he would be there whether she found it convenient or not. "Thank you for the warning," she said dryly, and heard his soft chuckle.

"Shall we go into the dining room?" Mrs. Royston rose to her feet and led the way to the table. While the guests seated themselves, Emma helped her bring out the bowls and platters of food, filling the room with their tantalizing aromas.

"Would you carve, Mr. Barclay?"

A disapproving frown marred Mrs. Allen's face and Emma surmised the lady felt the honor of carving the roast should go to her husband. Clearly, Mrs. Royston held Jed Barclay in higher esteem. She smelled a romance and heartily wished her landlady well. Mrs. Royston's housekeeping skills were wasted on the schoolmarm and a hired girl.

The burly shopkeeper picked up the bone-handled carving knife and set to slicing perfect, succulent servings of roast beef. Mrs. Royston passed around bowls of fluffy mashed potatoes, beets, carrots, and cabbage. The table practically groaned beneath the plates of pickles and relishes, mounds of freshly churned butter, and an overflowing bowl of gravy.

When Emma thought they couldn't possibly put anything more on their plates, Mrs. Royston passed the biscuits. "Mrs. Royston, you're a wonder. These are the best biscuits I've ever tasted." Jed slathered butter on another and munched blissfully as his hostess beamed and fluttered her eyelashes.

Emma glanced at Jed's girth and silently congratulated her landlady on having found the surest way to his heart. The man was going to explode if he ate any more, yet he didn't turn down the third helping of roast beef that his hostess pressed upon him. If Bella Royston had set her cap for him, Jed's fate was sealed.

"I could use a cook like you at the Rockingham," Grey remarked as he accepted just one more helping.

"Oh, Mr. North, such a compliment, but I couldn't consider going out to work."

"Not on a regular basis, of course," Grey tacitly admitted the loss of status such employment would mean for Mrs. Royston, "but for special occasions. Like when the Mining Association holds its annual dinner. Or perhaps a Christmas banquet for a select group of guests."

"I'm very flattered, Mr. North, but really . . ." She turned and cast a helpless glance at Jed. "What do you think, Mr. Barclay?"

"Perhaps you could cater for a fund-raising event," Grey persisted. "Miss Douglas here wants a piano for the schoolhouse. Now, she'll raise a few dollars at the Christmas concert, but if the hotel were to advertise a first-rate meal, prepared by one of Prospect's finest cooks and served in the hotel dining room, I'll wager we'd have miners laying down their gold nuggets by the fistful."

"I'd buy a ticket." Jed wiped the gravy from his plate with the last of the biscuits.

"I'll have to think about it."

"I'll call on you next week to arrange the details."

Against her will, Emma had to admire Grey's determination. He'd promised her he was the man to pry money out of Prospect's wealthier citizens, and if his handling of Bella Royston was anything to go by, he'd make good on his promise. It struck her that Grey North could accomplish most anything he set his mind to. He turned his head slightly and lowered one eyelid, a slow and deliberate wink that only she could see. Her cheeks flamed hot and she turned away. One thing he could not do was get around Emma Douglas.

"Any interesting guests staying at the hotel lately?" The Reverend Allen introduced a new topic of conversation.

"A gentleman from San Francisco left at first light this morning," Grey replied, sending Emma a significant look, "and we've had a number of railway men through, investors and surveyors and government officials. I hear they're looking for a route for a southern line."

"It sure would be a boon to Prospect," Jed said. "It takes four days to get supplies from the railhead at Gold City, now. Just think if we had our own line. Prospect'd become the center for the whole of the East Kootenays. Why, you could go visiting down to Vancouver or Seattle, Miss Douglas, and not have to trust yourself to a pack horse and a canoe."

"Or one of those frightful slings." Emma shuddered in reminiscence of her experience in crossing the river in a large basket slung from a cable across the current.

"A railroad would spark a boom in business and settlement," Grey conceded, "but I rather enjoyed crossing in a basket." He turned challenging eyes to Emma. "Didn't you admire the view from up there?"

"It had the potential of a thrilling experience," Emma admitted, "but I couldn't properly enjoy the scenery while terrified that the cable might break and we'd all end up smashed on the rocks below."

"I never opened my eyes at all," Mrs. Allen declared in a whining tone that grated on Emma's nerves. "I never want to see a view of a river if I have to hang in a basket in midair to get it."

"You must understand, Mrs. Allen is newly arrived from England," her husband rushed to explain. "She's not used to the rigors of frontier life."

"Nor likely to be." Mrs. Allen threw good manners and her husband's position to the wind as she went on to declare her dislike of all things Canadian, in general, and of Prospect, in particular. "I had no idea what sort of life we'd have when I accepted your proposal."

"Now, Mary," her husband chided her, "you don't really mean that. It's just the newness of it all that's upset you."

"I thought Cornwall was bad enough," his wife continued, heedless of the surprised faces around the dining room table, "but Cornwall is the height of civilization compared with this, this . . ." She fumbled for the right word to describe her view of Prospect and finally settled on "encampment." "Do you realize there are only Indian girls available to serve in the house? And they've been taught by Catholic priests. I wouldn't trust them out of my sight for a moment."

"The mission school does very good work." Emma surprised herself with her quick defense. "The impact of white settlers on the natives has been most distressing for them. They're not used to our ways, and there has been bloodshed because of it. The mission school was the first to build bridges between the two cultures."

"How can you defend them when it was the Indian children who destroyed your schoolroom?"

"That is only conjecture," she said sternly, as though reprimanding one of her more unruly charges. "There is no evidence to support such an allegation."

"Well said." Grey's soft words of praise brought a blush of pleasure to her cheeks followed by hot chagrin. She was not interested in Grey North's opinion.

"What part of England are you from?" Grey's question turned Mrs. Allen's attention away from her grievances.

"Hull."

"Ah," he nodded, "I understand."

Emma noticed Mrs. Allen flush slightly and wondered what powerful message Grey had conveyed with such few words.

"I notice you've a British accent yourself." The vicar strove to divert attention from his wife's ill-considered remarks. "Where do you call home?"

"Wherever I lay my hat," Grey answered. "And right now that is the Rockingham Hotel, Prospect, B.C., but I assume you were asking where I was born. The answer to that question is Hampshire."

"Very good," Mr. Allen nodded. "Some lovely estates in that part of the country."

"North," Mrs. Allen muttered to no one in particular. "North. The name seems familiar. Where did you go to school, Mr. North? Perhaps you knew my brother, Christopher Dalton?"

"No." Grey's reply seemed unusually curt, but before Mrs. Allen could pursue her genealogical enquiries, he asked Jed a question about the latest rumor of a gold strike and the conversation turned to tales of the fortunes made and lost over the past twenty years on the gold fields of the Kootenays. It was a topic guaranteed to stir the imagination. Even Mrs. Allen listened carefully to the details of where the biggest nugget, one weighing in at thirty-six ounces, had been plucked from the Wild Horse Creek.

Emma glanced at Mrs. Royston and, at that lady's nod, rose from her place and began to gather the used dishes. Her hostess was already busy collecting the bowls and platters. Mrs. Allen made no move to help.

She'll learn, Emma thought with grim satisfaction, carrying a stack of dirty plates through to the kitchen. It was a curious fact of life in Prospect that even the wealthiest women worked like skivvies in their own homes, cleaning, cooking, sewing, ironing, filling the role of laundress, gardener, and nursemaid, as well as wife and mother. Then, in the afternoon, they donned their best clothes and went calling on their neighbors with all the formality of a titled lady, leaving cards at each home they visited and pretending they hadn't a notion of hard labor. Mrs. Allen would have to give up her pretensions if she hoped to be happy in Prospect, and if she hoped to further her husband's work.

Over coffee and dessert talk turned once again to the increasing number of visitors passing through Prospect. "It's a good thing you're adding on to the hotel," Jed said to Grey. "When I came to Prospect there weren't more'n a three-room cabin for travelers. Most folks carried a tent or just a sleeping roll. Times sure is changing. The way the territory's booming, we'll soon be the capital city of the Kootenays."

"Do you mean you keep a saloon?" Mrs. Allen's eyebrows rose so high they nearly disappeared. Emma's temper rose with them. She might not be overly fond of

Grey North, but it annoyed her to hear Mrs. Allen, a definite outsider, criticize him, even obliquely.

"Better'n panning for gold." He lapsed into a vernacular form of speech just to annoy Mrs. Allen, Emma thought, and didn't know whether to be amused or irritated. "Mind you, the Rockingham is an expensive saloon," he elaborated, making Mrs. Allen's protuberant eyes seem to start from her face. "Only folks with money can afford my rates, miners and gamblers and railroaders, or men like Miss Douglas's friend from San Francisco. Now, if you're not so comfortably fixed, you could try the Gold Nugget. I believe that's where the traveling photographer is staying."

Emma choked and took refuge in her napkin, but Mrs. Allen seemed unaware of the gross insult she'd just been handed. Over the napkin Emma's glance met Grey's and she quickly lowered her lashes. Grey's eyes burned with fury. It was a side of him she'd never seen before. Despite the way he delighted in provoking her, she'd never known him to be mean or spiteful to anyone. Quite the opposite, in fact. Grey North was the first to support community initiatives, making his hotel available for civic functions, promoting free education, and organizing the Miners Association. There were rumors that he'd advanced a grubstake to many a miner down on his luck. His rudeness to Mrs. Allen was totally out of character.

She glanced at Mrs. Allen's supremely self-satisfied smirk and found herself siding with Grey. The woman's supercilious attitude cried out for a set down.

"Speaking of the Gold Nugget," Jed said, "I hear they've another visitor that might interest you, Miss Douglas. A feller from San Francisco."

She turned her head sharply in Jed's direction, the

image of the slight, dark figure she'd spied that morning looming before her mind's eye. "San Francisco's a big place," she said, striving to appear disinterested, especially with Grey's all too observant eyes upon her. "It's unlikely I would know him."

"Seems odd, though," Grey remarked, "two visitors from the same city within a day of each other." He tilted his head to direct a sideways glance at Emma. "Perhaps I should put an advertisement in a San Francisco paper: 'Visit Prospect, home of Miss Emma Douglas'. Could be good for business."

All her gentler feelings toward him vanished on the instant. "I'm afraid you have an exalted opinion of my importance," she said coldly.

"Still, I'll call around to the Gold Nugget tomorrow. That photographer wants to set up a room in my hotel to take pictures. I'll ask about the other chap when I see him."

"Prospect's leading citizens will have to go to your saloon to have their pictures taken?" Mrs. Allen's chilly tones ended the discussion of the visiting American but Emma couldn't put him from her mind. If it was Parnell Wilde at the Gold Nugget, she had no doubt Grey North would soon learn of her broken engagement and the events leading up to it. She dreaded seeing the same disdainful look in his eyes that she'd seen in the faces of her former friends in San Francisco. He annoyed her endlessly with his teasing, but, she realized with surprise, his good opinion was deeply important to her.

"The Rockingham is highly respectable, Mrs. Allen," Mrs. Royston said. "It is very generous of Mr. North to make his hotel available for the picture taking."

"Well, I'm sure you all understand that Mrs. Allen is not accustomed to the ways of the frontier," the vicar interposed, "but she'll soon fit in. Now, then, Mrs. Royston, I beg you will excuse us. My wife is not so robust as you ladies and it is time she went home to rest." He pushed his chair away from the table and stood up. It was the signal to break up the party.

"Really, Miss Douglas, I do think you should be more circumspect with your gentlemen callers." Mrs. Royston turned from peeking through the lace curtains in her front window the next morning. "Mr. North is a trustee, so there may be some excuse for your being in his company, but to have a complete stranger haunting your doorstep is testing the tolerance of the town."

"What do you mean?" After a sleepless night, Emma was in no mood to play riddles with Mrs. Royston.

"Out there." Mrs. Royston pointed at the window. "There's a man waiting for you."

"There can't be," Emma declared, but refrained from stepping outside to prove her point. Instead, she joined Mrs. Royston behind the lace curtains. Feeling like a snoop, she peered outside, then quickly dropped the curtain back into place. Grey North stood at the end of the walkway, deep in conversation with Parnell Wilde.

"I've no desire to test the town's tolerance," she said, and headed down the hallway toward the back of the house. For once she blessed Mrs. Royston's inquisitive nature. Thanks to her nosy landlady, she'd been saved from walking into the most embarrassing situation of her life. She took the coward's way and slipped out the kitchen door, cut across the neighbor's yard, and proceeded to the schoolhouse via a different route. Grey North could stand outside her door until noon if he chose. It would serve him right.

And what of Parnell Wilde? She could hardly credit that he was here, in Prospect, let alone haunting her doorstep, but she'd seen him clearly enough this morning. There was no mistake. Her erstwhile fiancé had tracked her down to the middle of nowhere. The question was, why? As far as she knew, Parnell hadn't the slightest interest in prospecting or railroading or homesteading. He must have come to find her. But did she want to be found? She'd wrestled with that question all night and hadn't found the answer. In one part of her mind, she was curious to see Parnell again, to test if her heart still beat faster in his company, to know if he regretted the break between them. In another, she wished he would just vanish. She had a new life. She didn't want reminders of the old.

She mounted the steps of the schoolhouse, unlocked the door, and entered its chilly interior. Without removing her coat or gloves she opened the firebox of the stove, stuffed in paper and shavings and kindling, topped it all off with a large piece of wood and struck a match. The paper and shavings caught instantly, then the kindling and round of wood. She closed the door to the firebox and adjusted the dampers with a sense of satisfaction. She hadn't exactly tamed the frontier, but she'd learned to work the heater in the schoolhouse.

She took off her coat, gloves and hat, and hung them on the clothes tree behind her desk, then spent the next twenty minutes writing her lessons on the blackboard. At nine o'clock she went to the door and rang the bell. As the children filed past her she saw Grey striding down the street. At the foot of the schoolhouse walk, he looked up at her with a broad grin, tipped his hat, and carried on without speaking a word. Emma nodded politely, returned inside, and closed the door. One up for her in her ongoing match against Mr. North. She smiled as she called the pupils to order.

Still, she couldn't help wondering what he and Parnell had talked about. All day long she found herself hovering near the window, seeking and yet dreading to find him lingering in the vicinity.

"It's time, Miss," Bessie Smith, the greatest clock-watcher in the class, announced the second the clock showed four.

Emma turned reluctantly from the window, for once she wished she'd had to hand out a detention during the day. It would have given her an excuse to remain in the schoolroom, protected by the presence of the naughty pupil. But today her charges had all been on their best behavior. She took her place behind the teacher's desk and dismissed classes. At least she hadn't seen Grey waiting for her again. Perhaps he'd finally taken her hints.

Once the schoolroom had emptied of children, she attended to her housekeeping chores, her ears on the alert for the sound of footsteps on the threshold, but no one came to disturb her routine. She put away the broom and stepped outside, hunching her shoulders against the cold. Briefly, she wished her teacher's salary stretched to include a fur coat, then buried her chin in her wool scarf, stuffed her hands deeper into her muff, and set off at a quick pace into the darkening street.

"Hello, Abigail. I've been waiting for you." Parnell stepped out of the shadows beside the school and fell into step beside her. The well-remembered voice brought no shiver of pleasure.

She stopped and looked hard at Parnell, trying to assess her feelings. He was still handsome, his eyes the color of bitter chocolate, his black hair thick and wavy, but he looked smaller now than he had at home. He was as tall as she'd remembered, but the slim, lithe body that had thrilled her in San Francisco now seemed gaunt and unhealthy. His fashionable suit appeared foppish and impractical against the backdrop of Prospect's spare, wooden buildings. She shook her head slightly, trying to dispel her unfair judgment. She'd become used to Grey's more robust frame, that was all.

"Abby? Won't you talk with me?"

"The last time we met it was you who walked by without a word."

"I'm sorry." Parnell tried to take her hand, but she buried them both more deeply in her muff. "I was upset and frightened and confused, Abby." He offered the apology she'd longed to hear, but it didn't touch her heart. "I worked with your father. He was my mentor at the bank. I was afraid the scandal would touch me as well. You understand."

"It was a distressing time for us all." She held herself aloof.

"I know, my dear." He reached for her hand again and this time she let him fold her gloved fingers into his. "And I'm a scoundrel for deserting you, but I am here now and you will forgive me, won't you, dearest Abby?"

She hesitated. He'd sought her out, apologized, asked her forgiveness. Why wasn't she glowing with happiness?

"Must I go down on my knees?" Parnell hitched up his trouser legs as though preparing to kneel before her right there in the street. A cynicism she hadn't known she possessed made her doubt he'd really soil his sleek black trousers and she was tempted to put him to the test.

"Miss Douglas?" She'd been so preoccupied with Parnell she hadn't noticed the approach of another woman. "Miss Douglas, are you in need of assistance?" The vicar's wife stared pointedly at her hand, still linked with Parnell's.

"No." Emma snatched her hand away and took a step backward, thankful that the near darkness hid her face. "Thank you, Mrs. Allen, but your concern is unnecessary. I was just on my way home and met an old acquaintance. Please meet Parnell Wilde." She made the introduction with the barest of detail. "I'm sure you'll forgive my not stopping to talk. It is so cold. Good evening, Mrs. Allen. Mr. Wilde." She nodded to them both, then hurried off, wondering what she might have said if Mrs. Allen hadn't interrupted. She risked a quick glance over her shoulder and saw the vicar's wife and Parnell Wilde deep in conversation. She gritted her teeth and hastened on, wondering what tales Mrs. Allen would be spreading tomorrow.

Mrs. Royston pounced the moment she stepped inside. "Ah, Miss Douglas, you're home. I've been waiting for you. Come into the parlor, I've something to tell you." The landlady seized her arm and practically dragged her toward the front room. "Leave your coat and hat for the moment. Goodness, you look chilled to the bone."

"It is very cold this evening." Emma moved to the fireplace and held out her hands to the heat, grateful for the warm and cozy parlor, bright with lamplight. Mrs. Royston could be a trial, but she kept a warm house and set a good table. She loosened her coat and unwound the woolen scarf from her neck, vowing to be more understanding of her landlady. "Now, what has you so excited?" She couldn't repress a sly question. "Has Mr. Barclay come calling?"

"No, well, yes, he has." Mrs. Royston fluttered her hands in confusion. "He called early this afternoon to thank me for the fine meal, but that's not what I wanted to tell you."

"What then?" Surely only a murder or an engagement would have her landlady so excited.

"It's Grey North. Do you know he's really an English lord and he killed a man in a duel?" Mrs. Royston's eyes were round and wide and gleaming with eagerness. "Have you ever heard such a thing?"

"No, I haven't," Emma said levelly, her newfound appreciation for Mrs. Royston vanishing as rapidly as the smoke up the chimney. "Where did you hear such a story?"

"From Mrs. Allen. She came around too, after Mr. Barclay left, and she told me she'd been mulling it over all night because she was certain she knew Mr. North from somewhere and it finally came to her just before dawn. He's not *Mr.* North at all. He's *Lord* Greydon North, the son of a marquess. His family disowned him."

So, Grey had his secrets too. She wasn't surprised. Why else had the son of a peer decided to live on the edge of the wilderness? What did surprise her was the sudden rush of protectiveness she felt for the annoying man. "I'd be careful of repeating that story," she said, hoping to dampen Mrs. Royston's ardor. "Mrs. Allen may be mistaken."

She might as well have saved her breath to cool her porridge.

"Oh no, she's sure of it. She said it all came back to her as clear as day. There was even an announcement in the *Times.* His father disclaimed any responsibility for his son's actions. Can you imagine?"

"No, I can't," she said repressively. "I'm quite warmed up now, Mrs. Royston. I believe I'll go and lie down for a bit before supper." She left the room, depriving the excited landlady of her audience, but it did no good.

As the week rolled on the story spread to every corner

of the town and with each repetition the tale grew until Grey was elevated to the rank of duke and the duel was reported variously as pistols at dawn, swords in the drawing room, or a round of fisticuffs in the boxing ring. By Wednesday, when Grey did not appear to escort her to or from the schoolhouse, Emma was both relieved and sorry. She had no wish to expose herself to gossip even if she did enjoy matching wits with her pretend suitor.

What intrigued Emma, despite her resolve not to listen to gossip, was the cause of the affair. According to the whisperers, Grey North had disgraced his family, given up his birthright and set sail for the New World over a woman.

While Grey kept his distance, Parnell continued to accost her at every turn, surprising her on her way to and from school, repeating his protestations of affection and regret when they were alone, but fading away into the shadows whenever anyone else approached. Any lingering feelings she might have had for him quickly died, replaced with a cynical suspicion. He could have been the one to ransack her room and the schoolhouse, though what he was looking for she couldn't imagine. Of all people, Parnell must know she had nothing worth stealing.

On Sunday morning, she went to church thoroughly fed up with Parnell and missing Grey more than she cared to admit. Mr. Allen's excellent sermon was wasted on her and she was among the first to leave the sanctuary and head for home.

"Good morning, Emma." The object of the gossips stood before her in the churchyard, not one whit ashamed, although she noted a certain tightness about his mouth, and the blue eyes, which generally twinkled with laughter, now glinted as hard and cold as ice.

"Good morning, Mr. North." She felt the scrutiny of several pairs of eyes, but a rebellious streak of her own sided with Grey. She would not give the gossips the pleasure of seeing her turn away from him. Having been a victim of rumor herself, she could not bring herself to participate in a character assassination, especially one built on nothing but the word of a small-minded, meddling and pernicious woman.

The blue eyes warmed a fraction. "Thank you," he said softly, dipping his head to her, then more loudly, "I believe we have some business to discuss about a piano for the school. May I walk you home?"

She hesitated for a moment, knowing she would leave herself open to censure, but her sense of justice outweighed her caution. "Of course." She inclined her head.

Something flickered across his face. Relief? Gratitude? Warmth? She couldn't say for sure, but when next she glanced at him the icy glitter had gone from his eyes and she felt ridiculously pleased.

Chapter Four

A scandalized whisper carrying clear across the churchyard shattered their rapport. "Would you look at that! And her the school teacher."

The icy fury returned to Grey's eyes; his voice snapped like a whip on a frozen morning. "I'd intended to offer you luncheon at the hotel, but I'm afraid your reputation could not survive such a meeting." He started to swing away from her.

A matching rage took hold of Emma, one she could not explain, but one that would not be quelled. It was as though all the taunts and slights and humiliations she had endured since the police had come to her home coalesced into this one moment. She lifted her chin and issued a challenge of her own. "I'd enjoy having luncheon with you, Mr. North. I believe such an engagement would be in keeping with our private understanding."

Grey wheeled about, then ducked his head to peer under the brim of her hat and study her face. The anger in his eyes receded, replaced with admiration and appreciation. "Emma Douglas, you delight and amaze me." He shook his head. "When I was Prospect's leading citizen you spurned my proposition. Now that I'm its most notorious cad, you're willing to defy convention and come to my aid."

"I don't know you for a cad, Mr. North. To me you appear to be a prosperous, civic-minded member of the community and, as a trustee of the school, my employer."

The hard line of his mouth softened into a self-mocking half smile. "Miss Douglas, you are a true lady and I am proud to offer you the very best the Rockingham has to offer." He extended his arm and with only the smallest hesitation she placed her hand on his sleeve.

As they swept down the walk and out onto the frozen mud of Prospect's Queen Street they passed directly under Mrs. Allen's hard-faced scrutiny. "We'll have to turn Presbyterian," Grey whispered as they turned up the street toward the hotel. "She'll probably have us expelled from the congregation by next Sunday."

Emma giggled. It was a foolish, high-pitched titter, born of nervous strain, but it set the mood for the rest of their trek to the hotel. Grey kept up a constant stream of inane jokes and she continued to smile and sometimes laughed aloud giving every appearance of enjoying herself as they traversed the two blocks from the church to the hotel. Yet, despite her resolve to defy the gossips, she could feel the eyes that watched from across the street or peered from behind parlor curtains or bored into her back.

By the time they reached the Rockingham there wouldn't be a woman in Prospect who didn't know the schoolmarm had been out walking with the rake and the two of them had entered the hotel together. "Are they going to fire me?" Emma hated the high quaver in her voice.

"Women aren't trustees," Grey growled, and held the door open. She slipped gratefully inside and out of sight of the town.

"But they can persuade their husbands." She couldn't accept his easy comfort.

"Not once they're out of sight. Don't worry, Emma. I can sway the school board in your favor." He ushered her to a table tucked into the corner by the fireplace and held a chair while she seated herself. For all Mrs. Allen's scandalized talk of a saloon, the dining room of the Rockingham was entirely separate from the tavern and as pleasant and proper as the vicarage parlor.

Emma turned her back on the only other patrons, three men hunched over a map spread over their table. A waiter appeared almost at once. "What would you like, Emma? I believe we're offering a roast of venison today," Grey said.

"Oh, no. Thank you." Her stomach clenched painfully at the thought of a large meal. She might be willing to defy the gossips with her head high and her step firm, but inside, her nerves fluttered like the leaves of an aspen. She doubted she could swallow solid food. "Just tea, please."

"Perhaps a bowl of soup? My cook is not as skilled as Mrs. Royston, but he makes good, thick soup. You need something to warm you."

She agreed to the soup and some bread and butter. Grey opted for the venison. "And make sure the tea is very hot," he said to the waiter. "Miss Douglas is quite particular about that." The look in his eyes invited her to join in his teasing. She shot him a quelling glance and assured the waiter that the hotel's usual tea would be quite satisfactory.

The heat from the fire warmed her back, soothing the knots from her muscles. She drew off her gloves and laid them in her lap, making a deal of work out of the simple act, keeping her head bent and her eyes fixed on her hands. In her rush to defy the gossips, she'd overlooked the fact that she was always uncomfortable in Grey's presence. Her father had often cautioned her about being too impulsive. She bit her lip and cast an anxious glance toward the table of three men.

"You've been very brave so far"—Grey drummed his fingers against the table, stretching her nerves to breaking—"don't chicken out now, Emma."

She brought her chin up and met his challenging gaze with a matching one of her own. "I'm not about to add to your disgrace, Mr. North, and will you please cease that annoying tapping."

"That's my Emma." His tight smile didn't reach his eyes, and although he moved his hand from the table to his knee, his fidgeting fingers still betrayed his tension. "I believe you should call me Grey now. We've long since passed the formalities." He paused, waiting while she wriggled in her chair.

"Very well, Grey," she muttered when the silence grew too long.

"Good." He leaned back in his chair, the picture of contentment if one ignored the tapping fingers and the tight clenching of his jaw. "Those men you're eyeing over there are the surveyors I mentioned, looking for a southern route for the railway. They won't blacken your name with the ladies."

"You sound as though you've experience with gossip." The words were out in a flash and instantly regretted when rage flared into Grey's face only to be instantly hidden behind a mask of bland indifference. "I'm sorry." She bit her lip so hard she tasted blood. "I had no reason to make such a comment."

The tea arrived and he invited her to pour, politely accepting the cup she passed to him. She had the feeling he would have preferred a whiskey. When he swallowed the tea in one quick gulp she was sure of it. "I suppose you think you've earned an explanation." The white line about his mouth reappeared.

"No." Her reply was swift and short.

"You don't want to hear the harrowing tale of my disgrace?" His bitter tone sent a shiver down her spine and an unexpected sympathy to her heart.

"As you said, Mr. . . . Grey, we all have our secrets. And we're all entitled to keep them."

The waiter appeared with their food and Emma tasted her soup, surprised to find she was hungry after all, and the hot broth took the chill from her better even than the fire. "Your cook is very good with the stockpot."

"Yes." Grey's own food was growing cold on his plate, but he seemed to have lost his appetite. He put down his knife and fork, pushed his plate away, and cleared his throat. "I prefer to keep my secrets, Emma, just as you do, but I can assure you I have never behaved dishonorably to a woman of virtue."

She raised her eyes and peered up at him. "Only to women of no virtue?"

He laughed, a short, hard bark of amusement. "Well said, Emma, but I'm not going to answer that one either."

She finished her soup, enjoying the sense of having topped Grey North at his own game. The waiter removed her empty bowl and Grey's untouched meal. Another server placed a fresh pot of tea on the table and withdrew.

"Did you come to Prospect directly you left England?" Since Grey had withdrawn into morose silence, she felt it incumbent upon herself to maintain polite conversation.

"Stop talking like a starchy matron, Emma." He scowled, and again she sensed his desire for a strong drink.

"Don't take out your temper on me," she snapped back. "I'm doing my best to restore your reputation."

"So you are." He drew a deep breath and expelled it on a sigh. "So you are. I'm sorry, my dear. I'm in a foul temper."

His few blunt words touched her in a way Parnell's fulsome excuses never could. She leaned forward, resting her elbows on the table, her voice soft. "What do you intend to do now?"

"Organize a fund-raiser for your piano." A wicked smile quirked the corners of his mouth upward. "Even if I can't persuade Mrs. Royston to cook for it, the gossips will be eager to buy tickets from the notorious Grey North."

"You won't go away for a while? Let the gossip die down?"

"Not on your life." The reckless look was back in his eyes. "I won't run, Emma. This is my home. Gossip won't force me out."

"Wasn't it gossip that sent you here?"

"Only partly." He frowned and looked beyond her shoulder, as though studying some scene in his memory. "I was already disillusioned with English society; it was too hidebound, too wedded to old ideas. The gossip merely gave me the excuse I needed. I was eager to conquer the frontier, determined to prove myself as a man without benefit of rank or privilege." His voice lost its hard edge, and he spoke with passion. "I've found my true home, Emma. It's right here." He stabbed a finger against the table for emphasis. "Sure, Prospect has its share of ruffians and schemers, but mostly it's filled with men of vision and big hearts. Can't you feel it? We're part of something here, a grand enterprise. The New World is set to rival the Old, and we're in the forefront."

"And yet you built a hotel instead of prospecting."

"And I bet every penny I had on its success. If the Rockingham fails, Emma, I'm destitute."

"You wouldn't go home to England? Throw yourself on your father's mercy? I take it the noble family part of the gossip is true?"

"Yes," he said shortly, "but, no. I will never go crawling back to my family. I chose this life, Emma, and I'll live by that decision."

"But Prospect won't stay raw and isolated forever. More people are moving here every year. The Mrs. Allens of this world are determined to civilize even your town, Mr. North."

"I don't mind the civilizing influence of common courtesy and decency, and more people are good for commerce." He gestured to the empty tables in the dining room. "It's not the hardships of the frontier I admire, Emma, it's the attitude. That sense of purpose and optimism." He leaned forward, his face intent with excitement, his eyes shining with fervor. "Can't you see it? This is a big land. It needs big dreams, not meddlesome busybodies trying to bind us all to drab little lives. Breathe deeply, Emma, spread your wings. On the frontier you'll learn to fly."

It was the longest speech she'd ever heard him make and the most revealing. He'd let down his guard for her, invited her to share his dream, allowed her a glimpse into his heart, but she shrank back, afraid. She wasn't ready to jettison all the old rules. Despite her impulsive championing of Grey North, she needed the security of a conventional life. Respectability, not liberation, was her watchword. She could not embrace the future that he reached for. She sat primly erect, her hands folded in her lap, her voice cool and distant. "Such passion," she said, managing to sound faintly amused.

The glow left his eyes. The sardonic mask slid back into place. "Silly, isn't it?" He sat back. "Now, about your piano." He launched into an explanation of his plans for the fund-raising dinner, his careless smile firmly in place, his words edged with cynicism, a sneer curling his lip. Emma listened with only half an ear, holding her reserve before her like a shield, keeping herself safe, and regretting, with all her heart, that she'd been found wanting in his eyes.

"Abby, please let me speak with you." Emma looked up sharply from her book on Monday and saw Parnell Wilde standing in the schoolhouse door. It was noon. The children had eaten their lunches and gone outdoors to play. She was alone.

"You shouldn't be here."

"You won't let me call on you at your boardinghouse. You won't go out walking with me. How else can I meet you?" He came closer, taking up a position midway down the center aisle of the school, the same place where Grey North had teased her and challenged her to flout the conventions only a short time ago. Her last parting with Grey had left her with a sore heart. She wished she could put him out of her mind, but seeing Parnell in the same place, she couldn't help but compare the two men. Grey was no taller, but he was broader than Parnell, his shoulders wider. Grey was fair, whereas Parnell was dark. Parnell spoke with the Gallic inflection of his New Orleans background; Grey with the precise tones of his English public school. But the outward differences were not what struck her most but the manner and character of the two men.

Grey had stood with his feet astride, his head thrown

back, a laugh in his throat and a challenge in his eye. Parnell seemed nervous, cringing and complaining, casting an anxious glance toward the door. "What are you afraid of?"

"I am not afraid, only you have told me that you are not allowed visitors. I do not wish to cause you trouble, but I must see you."

"Why?"

"Because I love you. I can't live without you. You must let me explain." He took another step down the aisle and she rose to her feet, regarding him from behind the safety of her desk.

"Don't come up here." She held up her hand and he halted.

"Then when?"

Whatever her feelings for him in the past, Parnell had betrayed her trust, proved himself a liar, with a false smile, and one who'd collapsed like a paper house when she'd needed him most. For all that, she couldn't bring herself to be rude. She had hoped, if she continued to avoid him, he would grow weary of Prospect and disappear as mysteriously as he'd arrived. Grey would call her a coward, but she had been taught all her life to avoid argument and confrontation.

She glanced at the clock. She needed to ring the bell for classes. "You may escort me home at half-past four."

"I will count the minutes," he said in the extravagant style she'd used to find so charming. "Until then." He kissed his fingers and blew the caress toward her. Then he turned and hastened away, leaving Emma with the sinking feeling she'd set herself up for disaster. Which was a foolish notion since she'd made no apologies for lunching with Grey North and he readily admitted to being a rake.

Men! She rang the school bell with unnecessary vigor. Perhaps the suffragettes had the right idea. A woman who could earn her own living was better off without a man in her life. She watched her pupils file into the classroom, grateful to them for needing a schoolmarm. It was a decent, honest living. She had a place in the community, a degree of respect usually reserved for married women, and sufficient income to see to her needs. Parnell, with his pretty phrases, and Grey, with his goading challenges, were mere distractions and best put out of her mind.

Once the children were settled, she strode to the big globe at the front of the room. A sense of pleasure and purpose brightened her smile as she began the lesson. "Today we'll study the routes of the explorers," she said. "Who can tell me where Champlain first landed?"

At four o'clock she dismissed her classes, then damped down the fire, cleaned the blackboards, and swept the floor without her usual resentment. At least she hadn't been reduced to taking in laundry or serving as a chambermaid. She looked about the tidy schoolroom with a sense of pride and then had to laugh at herself. Perhaps she was becoming a true pioneer after all, ready to fend for herself, an emancipated female. She shook her head at her fanciful musings and went to put on her hat and coat. Grey might want to pit himself against the wilderness, but she doubted her newfound independent streak would survive the first heavy snowfall. She had no appetite for shoveling walkways.

When she let herself out, Parnell was waiting for her, lurking around the corner of the schoolhouse, and only coming into the open when she descended the steps. "At last," he said, blowing on his gloved hands. "I am freezing out here, Abby. Why did you come to such a hard place?"

His complaints irritated her to the point she forgot her own aversion to the cold and stepped out briskly toward home, her footfalls muffled by the light skiff of snow on the boardwalk. "I wanted a challenge. What was it you wanted to say to me?"

"So brusque, my sweet?" Parnell hurried along beside her. "Are you so angry with me? Have you no room for forgiveness in your heart?"

"It's been nearly two years, Parnell." She kept her eyes focused straight ahead. "Why the desire for absolution now?"

"I would have come months ago, but you had disappeared." His remorse seemed almost genuine, but then his voice changed and he went on in an aggrieved manner. "I have suffered much, worrying about you, imagining all sorts of terrible things. You should have written to me, Abby. You have been unkind and selfish."

She stopped dead in her tracks and turned to face him, nearly breathless with astonishment. "You have the nerve to call me unkind?" She stabbed a finger against his chest. "After you took your ring back? After you refused to acknowledge me in the street? You accuse me of selfishness!"

"Yes, yes." He had the grace to look shamefaced. "You have a right to be upset. I will try to remember that you didn't know my anguish. But now we will put all that behind us. We will be happy again. You will come back to San Francisco, and we will go on as before."

She stared hard at him in the gathering darkness, a nasty suspicion forming in the back of her mind. "How did you find me?"

"Your friend, Mr. Jergens. I heard him book passage

on a ship to Vancouver and I followed him. I knew if anyone could find you, he could."

"You mean you spied on Everett." She made no attempt to keep the contempt from her voice. "Couldn't you just have asked him if he knew my whereabouts?"

Parnell shrugged, tucking his chin down deeper into the muffler he'd wrapped several times about his neck. "I was afraid he wouldn't tell me."

She began to walk again.

"Abby, I cannot talk to you like this, rushing along as though you're trying to escape and the frost freezing the breath in my lungs."

"Don't call me Abby. I'm no longer that girl."

"But you could be." His voice held a seductive whisper. "Come back to me, my sweet. We'll have music and moonlight and magnolia blossoms. I want you in a silken gown with pearls at your throat and stardust in your hair. Remember, my sweet? We danced as a warm breeze wafted in the window, your perfume filled my senses, intoxicating as wine. You fit in my arms as light as thistledown. We laughed together and we fell in love."

She slowed her charge toward home. Parnell's words pulled her into those heady days of their engagement, blocking out the pain of her father's death and obliterating the ice and toil of Prospect. He was a part of her. He'd known her as she had been, soft and pampered and carefree. Grey had almost convinced her that she belonged on the frontier, matching her wits and her skills against the harshness of the land. But was that her vision or his?

She halted and turned to study Parnell's face in the dim light of dusk. "And if by some magic I could conjure up that ballroom and the warm, soft night of San Francisco, what would you say to me, Parnell?" She gazed intently into his liquid brown eyes.

He caught her hand and carried it to his chest, holding it over his heart. "Then I would say you are beautiful, Abby. I would say I love you. I would court you all over again; I would get down on my knees and beg for your hand. Then I would cover you with kisses and sweep you off to a love nest. I would—"

"That's enough," she interrupted hastily, pulling her hand away. She knew what happened between a man and woman on their wedding night but she didn't want to hear it spoken of.

"Ah, you are shy?" He touched a finger to her cheek, sliding it down to graze the corner of her mouth, unbelievably intimate despite the gloves that covered his hands. "And yet you dined in the hotel with that notorious Mr. North."

She turned on her heel and set off again, marching determinedly down the street, her independent streak outweighing her romantic one. "So you have spied on me as well."

"There was no need." Parnell sounded peevish. "The whole town is talking of it. What were you thinking, Abb . . . Emma?"

"I'm thinking that you have no business censuring my behavior." They had reached the gate in the picket fence that surrounded Mrs. Royston's yard. "Good-bye, Parnell." She stepped inside the enclosure, clicked the gate shut with a snap, and strode up the walk with long, unladylike strides.

She stamped the snow from her boots without looking back and went inside, grateful for the heat and light that greeted her. "Good evening, Mrs. Royston," she called, surprised that her landlady wasn't lurking near the front of the house as was her habit. She shed her outer clothing and made her way to the parlor only to find it empty. She went on down the hall to the kitchen and found her landlady deep in discussion with Grey North. A pot of cooling tea sat at her elbow while Mrs. Royston sucked the end of a pencil and scowled at a lengthy list written out on a piece of lined paper. She looked up at Emma hovering in the doorway and dropped the pencil.

"Oh my goodness me! You're home already and the supper not even started." She bustled to her feet. "Mr. North, I'll have to think about this some more."

Grey also rose, but without the fuss and fluster of Mrs. Royston. Rather, he gained his feet in a smooth, languid motion that bespoke not only strength and agility, but also an ease and confidence with his body that set her nerves on edge. No man should be so self-assured, especially not one who was the center of the hottest gossip in Prospect. "Good evening, Emma."

"Grey." She tried to keep her tones as cool as his, but the sudden light that warmed his eyes at her use of his Christian name sent her into confusion. She dropped her gaze to concentrate on the pattern of Mrs. Royston's tablecloth.

"Mr. North was here talking about the fund-raising dinner," Mrs. Royston explained as she peeled potatoes. "I'm not sure about hiring myself out as a cook, but if you really want a piano for the schoolhouse . . ."

"You were serious about a fund-raising dinner?" She glanced up and then away again when he favored her with his brightest smile. It was very difficult to maintain an aloof attitude with Grey when he insisted on being charming and generous and, it would seem, totally indifferent of the sting of their last conversation.

"Of course. Don't you think it's a good idea?"

"Well, yes, but it's an imposition for you, and Mrs. Royston," she included her landlady in her apology, "and under the circumstances . . ."

"I told you I'd do it." He cut off her protests in a hard voice. "Or have you forgotten so soon?"

"I thought you were just venting your anger." Her cheeks grew warm. Apparently he hadn't forgotten their words over lunch at the Rockingham, after all.

"I always keep my word, Emma." He bent a hard blue gaze upon her as though offering a threat . . . or a promise. She shivered, and not from cold.

"I'm sure that's very generous of you." She picked up the teapot, lifted the lid, then set it down again, giving herself something to do that prevented her from meeting that hard look.

"Of course, you will attend." His voice softened, holding that note of intimate teasing she'd come to realize he used only with her. She glanced up and saw a slow smile cross his face. "As my guest of honor."

She had no choice, of course, and Grey knew it, but she wasn't about to meekly do his bidding, either. "I'll have to review the terms of my contract to see if such an outing would be allowable." She picked up the teapot again and carried it to the stove, uselessly pouring hot water on the spent leaves.

"Your contract says you are required to do all in your power to promote the learning and welfare of your students. Acquiring a piano for the schoolhouse will promote their learning opportunities." Grey closed that loophole.

"But I'm to keep an eight-o'clock curfew," she threw back at him.

"As a trustee I can make an exception." Laughter danced in his eyes. He seemed to take delight in their verbal duel. She hid her own smile. To be honest, she rather enjoyed matching wits with him.

"There is always the community to consider," she said primly, not willing to concede defeat easily. "What do you think, Mrs. Royston? Would it be proper for me to appear at the dinner with Mr. North?"

"I don't know why not," her landlady huffed as she plunked the heavy pot of potatoes onto the stove. "You've already dined with him alone, in a public place." Her attitude softened almost instantly. "Although Mr. Barclay says he admires you for standing up to the gossips, what I don't know is if it's proper for me to cook for it." Her face brightened, and she added, "I'll ask Mr. Barclay. If he approves, I'll be happy to cook the dinner for you, Mr. North."

"Thank you, Mrs. Royston." Grey nodded meekly but dropped another of those intimate winks in Emma's direction. "I'll get out of your way now." He set his chair straight to the table. "But I'll call on you in the next couple of days for your answer, if I may."

"Yes, fine." Mrs. Royston was busy stirring a pan on the stove. "After I've talked it over with Mr. Barclay. See Mr. North out, will you?" she asked Emma. "I've my hands full here. That Rose!"

Perforce, Emma accompanied Grey to the front door reflecting that Mrs. Royston's sense of propriety seemed a very convenient thing, allowing her to be a highly proper Victorian lady one moment and a practical, no-nonsense frontierswoman the next. She had certainly set Emma up for an unsuitable tête-à-tête.

"You look wonderful," Grey lingered in the front hall, apparently quite prepared to take advantage of Mrs. Royston's arrangements. "Your cheeks rosy with cold, your eyes sparkling with temper, and your mouth bright red because you chew your lips when you're upset." Before she knew what he was about he bent his head and softly brushed a kiss against her mouth.

She sprang back, face flaming, speechless with indignation. Her hands flew to cover her lips.

"I said you had a kissable mouth." He put his hat on his head and gave her the teasing smile that made his eyes twinkle. "I was right." He put his hand on the door. "Good night, Emma. I'll see you soon." A cold gust of wind, the click of the latch, and he was gone, leaving her to press her fingers to her lips and try to calm the wild beating of her heart. Of course, she was outraged, she assured herself. No gentleman would kiss a lady without first asking permission. It was indignation that made her breath come in quick, short gasps and vexation that twisted her stomach in the queerest way, but neither could explain her lifting of the curtain to watch Grey stride down the street. After he'd disappeared she waited a further five minutes while the heat died out of her cheeks, before daring to return to the kitchen.

"That took a while," Mrs. Royston patted biscuit dough into shape and slipped the pan into the oven.

"Mr. North is very enthusiastic about this dinner." Emma hoped the fib would explain her lengthy absence.

"Yes"—Mrs. Royston cocked her head to one side and studied Emma—"he is quite keen on the dinner, but what I want to know is whether it's a new piano for the schoolhouse he wants or an evening with the school teacher."

"Mr. North takes delight in teasing," Emma said with a repressive frown, "but as a trustee, he knows very well that I cannot receive his attentions." She went to the Welsh dresser and took down a couple of plates and set them on the table. Since Rose had left, the two women had fallen into the habit of taking their supper in the kitchen. It meant less work and was cozier. Emma found she preferred the arrangement to the formal dining room.

"I believe Mr. North writes his own rules." Mrs. Royston took the biscuits from the oven, slid them onto a plate, and set it on the table.

Emma had no doubt she was right, but she didn't want to talk about Grey North or his disturbing effect on her emotions. She dumped out the dregs in the teapot, spooned in more leaves, and refilled it from the kettle. "Have you heard anything from Rose?"

"That girl!" Mrs. Royston was off on a tirade about Rose's selfishness, laziness, stupidity, and a long list of other shortcomings. Emma listened with half an ear. Parnell's talk of San Francisco had unsettled her. If the new investigation cleared her father's name, would she return? Resume her old life, filling her days with the trivia of fashionable dress and afternoon calls and glittering balls? It was what she wanted, the safe and familiar. Yet something held her back. Something that cried for more in life. Perhaps she had caught some of the frontier spirit, after all.

"If I do agree to this dinner, what will I cook?" Mrs. Royston's question drew Emma away from her fruitless musings as they sat down to dinner.

"Personally, I think your shepherd's pie is a masterpiece." Emma sampled the chicken stew on her plate. "But for a gala event like Mr. North proposes, you'll want something more grand."

"There aren't a lot of choices in Prospect in December." Mrs. Royston pushed her mashed potatoes around on the plate, her brow furrowed in thought. "Roast beef, I suppose, but it would be nice to dress it up some."

"Maybe Mr. Barclay has some exotic canned goods that could help."

As a diversion, mention of Jed Barclay was a surefire winner. "Of course." Mrs. Royston brightened instantly and applied herself to her dinner with gusto. "That's the very thing, Miss Douglas. Thank you."

Upon leaving Emma, spluttering and furious, in Mrs. Royston's front hall, Grey walked into the dark street and turned toward the hotel in a fretful frame of mind. What had possessed him? He'd sworn never to get involved with a woman again. He'd only intended to pretend an attachment to Emma as a ruse to fend off the likes of Thelma Black. He hadn't bargained for Emma's eminently kissable mouth or the pleasure he took in her fine eyes or the exhilaration he felt when they matched wits. He'd have to call a halt to their supposed romance before it got out of hand. He'd do it, right after the Christmas concert.

A slight movement in the shadows drove all thoughts of dalliance from his mind and sharpened his attention.

It could be only a stray dog, but the criminal who'd vandalized Emma's property hadn't been caught, and he didn't agree with the police assumption of a disgruntled pupil. With every sense alert, he made another turn, stepping into the back lane, the one that gave access into Mrs. Royston's kitchen garden and allowed Rose to keep her trysts with Charlie Murphy. Snow crunched under his feet, masking any other footsteps as he made his way toward the cover of the chicken coop. Anyone hearing him would think he'd only come to check on the hens. On reaching his goal, he flattened himself against the darkest wall of the henhouse and listened, his eyes peering into the darkness, watchful for the least motion that would betray an intruder.

He stayed still and silent against the henhouse, patiently waiting for his quarry to betray himself. Other than the occasional flutter or cluck from the hens, he heard only silence. Had he allowed his imagination and an overprotective attitude toward Emma Douglas to conjure up danger where there was none? Then he heard it. Deep in the shadows, beside the Royston house, a muffled cough. There! A man crouched against the wall, just beyond the light from the kitchen window.

As silently as he could, he ran forward, but the crunch of his boots on the cold snow must have betrayed him, for the prowler, after one quick glance over his shoulder, sprinted away. Grey followed but the fellow had a head start and had vanished by the time Grey gained the street. The footsteps in the snow leading from the kitchen window to the front gate were plain even in the darkness, but once on the street it was impossible to distinguish one set of footprints from another. He searched the darkness but no more suspicious shadows moved along the street.

He spent a few more minutes investigating the yards and laneways of the neighboring houses, but even as he went through the motions he knew his mission was hopeless. The prowler was long gone. What he couldn't understand was why. If the thief wanted money there were better pickings than the schoolmarm.

Emma herself? His gut tightened. Anyone who harmed Emma Douglas would answer to him. But lust didn't explain the previous break-ins. There was something more, some secret that only Emma knew, and if his suspicions were correct, it was a secret connected with her past. Whatever she'd run from, it appeared to have followed her to Prospect. He wished she would trust him.

He turned his steps toward the Gold Nugget Saloon. He'd picked up no rumors in the tavern of his own hotel, perhaps a whiskey-soaked miner at the saloon would have something to tell him. Or perhaps he'd find a tall man with long legs and a cough and no explanation of where he'd spent the last half hour.

Chapter Five

"Couldn't you have worn something a little more festive?" Bella Royston frowned at Emma's neat gray skirt and high-necked blouse, the same outfit she wore with very little variation day after day to school. "I'm sure Mr. North expected his guest of honor to appear more stylish."

"I'm the school teacher," Emma responded, "not a fashion plate." She stood inside the large kitchen of the Rockingham Hotel watching while Mrs. Royston put the finishing touches to the dinner that had been sold out within hours of its being advertised.

"There's no need to look like a dowdy." Mrs. Royston sniffed and plucked at the stiff, shiny fabric of her own dress, which at the moment was covered with a huge apron. "Even in Prospect, a lady can keep up to date with the help of Mr. Timothy Eaton's new catalog. And what have you done to your hair?" She scowled at the severe bun Emma had adopted for the evening. "Rose, mind what you're doing." Mrs. Royston hustled over to the large stove and snatched the wooden spoon from her helper's hand. "Like this," she said, stirring the simmering sauce with slow, smooth strokes. She handed the spoon back to Rose, watched her with a critical eye for a moment, then came back to Emma. "Wasn't it thoughtful of Mr. North to fetch Rose to help me tonight? I don't care what Mrs. Allen says, the man's a gentleman."

Emma raised a hand to ease a hairpin that dug into her scalp. Perhaps she had overdone the schoolmarm thing. She winced as her hair pulled when she bent her head. Normally, she wore a looser, more flattering style, but that was before Grey had kissed her. She hadn't been alone with him since, and she intended to make it abundantly clear that she was here tonight only in her role of school teacher. "Are the Allens coming tonight?"

"No." Her landlady whipped off her apron with a sharp tug. "Not that anyone will miss them." She sniffed as though something smelled bad. "Such a sour-faced malcontent that woman is. Mind you, I feel sorry for her husband. He looks like he could do with a good meal." She patted her hair and smoothed her hands over her well-upholstered hips. "My Henry never had that lean and hungry look." For once, no tears accompanied mention of the long-departed Mr. Royston. "Now, Rose," she admonished her helper one last time, "you dish up the soup first, two of the hotel's waiters will serve it. There's no need for you to come into the dining room. I'll pop back between courses to see how you're managing. Is Mr. Barclay here yet?" She turned anxiously to Emma. "He bought one of the first tickets but he told Mr. North he wouldn't if I wasn't at the table, though how he expected me to cook a grand dinner and still sit down to eat it, I don't know. If Mr. North hadn't persuaded Rose to help out, I don't know what we'd have done."

"I believe Mr. Barclay has arrived." Emma couldn't suppress a smile. Mrs. Royston was as giddily in love as a schoolgirl.

"Ready, ladies?" Grey appeared in the doorway. He held out one arm for Mrs. Royston and the other for Emma. "Time to make our entrance." He raised his eyebrows as he assessed Emma's appearance, then grinned as though he knew just what she'd been thinking when she'd chosen a hairstyle guaranteed to give her a headache before the evening was out.

"This way, ladies." Instead of turning toward the hotel dining room, Grey walked them down a short corridor and into his private apartment. Emma couldn't help but cast a quick glance about, as curious as the rest of Prospect. She noted the same high ceilings as the public dining room, but the wallpaper was plain instead of flocked and of a pale green.

A gleaming white cloth covered a long table in the center of the room. Crystal sparkled in the light from a dozen candles; silver flatware bordered each fine china plate. It was like stepping into another world. "Where did you get all this?" she whispered to Grey, amazement overcoming her irritation.

"Do you like it?"

"Of course, but it's not what I expected."

"You thought I'd invite my guests to eat beans and bacon from a tin plate?"

"No, but . . ." She broke off and shook her head in resignation. "You're a strange man, Grey North." She turned her head to study the rest of the room. No paintings hung from the picture rail, but well-filled bookshelves lined one wall and several large maps of gold rush country adorned another. Nowhere could she see a photograph or portrait or coat of arms to indicate his family or background. As far as anyone could tell from this room, Grey North had arrived in Prospect with no history.

She hadn't really expected anything different. Grey

had made it clear he had no fondness for his family or for England. He'd embraced the New World and his new life without the slightest backward glance, cutting all ties with home. Or had he? Tucked into the corner of one of the bookcases she spied a miniature on ivory, a woman with soft golden hair and sad blue eyes. "Your mother?" she asked softly, inclining her head in the direction of the picture.

"Yes." The reply was brief and barely audible. His gaze skimmed the painting briefly before turning away. "Ladies and gentlemen," he called the room to attention, "may I present our guest of honor tonight, Miss Emma Douglas"—he urged her forward to greet the other guests—"and the lady responsible for the fine repast you are about to enjoy, Mrs. Bella Royston." Her landlady blushed with pleasure and curtsied slightly as the other guests applauded. Then Grey escorted them both to the table. With all the aplomb of a seasoned host, he seated Mrs. Royston on his left, next to Jed Barclay. Emma was on his right, with the inspector from the police detachment on her other side.

The Allens may have chosen to disregard the dinner, but fourteen of Prospect's other citizens seemed eager to enjoy Grey's hospitality. Farther down the table she spotted the newlyweds. Lottie wore the yellow silk from her wedding day, and Sean still looked at her with a mixture of pride and tenderness that made Emma's heart ache. If ever a woman had been transformed by love, that woman was Lottie O'Connor. She repressed a sigh and let her gaze pass on to the other guests. The setting might look like a London dining room, but the guest list was pure frontier, with the men outnumbering the women ten to four.

"Will you say grace, Father?" Grey nodded to the missionary from the Catholic mission.

The guests bowed their heads as the priest intoned a short blessing. As soon as the "amen" had been pronounced the waiters appeared, carrying bowls of Mrs. Royston's cream of pumpkin soup, artfully decorated with a swirl of sour cream in each bowl. Amid the clinking of silver on china, the room filled with the hum of conversation. Emma turned her attention to the inspector, resplendent in his scarlet dress uniform. Beside him, she felt drab and colorless and, for an instant, wished she'd followed Mrs. Royston's advice on the matter of dress. However, an acute awareness of Grey's shoulder only inches from her own put an end to such regrets. "Good evening, Inspector. How kind of you to support the school in this way."

"Not kind at all, Miss." The Mountie's speech was slow, his face a mask of correctness, but his eyes twinkled with engaging humor. "Any excuse to avoid the mess hall and dine with a lady is worth the price of admission."

Emma chuckled. "I think even Mrs. Royston would have trouble producing enticing meals for such a large contingent of men three times a day, every day of the week."

"P'raps, but she couldn't do worse. Have you ever eaten burned eggs, Miss Douglas?" He pulled a long face, although his eyes continued to twinkle with droll humor. "They taste even worse than they smell. Some days I envy the men out on patrol. Beans and bacon over a campfire would be a treat."

"Tell me about patrols." Emma relaxed under the inspector's indulgent gaze and gentle humor. It was a pleasure to speak with a man as entertaining and interesting as Inspector West and not have to deal with any undertones of flirtation. The whole town knew Inspector West was wedded to the Force.

"Mosquitos, black flies, poor grazing, washed-out roads, crazed miners, and angry Indians. Patrol is a real picnic, Miss, compared to life in barracks. There it's all drill, and morning parade, and green recruits misfiring their rifles, and endless reports."

"Any news on the break-ins?" Jed Barclay joined their conversation from across the table.

Inspector West shook his head, his doleful face becoming even longer. "Nor likely to be. Even if we knew who did it, it'd be hard to prove, since nothing was taken. There's no evidence to link the vandal to the crime."

"Your constable thought it might be a disgruntled student," Grey said, raising a speculative eyebrow in the inspector's direction.

"P'raps." The conversation ceased as a waiter served the succulent sirloin of beef that had been roasting slowly in the hotel kitchen for several hours. "Or not." Inspector West picked up his knife and fork and applied himself to the dinner, a sigh of satisfaction rumbling up from his large frame as he tasted the meat. "Mrs. Royston, you are a pearl among women."

Whatever the inspector thought about the break-ins—and he certainly had an opinion, Emma decided—there was a keen intelligence and a sharp mind behind his dry humor. He wasn't about to share his suspicions with his dinner companions.

As always in Prospect, talk shifted to the latest news from the gold fields. It seemed people never tired of telling and retelling the stories of fabulous finds and rumors of a new strike. "You went to the gold fields, Mr. O'Connor," the town banker said when they'd reached the dessert stage of the dinner. "Tell us about it."

"I went, sure enough," Sean replied, "but I'm home now." Emma observed the knowing look he exchanged with Lottie and felt that pang of envy again. "There's more to life than gold."

"Are your pupils ready for the Christmas concert?" Grey spoke at her elbow while the waiters cleared away the main course.

"As ready as they'll ever be," Emma sighed. "I'm counting on you, as master of ceremonies, and Mr. Barclay, as Santa Claus, to make people forget the off-key singing and the stilted dialogue."

"It'll be fine," Mrs. Royston said, watching with a critical eye as the waiters brought in the dessert. She prided herself on her cakes, and this time she'd used a week's worth of eggs and the bounty of her fruit tree to create a perfect apple chiffon cake, served with a warm cinnamon-caramel sauce. It looked and smelled divine.

"Bella, you've outdone yourself." Jed rolled his eyes in appreciation as he tasted the confection. "I've forgot what we were talkin' about."

"The school concert." Mrs. Royston's cheeks flushed pink with pleasure. "I was saying the audience is mostly parents and grandparents, and so long as each child gets time in the limelight, no one'll care if the singing isn't perfect."

"And Les Smith has promised to bring his fiddle," Emma said. "That will help."

"And next year, we'll have a piano," Grey announced with satisfaction. "Ladies and gentlemen"—he rose to his feet—"I thank you all for coming and hope you enjoyed this fine meal." He lifted his glass to Mrs. Royston and waited while the dinner guests applauded before continuing. "As you know, the price of your ticket bought you a fine meal—and the chance to make a contribution to the schoolhouse piano fund." There was a rumble of laughter around the table. "There is a box at the door where you may make your donation. I'm sure you'll be generous. The schoolhouse needs a piano, gentlemen, and Mrs. Royston's dinner deserves a proper appreciation."

"That fellow could talk a bear out of his skin," the inspector grumbled a good-natured protest as he pushed back his chair and reached into a pocket for his billfold. "It's been a pleasure, Miss Douglas." He bowed slightly before leaving her and making his way to the collection box. Others followed suit and soon the whole party broke up, leaving only Emma, Mrs. Royston, Grey, and Jed Barclay to watch the waiters clear the table.

"You did a fine job, Bella." Jed massaged his large stomach in appreciation.

"It was a labor, I'll say that." Mrs. Royston fluffed herself like a preening hen. "But it was all in a good cause."

"You must be worn out." Jed was all sympathy. "I'll see you home and Rose can tuck you up in bed with a cup of hot tea."

"Rose!" Mrs. Royston's good humor faded just a little. "I must speak with the girl. It's high time she came back to me. I hear her youngest brother is sickly and rations are mighty scarce at home." She hastened off in the direction of the kitchen, Jed trailing at her heels.

Alone with Grey, Emma felt hot and breathless, the high neck of her blouse suddenly too tight and her corset pinching her ribs. She couldn't forget that the last time they were alone he'd had the audacity to kiss her. "I'll just get my coat." She edged toward the door, giving Grey a wide berth. "Rose and I can walk home together. I've a feeling Mr. Barclay doesn't want us tagging along with him and Mrs. Royston."

"Running away, Emma?" Grey sent her a mocking smile. "Don't you want to help me count the collection?"

"I'm sure you can manage alone." She put her hand on the door handle, grateful to escape. "Good night, Mr. North. And thank you, on behalf of the school," she added in her best schoolmarm voice.

"I'll see you home." He dropped the teasing tone and stepped out into the hall behind her.

"Rose will . . ."

"Rose is a foolish girl who'd run at the sight of her own shadow. Until the culprit who wrecked your schoolroom is caught, it's not safe for you to be out on the streets after dark. Besides," his grin returned, "you're past your curfew. As a trustee, it's my duty to inquire into that."

"Perhaps while you're explaining my flouting of the rules, you'll also impress upon them that I'll need a raise to compensate for my additional duties as music teacher once the piano has arrived." She stuck her chin in the air and glared at him.

His grin widened and he chuckled before giving her a small bow. "One up for you, Emma. I'll be sure to raise the subject of your salary with the school board."

He walked with her to the kitchen where he had a few private words with the hotel's regular cook. The cook glanced at Rose, then shrugged his shoulders and wrapped the remains of the roast with butcher's paper and set it aside.

"Get your coat, Rose," Grey said. "You've done enough for tonight."

"Yessir." Rose dropped a plate into the soapy water, all too eager to abandon the washing up. She snatched her thin coat off a hook behind the door and hurried to join Emma and Grey for the walk home.

After leaving the women at their doorstep, Grey did a quick circle around the house, taking special care to check the bushes. Tonight he found no prowlers but did run into a policeman patrolling the quiet street. Apparently Inspector West had taken his complaints seriously. "Good evening, officer." He touched the brim of his hat as he passed the Mountie and set off for the hotel at a brisk pace. Since Emma was safely guarded, he could get on with his other business of the evening.

He entered the hotel through the kitchen door just as the cook set the big porridge pot ready for the morning's breakfast. "So did you make a lot of money with your fine dinner?" The cook cast him a malevolent look and then, pointedly, turned his back. George's mediocre skills in the kitchen didn't prevent him from having the chef's temperament.

"No need to be jealous, George." Grey dropped his empty saddlebags on the table in the center of the room. "Mrs. Royston was here to cater to a private affair. Your job's safe."

"I'd like to see her setting her fancy plates in front of a bunch of miners just in off the diggings," George continued to grumble as he reached for his coat and hat. "Plain cooking is what those boys want."

"And you provide it admirably, George." Grey picked up the remains of the roast and packed it into the saddlebags.

"Where you goin' with that, anyways?" the cook grumbled. "It'd make good soup."

"Not this time." Grey slung the loaded saddlebags over his shoulder and grinned at his cook. "You'll have to use the ox tail I saw in the larder." He gestured for George to precede him into the frosty night, then followed him out and locked the door.

"Feels like snow." George sniffed the air and looked up at the clouds scudding across the pale moon. "Not a night to go for a horseback ride."

"It'll only be worse tomorrow." Grey waved and set off toward the livery where he stabled his horses. The one thing he missed about England was the fine horseflesh. On the frontier he'd quickly learned that the high-stepping thoroughbreds of his native land were unsuited to the tough conditions of his new home. He walked into the livery, nodded to the stable hand, and went to saddle a tough little mustang.

"Whoa, Satan," he murmured as the horse shifted and stamped his feet. He held out a lump of sugar in the flat of his hand. It amused him to put the noble name on a horse who might better have been called Dobbin. "Let's go for a ride, shall we?" He patted the horse's long face, fitted on the bridle, and led him outside. A cloud obscured half the moon, making the night dangerously dark. "What do you say, boy? Can we make it to Rose's cabin and back again before we're lost or stuck in a snow drift?"

The horse snorted and bobbed his head up and down, rattling the bit and buckles on his bridle. "I think so, too," Grey murmured before he vaulted lightly onto his mount. He touched his heels to the horse's flanks and Satan moved off at a slow trot. Grey settled himself comfortably into the big Western saddle, another New World invention, and one infinitely more practicable for long days of riding than the flimsy bits of leather he'd grown up with.

He had to pay close attention to the few markings visible above the snow on the poorly traveled trail to the Beaton cabin. Still, Satan was a seasoned trail pony, and Grey trusted him to keep his footing. On the hour's ride through the patchy moonlight, he had plenty of time to think—about Emma Douglas.

She was a pretty thing. He liked her hazel eyes, even though they flashed green with temper every time she looked at him. He liked the thick auburn hair that normally framed her face in enticing waves. He grinned in the darkness. He'd seen her sneaking the pins out before they'd even reached her doorstep. He was pretty sure he'd not see that awful bun again. He liked the way she made him laugh and was even glad she scorned his attentions. She was the perfect foil to protect him from predatory females. His grin faded. He hadn't meant to kiss her.

But it was her own fault as much as his. Usually she drew her lips into a firm line, part of her stern, schoolmarm persona, but occasionally, when she thought herself unobserved, she relaxed her rigid demeanor. Then her mouth was soft and dewy and eminently kissable. It was the contrast that had fascinated him. He hadn't meant to kiss her. He shouldn't have. But he couldn't regret it either.

He scowled into the black night. He'd told Emma to keep her secrets, but she was so stiff and proper one moment and so appealingly vulnerable the next, he couldn't help but be intrigued. Besides, two men from her past had arrived in Prospect within a week of each other and Emma had been the victim of two break-ins. It strained credulity to think the two events were a mere coincidence. Perhaps he needed to enquire more closely of Emma's secrets—as a school trustee, of course. There would be no more kissing. After the fiasco of his youth, he was firmly resolved to remain a bachelor.

A vision of his mother's sad eyes during his last, terrible confrontation with his father crossed his mind. Even five years later his heart twisted with pain for her. He'd vowed then that he would give up the comforts of home and family forever before he'd put that look into the eyes of another woman. He'd paid dearly for a scandal that was not his fault, but he had no regrets. Besides, he bolstered his argument against marriage; he'd seen too many clever and charming women turn into nagging harridans once the knot was tied. He had no intention of sticking his head into parson's noose.

He swore softly as his horse stumbled over a snow-covered boulder. "Easy, lad," he murmured, tightening his knees. It was beginning to snow but he could spy the cabin just a little farther on. "Almost there." A few more minutes and he swung out of the saddle, unloaded the food from his saddlebags, and set it on the step. Then he knocked on the door before leading his pony out of sight behind a large fir tree. He couldn't just leave the food in case a wolf or a cougar found it, but he didn't want the Beatons' thanks, either.

He waited only a few minutes before the door opened and a man looked out, holding a lantern high in his hand, sweeping the snow before the cabin with its light. "Hello?" he called. "Anyone there?" Grey kept silent until he saw the man pick up the package on the front step and retreat to the interior of the cabin. Then he swung into the saddle and headed back to town, guiding his mount along their own tracks, already filling with snow.

The way back would be more difficult than the trip out. He bent his head and studied the trail, concentrating on getting back home and not getting lost and freezing to death in the bush. He felt no fear, only a strange sense of exhilaration. Pitting himself against the harshness of this land made him feel truly alive—rather like kissing Emma.

The schoolroom buzzed with anticipation all day. It had been snowing almost continuously since the night of Grey North's dinner, and the extra work of slogging through the drifted boardwalks and maintaining a fire had tired Emma out. Now the tumult in the schoolroom caused by the excited children as they prepared for the concert gave her a headache. But at least it was the last day before the school closed for the coldest weeks of the year. Unlike most school districts, Prospect set the school year by the weather, not the calendar. Classes were held until the end of June, exams were written in July, and in August the new term began. The long break in classes came during the icebound winter months.

"Try it again," she directed the smallest children, who'd mixed themselves into a mass of confused bodies in the center of their makeshift stage. "Janie, you turn to the left when you make the square." The eight little ones sorted themselves out into two groups, ranged along the side of the stage, and Emma tapped out a rhythm for their march. She fervently hoped Inspector West would not be present to see their laughable attempts at a drill.

From the back of the school she heard giggling and scuffling but pretended deafness. She couldn't deal with Bessie Smith and her cronies just now. "Michael," she said to Lottie O'Connor's son, "can you pretend your desk is a drum and rap out the beat?" She handed him her wooden pointer and went to join the small children, once again snarled into a knot on the stage. "All right, Janie. Follow me this time."

By the time she had the drill pattern sorted out the

giggling could no longer be ignored. "Bessie." She glared at the ringleader of the girls clustered near the back of the room, ostensibly studying their lines for the dialogue but more likely discussing boys. "Come up here, now."

The girls straggled onto the stage, taking their places in an imaginary parlor and conducting a stilted rendition of the lines that were intended to be funny but sounded forced and foolish instead. It was on the tip of her tongue to order them to stay in after school and practice, but she changed her mind. They wouldn't get any better and her headache was growing. "Try to speak more naturally," was all she said and sent the girls back to their seats.

"Everyone, line up and we'll practice our march onto the stage. You can sing 'Silent Night' and 'Away in a Manger.'" This time, with the bigger students nudging and whispering, the children managed to leave the rows of benches, where they would sit during the concert, and straggle onto the stage in a semblance of order, coming to a halt in three rows and facing the audience.

"Well done." Her spirits lifted. Maybe the evening wouldn't be a total disaster. As Mrs. Royston said, the audience would be made up of fond families. "Shall we try 'Silent Night'?" She hummed the opening note, then led the children in that most beloved of carols. The tension in the back of her neck tightened like a vise at the sour notes. She could only hope Les Smith's violin would overpower the voices.

"All right, children, march back to your places." She waited until they were reassembled in the front benches, then gave her good-luck speech and dismissed classes twenty minutes early with the admonition to be back at the schoolhouse a good half hour before the start of the concert. She rang the bell and the schoolroom emptied in seconds. The door slammed behind the last child and she winced, squeezing her eyes against the knife blade of agony that shot through her skull. Her head felt like it would explode. She closed her eyes and twisted her neck, trying to relieve the painful tension. It was no use. She felt like her head was clamped in a vise while sharp daggers of light pierced her eyes.

Of all the days to get a sick headache, this had to be the worst. Perhaps a drink of water would help. She walked to the water bucket at the front of the room and dipped out a glassful, then carried it back to her desk and sat down. She tipped the cold water down her throat, closed her eyes and rested her head against the back of her chair, waiting for the headache to ease off. Nothing happened. She sighed and opened her eyes. Then she blinked rapidly, trying to clear her vision. But no matter how many times she flicked her eyelids, when she opened them, Parnell Wilde was still standing inside the schoolhouse door, his arms crossed, a belligerent scowl marring his face.

She suppressed a groan. Not again and not now. She'd loved him once, but he'd let her down when she needed him most. She wanted nothing more to do with Parnell Wilde.

"I asked you before, Parnell. Please leave me alone."

"No." He turned and locked the door behind him, then walked part way down the aisle. "I must talk with you, Abby, properly. Not rushing down the street with the cold freezing your heart and every eye in this little town watching us. You must hear me out."

There was an unfamiliar wildness in his eye, and the locked door set off alarm bells in her head. Surely Parnell could mean her no harm, yet she lingered behind the desk, keeping its stalwart breadth between them. "Very well." She picked up the wooden pointer, a flimsy weapon, to be sure, but it felt good in her hands. "But I'm very busy. Please be brief." She threw a significant glance at the large clock just behind his head. "I need to tidy the schoolroom, bring in wood and water, and be on my way home in twenty minutes at the most."

He scowled, clearly offended by her abrupt words, but he did not apologize for surprising her in the schoolhouse or for locking them both inside. Instead, the glitter in his eyes grew brighter, a cunning look darkened his narrow face, and his voice took on a hard edge she'd never heard before. "Do not come the schoolmarm with me, Abby. I know your secret."

She blinked, caught entirely by surprise. "I beg your pardon?" She recovered herself and adopted her haughtiest tone. If he wasn't quelled by her schoolmarm stance, perhaps he would remember his manners when she played the society dame. She looked down at him, her eyes unwavering, her back rigid. He didn't retreat, but at least he lost some of the aggression in his stance.

"Sit down, Parnell"—she gestured to the row of benches below the platform—"and explain yourself." She took her own chair behind the desk and attempted to look unconcerned as he advanced down the aisle. She bit her lip as he grew nearer. If he refused to keep his distance but came up and laid hands on her, what would she do? What could she do? She tightened her grip on the pointer.

To her relief he stopped just at the edge of the platform and perched on one of the larger pupil's desks. "Come, Abby. Do not be coy with me. I know why Everett sought you out here in your wilderness. What did you tell him?"

Her bewilderment could not have been more complete if he'd suddenly accused her of murder. She stared in blank astonishment at this stranger with the face of the man who had once declared his undying love for her. "Truly, Parnell"—she shook her head in disbelief—"I've no idea what you're talking about. Do you know something?" She leaned across her desk, trying to read his mind. "Something about my father?" Her voice quavered ever so slightly.

For a moment, Parnell continued to watch her with the eyes of a cat stalking its prey; then his face changed, the cruelty vanished, the scowl replaced with softness. In an instant he was on his knees beside her, the anguished lover. He took the pointer from her weak fingers and cast it aside then pressed her hands to his chest. "Oh, my poor love, I am sorry." He was once again the companion of her happiest days. "I am a brute to cause you pain." He chafed her fingers between his own, making her conscious of how cold her hands were, how frozen her feet. If an Indian raid descended upon the schoolhouse at that moment, she would be powerless to help herself. "Forgive me, *chérie.* I thought you knew."

"Knew what?" she cried, unable to bear the mystery and innuendo any longer. "Tell me plainly, Parnell. What do you know? What has happened?"

"It's about the ledgers." He sat back on his heels and gazed up at her, his eyes intent and watchful. "Some sheets that disappeared at the time of your father's death and were never found. Now there has been another theft. The bank is reopening the investigation. You could get your fortune back."

She was overwhelmed. All the air left her lungs and she couldn't draw a fresh breath. After all this time, it would all be hauled out again, all the tiny details of her father's life exposed to censure and hostile curiosity. His character and his business spread out before an investigator to pick over like a vulture attacking a lamb.

"Why can't they let him rest in peace?" she whispered. "Why must it all be dragged up again?"

"No, no." Parnell caught her by the shoulders, shaking her slightly, forcing her to listen carefully. "You don't understand, Abby. They are reinvestigating because he could be innocent."

This time the shock was even greater. After all these months of bottling up her feelings, turning a calm face to the world, hiding her sorrow, trying to reconcile the father she knew with the villain described by the police and his bank partners, the notion that he could be exonerated left her gasping. She hardly dared to hope.

The bank officials had been so sure. Matt Douglas had access to the vault and the ledger sheets. He'd been seen leaving the bank late at night, on several occasions, long after everyone else. And the note he'd left behind had placed the seal on his guilt. "It pains me that we have come to this," he'd written, "but I can see no other course." The police had looked at his poor dead fingers clasped about the pistol and pronounced him a coward and a suicide.

His partners at the bank had informed her that they would keep the embezzlement a secret so as to avoid a run on the bank, muttering darkly about the threat to their depositors if word of irregularities ever leaked out. Then they'd hired an auditor to determine the extent of his theft. Emma hadn't waited for his report. The only thing she could do for her poor father was pay his debts. She hadn't hesitated. She'd sold everything and turned the money, along with his accounts and safety deposit box, over to the partners. All that had been left to her were his letters and a few photographs.

She'd left behind everything she'd known and everything she'd held dear and traveled to another country, hidden herself away in a remote frontier town to try to rebuild her life, and now Parnell Wilde stood before her and said it could all be a mistake? Tears sprang to her eyes. Grief, as sharp and poignant as the first, caught her by the throat. The defenses she'd so carefully built crumbled in an instant, exposing her sorrow, as fresh and raw as on the day her father died.

The tears poured unchecked from her eyes and she raised her hands to cover her face, rocking herself back and forth in an extremity, unable to still her weeping. Tears leaked from under her lashes, seeping between her fingers, soaking into the cuffs at her wrists. Her shoulders heaved in deep, wrenching sobs. All her repressed grief found expression at last. She'd thought she was healing, getting beyond the devastating sorrow and loss of those early days, getting on with life, putting the past behind her, but Parnell's words had wiped out all her efforts. For an instant she had felt hope, and then the realization that it was all too late opened in her a despair that could not be assuaged.

"Hush, hush." Parnell put his arms about her, drawing her head down onto his shoulder. "Why do you weep so, *chérie*? Is it not good news that your papa is innocent? That you could reclaim your home, your wealth?"

"He is still dead," she whispered, accepting for the moment the comfort of Parnell's embrace.

At last she drew away, drying her tears and staring toward the window. But she did not see the cold, dull light of Prospect's winter day. Instead, her mind filled with images of the blood-soaked carpet and her father's shattered face. She shuddered and turned away, rising from her chair, pacing restlessly across the platform, twisting her hands together. "Why?" she whispered, hugging herself and rubbing her arms for warmth. "Why? If he didn't steal the money, why did he pull the trigger?"

"Perhaps, he didn't."

She whirled about to stare in disbelief at his face. Forgotten words, impressions, suspicions all came racing from the dark recesses of her memory. Like an avalanche, the full implications of Parnell's words hit her, nearly knocking her to her knees.

"Do you think he was murdered?" She could scarcely say the word. It was too terrible. Her jovial, kindly father, shot to death by a . . . what? Who would do such a thing? Who would hate Matt Douglas so much? A business rival? A thief? A crazed customer from the bank?

"Oh, I can't think," she cried, raising a hand to her brow. Her headache had reached monumental proportions. Her eyes burned, her throat ached, and her stomach had tied itself into such a tight knot she doubted the cramp would ever leave her. If she didn't lie down and close her eyes soon, she feared she would embarrass herself by being sick on the spot.

But she couldn't seek her bed. The concert was set to begin in less than three hours. She had to be here tonight, smiling and encouraging and accepting the children's Christmas wishes, meeting the parents, showing to the community and the trustees that they had made a wise choice in their school teacher. There was so much still to do. The floor to sweep, boards to clean, the lamps to fill. She looked about helplessly, unable to focus.

Her father, branded an embezzler and a suicide—

her father could be innocent and a murderer could be running free.

She leaned her head against the cold glass of the window, hoping to ease the hot pain that burned behind her eyes. Down the street a familiar figure stepped onto the boardwalk. Mrs. Royston. "Oh no," she gasped, seizing on the immediate problem, one she could solve. "It's my landlady. Parnell, you must leave quickly. She must not find you here."

Parnell looked at her as though she'd become demented, and perhaps she had, but at this instant all her energies were focused on avoiding the inevitable questioning and prying if Mrs. Royston should find her locked in an empty schoolhouse with an old flame. "Quickly"—she rushed to the door and pulled the bolt free—"go. Please."

With a Gallic shrug and upraised hands, Parnell sidled down the aisle with good speed, stepped outside, and slid around the side of the schoolhouse out of sight of Mrs. Royston. "We'll speak again."

"Yes, yes," Emma promised, sending an anxious gaze down the street. Fortunately, Mrs. Royston was plump and the daylight was fading. She wasn't close enough to have seen him.

"When?" Parnell persisted.

"Later," she practically screamed at him. "Tomorrow." She said when he hesitated. She'd have promised anything to get him out of sight at that moment.

"Until tomorrow, then." He kissed his fingers toward her and finally disappeared around the back of the school.

Emma closed the door and tried to wipe the traces of tears from her cheeks, then hurried to the front of the room. She seized a rag and began erasing the chalk marks from the board, her ears attuned for the sound of the door. When Mrs. Royston spoke from the back of the room, she was prepared.

"Miss Douglas? Are you all right?"

"Oh, Mrs. Royston." Emma turned with feigned surprise, keeping herself in the shadow of the huge Christmas tree the children had decorated earlier in the day. "Am I very late? There's so much to do before the concert."

"Very late indeed." Bella surged down the aisle, squinting through the gloom. "What are you doing?"

"Oh, I wanted the schoolhouse to be perfect for tonight." Emma picked up the broom and made a great business of sweeping the needles under the tree into a neat pile and whisking them into a dustpan. "For the children."

"For everyone." Mrs. Royston opened the door on the stove and Emma dumped the needles onto the embers. "My goodness! You look dreadful." Even in the dim light her landlady had discerned Emma's pale cheeks and feverish eyes. "Are you ill?"

"I have such a headache." Emma placed her palm against her forehead and smoothed it back toward her hairline. It wasn't the whole explanation of her haggard appearance, but it was the truth.

"You must go home at once," Mrs. Royston declared, taking the broom from her hand and placing it in the corner. "A hot cup of tea and some ice on your neck will do wonders."

"But the wood and the water and the lamps . . ."

"Never mind all that." Bella hustled to the clothes tree in the corner and retrieved Emma's coat. "I'll see to everything." She bundled Emma into her coat, handed her her hat and gloves, and wrapped a warm scarf about her neck. "Come along."

Emma felt like one of the smallest children in her class being bustled about by an anxious mother, but right at this moment she felt only gratitude. It was such a relief to just do as she was told. Tomorrow she would speak with Parnell again. Tomorrow she would sort out her feelings. Tomorrow she would make a plan. Right now, she would follow her landlady down the snowy street, drink her tea, and lie down on her bed with a cold cloth on her eyes and rest.

Chapter Six

"Good evening, Miss Douglas." The parents of her pupils poured into the schoolhouse and quickly filled up the desks and benches. Emma stood at the door greeting each one, smiling, shaking hands, and trying to pretend her headache had receded in the past two hours.

Mrs. Royston had done her best, but no amount of hot tea and cold cloths could still the hammers pounding inside Emma's skull or disguise the shadows beneath her eyes. "Emma?" Grey's low voice spoke into her ear, "Are you ill?"

"We'll be ready to get under way in just a few more minutes." She ignored his question and turned to shake hands with the next group through the door. The room was growing increasingly hot and close. She should have let the fire die down. The heat made her head worse and the nausea was rising again.

"Emma?" Grey still hovered by her elbow.

"I'm fine," she snapped without turning her head. It was better to keep very still and her eyes fixed straight ahead. "Good evening, Mrs. Allen, Reverend." She greeted the vicar and his wife, smiling determinedly when Mrs. Allen stuck her nose in the air and refused to acknowledge her.

"Hello, Vicar." She heard Grey greet the frosty couple. "Good of you to come, since you've no children in school."

"As I explained to my wife," Mr. Allen replied, "we must support any project that benefits the community."

Much to her relief, Grey then led them away to a seat near the front of the room. Unfortunately, he returned to her side almost immediately. She bit her lip. Only a few more minutes and she could slip behind the curtain at the side of the stage, out of sight of prying eyes. So focused was she on keeping her composure while her migraine grew that she was completely unprepared when Parnell Wilde slid into the crowded room and pushed his way through the press of people about her. "Mr. Wilde!" She tried to keep her voice level but couldn't help the squeak of surprise. "I didn't expect . . ." She wished he hadn't come. The revelations he'd presented so recently were too much for her to absorb all at once. She needed time to carefully think, to work out the implications of her new knowledge, and to decide what she would do next. And she needed to do that without pressure from Parnell or distraction from Grey. She added that last thought as he reappeared at her elbow.

"I wouldn't miss the biggest event in town." Parnell took her hand and held it just a fraction too long. "Besides, it is an excuse to see you, my love." He whispered the endearment but she knew Grey had overheard by the sudden stiffening of his shoulder next to hers.

"Time to start." Grey edged by her, taking Parnell with him. "There's more space over there by the Christmas tree." He pointed to an unoccupied stretch of wall, a space offering a very limited view of the stage, and urged her unwanted guest toward it.

With relief Emma watched the two men move away, then took her seat amidst the excited children. Two more hours and she could go home and sleep for a week. Maybe she could be like Sleeping Beauty, and when she awoke all her troubles would have vanished. Except Sleeping Beauty was awakened by a kiss. Instantly, her lips tingled, remembering the brief touch of Grey's mouth to hers.

"Good evening, ladies and gentlemen." Grey's strong voice brought a hush to the room and the crowd turned expectant eyes to the stage. "It is my pleasure, on behalf of the school trustees and our teacher, Miss Douglas, to welcome you all here tonight. As you know, our school is in need of a piano. No offense, Les." He grinned at the Smith family patriarch, who tipped his head and drew his bow across the violin strings for a few lively notes.

The crowd chuckled, and Grey continued, "It would be a great boon to the children of Prospect to have a piano in the schoolroom. Miss Douglas is a trained pianist, and the trustees see no sense in hiring a teacher who can give musical instruction and not provide her with the means to do so. You know what a tightfisted lot we are." There were more chuckles and a few guffaws.

Emma had to smile. Grey had told her he was the one to raise money for her piano and he'd been right. He'd hit just the right tone with his crowd, teasing them, cajoling them, and finishing up with a challenge.

"I have here"—he held aloft a fat envelope—"the proceeds from a fine dinner held at the Rockingham last week. I believe we collected enough to cover seventy percent of the cost to purchase a piano in Vancouver and transport it to Prospect." He turned his hat upside down and dropped the envelope into it. "Now, it's up to you good folk to do the rest." He walked to the end of the first row of the audience and held out the hat. "We'll start with you, Sam."

Amid cheers and jeers, the owner of the livery stable added a few notes to the hat, then stood up, shoved his hands into his pockets, and turned them inside out for everyone to see there wasn't a penny left on him. A burst of applause greeted his gesture and he bowed to the room, then passed the hat down the row.

"Now, let's hear from the children." Grey left his hat circulating and announced the first number on the program, a welcome recitation by the smallest pupil in the school. The lines were so well-known the audience could have recited them by heart, but everyone listened with rapt attention while little Sally Gardener lisped through, "Although I'm very small, / And little I can do, / My teacher says to smile at you, / And welcome one and all."

The concert was off and running. Emma slipped behind the curtain to coach from the sidelines when the whole school marched onstage and sang "The First Noel" and "Joy to the World," sounding surprisingly confident and tuneful with the assistance of Les Smith's fiddle. The tiny drill team made a few wrong turns but managed to sort themselves out without any tears or tantrums. Bessie Smith got the giggles in the middle of her dialogue, but a quelling look from her mother brought her to order. Grey kept the audience in good humor with his wit and charm between acts onstage, and his hat continued to circulate through the schoolroom until it arrived back at the front where Grey scooped all the money into the envelope and dropped it into the top drawer of Emma's desk. "We'll count it at the end of the show," he promised, "and if it's not enough, I'll pass it again before you're allowed to go home."

Emma kept her smile pinned into place and, with one eye on the clock and another on the program, counted down the minutes until she could seek her bed. One more set of carols and Santa Claus would arrive. She peeked around the curtain for Jed Barclay. The seat beside Mrs. Royston was vacant. Good. The warm-hearted man had gone to put on his red suit and white whiskers. Earlier in the evening, Emma had put parcels bearing the names of each of her pupils into his sack and she'd added a few extras "from Santa Claus" just in case there were wee ones present whose parents had forgotten the gift exchange.

Her eye roved over the crowded benches and found yet another small Smith and a couple of Indian children who were too young to be in school. Someone had opened a window, thank goodness, allowing some of the heat to escape the overcrowded room. The last notes of "Silent Night" faded into the stillness, working their timeless magic, bringing a tender hush to the assembled crowd. The concert part of the evening was over.

Then Grey gave the signal and two stalwart men carrying full buckets of water came from the back of the hall and took up their positions beside the Christmas tree. She stepped forward and lit a match to set alight the dozen or so tiny candles that adorned the tall fir. It was time for Santa Claus.

Right on cue the tinkle of sleigh bells announced their burly visitor and the man in the red suit burst through the schoolhouse door. "Santa Claus!" crowed a dozen shrill voices, and every eye fixed on the jovial saint with a huge sack making his way to the stage.

"Ho, ho, ho." Jed Barclay was made to play Santa

Claus; his round tummy needed no extra padding and his hearty chuckle was infectious and genuine. He dumped the sack on the stage and bowed to the audience. "Merry Christmas," he boomed, while children squealed with delight. With a great show of surprise he reached into the depths of his sack. "What have we here?" He held up a small, flat parcel tied with a big bow. Every child held his breath. "Daisy Smith," he called, and the little girl, not yet of school age, rushed forward with a high-pitched squeak, then stopped three feet short in a welter of confusion. "Come on, Daisy," Jed coaxed, going down on his knees and holding out his hands. "Come and get your present."

"You get it for her, Les."

"She don't want it, I do."

"Toss it to her, Santa." The advice and encouragement poured forth as, reluctantly, Daisy inched forward until she could reach out and snatch the present, then hurtled back to her mother's knee. The crowd laughed and applauded while Jed got down to the serious business of handing out the rest of the presents. He had just reached the stage of tossing bags of homemade candy into the audience when someone yelled "Fire!"

In the ensuing pandemonium Emma could hear Grey shouting for calm and a dozen women shrieking with fear. On the far side of the tree, close to the wall, she saw a flame lick upward. Despite their precautions, one of the candles had set fire to a branch.

Some of the crowd broke for the door, threatening to trample each other. Others rushed forward to snatch their children from the benches and clutch them in their arms. Nearly all of the grade ones and twos were wailing at the top of their lungs. "Hush, hush." She moved along the benches of her pupils, trying to calm them. "Don't push. Everything will be all right."

"Order!" She heard Grey trying to restore calm. "Sit down, everyone. It's all under control. Order!"

She turned her head to survey the ruined tree and saw the emergency had passed as quickly as it had arisen. The hiss of dying flame and a whiff of smoke were the only evidence of the near catastrophe. The impromptu fire brigade had emptied their water buckets over the candles before the tree could become engulfed. Water dripped from the drooping branches in a spreading circle and a few gaily decorated boxes beneath the tree were transformed into sad, sodden blobs, but otherwise, there was no damage.

"Sit down, everybody," Grey ordered, standing on a desk to make himself seen above the melee. "Fire's out. Sit down."

Slowly, the frightened crowd returned to their seats, parents holding children on their laps, all eyes turned to the dilapidated tree with thoughts of what could have been, but the disaster had been averted and slowly the assembly relaxed. "Okay, folks." Grey was still standing atop a desk, a figure of calm authority. "You can all go home now, let's empty the building by rows so no one gets hurt in the crush. We'll start with the back."

"What about the money?" Sam from the livery stable asked. Emma saw some of the tension leave the frightened faces, replaced by reluctant grins. "Are we goin' t' have a pianer next year, or will we have to listen to Les Smith again?" There wasn't the usual laughter to greet this sally, but no one left the room either.

"Okay"—Grey opened the drawer of Emma's desk—"let's see." He looked into the drawer and Emma saw his jaw clamp tight, all the humor and cajolery wiped from his face. He pulled the drawer open further, then reached to the very back. He turned his head and murmured something to Jed Barclay, still perched on the edge of the stage in his Santa Claus suit. Then he opened another drawer and another.

"Where's the money?" The question was asked with irritation this time.

"There seems to be a little mix-up." Grey closed the drawers of Emma's desk.

"What do you mean? Where's the money?" The voices grew louder and more hostile.

"It's gone."

"Gone! Where'd it go?" Anger simmered in the air.

Emma stared blankly at Grey, who gazed over the crowd with a calculating stare; then he turned to look directly at her. "He's gone."

"Who?" she asked automatically, but with a sinking sensation in the pit of her stomach. Carefully she surveyed the room, looking for empty seats. Only Parnell Wilde had vanished. Cold air blew on her neck. She turned to the open window. He couldn't have climbed through it without being seen, but he could have thrown the money outside and then left the school in the general pandemonium without anyone noticing.

"Your friend, that's who," shrilled Mrs. Allen, standing to point an accusatory finger at Emma. "That man who's been hanging about the schoolhouse for the past couple of weeks. I've seen you with him."

All eyes turned on her, hostile and accusing. Not the friendly eyes of her pupils' parents, but the distrustful eyes of a town who felt duped and robbed.

"Her father embezzled from his own bank." Mrs. Allen wasn't done with her revelations and accusations.

The whispers ran around the room like wildfire, jumping from side to side, back to front, until the whole place was ablaze with anger and fear. She pressed herself against the wall, trying to disappear as the ugliness of suspicion turned its vengeful face toward her.

"Now just a moment." Grey tried to intervene.

"Thief!" Mrs. Allen shrieked.

"Call the police."

Someone seized her arm. The pain in her head exploded in a thousand blinding shards and everything went black.

"Emma. Emma, wake up." A voice kept calling her name, dragging her from the comfortable blackness. She wished he would go away. It was a he, the voice deep and rich as chocolate. She could drown in that voice, sink down into its molten depths, let its warm swirls envelop her, cradle her with tenderness. She never wanted to wake up again. "Emma!" The voice grew sharper, tugging at her consciousness, forcing her away from the warm darkness.

"Try this," another voice murmured, just at the edge of her senses, a female's, not nearly so velvety as the man's.

"Sorry, love." The man's voice was back and she sighed, then coughed, choked, and opened her eyes. Grey was there waving smelling salts under her nose. She pushed his hand away and coughed again, turning her head and attempting to sit up. A strong arm beneath her shoulders supported her, helping her struggle into a more upright position, keeping her steady and holding her close.

She realized that she was lying in a nest of buffalo robes in a cutter with Grey North holding her in his arms and Mrs. Royston peering anxiously into her face.

"What?" she started to ask; then memory returned with a rush. "Oh, no." She pushed against Grey's arm, wriggling into a sitting position. "The money. Where is it?"

"That's the question of the moment," Grey said. "The Mounties are doing their best to answer it."

"I didn't take it." Emma felt tears start to her eyes and blinked rapidly. After all the humiliation of this evening, she couldn't bear to begin bawling in front of Grey North, Mrs. Royston, and, she peered over her landlady's shoulder to the driver, Jed Barclay.

"Of course, you didn't." Mrs. Royston surprised Emma by her vehement defense. "That woman! There's been nothing but trouble and rumor since she came to Prospect. I've a good mind to write to the bishop."

"Here we are." Jed pulled back the reins and the cutter came to a halt.

Grey leaped out, then reached into the sleigh and swept Emma into his arms before she knew what was happening. "Put me down," she hissed into his ear as he held her high against his chest, his cheek only inches from hers. "I can walk."

"Maybe. Maybe not." Grey's warm breath fanned her cheek. "I'm not about to find out. You scared me out of a year's growth when you collapsed like that. I never took you for the fainting type, Emma."

"I'm not," she declared crossly as Grey stamped snow from his feet and Mrs. Royston held her front door wide. "I've had a miserable headache all day. The fire was the last straw."

"Just take her upstairs," Mrs. Royston instructed. "I'll see to getting her out of her things. Rose!"

"Really," Emma protested, wriggling in Grey's arms with the result that he tightened his hold, pressing his hands against her body in a way that provoked all kinds of disturbing sensations in her already overly sensitive person.

"Hold still," he muttered. "You don't want me to drop you down the stairs, do you?"

She subsided, biting her lip as Grey turned at the top of the stairs and strode into her room, while Mrs. Royston held the door. He set her gently on the bed, then stood back, gazing at her intently. She slid backward on the bed, bracing herself against the pillows. It wasn't seemly to be lying on a bed with a gentleman, especially one as attractive as Grey North, staring down on her. No matter that she was wearing drawers, a shift, two petticoats, a corset, a skirt, and a blouse, as well as a heavy woolen coat, warm boots, a thick scarf, and a fur hat. She felt naked.

"I still think I should call on the doctor." Grey looked over her head to Mrs. Royston. "She's very pale."

"*She* has a headache." Emma tried to glare at him but the effort was too much. She wished she could sink back into that pool of darkness where Grey's voice had soothed and comforted her, his arms had held her, and all her troubles seemed to have vanished. "Please, everyone," she softened her tone, "I'm very sorry to have caused you all anxiety, but I'm fine, really. I have a bad headache, but I'll be better in the morning, if you'll just let me get some sleep."

"Ah, there you are, Rose." Mrs. Royston took the warming pan from the hired girl's hands. "Put the tea on the dresser." Rose obeyed without a word and sidled out of the room. Mrs. Royston slid the warmer between the sheets and Emma flushed bright red.

If she'd felt naked lying on top of the coverlet, having Grey observe the inside of her bed made her feel positively wanton. "Now, then, Mr. North," Bella Royston finally remembered the proprieties and shooed Grey from the room, "it's time you were on your way. This is women's business. If you want to help, find out who stole the piano money and who started that ugly rumor about Miss Douglas's father."

"It's true," Emma whispered before Grey could leave. Much as she wanted to believe her father was innocent, she couldn't lie to her friends. Unlikely as it seemed, she had found friends in Prospect, and she would not betray their faith in her.

"Never!" Mrs. Royston dropped into the bedroom chair with a thud and threw her hands over her face. "Don't say I'm harboring a criminal in my best bedroom."

"You are not." Emma swung her legs over the side of the bed and tried to stand up, but a wave of dizziness overwhelmed her. She subsided on the bed, holding her head in her hands, her elbows resting on her knees, and waited for the nausea to pass.

"Oh, you're too ill to deal with this now." Mrs. Royston gathered herself together and came to help Emma back onto the bed. "Mr. North, I daresay there's a deal more we need to know, but we won't learn of it this night."

"Yes." Grey nodded curtly. "I'll call at the police detachment and speak to Inspector West." He turned on his heel and left the room.

Without his comforting presence, Emma felt bereft. "Mrs. Royston, I'm so sorry." She focused her attention on her landlady. "I never dreamed I would bring disgrace on you. I never guessed my past would follow me here."

"It's those visitors you've had." Mrs. Royston heaved herself out of her chair and came to pat Emma's shoulder. "Them and Mrs. Allen. That woman is nothing but a troublemaker. Still, she couldn't have done it on her own. You mark my words, Miss Douglas, old friends or not, those two men have brought this trouble on you." Mrs. Royston unlaced Emma's boots and pulled them off her feet, placing them neatly at the side of the bed. Her face creased in a worried frown, but her hands kept busy with the work at hand.

"I've thought of that." Emma managed to stand, holding on to the bedpost, while Mrs. Royston dealt with her outdoor clothes, then undid the fastenings of her skirt and petticoats, letting them slip to the floor. "But why? Everett Jergens was the only one of our friends to stand by me."

"What about the other one? Narrow-faced, weaselly sort if you ask me."

"We were once engaged." Emma blushed to admit her folly. "But I think he was more interested in the advantages my father could give him than in me."

"Think he ransacked your room and the schoolhouse?" Mrs. Royston stooped to retrieve the clothing from the floor.

"But what for?" Emma's headache began to throb more fiercely than before. "All of my father's property went to the bank. I've no money except what I earn as a school teacher, and I needn't tell you that's not enough to be worth stealing." She sat down on the edge of the bed and finished removing her clothes.

"There's something." Mrs. Royston eased a plain white nightgown over Emma's head. "In you go." The landlady held the covers with rough kindness while Emma swung her legs into bed. Mrs. Royston tucked her in, pulling the quilt firmly up under her chin. If she hadn't felt so miserable, Emma would have laughed. It was like having her mother put her to bed. She half expected Mrs. Royston to demand to hear her prayers. Instead, her landlady blew out the lamp and walked to the door. "Maybe it's a clue," she said, and pulled the door closed behind her.

Emma could hear her heavy tread as she made her way down the hall to her own room. A clue? What possible clue could anyone discover among her belongings? Whatever the robber sought, she doubted he'd found it, else why ransack her school desk as well?

Her head throbbed with the effort to think. Parnell's words had raised a wild hope in her breast, but had he really given her new evidence? Just because the police were reopening the case didn't mean her father was innocent. And what of Everett's news about the break-ins? And where were the ledger sheets? Could they prove Matt's innocence? And yet . . . always she came up against the one inescapable fact: Matt Douglas had killed himself. Why would an innocent man put a bullet through his head?

She moaned softly. *Oh, Papa, why?* Her head hurt abominably. Every muscle in her body ached. Her stomach clenched. She couldn't think anymore. She dropped into a heavy sleep with the question still unanswered.

"Miss. Miss?" Emma opened heavy eyelids to find Rose standing at the foot of the bed, a breakfast tray in her hand. "Mrs. Royston says to ask how you're feeling this morning and would you rather have tea than coffee." Rose recited her orders in a flat voice.

Emma sat up and Rose placed the tray in her lap. Toast, with Mrs. Royston's special gooseberry jam, scrambled eggs, two rashers of bacon, and a hot cup of coffee. Bella Royston's solution to every problem was good food and lots of it. Emma smiled and nodded her head. The pain from last night had gone at last, although she still felt groggy. "This is lovely, Rose. Please thank Mrs. Royston for being so thoughtful and don't bother to come back for the tray. I'll be up in a little while and I'll bring it down myself."

"Yes, Miss." Rose left her alone.

She nibbled on a crust of toast and found she enjoyed the taste. She felt tired but no longer feared she would faint or throw up. The eggs tasted delicious and Mrs. Royston's strong, black coffee went a long way to restoring her health, if not her peace of mind. She pushed herself higher on the pillows and gazed about the comfortable room, wondering if she should seek other lodgings. She wouldn't allow Mrs. Royston to suffer from the gossips because of her. Then again, perhaps lodgings were the least of her worries. The trustees could be meeting right this minute to fire her.

Seeking consolation, she turned her head to gaze at the photograph of her family, the one memento she'd salvaged from the wreck of her former life. A shaft of sunlight streaming through the window struck the frame, casting a shadow over the picture, hiding the faces she needed so desperately to see. She set the tray aside and got out of bed to retrieve the photo, then climbed back under the quilt.

The photo depicted Claire Douglas's features, but the black and white image didn't do justice to her mother's beauty. It failed to capture the sheen of her hair, as black and shiny as a raven's wing, or her startlingly blue eyes, fringed with long, dark lashes, or her lips as red and rosy as the dawn. Emma had loved listening to Claire tell stories of the many suitors who'd courted her, men of wealth and rank; but in the end, Claire had assured her daughter, she'd chosen Matt Douglas. Not the most handsome of her suitors, nor the wealthiest, but the kindest, the most steadfast, and her one true love.

It was a shame that her mother hadn't lived to see Matt rise to president of the bank or to enjoy the fine mansion he'd built on Nob Hill. Emma sighed with the inevitable sadness that colored her memories of Claire. Her mother had been the belle of the ball right up until she'd been struck down by acute appendicitis; but she'd never been a comfortable mother. Emma had never doubted her mother's love, but Claire had never kissed a sore knee or soothed a wounded ego. Instead, she'd preened for Emma, let her admire her hair and her pretty hands. All the tenderness in Emma's childhood had come from Matt.

She touched a finger to her father's pictured face. His hair had been the same dark auburn as hers when the photo had been taken, the silver at his temples came only after Claire's death. In the picture, Emma sat on his knee, her hand wrapped tightly in his, her mother standing beside them, one hand resting on Matt's shoulder, the other tucked into the folds of her skirt.

She frowned and examined the picture more closely. There was a touch of white in her mother's hair that shouldn't have been there. The picture had been marred by a slight tear in the paper. She turned it over and felt along the backing, discovering a slight bump behind the picture where something under the frame had poked through the paper.

Carefully, so as not to cause further damage, she slid the backing out of the frame. A single sheet of onionskin paper fluttered onto the quilt followed by a thin key. Mystified, she picked up the paper and unfolded it, instantly recognizing her father's handwriting. She gasped and stared at the paper, feeling as though she'd received a message from the grave.

"Sisters of Mercy Convent." She read the few scrawled words over and over, trying to discern their import. Why would her father's last message be the name of a convent? She had no doubt the sheet of paper she held in her shaking hands had been written just before Matt pulled the trigger that took his life. The ink was blotched, as though he hadn't had time to blot it properly before stuffing it into the picture frame. But why? The endless question beat against her brain. Nothing about Matt Douglas's death made sense. No matter what the evidence indicated, she had never been able to fully reconcile thieving and suicide with the man she'd known.

Even in her shock and grief she'd argued with the police and the bank partners, convinced in her heart that they were wrong; but in the end, she'd had to accept their version of events. She'd had no evidence to the contrary. Or did she?

She dropped the page and picked up the key, staring at it in thoughtful concentration, as though the notches in the strip of metal could speak to her. It looked like one of the many keys she'd seen in his office—keys to safety deposit boxes. But a convent? Why not the bank? Had he held a secret too terrible to trust to his own vault? Too terrible or too dangerous.

She touched a finger to the photo. Without its glass his face seemed clearer, his eyes gazing at her with a powerful message. "Oh, Papa. I'm sorry," she whispered, pressing her cheek against the picture. "I've let you down." She gazed a moment longer at his beloved face while a hard resolve formed in her heart. Her father had left her one final message. It was up to her to discover its meaning. Once and for all she would learn the truth, and the truth lay at the Sisters of Mercy Convent.

Carefully, she reassembled the photo and the frame, even slipping the letter back into its hiding place. The key she set on her dresser while she found her needle; then she sewed it firmly into her corset. She knew now, without the shadow of a doubt, that the break-ins had been because of that key.

Swiftly, she pulled on her shift and petticoats, poured cold water from the ewer into her basin, and splashed her face, washing away the last of the cobwebs from her headache. Then she finished dressing, collected her breakfast tray, and went downstairs, her mind churning with all she had to do. To begin with, she could consult Inspector West. The theft of the piano money gave her a perfect excuse to seek him out, and once closeted in the privacy of his office, she could tell him about the key and her suspicions. How ironic that while Parnell—she was convinced he was the culprit—was ripping through her belongings, the key was safely in her keeping, and she hadn't even known it existed. Her guardian angel must have been looking out for her the day she decided to take the framed photograph to school.

"Oh, Miss Douglas." Mrs. Royston sat at the kitchen table, her hands for once idle while Rose stood at the dishpan scrubbing the porridge pot. "I hope you're feeling better." Her landlady raised distressed eyes to Emma's face.

"Yes, I am." Emma carried her used dishes to Rose, then sat down at the table beside Mrs. Royston. "But you appear troubled. What has happened?"

"Oh, nothing really." Mrs. Royston made an impatient sound, but her worried frown stayed in place. "It's that nasty woman." She slapped the table with her open hand. "She's sent her husband around here with a message for me, offering to take Rose into her house while the 'shadow of suspicion,' as she puts it, hangs over me. Of all the nerve! She's just looking for a housemaid and is too uppity to hire one of the girls from the mission school."

"Oh, Mrs. Royston, I'm so sorry." Even though she'd been expecting just such a turn of events, Emma's heart still twisted with regret. "I wouldn't bring trouble on you, for all the world. Of course I'll seek other lodgings at once."

"No, you won't." Mrs. Royston crossed her arms over her bosom and glared at her. "Not that you're likely to find them, in any case, but I won't have that woman dictating to me." Emma felt like cheering but her landlady's defiance was short lived. The next moment her shoulders slumped again. "There's a Christmas tea at the church next week," she said sadly. "I usually take one of my famous cakes, but the vicar told me he wouldn't expect me to make a contribution in view of the present circumstances. That's her work, too, I'll wager. There's not a man in Prospect, including the vicar, who can resist one of my cakes."

"This can't be happening." Emma sagged into the chair opposite Mrs. Royston. She'd thought nothing could be worse than the humiliation she'd lived through in San Francisco, but to know she had brought trouble to Mrs. Royston's good-natured heart was worse. "I'm going to see Inspector West," she announced, rising abruptly to her feet. "Don't worry, Mrs. Royston, the Mounties will catch the thief." She also intended to go to Grey North and tender her resignation, better to do it now, before the trustees asked for it, but she decided to spare her landlady that distressing bit of news for now.

"Too bad the mining season's finished," Mrs. Royston grumbled. "News of a gold strike would eclipse the gossip, but during the winter there's nothing much to do in Prospect. A scandal is the best entertainment around."

"Do you need anything at the Mercantile while I'm out?" Emma sought the surest means of diverting her landlady.

"The Mercantile, yes." Mrs. Royston got hastily to her feet and cast a quick glance about her kitchen. "I'll go with you. I need . . . um . . . baking soda."

"Of course," Emma nodded encouragement. "You can't bake one of your famous cakes without rising."

"But, ma'am, the soda tin's fu—"

"Never mind, Rose," Mrs. Royston cut off the girl's protest. "Just see to the washing up and be sure you dust the front room thoroughly." She tapped her forefinger against her bottom lip for a moment. Emma could practically see the wheels turning in her heard. "I believe I'll drop some invitations to an impromptu tea while I'm out. The mayor's wife can't resist my baking, and she takes precedence over Mrs. Allen."

Despite her own distress, Emma had to smile. Bella Royston would not allow herself to be ostracized and humiliated without a fight. She pressed her hand against her ribs, feeling the edge of the key in her corset. This time, she decided with grim determination, she'd fight back, too.

A few minutes later, clad in warm coats, scarves, gloves, and fur hats, the two women stepped out into the winter sunshine, backs straight, resolute smiles pinned to their lips, and set off toward the center of town. It was still too early in the day for ladies to be out calling, so they were spared the need to stop and converse with passing acquaintances, and thus avoided any embarrassing situations, although Emma did see one other early walker dodge into the millinery shop as they approached. She glanced sharply at her companion, but Mrs. Royston didn't appear to have noticed.

"I believe Mr. Barclay has a new shipment of yard goods." She hustled Mrs. Royston through the door of the Mercantile. "Maybe sewing a new dress would be a good occupation over the winter. Something other than black," she added, remembering her landlady's pride in the dress she'd worn for Grey's dinner.

"You could be right." Mrs. Royston pursed her lips in thought. "Mr. Barclay was saying just last week that he admired color in a woman's dress. Good heavens," she exclaimed, shaking her head, "was it only a week since our dinner at the Rockingham? It seems like an age."

"It does, indeed," Emma agreed, and cast her glance about the Mercantile. A few miners clustered about the potbellied stove in the middle of the store, but there were no other women in the place. "I'll leave you here, then, and go on to the fort. Don't wait for me. I could be some time."

"Yes, yes." Mrs. Royston waved her off, already drifting toward the counter and Jed Barclay.

Emma went back outside and proceeded on her own. The cleared boardwalk ended just a few doors past the Mercantile, so she was forced to slog through deep snow for the remainder of the journey. She arrived at the police station slightly out of breath and with a rim of snow clinging to the hem of her skirt. As she paused in the doorway to catch her breath and shake off the snow, she overheard a shout from the cells at the back. "This is absurd. I am an American citizen. You can't arrest me."

She recognized Parnell's distinctive accent and halted,

standing stock-still, absorbing yet another blow to her peace of mind.

"You're a thief and a scoundrel, that's what you are," growled another voice, "and I don't care if you was born in the antipodes, you're still under arrest. Now get in there." A door slammed shut and the sound of boots coming toward her sent Emma scuttling back into the frost-laden outdoors. She didn't want to give the appearance of eavesdropping.

"Miss Douglas?" Inspector West dismounted from his horse and stood before her, his eyes watchful but filled with concern. "Are you looking for me?"

"Yes." She drew a deep breath, forcing herself to appear calm. She was no longer in love with Parnell, but she hated to think of him in a jail cell. "I wanted to know if you'd solved the theft of the piano money and . . ." her voice faltered as she imagined the disappointment in Inspector West's face when he learned her story, but she pressed on, "and I need your advice on another matter."

"Come inside, Miss Douglas." Inspector West looped the reins of his mount over a hitching post, opened the door, and called to the constable. "Take my horse around to the stables, Grimsby."

"Yes, sir!" The constable shot to his feet, saluted smartly, and marched outside.

"This way, Miss Douglas." The inspector escorted her through a second door and into the small, square space that served as his office. "Now, sit down and tell me what's troubling you."

"The money from the school concert . . ." she began, but the inspector waved her explanations aside.

"You can set your mind at rest on that score. We've got the fellow." He hunched forward, fixing her with a stern yet kindly gaze. "Now, why don't you tell me the rest of the story?"

"Am I so transparent?" She made no attempt to argue with the inspector's assessment. In an odd way it was a relief to drop her facade of calm and to confess her troubles.

"I'm a policeman, Miss. There's not much gets past me. That Wilde fellow, now I figured him for a rum one the minute I laid eyes on him. No offense, Miss," he hastened to add, "I understand he was an acquaintance of yours."

"I thought he was my friend." She bit her lip. "Apparently I was wrong." She gripped her gloved fingers together in her lap and proceeded to tell the inspector everything she knew and everything she suspected, except for the fact that she had a key sewn into her corset. On her way to the police station, she'd decided to visit the Sisters of Mercy herself. Her father would have wanted it. "I've had to accept what the police told me," she concluded her account, "that my father committed suicide," her voice cracked on the word, and she took a deep, steadying breath before carrying on, "but if there's a chance he was murdered instead . . ." She raised pleading eyes to the policeman. "You understand?"

"Yes, my dear, I do." Inspector West stroked his mustache. "My condolences, Miss Douglas. You've had a rough time." His soft drawl held a deep sympathy. Then his manner changed, becoming brusque and businesslike. "Now, we might have something for you. When we caught up to Wilde—it wasn't hard, the idiot left a trail in the snow as plain as day, we just had to find the evidence on him—anyway, as I was saying, we conducted a search of his belongings and found a bank passbook with the name of Matthew Douglas on the inside page." Emma gripped the edge of the inspector's desk, her mind teeming with surmise. "Now, don't get too excited," Inspector West cautioned her before she could ask the questions that trembled on her tongue. "The last page of the book was stamped CANCELED, and there's nothing illegal in having an old passbook as a souvenir, which is what our Mr. Wilde claims, but it does make a body wonder."

"He said it was a souvenir?" Emma fixed on the trivial detail while she tried to understand the larger implications of Parnell's actions. "Of what?"

"Exactly, Miss. Now that I've heard your story, I think we'll let our Mr. Wilde contemplate the inside of a jail cell for a time. Could be he has something else he wants to tell us. In the meantime, I'll send a man to the telegraph office in Gold City. Maybe the police in San Francisco will have some information for us."

"Can you send him back? Mr. Wilde, that is." Emma was somewhat hazy on the legalities of the criminal code.

"Depends on what he's done. We've an extradition treaty with the United States, signed in 1877. The days of committing a crime in one country and escaping prosecution by fleeing across the border are no more, Miss Douglas. Don't you worry. Justice will out."

The enormity of Parnell's betrayal left her breathless. First, he'd stolen the money for the school piano, costing her the trust and good will of the community and likely her job. Now, she learned that he might also have information about her father's tragedy. And he'd said nothing. Nothing to bring a possible criminal to justice. Nothing to exonerate a decent man from false accusations, and nothing to ease the anguish of her grief. Anger, pure and hot and unyielding, flooded through her, washing away the confusion that had surrounded her feelings for Parnell. "I want to see him," she announced, rising abruptly to her feet, her hands clenched.

"Oh, that wouldn't be proper, Miss Douglas." The inspector heaved himself out of his chair. "You go along home, now. If there's anything to report, I'll call on you personally." He surged around the desk and swept her before him, out of his office and out of the police station before she could protest.

She blinked in the bright sunshine, squinting her eyes against the glare of light from the snow, feeling rather like a puppy who'd been roused from his nap and unceremoniously dumped outside. She turned her head. The door behind her was firmly shut.

"Emma?" She spun about and raised a hand to shield her eyes. Grey North stood before her. For one crazy moment she considered hurling herself against his chest and sobbing out all her troubles and begging him to make everything right again. Her foolishness made her cross.

"What are you doing here?"

"I could ask you the same thing but I suspect I know the answer. The Mounties have caught their man. I'm here to corroborate the evidence. You know it's your friend, Parnell Wilde."

"Yes." She stared down at her boots.

"I'm sorry. I believe you cared for him." The gruff sympathy in his voice threatened to break through her reserve. But Grey was only playing a game, she reminded herself, using her to dissuade the marriage-minded ladies of Prospect. It was a lowering thought but one she must keep in mind lest she let herself be flattered by his attentions.

"I cared for the man I thought he was." She turned her head to look off toward the mountain peaks. "I don't know the man in the cells back there."

"Betrayal stings worse than outright enmity."

"Yes." His understanding surprised her, but she was grateful for it. The pain in her heart eased, just a little.

She drew in a long breath and expelled it in a short puff. "The inspector's sent me home." She turned a wry smile toward Grey. "I'm to wait quietly like a good girl until he calls on me."

"I take it you're not enamored of that plan." The corners of Grey's mouth quirked upward.

"No." She gave him a wry smile. "I've become infected with this frontier mentality of yours. I want to be in the thick of the action. I want to ask the questions myself and I want the answers now."

"Sorry," Grey actually chuckled, "I can be very persuasive, but when the inspector makes up his mind to something, that's an end to it."

"You're going in there." She tilted her head toward the door Inspector West had closed so firmly behind her. "Let me come with you."

"Wouldn't do any good." Grey shoved his hands in his pockets and rocked back on his heels. "The inspector has very precise ideas about what's proper for a lady. He won't let you anywhere close to his prisoner."

"I'm not going home to twiddle my thumbs while everyone else in town discusses my business." Emma stamped her foot in frustration, sending a cloud of snow swirling about them both.

"Go to Barclay's Mercantile, then." Grey slapped his gloves against the snow she'd showered over his trousers and grinned. "I'll come and fetch you the minute I've finished my business here. I'll report every word your criminal says. I promise."

It wasn't what she wanted, but she accepted the offer. It was the best she could do for the moment. "There is another matter," she said, squaring her shoulders and lifting her chin at a proud angle. "I wish to submit my resignation without delay. I'll have a letter for you this afternoon."

"Why?" Grey's good humor vanished in the instant. His sharp question bristled in the air between them.

"I can't do my job without the trust of the parents and the trustees."

"Has anyone accused you of wrongdoing?"

"You mean apart from everyone who attended the concert last night?"

"That was just the shock of the moment and Mrs. Allen's spite."

She shook her head sadly. "It's more than that, you know. Parnell Wilde is here because of me," she faltered and dropped her gaze, biting her lip.

"And?" Grey prompted, his voice low and compassionate.

"And my father was accused of embezzlement. He committed suicide because of it." She drew a long breath and raised her head, although she still could not meet his gaze. "I think it's best if I resign before Mrs. Allen and her cronies force me to."

"We can't discuss this here." His words were as hard as ice. He glanced about as though seeking a shelter in the snow drifts piled against the jail. "Look," his voice grated with irritation, "you can't hang about here while I identify the evidence Inspector West has for me. Go on to the Mercantile and wait for me there. All right?" He gripped her shoulders between his hands and peered under her hat brim for a better view of her face. "All right?" he said again when she didn't answer.

"Yes, all right," Emma capitulated when she could think of no better alternative.

"Good." Grey moved past her to the station door.

"Ask him . . ." She paused until Grey gave her his full attention. "Ask him if he killed my father." Her knees trembled and she clapped her gloved hands to her mouth when she'd put the unthinkable into words, but when Grey made a move to support her, she waved him away. "Just ask him," she said through gritted teeth; then turned and headed back into the main part of town following the same path she'd trampled in the snow on her way out. She kept her head down, concentrating on her footsteps, looking neither left nor right until she gained the boardwalk.

"Good morning, Miss Douglas." She looked up in surprise and found herself facing Sean and Lottie O'Connor outside the Mercantile. "That was a fine concert the young'uns put on last night. Congratulations."

She murmured a polite thank you to Sean and cast a quick, assessing glance at Lottie. The men in town might not brand her with the disgrace of her father, but the women were another question. Lottie looked back at her with frank, understanding eyes. "I hope you're feeling better today," she said. "The ruckus at the school last night must have distressed you, especially after all your hard work and Mr. North's persistent arm-twisting.

"Much better," Emma assured her, trying to present a composed face, "and I believe the police have traced the thief and recovered the money."

A pair of ladies approached the Mercantile, then hesitated and whispered to each other when they saw Emma and the O'Connors standing in the doorway. Emma ducked her head. This was exactly the reason she'd offered Grey her resignation.

"Hello, Mrs. Johnson, Mrs. Smith." She jerked her chin up when she heard Lottie's unmistakable challenge to the two ladies. "Do come and join us. We were just congratulating Miss Douglas on a splendid entertainment last night. You must be particularly grateful to her, Mrs. Smith, considering how many of your children took part." The fire in Lottie's eyes was hot enough to scorch the feather in Mrs. Johnson's hat.

The discomfitted ladies greeted Emma and murmured their perfunctory gratitude, then scuttled into the store as quickly as they could. If she hadn't been so miserable, Emma would have found the situation funny. As it was, she was merely thankful to have avoided a confrontation.

"Don't let them distress you," Lottie advised Emma with a grim look, "and if you're looking for a Christmas dinner, we'd be honored to have you as our guest at Pine Creek Farm. Sadie and Ab Gardener will be there. I've a notion to invite Jed Barclay as well. What do you say, Sean?"

"I'd say you do me proud, girl, and if you invite Jed, you'd best include Mrs. Royston, too." He smiled with fond indulgence at his new wife, then echoed her invitation to Emma. "My wife was the school teacher in Prospect years ago," he explained. "She has strong views on the proper treatment of the schoolmarm."

"I'm very grateful." Considering the nasty whispers she'd heard about "Crazy Lottie" when she'd first arrived in Prospect, Emma felt humbled by Mrs. O'Connor's brave championing of her. "But I intend to go back to San Francisco over the long school break. I have some unfinished business."

"In that case, I'll wish you a Merry Christmas, but if your plans fall through, the invitation to Pine Creek Farm is still open."

"Ah, the newlyweds." Grey North joined them on the boardwalk. Although he didn't touch her, Emma was aware of his solid bulk behind her and instantly felt better. His supreme self-confidence, which used to irritate her, now offered her reassurance and strength. "I was just going to offer Miss Douglas luncheon at the Rockingham," he said. "Would you care to join us?"

Lottie glanced first at Grey and then at Emma. A hint of a smile curled her lips and she shook her head. "I wish we could"—she slipped her hand into her husband's—"but we've a deal of business to see to today and we want to be home by dark. There's a pack of coyotes out there. Been worrying our cattle."

Emma and Grey took their leave of the O'Connors and crossed the street to the Rockingham. Emma, impatient for news from the police station, forgot to be annoyed with Grey's high-handed ways. "What did you learn?" she demanded the minute they were seated and the waiter was out of earshot.

"Inspector West was right about Wilde." Grey's lip curled with contempt. "The minute I confirmed the envelope they'd found on him was the one I'd placed in your desk drawer, he folded up like a deck of cards. He admitted stealing the money from the schoolhouse."

"What else?" After all she'd learned this morning, the piano money seemed of least importance.

Grey pursed his lips and shook his head, his eyes thoughtful. "He swears he never broke into your room at Mrs. Royston's."

"Do you believe him?" She rapped out the question.

"Strangely enough, I do." Grey sat back and waited while bowls of hot soup and a plate of crusty, fresh bread were placed on their table. As soon as the server withdrew, Grey explained, "Since he's already confessed to the more serious crime, I see no reason for him to lie about the mischief charge. Maybe the police were right and it was just a disgruntled student." He picked up his spoon. "Eat up, Emma. The soup is good and you're far too pale."

Obediently, she dipped her spoon into the hot broth and carried it to her mouth, but she barely tasted the prized Rockingham corn chowder. "I need to speak to him myself."

"Inspector West won't like that."

"I don't care! There are things about my father's death that I need to know. Parnell may have the answers."

"Eat your soup," Grey advised, his eyes thoughtful.

A waspish retort hovered on her tongue, but she studied his face before speaking and decided to hold her peace. She could practically see the wheels revolving in Grey's mind. Her tension eased and she concentrated on the soup, confident that he would find a way to help her. She'd swallowed every last spoonful before he spoke again.

"The inspector's a stickler for propriety," he said, "but his constable's more easygoing. The thing to do is wait until the inspector is out of his office, then go and bat your eyelashes at the constable. If you do it right, he'll let you speak with Wilde."

"And how am I supposed to do that?" Disappointment sharpened her voice. She'd expected something more from Grey, something bold and daring, something befitting the adventuresome spirit of the frontier he was so fond of extolling. "Do you expect me to lurk about the police station like a prowler, waiting for the inspector to go for a walk?"

"I suppose that could work." Grey's eyes brimmed with laughter. "But I had something more practical in mind."

"What?"

"A crime."

"You call that practical?" She pushed her empty bowl away and rested her elbows on the table in a most unladylike pose. "And how long do you think it might take before just the right felony occurs in Prospect?"

"I expect it will happen tomorrow, about mid-morning." His lips twitched. "Would that suit you?"

"You're going to commit a crime just to get me an interview with Parnell?" She leaned forward and lowered her voice to a whisper before sending a guilty glance about the dining room. Fortunately, the table by the fireplace where they sat was somewhat separated from the other diners.

"Not necessarily 'commit,'" Grey prevaricated, "but I can report a very serious occurrence that will require Inspector West's personal attention."

"What?" She couldn't contain her curiosity.

"Probably better for you not to know." His eyes twinkled with mischief. "That way, if I'm arrested for being a public nuisance, you can claim ignorance. Have you finished?" At her nod Grey came round the table and held her chair, then escorted her outside. When he would have walked home with her she forestalled him.

"There's no need for you to see me to my door. It's broad daylight. No one will molest me on such a short journey."

"Good." Grey seemed relieved to leave her. Being of a contrary mind, she was piqued that he'd accepted dismissal so easily.

He touched the brim of his hat in a brief salute and set off in the direction of the livery stable. Emma walked home in a deep fog, her mind busy surmising the schemes Grey might engineer to call Inspector West from behind his desk at mid-morning tomorrow. Everything she concocted, like horse stealing or arson or kidnapping or claim jumping, was far too improbable or too dangerous to contemplate. If Grey committed any one of the offenses she pondered, he could end up with a noose around his neck.

She shook off her useless musings and considered the more urgent matter of her resignation. She should have discussed it with Grey over lunch, but he'd managed to distract her. She would write a proper letter the instant she got home and give it to him tomorrow. He could inform the rest of the trustees. She quickened her step and was soon letting herself in the front door of Mrs. Royston's home.

But before she could get to paper and pen Mrs. Royston called her to help put the finishing touches to their impromptu tea. "Now, then, Miss Douglas"—her landlady stood back to admire a high yellow cake, beautifully frosted and decorated, sitting on her prize crystal cake plate—"that's one of my best, if I do say so myself."

"It looks scrumptious." Emma admired the delicate swirls in the icing. "I could almost wish your friends would stay home so we could have the cake all to ourselves."

"Well, you can't have your cake and eat it, too," Mrs. Royston quipped and laughed out loud, delighted with her own wit. She left the cake on the dining room table with the tea things, all laid ready, and went to take up her usual position just inside the front windows, where a judicious lifting of the lace curtains allowed her a full view of the street.

"Ah, there's the mayor's wife turning in the gate, just on time and . . ." she broke off with a small shriek. "Of all the nerve!" Before Emma could take in what had happened, Mrs. Royston had darted to the front door and yanked it open. "Mrs. Carlton," she shouted a greeting to the mayor's wife. "Punctual as always. Do come in." She held the door wide and Emma could see Mrs. Carlton hovering uncertainly at the foot of the well-swept walk. Mrs. Allen, on the other side of the half-buried picket fence, watched with daggers in her eyes.

"Lemon cake!" Emma exclaimed in a voice loud enough to carry to Mrs. Carlton's ears. "My favorite."

The battle was won. The mayor's wife surged up the walkway, resplendent in a beaver hat and fur collar.

"Oh, Mrs. Allen, I didn't see you there." Mrs. Royston drove home the knife. "Would you care to join us? I'm having a few of Miss Douglas's most ardent supporters in for a small tea. You may know some people in town are raising questions as to her suitability since news of her father's demise has surfaced. Such murmurs are so un-Christian, as I'm sure you'll agree."

It was a bold stroke and left Mrs. Allen no way out. Emma smothered a smile as the vicar's wife grudgingly set her foot on the path to Mrs. Royston's parlor. From the look on her face she considered that she had set her foot on the road to perdition as well. However, there was no turning back as two other guests arrived and swept up the walk behind her.

The ladies drank their tea, ate their cake, and plied Emma with questions about the robbery—now that the culprit was safely behind bars, it was not only a safe topic, but one of the most exciting as well. Mrs. Allen made one last attempt to discredit Emma by asking about San Francisco and the people she'd known there, but the arrow missed its mark. Emma became the center of attention and a minor celebrity as she described the modern city of her birth.

"They have streetcars?" Mrs. Carlton exclaimed. "And a telephone service? Imagine!"

"It's quite wonderful, to be sure," Emma said. "Not many people are subscribed to the telephone, but it means that if someone in the household is ill, you can telephone the doctor and speak to him immediately rather than waiting while a messenger carries notes back and forth."

"Newfangled nonsense if you ask me." Mrs. Allen brushed cake crumbs from her skirt.

"I'd love to go to a concert such as you describe," Mrs. Roberts sighed.

"Well, now that we're going to have a piano in the schoolhouse and Miss Douglas plays, we can get up our own concerts." Mrs. Royston leaped into the debate. "Les Smith can bring his fiddle and you could sing, Mrs. Carlton. I believe you have a very fine voice."

The idea was an instant hit and the ladies were so voluble in their enthusiasm Emma almost didn't hear the knock on the door that announced Inspector West. She took him through to the kitchen, leaving the parlor to the organizing committee of Prospect's First Annual Victoria Day Concert. "In honor of the Queen's birthday." She heard Mrs. Allen's firm voice dictating the choice of date and theme.

"What's all that, then?" The inspector cocked his head toward the parlor.

"Mrs. Royston preserving my reputation." Emma gestured to the kitchen table. Inspector West pulled out a chair and seated himself, stretching his long legs toward the stove. "Would you care for a piece of her lemon cake?"

"Wouldn't say no. Mrs. Royston's cakes are famous."

When she had fulfilled her hostess duties and the inspector was provided with tea and a slice of cake, Emma sat down opposite and waited for him to state what he'd come to tell her. Most of it she already knew from Grey, but she forbore mentioning her meeting with him. No point in putting Inspector West on his guard. "As for your father's passbook"—the inspector pushed away his empty plate—"Wilde maintains he picked it out of the wastebasket on a whim." He pursed his lips and raised a weary eyebrow. "Seems dodgy to me. We'll know more when we hear from the San Francisco police." He stood up and reached for his hat. "Thanks for the tea, Miss Douglas."

After seeing the inspector out, Emma returned to the parlor, just in time to witness the breakup of the unofficial steering committee for Prospect's first ever Victoria Day celebrations. "It's the Queen's golden jubilee year," Mrs. Allen repeated as the ladies gathered their winter coats. "It's only fitting that all her loyal subjects should mark the occasion." There was a flurry of good-byes and the ladies at last departed.

"Well!" Mrs. Royston flopped onto her horsehair sofa with a most unladylike grunt and fanned her face with her hand the minute the door closed on the last of her guests. "There'll be no more talk about our suitability after this afternoon, *and* I'll be taking a cake to the Christmas tea."

"Mrs. Royston, you are magnificent." Emma dropped onto a low chair and gazed at her landlady with new respect and gratitude.

"Oh, call me Bella." Her hostess waved a dismissive hand. "After all we've been through, formal titles seem a bit silly."

"Bella, then, and thank you." Unaccountably, Emma felt weepy. For all her faults, Bella Royston had proved herself a staunch friend, and goodness knew Emma could use all the friends she could find. She would be sad to say good-bye, but she had no choice. If there was a chance to clear her father's name, she must take it, whatever the cost to herself. She felt the outline of the key in her corset and allowed herself just the tiniest spark of hope.

But that was for tomorrow. Today was for her landlady. "Wait there," she said and left the room. A moment later she returned with two glasses of sherry. She handed one to her friend and raised the other herself. "To Bella and Emma."

"Emma and Bella," Mrs. Royston chuckled, and raised her glass in a toast, "and to the First Annual Victoria Day Concert."

Chapter Seven

The next morning Emma watched from the doorway of the Mercantile as Grey North and Inspector West rode down Prospect's main street and headed out of town. As they passed Grey flashed her a conspiratorial wink. Whatever he'd told Inspector West, the ruse had worked. She picked up her skirts and hurried toward the fort. It hadn't snowed for two days, so the path was well tramped down. Within ten minutes she was standing before the constable and acting the heartbroken maid with such conviction that she was shown into the cell area of the jail, offered a chair, and given the constable's sympathy before you could say North West Mounted Police.

"I can't let him out of the cell, Miss," the constable apologized, "but I'll close the door into the front. You can have a few minutes in private."

"Abigail!" Parnell leaped to the barred door of his cell the moment the constable withdrew. "You have come to get me out."

"Of all the nerve!" Emma dropped her heartsick demeanor and glared at the man behind the bars. "You stole from me and you think I'll come to your rescue? How could you do that, Parnell?"

"I'm so sorry." Did she actually see tears in his eyes? "I don't know what came over me. There was the money and the open window and the proprietor of the Gold Nugget hounding me for payment." He spread his hands and shrugged helplessly. "What else could I do?"

"You set the tree on fire." Even yet she couldn't get over the enormity of what could have happened because of his self-centeredness.

"It was an excellent distraction." He appeared unmoved by her expostulations.

"People could have been hurt! What if the fire hadn't been doused so quickly? The whole place could have gone up. Have you no conscience?"

"If you have only come to scold, Abigail, I've no wish to speak to you." His face turned sullen and she knew she had to control her anger or he would refuse to tell her what she needed to know.

She gripped her fingers tightly together, controlling the urge to scream. "No, I didn't come to scold." She did her best to sound placating, trying to appeal to the man he used to be, or at least the man she'd thought he used to be. "I've come for your help." She drew a deep, steadying breath. "Parnell, the police told me you were carrying my father's passbook." The pleading in her voice was no longer an act. "Where did you get it? And why?"

"I was not stealing from the bank, if that's what you're asking." His sullen look rivaled Bessie Smith at her worst. He walked to the back of the cell and lounged against the wall. "I found the passbook the day your father died and kept it on a whim. Then when I heard the partners talking about reopening the case I thought, if your father were found innocent, after all, they would have to restore to you your papa's money. I kept the passbook to show how much was owing. I did it for you, Abigail. For us."

His voice was filled with passion, his gaze soft and sentimental, but she wasn't fooled. Not anymore. Her erstwhile fiancé might try to persuade her it was true love that had brought him hotfoot to the Kootenays, but, she suspected, it was really the dollars recorded in her father's old passbook.

"You haven't told me how you came to have it."

He drew back and cocked his head, studying her with a calculating look. How had she ever thought his eyes soulful? They were as cold and as hard as pebbles in a stream. "If I tell you something, will you get me out of here?"

She flinched. She hated duplicity, but she had to promise him something if she hoped to learn what he knew. "I don't have the power to have you released," she said slowly, "but I'll vouch for you with Inspector West. Perhaps he will reduce the charges."

"And I will languish here in this oh-so-boring little cell until the circuit judge pays a call? Bah." He kicked at the leg of the wooden cot.

"It's the best I can do."

"These Canadians with their red-coated policemen and fancy courts and judges in black robes in the middle of the wilderness. It's ridiculous."

"Please." She glanced nervously over her shoulder. How long could Grey keep the inspector away? How long before the constable grew suspicious and ordered her out?

Parnell stopped grumbling about the administration of justice in British Columbia and looked at her anxious face instead; then seemed to come to a decision. "Very well." He pushed himself away from the wall and sauntered to the barred door, hands in his pockets. "But I must have your promise, Abigail."

"I promise." She licked her dry lips, her stomach churned.

"You'll have to say better than that."

"I promise I'll put in a word for you with Inspector West." She took a deep breath and returned to the chair in front of the cell. "Now it's your turn, Parnell. Tell me what you know. Please." Her voice quavered ever so slightly, but she bit her lip and would not allow the tears to come.

"I didn't kill him if that's what you think." Parnell scowled in sullen petulance. "When I entered the study, your father's desk had already been rifled. There was a paltry bit of money strewn about and the passbook. I took it. I'll admit that, but nothing more."

"You took it from his desk? Not from the trash as you told the inspector?"

"Yes."

"But where was Papa?"

"He was dead." He turned his back and walked to the farthest wall of the cell, as though unable to meet her eye. "When I went in I saw him, lying on the floor, the gun in his hand and the desk drawers open with the money lying there. What was I to do?"

She stared at him, aghast at his callous disregard for common decency. "You could have called the police," she croaked. "You could have come for me." Tears closed her throat, reducing her voice to a bare whisper. "You could have given me one last moment with my father."

"It was too late, Abigail." At last he spoke gently,

coming to the door of the cell and holding out his hand to her. "Your papa was beyond knowing, even if you had been there to hold his hand."

"Then the police." She jumped from the chair, unable to sit still while Parnell poured out his horrible words.

He backed away, shrugging his shoulders as though trying to shake off an irritating mosquito. "If I'd called the police, they would have accused me. There had been trouble at the bank earlier that day. Your father, he left his office in anger, then your friend, Mr. Everett Jergens, he came to me where I worked in the accounts and ranted at me like a madman over an error in the accounts that was not my fault. That is why I called on your papa, to complain about such treatment. But . . ." He shrugged and turned his hands palm upward. "Your papa could no longer help me."

The enormity of his betrayal nearly knocked her to her knees. To have walked away, without the slightest remorse, and left her to find her beloved father after his body had grown cold. His lack of pity was monstrous. Even a stranger would have shown more compassion. She felt she looked through a veil as she studied his well-known features, the slim, straight nose she'd admired, the soft lips she'd kissed, the dark eyes she'd thought so romantic, and realized she gazed upon a man she'd never met. The soul inhabiting the body of Parnell Wilde was totally alien to her.

She shivered, wishing she could run away. But she wouldn't abandon her father a second time. She must learn what Parnell could tell her. "And you saw or heard nothing?"

"Like I told the police, I went to talk to your Papa. Your housekeeper let me in the front door. I said I could find my own way to the study. She went back to the kitchen. I heard a noise, but when I got to the study it was as I said. Your father dead, the desk drawers open, money scattered about. I took it and left."

"Is that all?" she whispered when she could trust herself to speak.

"Not quite." Having begun, Parnell seemed determined to make a clean breast of it. Perhaps somewhere at the bottom of his selfish heart was a kernel of regret for the pain she'd endured. "I've been asking myself about the desk, Abigail. If your father shot himself and left a suicide note, why did he ransack his desk?" She gripped the bars of the cell for support, bracing herself to hear the words she dreaded.

"You think it was murder?"

Again, he shrugged. "Who is to say? But when I got home and counted the money, I discovered I'd taken some other papers as well. There was a report from the bank auditor."

"Of course." She almost wept with disappointment. She'd been so sure Parnell could tell her something to clear her father. The auditor's report only confirmed the embezzlement/suicide theory.

"Abigail, if the auditor suspected your papa of embezzlement, he would not have sent the report to him."

The simple statement of fact left her breathless. Her mouth dropped open and she could only stare in disbelief. She had her proof. At least, Parnell had the proof that would clear her father's name. "Who?" She forced the single word past suddenly parched lips.

"Don't know." He shrugged and braced his shoulders against the cell wall. "The report said they'd found accounting irregularities but they hadn't traced the source as yet."

She sat down hard on the chair the constable had so

thoughtfully set for her. The proof she needed was so tantalizingly close, yet still beyond her grasp. "The embezzler knew he'd been found out," she said in a flat, dull voice, "and he murdered Papa to keep his secret."

"It's probable."

"Then why did the bank accuse Papa? Surely the auditor could have told them he was innocent?"

"From what I know of the bank, Abigail, the partners would do everything possible to avoid publicity. If your papa was the thief and he killed himself, they would be happy to sweep the whole affair under the carpet."

"Where is the auditor's report?"

"It was of no use to me. I burned it."

"And you never reported what you knew?" She could hardly credit his callousness.

He scowled and turned his back on her. "You have changed, Abigail. Always nagging me for what I could not help. You are not so charming anymore."

She rose and stood behind the chair. Her hands gripped tightly about the back post, she fought the tears and the anger and the grief. None of it could help her father now, but deep in the primitive part of her soul she wanted to rail at Parnell Wilde, to scratch at him with her nails, to pummel her fists into his two-faced smiling mouth and force him to get on his knees and admit his shame, to her and to the world. But it would do no good. He had no conscience. "I must go." She loosened her white-knuckled grip on the chair and called for the constable.

She walked the length of the jailhouse, hardly noticing when the constable jumped ahead of her to open the outside door. She stepped out into the crisp, cold air of the mountains and drew a deep breath, trying to cleanse her soul of the ugliness she'd heard. She raised her eyes to the snowcapped peaks, glinting against an

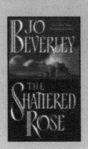

impossibly blue sky. God's handiwork, so far removed from man's sordidness. No wonder Grey loved the frontier. Here the fight was for survival against the elements, pure and clean and lethal, but without the viciousness of man against man. She stepped out into the new snow, forgiving its cold and inconvenience, embracing its purity.

"A visit to San Francisco? At this time of year? Impossible." Bella stood in the doorway to Emma's room, her arms folded across her chest as though she could physically bar Emma from committing such a folly. "It will take three or four days just to reach the railhead."

"I know"—Emma continued to stuff blouses and underclothes into a satchel—"but it's something I must do."

"And when will you get back? The school is closed now for the coldest part of the winter, but the trustees will expect you to be here as soon as the days begin to lengthen."

"I have my letter of resignation ready. I'll deliver it to Grey North today." She didn't pause in her packing but her hands trembled.

"Resign!" Bella shrieked. "You can't! It will make you look guilty. And after all I've done to preserve your reputation." She fanned her face with a lace-trimmed handkerchief.

"I'm sorry." Emma closed the handles of the satchel and set it on the floor. She stepped to her landlady's side and put an arm about her shoulders in an awkward hug. "You have been so kind, Bella, I can't begin to thank you. But this is something I must do. It's for my father."

"You told me you were an orphan."

"I am," she smiled slightly, "although I'm not sure the term applies to someone past her eighteenth birthday." She hesitated, torn between a desire to set her landlady's mind at rest and the need to keep her mission a secret. She'd already suffered two break-ins, and she believed the thief had been seeking the key now secured in her corset. Oddly enough, she believed Parnell's protestations of innocence when it came to the break-ins, which meant the thief, and possibly the killer, was still at large. "Listen, Bella"—she drew her landlady into the room and closed the door—"you must keep this a secret, but I believe whoever broke in here and ransacked my room may have murdered my father."

"Merciful heavens!" Bella's face blanched and she touched the handkerchief to her mouth.

"Don't repeat what I've told you," Emma cautioned. "I could be in danger if the killer knows of my plans, but I wanted you to understand, I have no choice. If there is a chance to clear my father's name and bring his murderer to justice, I must take it. I must go back to San Francisco."

"Couldn't you leave it to the police?" A shimmer of moisture darkened Bella's eyes.

"Papa trusted me."

"And what if you get caught in a snowslide, or your ship sinks on the way, or your horse throws you down a canyon?" Mrs. Royston sniffed and dabbed at her eyes with the hankie.

"I must go."

"Very well." Bella seemed to recognize the futility of argument. "But you cannot make the journey alone and I'm not able to go with you. You need a male escort, Emma. Someone to deal with the rigors of the trail and protect you from unsavory characters on the journey."

"I've talked to Mr. Paget. He's taking a team of pack animals to the railhead at Gold City tomorrow. I can go with them."

"You're too inexperienced to undertake that journey, even with Mr. Paget. He'll be too busy keeping his horses together and tending to his cargo to cater to a tourist."

Emma picked up the photo and touched a finger to her father's face before opening her satchel and tucking the photo inside. "I'll manage."

Bella threw up her hands in defeat and left the room. Emma heard her stomping down the stairs, shouting for Rose.

She spared a moment's sympathy for the girl who would take the brunt of Mrs. Royston's displeasure, but she would not allow herself to be dissuaded. She glanced toward the window, noting the frost on its panes. Bella hadn't told her anything she didn't already know about traveling through the mountains in December, but her determination to vindicate her father was stronger than her fear. The worst part would be the trip from Prospect to Gold City. In comparison, the train from Gold City, down the Fraser Canyon to Vancouver, and then a steamer to San Francisco would seem like a picnic.

She checked her purse, spreading its contents on the bureau. She counted out her dollars and tried to calculate the cost of her fare. A school teacher on the frontier was not lavishly paid, but she had been frugal and her lodgings with Mrs. Royston were reasonable. She would have enough, at least for a third-class fare. She sat down on the edge of her bed, her gaze roving restlessly over the room. She had nothing to do until tomorrow morning and it was barely past noon. Having made up her mind to take action, she found the waiting set her nerves on edge.

"Miss Douglas!" Rose knocked on her door and opened it a crack. "Miss Douglas," the girl was panting from her rush up the stairs, "there's a man downstairs for you. Mrs. Royston says could you come."

"Of course." Emma followed the girl to the parlor and found Grey and Mrs. Royston waiting for her.

"I don't want to seem interfering," Bella hastened to assure her, "but I can't let you go haring off into the bush, in the middle of winter, alone. I told Mr. North your plans and he agrees with me."

"You told him?" She couldn't believe Mrs. Royston had betrayed her confidence so easily.

"Yes, I explained your attack of homesickness," Bella offered the lie with a meaningful glance, "and he agrees with me. The trip is too dangerous for you to undertake alone."

"Oh, I see." Emma dropped her gaze and attempted a woebegone look.

"That's why I asked Mr. North to go with you," Bella declared smugly.

"But I can't ask you to do that." Her glance flew to Grey's face, aghast at the thought of spending three days traveling through the wilderness with Grey at her side and even more disconcerted by her eagerness to do just that. She ruthlessly squelched her foolish longings. "What would Mrs. Allen think?"

Grey's eyes glinted and he snapped his fingers. "That for Mrs. Allen." He stood with his feet planted wide, his shoulders thrown back, hands resting easily at his sides, the epitome of male confidence and power.

"But it's such an imposition." She made one last protest, more to salve her conscience than to dissuade Grey. She was certain no amount of threatening or tears or bombast, even from those he loved, could persuade him against his will, and to be honest, she would welcome his escort. No matter her brave words, the wilderness terrified her.

"Stop quibbling, Emma." He moved to the fireplace, resting one elbow on the mantel. "We need to discuss the arrangements."

"I've already hired a horse from the livery stable." All her softer feelings vanished in the face of Grey's high-handed assumptions.

"Won't work." He dismissed her preparations. "You haven't ridden since you came to Prospect. You're in no condition to undertake this trek on horseback."

"Well, I can't walk." She barely refrained from stamping her foot.

"Temper, temper." His lips twitched. "We can take a sleigh and my team. It's slower than on horseback and you'll feel the cold, but it's still a wiser plan. With Paget going ahead, the wagon road will be well marked and any fresh snow tramped down. We'll catch up to him when he stops for the night."

"Don't you have a hotel to run?"

"I don't exactly change the sheets myself, Emma." He grinned. "My staff can run the Rockingham for a few days without me."

"But you'll miss the Christmas festivities." She suddenly recalled an advertisement for a sleigh ride and tree-trimming party followed by refreshments at the hotel for the day before Christmas.

"So will you." He sauntered toward her. "Perhaps we can console each other."

"Now stop making difficulties, Emma." Mrs. Royston stepped between them. "Mr. North's plan makes sense and you know it. With any luck you can go to San Francisco and do what you have to do and be back here in time for the new term. And don't forget, I'm counting on you to entertain at the Victoria Day concert." She dusted off her hands, apparently declaring an end to discussion. "You just listen to Mr. North and stop making difficulties." She nodded to Grey. "I'm trusting you to behave like a gentleman, Mr. North."

Grey swept them a mocking bow. "Word of honor." His lips still curved in a smile but his eyes were somber. "I'll be here first thing in the morning." He nodded and took his departure.

"Come along, Emma. We'll check the larder and decide on provisions." Mrs. Royston led the way to the kitchen and Emma followed meekly. "I'll put bread to bake tonight so you'll have fresh loaves in the morning." She clicked her tongue in disgust. "The miners seem to live on beans and bacon, but I can fix you up with better than that." She pulled down several jars of preserves from the shelves, then set about slicing up a roast of beef. "One thing about traveling in winter, your food won't spoil. You'll just need to make a fire to thaw it out."

With her trip planned for her, Emma had nothing to do but comply and be grateful. She spent the rest of the day helping Mrs. Royston prepare a large hamper of food and pressing her fingers to the key sewn into her corset, to remind herself of the purpose of her journey, and tried not to think about spending the next three days alone with Grey.

At first light the next morning she was ready and waiting in Mrs. Royston's front hall, the hamper of food at her feet. As well, her landlady had provided her with two hot bricks, wrapped in blankets, ready to place on the vehicle floor. They would help keep her warm, at least for a little while.

The jingle of sleigh bells alerted her to Grey's arrival. She wrapped her scarf more tightly about her neck, hugged Mrs. Royston in farewell, and did her best to assure that lady she would return. Grey loaded her luggage, then handed her up into the sleigh. She settled into the seat and they were away. The horses were fresh and they skimmed down the empty streets of Prospect in a whirl of flying snow.

"There's Mr. Paget's pack team." She pointed ahead to the dark shapes moving steadily down the snow-packed wagon road as they left the last of Prospect's buildings behind.

"We'll keep fairly close to them for the morning anyway," Grey said, "but we need to spare the horses for the long haul."

Emma snuggled under the buffalo robe Grey had provided, glad for the hot bricks at her feet. The frozen landscape awed her with its stark beauty. The dark forest marched in silent majesty down the mountainsides to the very edge of the rough road. The dawning sun, reflected from the snowy peaks, sent blinding rays of light into the sky. "Everything is so grand," she whispered, reluctant to disturb the great cathedral of the mountains with the sound of her voice.

"Exactly." Grey's voice held a tinge of excitement, and she glanced sharply at him. He sat comfortably, his back resting against the sleigh's plush seat. His hands, holding the reins, looked relaxed; his eyes scanned the way ahead with an alert gaze.

"You love it, don't you?" It wasn't really a question even though she inflected the last word upward. The answer was written clear in his sparkling eyes and eager face.

"Yes." He turned his head slightly, watching her from the corner of his eye. "You can stretch to your fullest in this land, Emma, and not touch any edges. There's no dream too big for the wilderness. I'd hate to see it tamed and carved up into little fiefdoms."

"But don't you own just such a one in England?" She didn't credit that he was the son of a duke, but Mrs. Allen had insisted he had a title of some sort and she couldn't resist the urge to probe. Alone in this immense space, conventional good manners seemed meaningless.

"My father does." His lips tightened and he stared straight ahead again, concentrating his attention on the horses. "But I left all that behind." His manner changed again and he waved a hand to encompass the sky, the mountains, the forest, and the snowy surface of the lake lying off to their left. "Just look at this, Emma. It is far too grand for a mere man to control."

"You're a strange one, Grey North." She snuggled deeper into the folds of the buffalo robe as the cold penetrated her layers of clothing. "Most men of rank and privilege fight to the death to keep it."

"I'll fight for what I've earned, not what I've received by an accident of birth." She heard the scowl in his voice.

"You sound like an American."

He threw back his head and laughed aloud, the rumble of his mirth echoing off the mountain slopes, filling the valley with the sound of good cheer. "I knew you'd understand. You've the revolutionary spirit in you, even though it's hidden beneath layers of manners and city living."

"Perhaps," she conceded. She'd always loved to listen to tales of the pioneers. Men and women who'd come from humble beginnings, yet rose to prosperity and prominence through hard work and determination. "As a child I used to imagine myself homesteading or joining a cattle drive on the open range." She shook her head at her foolishness.

"You'd have made a delightful cowgirl." Grey ran his gaze over her. Even though she was swathed in layers and layers of clothing and covered with a thick robe, she felt as though he'd inspected every intimate curve of her body.

"Nonsense." She blushed and thrust her chin in the air.

"So, instead, you learned to hide your feelings behind a polite mask of manners and gushed over the latest fashions and went to any number of parties and balls. Pity." He raised one expressive eyebrow.

"I also read, a lot." She wished she'd bitten her tongue rather than defend herself and admit his opinion of her mattered.

"Dime store novels?"

She knew he was goading her but rose to the bait anyway. "The public library, if you must know," she shot back and smiled in satisfaction when she saw his surprise. "That's why I was able to challenge the teacher's examinations and pass on my first try."

"I'm impressed." He reached out a hand to tuck in the end of her scarf that had worked free. "Did you talk to your friends about your reading tastes?"

"No." Her satisfaction ebbed away, leaving her cross. "What about you?" It was time to turn the tables and probe into his past. "What were your childhood dreams?"

"To hear my mother laugh." His sharp intake of breath told her he'd spoken more freely than he intended.

"I'm sorry." She laid a hand on his arm, feeling the sinewy strength of muscle as he guided the team along the snow-packed trail.

"For asking? Or for hearing the truth?" She heard the familiar cynicism in his voice.

"A little of both, I guess. You're right about the wilderness. It makes the rules of polite behavior seem irrelevant."

"Exactly." His approving smile made her forget the cold that was slowly but surely seeping into her bones. She risked another question. "Still, don't you ever long for home?"

"You sound wistful. Look!" He broke off and pointed to a pair of golden eagles riding the airstreams, soaring and floating between the mountain peaks, gliding effortlessly over the valley, savage and free.

"They're magnificent." Emma shaded her eyes, watching the noble creatures. For the moment she forgot that her feet were cold, her face burned from the wind, and her back ached from struggling against the swaying of the sleigh.

Grey drew in the reins and they came to a halt. For several minutes they sat still, watching the aerial display, perfectly in tune with the land and each other. Then the eagles soared out of sight. He shook the reins and they were moving once more. "Cold?"

"A bit," she confessed, "but I don't mind." Watching the eagles seemed to have made up for her discomfort—seeing them and sharing the moment with Grey.

"That's the wilderness experience." His smile warmed her even more than the hot bricks at her feet. "After a day on the trail, the fire will feel warmer, the food will taste better, and the beds will seem the softest you've ever slept in. To answer your question, Emma, no, I don't want to go home. Here is where I'm truly alive."

She turned slightly in her cocoon of coverings and studied his face. Wind and cold had reddened his cheeks and set ice crystals in his eyebrows, but the blue eyes glistening below those frosted brows were alight with vitality. His mouth had lost its cynical twist. He looked full of eager confidence. In town, she'd resented his supreme self-assurance. Here, on the open trail, she found it heartening.

She wriggled her toes, forcing the blood through her frozen extremities, and relaxed against the well-padded seat, letting her head rest against the high back while she watched the magnificent scenery. If she let her body move with the sway of the sleigh instead of fighting it, the movement was as soothing as a rocking chair.

At noon they stopped to rest the horses and replenish themselves. Mr. Paget already had a fire going when they arrived at the halt and water boiling, ready for their tea. Emma unpacked the generous sandwiches Mrs. Royston had placed in the hamper and placed them close enough to the fire to thaw while Grey tended to his team.

"Here you go," he said, carrying the buffalo robe from the sleigh and laying it over the downed log Mr. Paget had set as a seat for her beside the fire. "All the comforts of home."

Mr. Paget handed her a cup of tea in a porcelain mug while he and Grey drank theirs from tin cups. She spared a grateful thought for Mrs. Royston's consideration in supplying a proper cup and hoped it wouldn't end in disaster. If she broke the fragile piece, she'd not only need to drink her tea from a tin cup, but share it as well.

She bit into a thick sandwich loaded with Mrs. Royston's roast beef and her pickled string beans. The homey meal tasted like a feast of finest herbs.

"Perfect." Gray sat beside her, munching his own sandwich.

"Aye, it's a great day for the mountains." Mr. Paget cast an experienced eye toward the heavens. "And the weather should hold for a couple more days. You'll be lucky, Miss Douglas. We'll reach the railhead without having to weather a blizzard. I just hope that sunshine doesn't trigger an avalanche."

"Avalanche!" She looked up the mountainsides in alarm, as though expecting a river of snow to come crashing down at any moment. "Aren't you worried?" She turned to Grey.

"It's what makes the journey worthwhile," he teased, but she sensed a deep truth behind his lightly spoken words. "Danger sweetens the day."

"If you say so," she muttered dryly, and turned her eyes to study the deep drifts of snow hanging off the mountainsides.

"I don't suppose Mrs. Royston slipped any of her famous cake into that hamper?" Grey drew her attention back to their unusual picnic.

"As a matter of fact, she did." Emma opened the lid on the basket and drew out three slices of chocolate cake. "No frosting but, as you say, eating it beside an open fire under a blue sky adds its own accent."

"Good girl." Grey accepted the wedge of cake. "You're learning."

"Better make the best of the daylight." Mr. Paget emptied the last of the tea onto the fire. "It'll be getting dark by four o'clock. I aim to be at Mrs. Hunter's by then."

"You go ahead," Grey said. "I'll finish up here."

"Fair enough." Mr. Paget nodded to Emma, then went to tighten the ropes on his pack team.

Grey retrieved the bricks he'd placed beside their campfire to warm and loaded them into the bottom of the sleigh, then smothered the last embers of the fire. "Ready?" He held out his bare hand to help her rise from her makeshift chair.

"Ready." She placed her hand in his and felt a jolt of awareness race through her body as their fingers touched. She pulled away quickly and hastily donned her thick gloves. Grey gave her a quizzical look but for once didn't ask her any embarrassing questions.

The rest of the day passed without incident. Mr. Paget had cleared the few fallen trees from the track, and there were no deep ruts to catch the sleigh's runners. They made good progress and arrived at Mrs. Hunter's lodge by dusk. "Not the Ritz or even the Rockingham," Grey said with a nod to the single-story log structure as he drew rein, "but I believe you'll find it adequate."

"If it has a fire, hot water, and a warm meal, I'll consider it a palace." Despite her resolve to remain cheerful, the last hour on the rough road had stretched Emma's reserves. She was cold, hungry, and weary.

Grey secured the reins and vaulted easily out of the sleigh, as supple and vigorous as he'd been at the beginning of the day, although she knew he had to be cold and tired, too. He put his hands at her waist and swung her to the ground at the steps of the lodge. "That's not necessary . . . oh!" She made her habitual protest and then realized that his assistance was very necessary. Her legs had grown stiff, numb from the knees down. Without Grey's support she might have lost her balance. "I'm sorry," she apologized as she clutched at his arm.

"Come on." He picked her up and carried her the three steps up to the lodge front door, shouldered it open, and walked inside, setting her on her feet only when they reached the big fireplace, ablaze with a roaring fire. Her legs still trembled, and he kept his arm about her waist for support. "You'll do better as soon as you thaw out. Mrs. Hunter will see to you." He nodded to the spare, gray-haired woman hastening toward them with a cup of steaming tea in her hands and a welcoming smile on her face.

"There you go, dearie"—she handed Emma the tea—"get that inside you and you'll soon feel better. I'd offer you whiskey if you preferred, but Mr. Paget tells me you're the schoolteacher and not used to strong spirits. I'll save that for the men of the party. Don't be alarmed," she continued when she rightly interpreted the look of misgiving on Emma's face. "Nobody gets drunk in my house, but there's nothing like a little whiskey to take the chill off after a long day in the open."

"I'm sure," Emma said weakly. She was rapidly growing too warm, though whether from the fire or from Grey's closeness she didn't dare to say. She stepped away and removed her gloves and scarf, keeping her back to him, suddenly self-conscious.

"I've put you in the first bedroom." Her hostess pointed to a short hallway leading down the left-hand side of the fireplace. "If you're warm enough, you might like to freshen up."

"Yes, thank you." Although Grey had stopped the sleigh twice without asking, and remained politely oblivious while she'd waded through the snow to seek the shelter of some bushes, traveling all day in the company of men made her more than eager for the privacy of a bedroom.

"I'll see to the horses." Grey headed out the door, leaving her alone with her hostess.

"There's hot water in the kettle and cold in the ewer," Mrs. Hunter explained. "The privy's through the door at the end of the hall. I'll leave you to yourself, if you don't mind. I've dinner cooking in the kitchen."

Having attended to her personal needs, Emma returned to the bedroom and removed her outer clothing, took off her boots, and loosened her stays. She washed her hands and face, grateful for the warm water, and stretched out on the bed, letting its soft mattress ease her tired body. The room was cozy, the log construction providing a soothing contrast to the elaborate wallpaper Mrs. Royston favored. A tiny window cut into the thick logs afforded her a glimpse of snow-laden forest and a glimmer of the rising moon. She sighed and stretched her arms over her head. Just at this moment she wanted nothing more than to sink deeper into the pillows, pull the quilt over herself, and go straight to sleep—maybe for days.

A tap on her door put paid to such languishing notions. "Emma." It was Grey's voice. She scrambled to her feet, hastily refastening her clothing.

"Just a moment." She stuck her feet into her boots and stumbled to the door without bothering to do them up. She barely cracked the door and made sure to position herself in the opening, not wanting him to see the rumpled bed. "Yes?"

"I've brought your satchel. I'll put it inside for you."

She had no choice but to step aside and he walked in, placing the small bag at the foot of her bed. "Tired?" He grinned and cocked his head toward the dishevelled quilt and squashed pillow.

"Aren't you?" She couldn't help the waspish tone. Despite having spent the entire day snuggled next to him in the sleigh, she was uncomfortable with him in her bedroom. Besides, it irked her that a day of travel had exhausted her but seemed to have left Grey untouched, even though he'd had the extra task of driving the team.

"I'll sleep well tonight," he conceded. "There's nothing like fresh air to call up Morpheus from his domain, but don't miss your supper. You'll find Mrs. Hunter serves a hearty meal and you'll need it to keep up your strength. If you're hungry you'll feel the cold more."

He withdrew, leaving Emma the choice to lie down again, and run the risk of sleeping past dinner, or to tidy her hair and join her fellow travelers around the big fireplace in the front room. Despite her weary bones, she wisely chose the latter.

"There you are, dearie." Mrs. Hunter greeted her as soon as she stepped around the corner of the fireplace. "Sit ye down here." She pointed to a curious-looking chair made of bent wood twigs with a deer hide seat and back. "You'll find that seat surprisingly comfortable. Now, then"—she snapped her fingers—"just you rest there and I'll have supper ready in two shakes." She patted Emma's shoulder, then scuttled out of the room, a veritable whirlwind of energy.

Emma and Grey were left alone before the fire. She squirmed in Mrs. Hunter's comfortable chair. The roaring fire, the glass of whiskey in Grey's hand, and the cozy room felt altogether too intimate. If she wasn't careful, she'd become accustomed to Grey as a permanent fixture in her life, and that was pure foolishness. He wasn't the marrying kind, and she needed to focus on the reasons for her trip to San Francisco. "Where's Mr. Paget?"

"With his horses. One of them has a cut on his leg where he broke through the crust on the snow."

They fell silent. Her eyelids drifted downward and she jerked herself upright, turning her head away from the mesmerizing leap of the flames.

"Let's go for a walk," Grey's voice held laughter, "just to keep you awake until we eat." He held out his hand, drawing her from the chair. She came to her feet much too close to him, her heart setting up a wild flutter in her chest. She'd always considered him a well-made man, but here in the confines of the log house his size and strength seemed overwhelming.

She stepped back quickly, looking for space, seeking air.

"What's the matter, Emma? Afraid I'll bite?" His voice was low and seductive.

"Don't be ridiculous." She crossed the room to the window, looking out over the shallow verandah. "Look!" She pointed to a horse looming out of the distance, the rider bent low over the saddle horn. "Someone's in trouble."

In a flash, Grey sprang into action. "Mrs. Hunter!" he bellowed before sprinting out the door and across the short expanse of snow toward the unexpected visitor.

"What's the matter?" Mrs. Hunter, swathed in a huge apron and with flour on her hands, hastened into the room.

"Out there"—Emma pointed—"someone's in trouble." She turned back to the window in time to see Grey guide the horse to the foot of the stairs leading into the house.

"Oh, my goodness me. Bring him in. Bring him in." Mrs. Hunter hurried to help Grey support the young man staggering up the steps.

Emma pulled up the deer hide chair, and together they lowered the stricken traveler into it.

"What's happened to you, poor man?" Mrs. Hunter unlaced his boots and drew them off, placing them on the hearth. "Look, your socks are soaking wet." She pulled those off as well and laid them against the hot stones. "Mr. North, help him out of his coat, I think that's wet too."

By this time Emma could tell the young man's teeth were chattering so hard he couldn't speak and his hands shook so he could barely draw them out of his coat sleeves. "Here"—she picked up Grey's unfinished glass of whiskey and proffered it to Mrs. Hunter—"perhaps this will warm him."

"That's the spirit." Mrs. Hunter nodded her approval. "Now, dearie, could you fetch the quilt from your bed and wrap him up while I get some hot water."

She hurried to do her hostess's bidding, her lethargy dispelled by the need for action, and though she hated to admit it, the look of approval in Grey North's eyes. "Here you go." She returned to the fireplace and handed the heavy blanket to Grey. They'd succeeded in removing the man's wet outer clothing, but it looked to Emma as if he was soaked to the skin.

"However did you come to be in such a pickle?" Mrs. Hunter placed a basin of water at the man's feet and lifted them in. "It's only lukewarm," she said, "but it'll feel hot to you. I only hope we can thaw you out before any permanent damage is done."

"Th . . . th . . . thank you," the stranger gasped through his chattering teeth. "Name's Wesley. Frank."

"Well, Frank Wesley, you're lucky you found us this night. How'd you get so wet?"

"Went through the ice."

"The temperature has been well below zero for weeks. Where'd you find thin ice?" Grey draped the quilt over Frank's shoulders.

"T . . . t . . . tried to take a shortcut and ended up on a hot creek. M . . . my horse had enough sense to throw me off."

"There's hot springs a few miles east of here," Mrs. Hunter explained for Emma's benefit. "Even in winter they don't freeze hard."

"Apart from a dunking, are you hurt?"

"D . . . don't th . . . think so. I'll know better when I

thaw out. Can someone see to my horse?" The violent shivering had stopped.

"Mr. Paget's already done it," Grey said. "Now, we need to get you into warm, dry clothes."

"I've kept some of Mr. Hunter's things." Mrs. Hunter gave up chaffing Frank's hands and got to her feet. "If you can take the young man to your room, Mr. North, I'll fetch them to you there."

"Up you go, lad." Grey got an arm under Frank's shoulder and hoisted him to his feet. The poor man was still wobbly but managed, with Grey's support, to make the short walk down the hall to the room next to Emma's.

"I'm sorry, dearie." Mrs. Hunter gathered up the basin of water and Frank's socks. "Dinner will be a bit late."

"Can't I help?" Being the only idle person at the inn made her feel too much like Mrs. Allen.

"Well, now, that you can." Mrs. Hunter's cheery face wore a warm smile. "Come to the kitchen and I'll show you where the plates are kept. You can lay an extra place for Mr. Wesley."

By the time they all sat down to dinner of chicken and dumplings a half hour later, she felt as though Mrs. Hunter were an old friend. "So tell us, Frank"—their hostess moved around the table pouring out cups of tea—"how did you come to be here alone in the middle of winter?"

"A greenhorn's mistake." Frank hunched one shoulder and looked sheepish. "The old-timers told me to bide my time, but I'd heard there was a grand strike at the Big Bend and I thought I'd get the drop on the other fellows if I got as far as Placerville before spring. I got dropped all right." He shuddered. "Can't believe how close I came to dying. Thank goodness my horse didn't bolt after he'd thrown me. You can't know what a miracle it was when I smelled the smoke from your chimney and spied a pinpoint of light."

"You should have built a fire and dried out the minute you got out of that creek." Mr. Paget waved his fork for emphasis. "That's another greenhorn mistake."

"Only one of many," Frank confessed. "I didn't pack extra matches in my saddlebags."

"At least you're learning from your mistakes." Emma tried to ease his embarrassment.

"So, are you still heading for Placerville?" Grey scowled when Frank smiled in Emma's direction.

"You bet." The young man's enthusiasm was undampened. "Except, I'll wait until spring."

"Good thinking," Grey muttered.

"We're heading for Gold City," Mr. Paget said. "You can ride with us if you've a mind."

"Thank you, sir. I'd surely appreciate it."

"Oh, Mr. Paget, what a wonderful idea." Emma beamed happily at their normally taciturn guide. "Mr. Wesley, you couldn't ask for a better mentor."

"See that you heed his advice," Grey growled, "and don't go causing him trouble."

Emma turned her head sharply to stare at Grey, seated beside her. A dark frown marred his usually cheerful countenance. Perhaps the day's driving had fatigued him more than he'd admitted.

"I'll do my best." Frank reached for the pot of chicken and took another healthy serving. "Mrs. Hunter, this's the best stew I've tasted in my life. How do you do it out here in the middle of nowhere?"

"I've learned a thing or two from the Indians," their hostess replied. "There's good herbs growing here in the forest if you know what to look for, and of course, I've my garden in the summer and a good root cellar for winter."

Talk turned to survival techniques on the frontier and tales of other misadventures Mr. Paget and Mrs. Hunter knew. Emma listened, fascinated by the tales of grit and determination of the men and women who'd pioneered this vast territory. Twenty years ago, when Mrs. Hunter had built her first house with her husband, there'd been no railroad anywhere. Supplies had been packed in by canoe and horseback. There hadn't even been a proper wagon road. Mrs. Hunter had lived as the only white woman in the area for five years. She still had no close neighbors. When Mr. Hunter had been killed felling a tree, she'd buried him herself.

"Why did you stay?" Emma couldn't help asking.

"I thought about leaving," Mrs. Hunter sighed, then shrugged her shoulders, "but where was I to go? Down in Vancouver I'd've had to take work in someone else's hotel for poor wages and a tiny room. The wilderness was in my blood by then. I couldn't see myself all cramped and crowded in. Besides, by then there was a wagon road and people passing by pretty regular. I decided to stay."

"Any regrets?" Grey's question surprised Emma.

"Sometimes I wish for music. My husband . . ." She took a shaky breath before continuing, "He played the fiddle. That's it over there." She pointed to the instrument hanging on the wall. "I miss that."

"Well, Mrs. Hunter, perhaps I can repay you in a small way, after all." Frank pushed back from the table and took the violin down from its hook and touched the strings. Then he drew the bow across them, experimenting, tuning them until the mismatched noises blended into melodious sound.

"You happen to know 'Nelly Bly'?" Mr. Paget dug deep into his pocket and produced a harmonica.

To Emma's delight, the two men struck up a lively harmony, setting the rafters ringing with the sound of Stephen Foster melodies, snatches of operetta, and familiar hymns. Mrs. Hunter's face melted with joy. She alternately tapped her toe or sat absolutely still, soaking in the music, ignoring all else. Quietly, so as not to disturb, Emma cleared the table. On her second trip to the kitchen she met Grey, hands laden with the stew pot, bent on the same errand.

When the table was cleared, Emma filled the dishpan with water from the pump, added some boiling water from the simmering kettle, and set about washing up. Grey retrieved a tea towel from the line that hung over the stove and dried. "I'm so glad for Mrs. Hunter." Emma kept her voice low, not wanting to interrupt the music; not wishing to recall the landlady to her duties.

"It's a privilege to witness such pleasure." Grey surprised her with his quick understanding. "Makes one humble." He smiled at her, his dark mood forgotten.

Setting another plate on the drainboard, Emma nodded. She'd attended wonderful symphony concerts where upward of thirty musicians had played the music of Mozart and Beethoven. She'd heard the legendary singers of her day and laughed at the antics of the actors in musical theater but she'd never witnessed such pure joy in music as that exhibited by Mrs. Hunter and her impromptu orchestra in the middle of the Kootenay mountains. She smiled back at Grey, perfectly in tune with his mood.

They finished the dishes and returned to the front room just in time to watch Mr. Paget put down his harmonica. "That's about it for me tonight," he said with an apologetic nod to his hostess.

Mrs. Hunter started, as though coming out of a trance. "Oh, of course." She jumped to her feet and looked at the cleared table and her two guests standing in the kitchen doorway grinning at her. "Oh, I've neglected you all shamefully. Mr. Paget, Mr. Wesley, I do thank you for your music." She wiped her eyes with a handkerchief, then tucked it back into her apron pocket. "Now," she looked about herself, a little flustered, "we've four guests and only three rooms."

"Not to worry," Grey hastened to reassure her, "Mr. Paget can share my room and you can put Frank in his."

"Suits me." Mr. Paget slid his harmonica into his pocket, stood up and stretched. "And if it's all right with you all, I'll head for my bed now."

After bidding Mr. Paget good night, Mrs. Hunter turned to Frank. "I've hung your wet clothes to dry around the stove, Mr. Wesley. They should be fit for you to wear in the morning. Now, I'm sure you're all ready for bed. I'll just go down to the barn and feed the dog. She has pups and needs extra coddling.

"Let me feed the dog," Grey offered.

"Well, if you don't mind," Mrs. Hunter hesitated only briefly, "that'd give me a chance to set the porridge ready for breakfast and make up sandwiches for you all to take with you tomorrow."

"Come with me," Grey whispered to Emma as he followed Mrs. Hunter to collect the bowl of scraps for her dog. "You won't regret it."

It had been such a strange day so far, Emma didn't protest his odd invitation, but went meekly to fetch her coat, then followed Grey out into the night and down the short path to the stable. When they stepped out of the cold mountain air into the warm, animal-scented barn, it was as though they entered a different world. A world of shadows and rustlings and peace. A world far removed from their everyday lives.

Grey carried a lantern and hung it on a nail just inside the barn door. To her left, Emma could see the horse stalls housing Mr. Paget's pack horses and Grey's team, all well-bedded with fresh straw, their mangers full of hay. She turned to her right and took a step toward a stack of sweet-smelling hay. Curled into its base she saw a black and white dog with three roly-poly pups snuggled into her belly.

"Oh, Grey, look! They're adorable." She dropped to her knees and reached for a puppy.

"Careful," Grey cautioned as the mother dog curled back her lip and growled deep in her throat. "Let her get used to you. Hold out the back of your hand for her to smell."

Emma did as she was bid, and in a matter of minutes the mother relaxed her defensive attitude, even sweeping a wet tongue over Emma's fingers.

"Okay, now reach for a puppy, only slowly."

"Aren't you wonderful?" Emma crooned to the mother as her fingers stroked over the silky fur of the first pup. "Such a clever girl." She rubbed the ears of the second sleepy youngster. "Oh my." She felt like laughing and crying at the same time when the third puppy waddled over to her and tried to climb into her lap. "Oh my," she said again as she scooped the wriggling pup into her arms and felt his wet little nose nuzzling into her neck. "I think he likes me."

She raised her eyes to Grey's in wonder and delight.

"It's a she, and I'd say she does . . . like you, that is." His own smile was more gentle than Emma had ever seen it. "And from the mist in your eyes, I'd say the feeling is mutual."

"Of course," she tried to sound matter-of-fact to hide her emotions, "who doesn't like puppies."

"What's the matter, Emma? Afraid to show your tender feelings? Do you think I'm so hard?" He leaned down and put a finger under her chin, bringing her face close to his, his breath feathering her cheek. She should pull away. His hold on her was light and easily broken. But she couldn't move.

"You've never. . . that is, you're a survivor, you . . ." She broke off in confusion wishing she could read his expression in the shadowed barn.

"You misjudge me, Emma. I'm not some hard-hearted adventurer ready to pounce on honest emotion as a sign of weakness. I'm glad to see you capture your own moment of joy, to drop your reserve and your rigid notions of propriety and go all misty-eyed and mushy over a mongrel pup. It's endearing, Emma, and genuine." He traced his thumb from the dimple in her chin to touch the corner of her mouth.

The puppy squirmed and yelped. Hastily, she returned it to its mother, glad to have an excuse to draw away from Grey and from her own unruly emotions. She avoided looking at him, concentrating instead on watching the puppy fasten herself to a milk-filled teat and suckle vigorously, drinking in the reassurance of its mother's presence along with the nourishment.

"The mother needs the extra food," she said, avoiding his eyes, evading a direct reply.

"Don't worry, Emma. I won't press you to anything more than you want. But"—he set the bowl of scraps close to the dog, then stood up, drawing Emma to her feet with him—"I'm betting you want more than caresses from a puppy, however charming she might be."

She felt her face flame red. Grey North had made it no secret that he found her attractive, but she'd assumed it was all part of the act, the charade to keep the ladies of Prospect from looking to Grey North for a husband. She wasn't ready to believe he might have developed real feelings for her. "We should go now." She looked past him toward the door.

She heard him sigh before he stepped away from her. "You're right." His voice had lost its soft quality. "It's much too late for soul-searching. We'll have plenty of time on the road tomorrow to discuss my character and yours. He took the lantern off the wall, opened the door, and together they stepped outside into the moonlight. The silvery swath across the snow was so bright he extinguished the lantern. "No need for that." He paused and tipped his head back. "Look at the sky, Emma. Have you ever seen anything like it?"

A full moon sent a swath of silver over the snowy path leading to the barn. Stars twinkled from a velvet sky. She felt as though she'd landed on a fairy landscape, except for the cold.

"Beautiful, isn't it?"

"It seems unreal."

"See that group of stars over there?" He pointed to a squarish formation. "That's Ursa Major, more usually called the Big Dipper. Follow the line from the two end stars and you'll see Ursa Minor, the Little Dipper. See it?"

She shook her head. "Follow my finger." He stood close beside her, his arm about her waist, his head pressed close to hers, setting her gaze in the right direction. As she looked heavenward she forgot about the cold, forgot her grievances against Grey North, and let herself float in the magic of the night. "See it?"

She nodded as the smaller version of a long-handled cup popped into view.

"Now, follow the handle back. The last star is the North Star. Wherever you are in the Northern Hemisphere, that star is constant. The rest of the constellations swing around it, but the North Star never moves. Find your north star, Emma, and you'll never lose your way."

He stood before her, his features cast into sharp black and white by the light of the moon. The night and the stars and the cold isolated them, creating a world of two where only this moment seemed real. When he bent his head and touched his lips to hers it seemed natural and inevitable. Her mouth softened, welcoming him, inviting more. She stepped closer, moving easily into his arms as the kiss deepened. Her heart pounded against her ribs. Her breath caught in her throat.

She lifted her hands to rest them on his shoulders, then reached higher, sliding her fingers behind his neck, touching her thumbs to the thick hair at his nape, pressing herself into the firm strength of his body, letting her back arch to accommodate the breadth of his chest, losing herself in the power of his embrace.

"Ah, Emma," he groaned, his mouth leaving hers to trace a row of kisses across her jaw and downward to her throat, then returning to lay claim to her mouth in an embrace that plundered the depths of her being. Imprisoned by the power of passion, she returned his kisses with matching fervor, discovering an ardor in herself that would have shocked Miss Emma Douglas, respectable schoolmarm in Prospect, British Columbia.

But here, in the primeval forest, under the vastness of the northern sky, the proper schoolmarm did not exist.

Here, she was Emma, a healthy, vital woman with a woman's passions and a woman's desires. She responded without inhibition to the man she recognized as a worthy mate. Strange sensations curled through her, building a heat in her loins, leaving her legs weak and her body yearning for something she could not name.

When Grey lifted his head and whispered, "Listen," she felt as though she were coming out of a trance. She looked at him, bewildered and bereft by the loss of his kiss. His head was cocked to one side, alert and attentive. "Do you hear it?"

Dimly, through the haze of her emotion, carried on the frosty air, she heard a spine-tingling howl, calling to all that was wild and free in the universe.

"What is it?" she whispered.

"Wolves."

"Aren't they dangerous?"

"Yes," his teeth gleamed in a sudden smile, "but magnificent."

She shivered, not from the cold, but from the sense of primal wildness that lifted Grey's chin and thrilled his soul, making him one with the savage land and its creatures. She shivered again, from fear and from a forbidden excitement.

"You're cold." He touched a finger to her cheek, drawing a circle of heat.

"Yes." She drew away from him, recalled to herself, her cheeks burning. "We must go in."

"I expect you're right." She thought she could detect a note of regret in his voice but he didn't argue. "Come." He placed a hand beneath her elbow and guided her, in silence, along the short path to the house. Inside, they found Mrs. Hunter had already banked the fire and turned down the lamp on the big table. On tiptoe, they crossed the floor of the front room and walked down the hall. At her bedroom door Grey wished her good night.

"I'll see you in the morning," he murmured, then rolled his eyes as a burst of loud snoring emanating from his own room assailed their ears. "Perhaps I'll just get a blanket and sleep in front of the fire, or . . ." He grinned and looked suggestively toward her opened door.

"Good night!" She backed up so hastily she nearly stumbled, closed the door firmly and leaned against it, her hands to her burning cheeks. Softly, through the sturdy planks she heard Grey's laughter.

"Sleep well, Emma."

She didn't move until she heard him walk away. Then she rid herself of her clothes, without bothering to light a candle. The moonlight through the window was sufficient to allow her to scramble into her nightgown and scurry into bed. With the covers pulled tight to her chin she stared into the shadowed corners of the room and tried not to search the shadows of her heart. It was only the moonlight and the strangeness of the night that had made her forget her inhibitions and filled her with ridiculous longings. She couldn't be so foolish as to fall in love with Grey North.

Chapter Eight

"There you go, dearie." Mrs. Hunter set a cup of hot tea on the washstand. "Breakfast's on the table. Mr. Paget and Frank have already eaten and are out in the barn loading the pack horses, but Mr. North is waiting for you." She withdrew, leaving Emma to hustle out of bed and into her clothes. After the turmoil of last evening, she couldn't believe she'd overslept. She'd expected to lie awake all night. Instead, she'd fallen into a deep slumber and stayed there until well past dawn. Now she would have to meet Grey over the breakfast dishes without the mediating presence of Mr. Paget or Frank Wesley. She ground her teeth. How could she have been so foolish as to fall in love with a man who'd told her right from the beginning he intended never to marry? She left her room with a quick step. She was *not* in love with Grey North. She'd simply been bemused by moonlight.

"Good morning, Emma." His words and tone were cool, but the warm look in his eye made her blush.

"Good morning, Mr. North." She took her seat as far away from him as possible. Mrs. Hunter bustled in with fresh toast and hot coffee. "I'll just see to packing you a good lunch," she said, and hurried back to her kitchen.

"Going all starchy again, Emma?"

"In our present circumstances, I believe it's best to observe the proprieties." She sipped her coffee, hiding her face.

"And what circumstances are those?"

"You know very well what I mean." She set down the coffee cup and glared at him. "We've been thrown together, without a chaperone, out here in the middle of nowhere. We need rules."

"Ah, yes, your rules." He flashed a wicked grin. "Does your etiquette book have rules for how to behave with a gentleman when you're gazing at the stars?"

She licked her suddenly dry lips. "About last night . . . "

"Yes?" His brows rose in amusement. "What about last night, Emma? Did I forget something?"

She colored up to the roots of her hair. Why hadn't she just pretended their kisses in the moonlight had never happened? Now she'd forced the situation between them into the open and only made herself look ridiculous. "I would like you to forget last night." She turned her attention to buttering a slice of toast, keeping her eyes firmly fixed on the table in front of her.

"I couldn't do that." Grey's voice was soft and enticing. "I'll remember last night for as long as I live. I rather hoped you would, too."

"I will do my best to put it out of my mind. In fact," she told a bare-faced lie, "I'm already uncertain of what passed between us. I was so tired and so cold, I'm sure I was not fully in control of my faculties."

Grey chuckled and she risked a quick glance in his direction. "I believe you, Emma, love. Not about being tired and cold, but as for the rest, I'm quite convinced."

"Then we'll say no more about it." She tried to sound

decisive, but even in her own ears her voice sounded plaintive and uncertain.

"Until I find you in the moonlight again." She heard the seductive note in his voice and silently vowed never to admire the moon again. His chair scraped against the wooden floor as he left the table. "Relax, Emma. I'm not about to ravish you in the snow. Finish your breakfast and then get ready to leave. I'll go and have a word with Paget."

With Grey out of the room she hurried through the rest of her breakfast and hastened to prepare herself for the day's journey. When Grey brought the team to the door she was ready. Mrs. Hunter brought out the bricks, heated in the oven and wrapped in cloth to place at their feet. "Safe journey," she called, waving from the bottom step of the lodge. Grey flicked the reins and they were off.

"What a gracious lady she is," Emma exclaimed as she watched the figure of their hostess waving until they were out of sight. "I don't know how she bears the loneliness."

"She's one of those rare people who can be alone without being lonely." He slanted an intent look toward her. "She has found her own north star."

"Do you think the weather will hold?" Emma steered the conversation into that inexhaustible and quintessentially safe topic.

Grey threw back his head and laughed, a rich, rollicking sound that startled a flock of chickadees from their cover. She sat stiffly, back ramrod straight, eyes fixed on the point between the horses' ears and refused to feel ridiculous. "Relax, Emma. You'll give yourself a backache again. Yes, I do believe the weather will hold. Look to your left, that's where the systems come from. Moist air off the Pacific Ocean comes in on the prevailing winds, hits the coastal range of mountains, rises and cools, dropping rain and snow along the coast." He went on to give an exhaustive discourse on the winter weather patterns for the Kootenay mountains and ended with a series of local folklore methods for predicting snow.

By the time he finished she'd allowed herself to rest her back against the seat and give in to the rhythmic swaying of the sleigh. She had no real reason to be uncomfortable. It had been only a kiss, after all, and since neither she nor Grey was interested in marriage, it wouldn't lead to anything more. Still, she was grateful that Grey seemed preoccupied this morning. The miles slid by under the runners with only the steady tramp of the horses' hooves and the jingling of their harnesses to break the silence.

They caught up to the pack train at noon and shared their meal and a pot of strong tea beside a small fire. The bricks were taken from the sleigh and reheated. Emma took the opportunity to walk about, stretching her legs, warming herself with exertion. Frank Wesley joined her on her perambulations and entertained her with news from the world outside. "We live in an amazing time," he said. "Here it's as though we lived in the last century, but when we make it to the railhead we jump right into the modern age."

"We're moving with the times in Prospect, too, Mr. Wesley. We have a new weekly newspaper, the Miners Association is lobbying to get a railroad through town, and I have it on good authority that we will stage our first annual Victoria Day Concert this spring." Emma smiled, grateful for Frank's easy camaraderie, with none of the undercurrents that swirled around her and Grey North.

"Such enterprise." Her companion grinned and offered his hand to help her over a clump of frozen snow. "Maybe I'll winter in Prospect next year."

"Ready, Miss Douglas?" Grey was beside her, his tone brusque. "Paget could do with a hand, Wesley."

"Oh, right." Frank hurried off.

"Wasn't that rather rude?"

"He's already had one near catastrophe. He'd be better off learning the business of survival from Paget than doing the society stroll with you."

"You're jealous." Her mouth dropped open in amazement. Grey North, the master of self-confidence, object of every female heart he encountered, jealous of a green boy. She wanted to clap her hands in glee. Grey had a weakness. It evened the odds between them.

"Don't be ridiculous." He handed her up into the sleigh, then walked around the team, checking their harness and talking quietly to them before taking his seat beside her and lifting the reins. "We should reach the Hodder ranch by sundown."

"I'm pleased to hear it." She raised innocent eyes to his profile. "Frank tells me he plans to spend next winter in Prospect. Won't it be lovely? With the new piano in the schoolhouse, we could hold concerts. I'm sure everyone would enjoy hearing him play the violin."

"Don't bet on it." Grey scowled at the fat rumps of his horses and flicked the lines, urging them to a faster pace. "Boys like Frank Wesley aren't likely to remember a promise from one week to the next, let alone for a whole year."

"Maybe." Emma smiled secretly and settled back in her seat. It was lovely to have the upper hand with Grey North, just this once.

"Do you intend to spend next winter in Prospect?"

"Yes, of course."

"Maybe you'll find you don't want to leave San Francisco a second time."

"Are you asking for my resignation?"

"I'm asking your intentions. How long will it take to assuage your homesickness? Or is it really homesickness that takes you away?" He glanced sharply in her direction. "Is Parnell Wilde the real reason? Are you making this journey on his behalf?"

"No!"

"Then why? And don't give me some tale about missing the city."

She studied the belligerent jut of his chin and knew he wouldn't be put off with a simple lie. She would have to tell him the truth, or at least part of it. "No, it's not homesickness," she said. "Mrs. Royston made that up so it wouldn't seem I'd had something to do with the robbery at the school. I have business in San Francisco."

"Couldn't it wait until a better time?"

"No." She took a deep breath and expelled it on a sigh.

"Are you in trouble, Emma?" The harshness had left his voice, and for a moment she was tempted to pour out her story. But it wasn't only her story. Until she had cleared her father's name, she would not add to his disgrace by discussing his death.

"No," she whispered.

"When will you be back?"

"I don't know." She turned her head away. Grey's question forced her to face the reality she'd tried so hard to avoid. Whatever awaited her at the Sisters of Mercy Convent would change her life. She might never return to Prospect, never see her pupils graduate or taste another of Mrs. Royston's cakes or match wits with Grey. She would miss them. Bella and Grey had proved truer friends than she'd ever known. She felt like a traitor to them. She pressed her hand to her ribs, feeling the outline of the key. *I'll see it through, Papa. I won't let you down.* "I'll write my letter of resignation tonight." She bit back a sob. "Mrs. Royston will be disappointed in me."

"Never mind," Grey's terse words cut through the frosty air. "If you're delayed too long, I'll ask the other trustees to consider it a leave of absence."

"Thank you." She made sure he couldn't see her face.

As Grey had predicted, they arrived at the Hodder ranch just as the sun dropped behind the highest mountain peak, casting the valley into instant shade. The ranch house was a mean affair with no welcoming verandah or smiling hostess to greet the travelers. Emma could see the tracks of Mr. Paget's pack team leading off to a lean-to attached to the barn. "You can get out here while I take the team straight on to shelter," Grey said, pulling rein at the house. They were the first words he'd spoken since she'd been unable to name a date for her return to Prospect.

She scrambled to the ground, unaided, determined to prove her independence, but after a swift glance at the inhospitable door, wished Grey was beside her. She bit her lip and silently chastised herself for being ridiculous. The ranch was accustomed to providing lodging for travelers. Mrs. Hodder was probably too busy preparing the evening meal to stand by the doorway awaiting their arrival. She stepped up to the door and knocked loudly, then waited. After several minutes, she raised her fist for a second assault on the rough planks when the door opened. A thin-faced woman allowed her into a cheerless room devoid of a welcoming fire.

"Mrs. Hodder?" Emma held out her hand. "I'm Emma Douglas."

"You're room's down here." The woman turned her back and walked away. Bewildered by her hostess's unfriendly attitude, Emma followed her through the kitchen and into a windowless space at the back of the house. "Dinner's in thirty minutes." Mrs. Hodder withdrew and closed the door. The space was so cramped Emma could barely get around the narrow bed to the washstand, and when she did, she found the water in the ewer stone-cold.

One more day, she reminded herself as she splashed her face and shivered; one more day and she'd be on the train. She banged her shin against the edge of the cot and sat down to rub the bruise. The bed was hard, the blankets thin, and the pillow next to nonexistent. Why in the world would the Hodders open their ranch to visitors when they were so plainly inhospitable? The lack of air in the tiny room made her claustrophobic, so she decided to brave Mrs. Hodder's black looks and venture into the kitchen. At least it would be warm there.

"You can sit over there." Mrs. Hodder pointed to a rough wooden table set up close to one wall of the kitchen and laid with plain crockery.

"Can I help?"

"I'm used to managing on my own." Mrs. Hodder turned away and stirred something in a big black pot at the back of the stove.

"Do you have many visitors?" Emma tried again to be sociable.

"Some."

Struggling to maintain at least the appearance of good manners, Emma looked about the room seeking some topic of interest to Mrs. Hodder. There was nothing. No hooked rugs adorned the floor, no books stood on a shelf, and no painted picture graced the wall. Even the cookstove looked neglected, its chrome trim sadly in need of polishing. "Have you lived here long?" Perhaps her hostess hadn't had time to decorate her home.

"Nigh on twenty years." Mrs. Hodder spoke the words as though they marked a prison sentence.

"Do you have children?" Emma made one last, desperate attempt.

"Three, buried out back." Mrs. Hodder jerked her chin toward the hill rising behind the house. "One girl in boarding school in Vancouver."

"I'm so sorry." Her heart clenched in pity. "I can't imagine the pain of losing your children."

"Diphtheria." Mrs. Hodder clamped her lips tight together and stirred harder at the stew pot.

"How old is the girl at school?"

"Six." The single word vibrated off the bare walls.

Such a young age to be sent away from home. "You must miss her."

"At least she won't have to slave her life away in the wilderness," Mrs. Hodder hissed through clenched teeth.

The entrance of the men into the room put an end to any more confidences. Mrs. Hodder placed the stew pot in the center of the table. Grey, Mr. Paget, and Frank Wesley slid onto a wooden bench at the back, Mr. Hodder took the chair at the head and Mrs. Hodder the one at the foot, leaving Emma in possession of the only other seat.

"Grace," Mr. Hodder announced, and bent his head to mumble a few words before proclaiming "amen."

Mrs. Hodder jumped to her feet and picked up a large ladle. "Rabbit stew." She spooned a serving into a bowl and handed it to Emma. Then she filled five more plates and returned the pot to the stove without saying a word.

Emma looked at the gray glob of food before her and hoped she wouldn't be expected to eat rabbit stew for breakfast as well.

Thick slices of bread and butter were the only accompaniment to the stew, but at least the bread was light and tasty enough to make up for the unappetizing meat. Like his wife, Mr. Hodder was a man of few words, but Grey and Frank and Mr. Paget kept up a conversation regarding the state of the wagon road, the prospects for reaching Gold City tomorrow, and the vagaries of pack animals. "You always place your animals in the same place in line," Frank said. "Why?"

"They like it that way." Mr. Paget wiped the last of the gravy from his plate with the bread and popped it into his mouth. "I mind one time I had a new helper with me. He put the number two horse in the number three position and all hell broke loose. As soon as we hit the trail, she started pushing and shoving to get to her rightful place. I nearly lost the number three animal. He got pushed right off the trail and down into a ravine. Had to unload him and get him back up on the trail, then carry all his cargo up the slope and repack the whole lot. Now I always check the order of the horses myself."

"What will you do when the railroad comes through?" Emma asked, worried for her guide's prosperity.

"Oh, I figure there'll be plenty of work for horses still. We get freight comin' into Prospect, somebody's still got to cart it out to the ranches and the mines. Business will get better. Same as you." He pointed his fork at Grey. "Your hotel'll be bursting with tourists come to get a look at the wilderness."

"Mmm." Grey's uncharacteristic mumble had Emma wondering if he was ill. She'd never known him to miss an opportunity to wax on about the bright future of Prospect.

Before she could question him, Mrs. Hodder broke into the conversation. "You figure the route will follow the wagon road?" There was a hint of fear in the question. No doubt, Mrs. Hodder depended on the income from her unwelcome guests to keep her daughter in boarding school. It was a cruel choice, and Emma's heart ached for the bitter, lonely woman.

"No telling," Mr. Paget grumbled. "Them government fellows will be stickin' their oar in, gettin' favors for their friends. Never mind where the best route is."

The meal ended on that sour note. There was no music tonight. Mr. Paget went to tend to his horses as soon as the last of the tea had been drunk. Frank went with him, saying he needed every opportunity to learn from a trail-savvy packer. "Care to step outside?" Grey asked Emma. "There's a full moon."

Even if she'd a mind for more kisses, Emma recoiled from the cynical gleam in his eye. Tonight he was not the man who'd shown her the North Star and drawn her into fairyland with his kiss. Tonight he was a cold, hard stranger. "No . . . thank you," she stuttered, hastily leaving her place at the table. "It's been a long day. I'll bid you good night." She tried not to scuttle like a frightened hen, but she feared her retreat was less than dignified. She could imagine the sardonic curl of Grey's lip as he watched her cross the room.

Once entombed in her cramped quarters she wondered if she'd made an error. Even the cold of the night and the sharp side of Grey's tongue might be preferable to this confined little space. She shook her head and lit the candle on the washstand. Grey North was an enigma. She was much better to keep her distance from him, especially now that she knew herself susceptible to his charm.

She removed her clothes and laid them across the bottom of the bed as there was no hook or chair for that purpose, washed in cold water, again, blew out the candle, and climbed into her narrow bed. There was no silver moonlight in the windowless room, no music from Mr. Paget's harmonica, and no lingering kiss on her lips to send her to sleep. Instead, she lay rigid and wakeful, listening to the clatter of Mrs. Hodder in the kitchen. She recognized all the sounds, the damper in the stovepipe, the rattle of wood in the firebox, the whish of the broom over the bare floors; ordinary, homey sounds that signaled peace and security in Mrs. Royston's kitchen, but in Mrs. Hodder's beat out a tattoo of anger and frustration.

"What a sad place," Emma exclaimed the next morning as Grey drove them away from the Hodder ranch. No smiling hostess waved them good-bye, and the bricks in the bottom of the sleigh were barely warm. "I wonder why they don't pack up and leave."

"That's what happens when you don't find your own true star." Grey's face was set into hard lines. "Mrs. Hodder resents the life her husband has provided, her resentment makes him silent, his silence makes her angry, her anger makes him resentful. Round and round it goes."

"The voice of experience?" She turned her head to study his face.

"Close observation, at least." He squinted into the sun, his eyes like blue ice chips. "You see this team of horses?" He nodded toward the sturdy Belgians pulling the sleigh with ease. "Look how well their strides match; the weight of the load is shared evenly, neither one lunging ahead or lagging back, no jostling, no lashing out at each other. They're a well-matched team. Mr. and Mrs. Hodder are not."

"Maybe they were once." Emma thought of the little ones buried on the lonely hillside. "Maybe it was the harshness of life that destroyed their harmony."

"Then it was a poor match to begin with. Adversity only tightens the bonds between two people who love honestly."

"Don't you think you're being unjustly harsh in your criticism? As a bachelor you're hardly in a position to pass judgment on a marriage?"

"Maybe, but then everyone who enters into a marriage is untried. Doesn't stop them from thinking they know what they're doing."

"Why so bitter, Grey?" She turned her head to look up at him, studying the planes of his face, wondering what had brought the set, hard line to his mouth.

"Sorry." He puffed out a deep breath. "It's just that house. It reminds me of things I'd rather forget."

"You mean you're not a duke with a mansion and a fortune and a host of servants?" She tried to lighten the mood.

"Hardly," he said, with a derisive growl. "Not that I grew up poor. My father is a minor baronet, not a duke, as the gossips would have it, but I am heir to a fortune. It's not the meanness of the Hodder house that is familiar, but the unhappiness."

"How so?" She didn't want to pry, but she felt an overwhelming need to understand this complex man.

Grey didn't answer immediately. Emma watched a small muscle clench and unclench in his jaw as he stared straight ahead. "I'm sorry," she said, impulsively laying her hand on his sleeve. "I've no right to ask."

Under her touch his tension seemed to ease. His face softened. "Perhaps you do." He drew a deep breath and refocused his attention on the horses. "My father's estate may be small, but his sense of importance is large. I've been a disappointment to him since I was five years old and struck up a friendship with the ostler's son." His lip curled in disdain. "People like us don't associate with that sort," he said in a self-righteous tone, and Emma could hear the fury behind his mimicry.

"I refused to give up my friend and was handed a beating for my impudence. It was the beginning of a long battle: father trying to thrust me into the 'right' circles; me choosing my friends for their character and not their circumstances."

"What about your mother?" She couldn't imagine the gentle-faced woman she'd seen in the picture condoning violence.

He sighed. "She was no match for my father. Every time we quarreled she suffered. I learned not to tell her of our clashes, presenting a smiling face and tales of boyish misadventures to account for my bruises. I suspect she knew the truth, but it suited her to pretend."

"Is that why you left? Because your father beat you?"

"Ha!" His short bark of laughter held no mirth. "It was more than that." He stared off into the distance, but Emma didn't think he saw the pristine mountains of British Columbia. She suspected his mind dwelled on some old, unhappy scene. His next words, spoken in a hard tone, confirmed her suspicion. "There was a certain well-born lady of my acquaintance who committed the unthinkable and then tried to name me as the father of her unborn brat." His hands tightened so hard on the reins the horses faltered.

When he had both himself and the team under control, he continued, "My father refused to believe me." The bare words contained a world of bleak disillusion. "He insisted I marry the baggage. Said even if the child wasn't mine, the connection was a good one. The Norths would move up in society." His mouth twisted. "I was nineteen."

"Oh, Grey, I'm so sorry." Her heart ached for the hurt youth behind the hardened man.

He fell silent and stared so long and so intently at the shiny brass of the ring on the right horse's bridle that she believed he had reconsidered and would not tell her the end of the story. She stirred. Should she let him brood in silence or prod him to release his bitterness? Before she could decide, he spoke again, a white-hot anger burning through his clipped words.

"Suffice it to say, I discovered the identity of the real father. There was nothing so noble as a duel. We brawled. I dragged him to the lady's house and stood over him until he did the right thing. My father and I had our fiercest row ever, and I departed the family estate for good."

"You haven't kept in touch? Even with your mother?" It hurt to think of him as a green youth, making his own way in the world, but it hurt even more to think of the softhearted mother who must wonder every day what had become of her son.

The anger faded from his face, replaced by a deep sadness. "I send her a letter, once a year. Tell her I'm still alive. I've no way of knowing if she receives them."

"She doesn't write back?"

"I've never given her an address." He drew a deep breath, his shoulders drooping as under an unbearable weight of weariness. "After I left home, I went to London, hoping to find a life that would suit both me and my family. I even considered a career in politics—as a Reformer, of course." He smiled slightly at the absurdity of his youthful ambition; then his expression turned cynical. "My reputation had preceded me—I was deemed a rake and a despoiler of innocence—but that didn't stop the marriage-minded mamas from parading their daughters before me and angling for a proposal, decent or otherwise. It seemed money could overcome the nicest of scruples."

"Surely other wealthy young men have been targeted for matrimony. They aren't all self-banished and cynical."

"More fool them," Grey muttered through gritted teeth. "The final straw came one evening as I left the theater. I found an enterprising young miss, whom I'd barely met, concealed in my carriage. No doubt, she hoped I would offer marriage to save her reputation. I didn't, but that night I decided to leave England."

The bleak look left his eyes to be replaced with excitement and a determined idealism. "I struck out for Canada, filled with visions of ice and snow and wild rivers and great prairies and vast empty spaces. I pictured myself in deerskins and a birch bark canoe, forging my way through the wilderness." He chuckled and glanced at her with his usual good humor. "I was almost disappointed to discover I was two hundred years too late. The country now boasted cities and farms and a railroad." He cocked his head to give her a half smile. "Still, the frontier was rugged enough and gave me the chance to prove myself, without benefit of rank or fortune."

"And you've succeeded very well."

"Hah!" The scornful exclamation carried a wealth of

pain. "My father would be appalled by the Rockingham. Just like Mrs. Allen, he would see me as a common saloon keeper." He slanted her an ironic glance. "You understand, I am a saloon keeper and not ashamed of it. It's the 'common' I object to."

She smiled at the jeering words, but she heard the bitterness behind them. "What about the estate?" she asked. "Do you intend to claim your inheritance when the time comes?"

"No doubt, my father will have disinherited me by now. He had a cousin. I expect the land will pass to him."

"Don't you care?" She studied his face for any sign of interest or regret.

"No, I've told you. The new world is my home. There's nothing for me in England."

"Not even your mother?"

He scowled, the anger and bitterness banishing the brightness from his face. "She has all she needs." His harsh tone made clear the discussion was over.

For a while they drove in silence, Emma lulled by the steady plop, plop of the horses hoofs, Grey apparently absorbed by unhappy thoughts if the grim look on his face was any indication. "I've been watching your horses," she said at last, "and your analogy is unfair."

"What are you talking about?"

"The Hodders. You said they weren't well-matched, but you can't compare them to your team. When you harness these two together, they're equal—equal in strength and size, equal in health and training, and equal in treatment. When you pair a man and a woman, that equality is missing. In our world, even if a woman possesses strength and skill equal to a man, she remains without power. Mrs Hodder is harnessed to a life she doesn't want because she hasn't the power to change it. She is balancing that lack of power with misery."

"And is that your argument in favor of marriage?" The light of challenge was back in Grey's eyes.

"No, of course not. That's an argument against marriage—for a woman." She emphasized the last point. "For a man, marriage is the best possible arrangement. He gets a housekeeper, a cook, a mistress, a mother for his children, everything he wants, without the slightest sacrifice or effort on his part."

"Rubbish!"

"Perhaps, since you're so averse to women, you should have entered a monastery."

"Oh, I've nothing against women, Emma love." He turned to regard her with a hot look that reminded her uncomfortably of their kiss in the moonlight. "I find women endlessly enticing. It's the persona of wife I reject."

Hot embarrassment flooded her at the outright suggestiveness in his eyes. She shifted in her seat, as far from him as the confines of the sleigh allowed, turning her face away. In a moment she heard him draw a long breath, and when he spoke again the harshness had left his voice. "I'm sorry, Emma. I had no excuse to take out my anger on you. Please forgive me."

"I'm sorry, too," she murmured. "Sorry that you harbor such bitterness. It's not the institution of marriage that warps your mind, Grey. It's something in you."

They didn't speak again until the noon halt, when the presence of Frank and Mr. Paget eased the tension between them. By the time they started the last leg of their journey, Grey seemed restored to his usual good humor, pointing out sights of interest, showing her wolf and rabbit tracks in the snow, and entertaining her with his impressive knowledge of the land. She began to relax and enjoy herself.

"What are those?" She pointed to a dozen little gray birds twittering in a lone spruce tree close to the road.

"Whiskey jacks. They're very friendly birds. In the lumber camps, where the men throw them crumbs, they're almost tame. Their true name is Canada jay. If you keep your eyes peeled, you may see a Stellar's jay as well. It's a little larger, blue with a black head and neck. You can recognize it in profile by the crest." He raised his eyes to let his glance rove over the mountainside.

"Damnation!" He hauled on the reins, bringing the team to a halt, and vaulted out of the sleigh. "Hold them." He thrust the lines into Emma's hands.

"What are you doing?" she squeaked in alarm. The horses stamped their feet, backing and sidling as they sensed her inexperienced hands.

"There." Grey pointed up the slope. "See it?"

She followed the line of his pointing finger but could see nothing except a mass of snow-covered hillside extending about twenty feet up from the roadway and ending at the edge of the omnipresent forest. Large black birds circled overhead. The scene was the same one they'd been traveling through for the past three days. She was about to ask again what had caused their sudden halt when a movement at the edge of the woods caught her eye. "What is it?" She squinted against the light.

"A bighorn sheep." While she'd been searching the landscape, Grey had rummaged through his gear. "He's got his head stuck in those branches. He'll starve if he can't get loose. See?" He swore as the animal ceased his struggle and sank to its knees. "Already he's weakened."

With an axe in his hand he set off up the slope, his progress slow and difficult as he waded through knee-high snow. "Grey, he could kill you!" she shouted after him, but her warning fell on deaf ears. She could do nothing but watch as he climbed higher up the mountainside.

As Grey drew nearer, the ram lunged to his feet. His mighty horns were stuck fast in the tangled branches of a thicket but he lashed out viciously with his hind legs. "Watch out!" she shrieked, then screamed again as the horses surged forward. "Whoa! Whoa!" She hauled on the reins with all her strength, bracing her feet against the high front of the sleigh and exerting every ounce of power she could muster to force the galloping horses to a halt. They were a hundred yards down the road before a fresh drift of snow slowed their dash. "Whoa, now!" she said sternly, trying to emulate the calm, commanding tone she'd heard Grey use with the team. "Whoa up."

To her unmitigated relief, they responded, coming to a halt, up to their fetlocks in snow, their flanks heaving from the sudden and unexpected gallop. Her arms felt as though they'd been torn from their sockets. Her breath came in hard, panting gasps, and the taste of fear in her mouth was dry and bitter as gall. If the ram didn't kill Grey North, she'd do it herself. She gritted her teeth and took a fresh hold on the reins. "Whoa, laddies," she crooned while risking a backward glance.

Grey had reached the stricken sheep and worked his way around the animal to its head. She held her breath as he raised the axe and hacked at the tough, scrubby brush. Once he freed the ram it might very well charge him, killing him with a single blow from its massive head. She'd seen the rams jousting with each other in the rutting season, setting the mountainsides echoing with the force of their combat.

One branch came loose. The animal lunged and twisted.

Grey dodged, taking cover beside a sturdy fir. The ram managed to heave itself free and stood, feet planted wide, head hanging, nostrils flaring, eyes fixed on Grey. Emma tensed. The two faced each other, challenge and respect in their stance. Then the ram leapt high, pivoted, and charged up the slope, disappearing into the forest with two mighty bounds.

Grey watched for a minute, then turned and half-slid, half-walked back down to the roadway following his own footsteps. Once on the road he sauntered easily toward her, reaching the sleigh and restoring the axe to its proper place as nonchalantly as if he'd been out for an evening stroll. "Want to drive?" he asked, his eyes alight with vitality, his mouth stretched into a broad grin. His cocky self-assurance made her fingers itch to slap the reins over the horses' rumps and drive off. Never in all her life had she met a man who could stir her to such extremes—passion and longing one moment, red-hot fury the next.

"Don't glower." He took his seat beside her and took the reins from her hands.

"You could have been killed," she shouted, then clamped her lips shut, staring straight ahead, her back rigid and her chin in the air. She refused to care about Grey North.

"I know." All the lightness had left his voice.

"It was a foolish risk." Tears stung her eyelids.

"It was a necessary risk. I couldn't leave him to die an ignoble death. He deserved better."

She turned to look at him then, shaking her head in bewilderment. "I can't understand you, Grey. You care so deeply about a stricken animal, yet you sneer at your fellow men. You snap your fingers at a fortune and risk your life on a whim. Is there anything in this world that truly matters to you?"

They traveled in silence for some minutes with only the squeak of the runners against the snow and the tramp of the horses' hooves to break the stillness. She thought he would refuse to answer, but just as she'd hardened her heart to his rudeness he surprised her. "Honesty," he said, "I care about honesty."

This time it was she who had nothing to say.

They had nearly reached Gold City when she spotted Frank Wesley at the side of the wagon road. "Look"—she pointed ahead—"Frank's waiting for us."

"And letting his horse stand about in the cold," Grey muttered. Then his voice sharpened. "Damn fool!" He urged his tired team into a gallop. Emma gripped the seat as they hurtled forward, swaying dangerously close to the steep drop at the side of the road.

"Grey! What are you doing?" she shrieked just as a rifle shot echoed between the mountain peaks.

"Avalanche!" Grey whipped his horses to greater speed.

She jerked her head up and saw a torrent of snow roiling down the mountain directly above them. A low rumble quickly swelled to a deafening roar, filling the valley with its awesome power. The snowslide swept onward, uprooting trees and boulders in its path, relentless and unstoppable. Emma's heart filled with terror. If the slide caught them they would die, smothered under tons of snow. She clung to the sleigh's rail and willed the horses to greater speed, praying that Grey's strength and skill might still save them. Frank Wesley's riderless horse pounded down the road ahead of them.

"Frank!" she screamed as she spotted him standing in frozen panic at the edge of the road, his eyes stretched wide in horror.

"Come on!" Grey shouted, and Frank leaped for the back of the sleigh. The impact of his weight was too much for the swaying sled. With a sharp crack the box broke loose. One runner slid over the edge of the road, and the entire equipage tilted. "Jump!" Grey yelled at her, leaning far out to the side, trying to keep them from tipping over completely. "Jump!" he shouted again, grabbing her with one hand and practically flinging her into the road. She leaped just as the box broke free entirely and went sliding and jolting down the river bank, taking Grey with it. The terrified team thundered down the road, taking the remains of the sleigh with them.

"Grey!" She clawed her way out of the soft snowbank where she'd landed. She looked behind her and saw the churning snow of the edge of the avalanche roar across the road just a few yards behind them. They'd escaped being crushed by the snow and ice, but Grey was gone.

"Miss Douglas!" Frank Wesley was on his knees beside her, brushing the snow from around her. "Miss Douglas, are you hurt?"

"I'm fine." She scrambled to her feet. "Find Grey! He went over the bank!" She lunged toward the roadway and lay down flat on her stomach to peer over the edge of the embankment. About fifteen feet below the wreckage had come to rest against a downed tree, the splintered wood pointing a jagged edge to the sky. Of Grey there was no sign.

"Grey!" she shouted as loud as she could, then scrambled off the roadway to slither and slide her way down to the ruined vehicle. "Get help!" she screamed to Frank as she sank waist deep in snow. She practically swam the last few yards to the sleigh. "Grey!" She sobbed with terror and exertion. "Grey, where are you?" There was no reply. After the great roaring of the avalanche the valley seemed ominously silent. "Grey," Emma whimpered, working her way around the ruined conveyance, trying to peer underneath.

Just when she was convinced he must be buried in the snow somewhere between the road and the sleigh, she saw him on the other side of the tree that had halted his descent. "Grey," she shouted, plunging toward him. "Oh, Grey, thank God I've found you." She reached his side, but her relief was short lived. He lay utterly still, while the snow beneath his head turned crimson. "Oh no!" she sobbed. "Please, God, don't let him be dead." She pulled off her mitts to clear the snow from around his face. Her fingers sought the pulse below his jaw. Desperately, she pressed her hand to his neck. Her own breath was so loud she couldn't hear his, but at last she felt a pulse, faint but steady, beneath her fingers. He was alive.

"Grey, wake up, please." She pressed her face against his, aghast at the coldness of his skin. She looked at the blood-soaked snow and tried to determine if the stain was growing. She couldn't move him by herself, but she could try to bandage the wound. Leaving his side, she floundered about until she found her satchel half buried under a mound of snow, then struggled back to his side. She opened the bag and drew out a fine lawn petticoat. Without a second's hesitation, she ripped it from hem to waist, repeating the action over and over until she had a series of long strips. She folded one into a thick pad and pressed it against the source of the oozing blood, a wound just above his ear. Carefully, lest she injure him further, she wound a strip of cloth around his head and tied it with a tight knot. It wasn't the prettiest of bandages, but it would do the job.

She blew on her fingers to warm them, then pulled on her heavy mittens. With her back to the sun, she cast a long shadow. Another half hour and it would be dark. She hoped Frank found help quickly. Surely Grey's horses would stop their pell-mell gallop once they were free of the lurching sleigh and the roaring sound of the avalanche. "Grey," she whispered, leaning over him, "wake up, please." Not by the flicker of an eyelash did he respond to her plea. She leaned closer, taking solace in the faint stir of his breath against her cheek. Gently, she touched her lips to his, hoping to draw a response from him, seeking to ease the ache in her heart. She couldn't bear it if Grey were to die. There was no use pretending any longer. Despite her best resolve, she'd fallen hopelessly in love with Prospect's most committed bachelor.

She sat back on her heels and watched his face a moment longer, then left him to look for the buffalo robe. They could be here a long time, waiting for rescue, and she wasn't about to let him die of cold. She found the heavy wrap and dragged it over to the log. Then she retrieved the axe, still wedged under the seat, and used it to hack two small branches from the fallen tree. Panting with effort and frustration, she managed to drive the small poles into the snow; then she dragged the buffalo robe over them, creating a lean-to shelter. Finally, she used the axe once more to chop out some wood and kindling and carefully constructed a fire, mimicking the pattern Mr. Paget had used on the trail.

She reached into her coat pocket for the box of matches Grey had insisted she carry. "Always be prepared for emergencies," he'd said. She'd never dreamed she'd need them for him. She took out a match, struck it, and watched it flame and die before she could touch it to her little pile of shavings. Panic gripped her by the throat, but she fought back. Moving to the other side, using her body to shield the match from the wind, she tried again. This time she managed to drop the lit match onto the thin sticks, but it didn't catch. She bit her lip, hard. Thank goodness her matchbox was full. With painstaking care she searched the length of the fallen tree until she found a few twigs with dried needles. She stripped the needles into her hand and brought them back to her campfire, placing them carefully in a curl of thin wood. She lit one more match and watched with dawning relief as the needles caught. She fed more tiny twigs into the fire until the shavings and kindling she'd so laboriously hacked out of the tree began to smoke and then burst into flame.

She sat down in the snow with a thump. She'd done it. With no one to help her, she'd built a tent and a fire, and by heaven, she glanced at Grey's unconscious form, she'd keep him alive until help came, even if it took all night. She rolled onto her knees, pushed herself to her feet, then went to chop more branches, enough to keep her fire going until rescue arrived. At least she could be grateful the avalanche had provided her with an easy supply of firewood. She doubted she'd have been able to fell a tree with the small axe.

"Halloo!" The shout came from the roadway above.

She dropped the small bundle of sticks she'd collected and waved her arms. "Down here!" she screamed. "Help!"

Mr. Paget's worried face appeared over the edge of the embankment. At that precise moment she thought she'd never seen a more beautiful sight. "It's Grey," she shouted. "He's hurt and unconscious. We have to get him to a doctor."

"Hang on, Miss." Her guide disappeared briefly only to reappear a moment later, a rope around his waist, and rappel down the bank to her side.

"Oh, Mr. Paget, I'm so glad to see you." Emma felt tears of relief gather along her lashes.

"We're not out of the woods yet." Mr. Paget assessed the upended sleigh and the unconscious man. "You did well to get a fire going."

A flush of pleasure warmed her from within. "He's breathing," she said, kneeling beside Grey again, "and I've bandaged the cut on his head, but he's unconscious. I'm afraid he has a concussion."

"Hmm." Mr. Paget stroked his beard and looked up the steep slope. "Lucky thing young Frank's horse caught up to the pack team. I knew something was wrong right away and headed back. Caught Grey's team, too, so we've lots of horse power. What we need is a sled. Hand me that axe, Miss Douglas."

Emma surrendered the blade and watched as Mr. Paget attacked the ruined sleigh and quickly fashioned a simple sled. He positioned it beside Grey, pushing it down into the snow. "Now, Miss, if I take his shoulders, can you take his feet and we'll slide him onto this contraption?"

Emma nodded and grasped Grey's ankles, pulling him sideways on Mr. Paget's command. "Now, then, we'll just tie this rope on and let the horses haul him up." While he talked, the packer slipped the rope from around his waist and secured it to the sled. Then he took the buffalo robe, wrapped it over Grey, and tied that down, too. "Haul away," he shouted, and grasped the back of the sled, steadying it as the rope tightened and the makeshift litter began the slow ascent to the roadside. "I'll come back for you, Miss," he said over his shoulder.

With her heart in her mouth, Emma watched the sled skid up the almost vertical embankment until it disappeared over the crest. A moment later the rope came hurtling down toward her. "Tie it around your waist." In the dying light she could barely make out Mr. Paget's face as he hung over the bank, but she could hear him plainly enough in the cold air.

Quickly, she wrapped the rope around herself and tied a secure, if somewhat clumsy, knot. "Ready," she shouted, and gripped the rope with both hands. She stumbled the first few steps, then rolled onto her back and hung on while Mr. Paget shouted encouragement. It took only a few seconds until she felt his strong hands grasp hers and pull her onto the roadway.

"Well done, Miss," he exclaimed, and helped her to undo the knots since her own hands shook so badly she couldn't manage herself. Then he rigged Grey's litter to the runners still harnessed to his team. "Now, then," he checked the ropes to be sure they were secure, "you can ride Wesley's horse and he can straddle one of Mr. North's. If he can't walk in the morning, it'll serve him right for doing such a damn fool thing as firing a rifle at a snow drift."

"I was aiming at a cougar," Frank said, weakly, as he helped Emma to mount his horse. "I never meant to cause such a disaster." He was greatly distressed, his woebegone face pleading for understanding, but she was in no mood to comfort him. Because of his ignorance, the man she loved might die.

"Let's go." Mr. Paget mounted his own horse and took the reins to lead Grey's. Emma fell in behind, where she could watch Grey. In silence they trekked the last few miles into Gold City, completing their journey by the light of the moon and Mr. Paget's consummate knowledge of the road.

When they arrived at the luxurious hotel, the doorman hastened to help them get Grey inside while the desk clerk dashed off to summon a doctor. The men carried Grey upstairs to a well-appointed room while Emma hovered at his side. Only when they began to undress him, did she hasten across the hall to the room assigned to her. She stripped off her outer garments, washed her hands and face, and was ready to take up the post of nurse as soon as the doctor arrived.

"Whoa," Grey shouted and knotted his fists, straining against a set of imaginary reins. "Emma!" He struggled to sit up but she pressed him back against the pillows.

"Sh, it's all right now." She smoothed the hair back from his forehead, noting the unnatural heat of his skin. He was feverish, had been almost from the moment the doctor had left them. Feverish and delirious. No matter how often she assured him, he seemed to think they were still in the careering sleigh, hurtling toward the edge of a cliff.

She sighed and drew the covers over his powerful shoulders and shuddered. It was only because of Grey's strength she'd escaped the final plunge over the embankment. And if he hadn't used those final moments to throw her free, he might have saved himself. She couldn't bare to think how close she'd come to losing him. She gulped back the terror that filled her mouth as her fingers touched the bruise purpling his cheek. Just an inch higher and he might have lost his eye. An inch to the right and he would have been killed. He murmured at her touch and turned his head, his mouth finding the palm of her hand. She didn't draw back. Let him find what comfort he could in the touch of her cool fingers against his hot skin. She took solace for herself in the steady beat of his pulse beneath her hand. His eyes were closed: his breathing deep and steady, but when she would have moved away, he groaned softly in protest.

"Grey?" she whispered. "Grey, are you awake?"

"No," he muttered. His eyelids flickered but did not open. "I'm dreaming of an angel. I can't be awake."

"Oh, Grey, please wake up properly." Her voice shook as the horror of the accident washed over her anew. "Please look at me and tell me you're all right."

He made no response, falling back into oblivion. "Please wake up," she whispered again, mindful of what the doctor had told her. If he didn't regain full consciousness within twenty-four hours, he might suffer permanent brain damage.

She dipped a handkerchief in water and bathed his face, seeking to cool the fever that heated his skin and muddled his brain. A trickle of water ran down his cheek. She leaned forward to catch it, touching her lips gently to the corner of his mouth. His lips parted slightly and she drew back, studying his face, searching for a flicker of the vitality and zest that were so much a part of him. Her heart squeezed tight. He was so pale and still. The bruise on his cheek so vivid.

"Grey, wake up!" She nearly sobbed in her distress, clutching his shoulders.

"Emma? Emma! Where are you?" He thrashed his arms against her restraining hands, clutching at the empty air. "Emma." It was a long, drawn-out cry.

"Hush, hush. I'm here. It's all right." She caught one flailing hand in both of hers. "I'm all right, Grey. I'm here. I won't leave you."

His eyes opened, his cloudy gaze searching her face. "Ah, my angel." His eyelids fell shut, his body grew quiet. She studied his face, trying to convince herself that there was color returning to his skin. She tried to make herself believe his breathing was deeper and more natural.

She sank down in her chair, his hand still clasped in hers. He'd been like this for a night and a day. Now night was falling again, the light from the window nothing more than a pale square in the wall. The shadows in the room drew in, shutting her off from the world. Her eyes burned with weariness. She'd dozed off and on the previous night, sitting in the easy chair by Grey's bed, but she hadn't had a proper sleep in nearly two days. Frank had tried to relieve her at supper time today, but Grey became so agitated she'd made haste to hurry back, taking time only to swallow a few bites before repairing to her room to wash her hands and face, ready to spend the night by his side once more. The only concession she'd made to her own fatigue was to remove her tight corset and dress herself in a loose wrapper before taking up her post again.

Her back ached. Her shoulders slumped. It must be nearly midnight. She stretched to relieve her cramped muscles. Her eyelids drifted closed. Just for a minute, she promised herself. She could doze for just a few minutes. With Grey's hand in hers she would know instantly if he stirred. She leaned her head against the back of the chair, easing the strain in her neck.

She had no idea how long she slept, but she woke with a start, staring into the unfamiliar darkness, disoriented and confused. She was cold and for a frantic moment thought she was still on the trail. As her senses cleared she pulled her wrapper more tightly about herself and looked at the fireplace. The hearth held nothing but a few glowing coals. She must have drowsed longer than she'd intended. Horrified that she might have slept when Grey needed her, she lunged forward, touching the pulse in his throat, listening to his breath. He still slept. She couldn't see the pallor of his skin in the dark, but she was sure the rise and fall of his chest was deeper. She prayed that this sleep was normal, healing rest and not the awful delirium of the past hours. Hours in which he'd drifted in and out of consciousness. Hours in which he'd called her name but hadn't known her, apparently convinced she was some heavenly visitor. She almost smiled at the irony. In his right mind, Grey would never confuse her with an angel.

She shivered. She was so cold. Her feet felt like ice. She inched closer to the bed, pulling an edge of the blanket over her knees. It wasn't enough. She eyed the covers beside Grey. It was a big bed and he took up only one side. She could just slip under the blanket and he'd never know. She dared not leave him until she knew for certain that he had regained consciousness, but she didn't have to freeze to death in the meantime.

She released her fingers from his and tucked his hand under the covers. Quietly, she slipped around the end of the bed and slid beneath the blankets. He stirred and moaned, clutching convulsively at the air. "Hush, my darling." She caught his arm. "I'm here."

"Ah, my angel." He turned toward her, his arms reaching out with surprising strength, pulling her tightly against his body.

She let out a small gasp when she felt his mouth against her neck, his hands cupping her hips, pulling her hard against him. Her eyes opened wide as he brushed aside her wrapper, trailing kisses down her throat until he reached her breast. His mouth fastened over her nipple, tugging gently and sending ripples of pleasure coursing through her body.

"Grey," she protested in a horrified whisper, wriggling a little, trying to pull away, but he wasn't hearing Emma Douglas. In his befogged mind she was merely "his angel." He ran his hand down her side, skimming her hip and thigh, then trailing back up the inside of her leg. From freezing cold, her body now felt as though she were on fire. She trembled beneath his touch but no longer tried to pull away.

What did it matter, here on the edge of the wilderness? Who would know? Having come so near death, she longed to embrace life, to touch and feel and taste. In her deepest being she wanted to know Grey North, to hold him close, to feel the life in him.

She arched her back, pressing the center of her body against his, inviting him to taste and take. His hands spanned her waist, then slid over her stomach, exploring and probing. She lifted her arms to run her fingers lightly along his jaw, feeling the scratchy stubble of his beard. "Angel," he groaned, and buried his face into the curve of her neck. She felt his lips exploring the hills and hollows of her collarbone, dragging a trail of fire toward her breast.

Her pulse fluttered in her throat, her breath came in ragged bursts, and her bones felt as though they'd melted into useless jelly. Her breasts swelled and strained toward the source of their pleasure. Her nipples had grown so hard they hurt and only Grey's mouth could relieve the pain. "Please," she whispered.

In the darkness she reached for him, aching with need. He touched her swollen nipples, first cupping her breast and massaging in small circles with his thumbs, then, with a sigh, drawing her breast into his mouth, sucking gently, kneading, caressing, driving her wild with a desire she did not know or understand, but one that demanded fulfilment.

She had thought when he kissed her breasts the ache would cease; instead, it grew stronger, making her whimper with frustration, sending her out of control. She grasped his head, holding him tightly to her bosom, thrusting her nipple deeper into his mouth, twisting her body under his, seeking the one place that would bring her release.

When he rolled on top of her she wrapped her arms about him, holding him close, taking comfort in the steady pounding of his heart, assuring herself of his vitality. "Grey?" she whispered his name.

"Angel." He pressed his knee between her thighs, opening her to himself.

Without conscious thought she began to rock beneath him, feeling as though a flood were building in her loins, dammed up and spreading backward. She would drown if the dam wasn't broken, and only Grey had the power to save her. "Oh," she gasped when, with one quick thrust, he laid waste to the thin barrier that held them apart, driving himself deep inside her, burying himself in her flesh.

There was an instant of pain, a sharp, stabbing pang; but then it was gone and there was only the reality that was Grey and a sweet, savage, life-affirming joy. They rocked together, riding on a bounding sea, each wave taking her higher and higher until at last the dam broke, washing her away on a tide of delight.

"My angel." He shuddered and bore down on her, driving her into the mattress. She welcomed his weight, offering her body as a cradle for his. Accepting and receiving, reveling in her power to please and comfort him.

The wild rocking of their bodies slowed to a gentle sway. The frenzy of their lovemaking easing to tenderness and peace. In the aftermath of their loving her body grew languorous, melting into the mattress, quiescent beneath Grey's weight. She sighed when he shifted off her, then snuggled her head against his shoulder and listened to his deep, steady breathing.

When next she woke his skin was cool beneath her cheek. The fever had broken. She stirred, easing herself away from him, smiling secretly. He would be all right. Far off she heard the sound of a delivery wagon. Dawn was lightening the sky outside the window. People would be up and stirring soon. They mustn't find her here. She turned her head to gaze for another long moment on his face, then slid from the bed and fled across the hall to her own room. By the time the doctor came to check on his patient, she was washed and dressed and sitting serenely in a chair beneath the window. No one would guess at the storm that had taken her during the night.

"How's the patient?" The doctor was a bluff, hearty man. "Give you any trouble?"

"Not much." She bit back the gurgle of mirth that threatened. "He was restless for most of the day and part of the night, but by dawn he slept peacefully."

"Well, let's have a look at him, then." The doctor turned to the bed and shook Grey's shoulder.

Emma hovered behind the doctor until she saw Grey open his eyes. They were clear and blue and brilliant. She slipped out of the room, leaving the patient to his doctor. He had no more need of her.

* * *

It was nearly dinnertime when a porter knocked at her door to convey the message that he'd brought dinner for two to Mr. North's room and the gentleman requested that she join him.

"Tell him I'll be along shortly." When the porter withdrew, she whirled to examine herself in the big mirror over the dresser. Once the doctor had assured her Grey needed only rest to see him fully restored to health, she'd sought the comfort of her own bed and slept for several hours. Now the face that looked back from her mirror was refreshed, the eyes glowing with a secret knowledge, the dewy lips curled into an irrepressible smile. She touched her fingers to her ribs, feeling the hard edges of the key in her corset. Nothing that had happened last night changed her determination to travel to San Francisco and clear her father's name. But she couldn't stop smiling. She patted her hair into place, then went to join Grey for dinner.

"Come," he called in response to her gentle tap on his door.

She walked into the room and stopped short in astonishment. Grey was standing before the fireplace, his cheeks freshly shaven, dressed in clean clothes and looking completely in control. If it hadn't been for the bruise on his cheek, she would never have guessed he was the same man who'd frightened her half to death by refusing to wake up for two days. "Grey! You look wonderful."

"Thank you, madam." He swept her a low bow, his mocking smile firmly in place and his eyes as cold and cynical as she'd ever seen them. He gestured to the small table, covered in crisp white linen and glistening with silver, before pulling out a chair then standing stiffly behind it until she was seated. Then he took his seat opposite and lifted the covers on the dishes. "I trust you'll find the meal to your liking," he said with all the cold formality of a paid waiter.

Her smile faltered and she peered sharply at him. Perhaps he wasn't as recovered as she'd thought. "What did the doctor say?"

"He assured me I'd had a lucky escape and could expect a speedy recovery." The words were clipped and sharp, almost as though he regretted the necessity to speak.

"Are you in pain?" She couldn't understand his hostility. She didn't expect lover-like behavior from him, especially since she suspected he didn't remember their lovemaking, but she did expect a friendly dinner companion. "Would you rather skip dinner and go back to bed?"

"Would that please you?" Even in the candlelight she could see his face change from cold courtesy to furious anger. "Let me assure you, it won't be necessary. You've accomplished your aim."

"Grey, what are you talking about?" She gave up pretending they were having a normal conversation. "If you didn't want to see me, why invite me to dinner?" She chewed on her bottom lip, totally bewildered.

"Don't dissemble, Emma. I admit I wasn't totally conscious last night, I thought I was dreaming; but when the doctor pronounced me fit to leave my bed, I found the blood on the sheets. Congratulations, Emma. You've succeeded where many before you failed. We'll be married immediately."

A fury to match his gripped her as she finally understood. She stood up so quickly she jostled the table, setting the dishes rattling and upsetting the glasses. "You insult me, Grey. I have no wish to couple myself with such an arrogant, ungrateful, odious *gentleman* as yourself." She whirled away from the table, intent on putting as much space between herself and Grey North as possible, but he was too quick for her. His hand shot out, grasping her arm and forcing her to a halt.

She stopped, standing stock-still, refusing to disgrace herself with an undignified tussle. "Let me go."

"Never." His eyes bored into hers. "I told you before, I'm no despoiler of innocence, and since you were a maid, I'll do my duty. Congratulations, madam. You've snared the *Honorable* Greydon North." His lip curled in derision and his eyes raked her from head to foot, lewd and insulting. "You cheated, Emma, but you've won the prize. I've no choice but to marry you, but by heaven, you'll find no joy in the union." He dropped her arm and turned his back. "It's Christmastime. It may take a day or two until we find a vicar willing to perform the ceremony. You'll have to delay your trip to San Francisco."

Without a word she walked out of the room, closing the door with a gentle click when every nerve screamed to slam it shut with enough force to rattle the rafters. How dare he make wild, passionate love to her and then defile the act by pretending she had set out to seduce him?

She flew into her own room, closing the door behind her and turning the lock with a vicious twist. Angrily, she paced up and down the floor, devising and rejecting schemes to revenge herself on Grey North. Their lovemaking had been born of fear and loneliness and isolation, but it had been beautiful. She would not let him make her ashamed. And she certainly had no desire to marry him! She pulled open the drawer of the dresser and slammed it shut just for the satisfaction of making a noise.

First he harangued her about the foolishness of polite conventions and meaningless decorum, and then, when she'd responded to her natural instincts and succumbed to the magic of the wilderness, then, he had the gall to turn priggish and proper and accuse her of corrupting his good name. She kicked at the footstool before the fireplace, furious with Grey North and even more furious with herself. How had she ever allowed herself to fall in love with such a hateful man? Despite everything, she couldn't deny that she loved him. With ruthless honesty, she stripped away all her excuses for sharing Grey's bed and admitted she'd allowed him to make love to her because she loved him. She sat down on the hapless footstool and rubbed her abused toes. Love him or not, she would not marry a man who despised her. Her life was her own and to hell with Grey North.

She looked toward the window, trying to determine the time, but the heavy curtains obscured the sky. She crossed the room and shoved the heavy draperies aside. Outside the night was dark, but light spilled from the lighted windows of the hotel, throwing long rectangles of gold across the snow-covered street. In the sky she could see a crescent moon directly overhead. Below her someone whistled and a dog barked. Dawn was hours away and the train to Vancouver didn't leave until noon. She was stuck in this hotel with Grey North for another ten hours at least. She leaned her shoulder against the window frame and stared down the empty street.

She wasn't marrying Grey North, not even if he presented her with a whole raft of priests and judges. He couldn't force her to say "I do." Still, she didn't want to have to explain to a man of the cloth that her proposed groom intended only "to make an honest woman of her." As if she hadn't already been humiliated enough to last a lifetime.

A train whistle blew in the distance, its mournful note

echoing between the mountains a perfect reflection of her doleful mood. If only she could get on the train and be on her way before Grey . . . She leapt away from the window as a sudden thought struck her. There was only one passenger train from Gold City, but if she could get to the station, she just might be able to get a ride on the freight.

In a fever of impatience, she snatched up her belongings and jammed them into her battered valise, then opened the door a crack and peeked into the hallway. Seeing it was empty, she threw her heavy outdoor clothes over her arm, grabbed the valise, and tiptoed past Grey's room to the broad, sweeping stairs at the end of the hall. She skimmed down the steps on light feet, her ears attuned for the slightest sound from Grey's room and her heart in her mouth lest he intercept her. When she reached the lobby, the night porter was invisible and she was forced to ring the bell, praying the tinkling sound wouldn't carry upstairs.

To her stretched nerves it seemed an eternity before the night clerk appeared, tucking in his shirttail and looking annoyed. "It's nigh on two in the morning," he grumbled. "What do you want?" He didn't bother to add the polite "Miss."

"I wish to pay my bill," she replied tartly, "and I'll thank you to remember your manners or your employer shall hear of it."

"Yes, Miss." The rejoinder was hardly an improvement on his original question but she let it pass. "What room?"

"Twelve."

She waited while he dragged a finger down the register, wanting to scream at him to hurry up.

"Name?"

"Miss Douglas." What was so hard about finding the

number twelve on the ledger page and reading out the charges noted beside it?

"Bill's been paid . . . Miss." He added the last when she glared at him.

"Perhaps it wasn't entered properly. I arrived two days ago with an injured man. Look again."

"Ain't no charges, Miss."

"Let me see that." Despite the porter's protest, she grasped the register and turned it so she could read the entries herself.

"Oh!" She nearly stamped her foot in frustration. Beside room twelve was the notation, CHARGED TO MR. G. NORTH IN ROOM 10. "Very well. Please bring me an envelope and a sheet of paper and a pen."

Glowering, the clerk pointed toward a writing desk set in an alcove of the lobby. "Over there, Miss."

Not bothering with her valise, she hurried to the desk, found the required writing materials, and penned a short note of resignation to the Prospect School Trustees, saying she regretted leaving them with short notice, but she feared her business in San Francisco would take longer than she had anticipated. She was sure the trustees would wish to replace her rather than have classes suspended while they awaited her uncertain return. She blotted the ink, folded the page, and stuffed it into an envelope. Then she withdrew several of her remaining bills and placed them inside with the letter. She would not be beholden to Grey North. She sealed the envelope, wrote Grey's name on the front, and returned to the reception desk.

"Please see that Mr. North gets this." She handed the envelope to the porter. She felt a pang of regret as she watched him place it in the appropriate pigeonhole. She had just burnt her first bridge. Who knew how many others still awaited the torch? She set her shoulders, handed in her room key, and walked smartly to the front door and out into the street. This was not the time for looking backward.

Fortunately, the Canadian Pacific Railroad put its hotels close to its train stations. She merely had to cross the street, pray the incoming freight contained one passenger car, persuade the station agent and the conductor to let her board, and she could put the *Honorable* Greydon North out of her life forever.

Chapter Nine

After Emma had fled from his room, Grey tried to relieve his frustration with a tirade of invective. He swore with passion, with imagination and vehemence. He called up every oath he had ever heard and then created new ones. He cursed his father, the fates, himself, and Frank Wesley. But no matter how eloquent his condemnations, the fact remained, he'd been duped. Emma Douglas, the prim and proper schoolmarm, had cozened her way into his bed, and he was now committed to marry her.

He kicked viciously at the coal scuttle, sending it crashing and banging across the hearth. He liked Emma. She was good company, amusing, clever, pretty, and intelligent. She was kind and understanding with those less able than herself and quick to see through pretension and falsehood. She also made his blood sing, and if his vague memories of last night were any measure, they would enjoy each other in bed. In short, she was everything he would want in a wife. Except, he didn't want a wife. The minute he slipped a ring on Emma's finger, all their pleasure in each other would vanish.

He stalked to the bed, flinging himself onto the mattress, hands behind his head, staring at the ceiling. He could just disappear. Plenty of men lost themselves on the gold fields or evaporated into British Columbia's vast forests. He gritted his teeth and swung his legs over the side of the bed, to sit with his head in his hands. He couldn't do that. He'd betrayed Emma's innocence. He would pay the price; the devil of it was, so would she.

Dimly in the distance he heard the sound of a train whistle, long and mournful in the silence of the mountains. It touched his soul, just like the cry of a wolf, connecting him to the wilderness, stirring a deep longing in his heart. He swore again and punched the pillow at the head of the bed. Within three days, a week at most, he'd be a married man, tied hand and foot to dull duty and meaningless formalities. With each passing day he'd lose a little more of himself, the heart leeched out of him by gossiping matrons and a nagging wife.

If his father could see him now. His mouth filled with bitterness. At least his bride didn't come with a half-dozen sisters all looking for an *entré* into London society. No, his mouth twisted in contempt, she only came with a suicide for a father, a thief for an ex-fiancé, and an old friend who roused every suspicious nerve in Grey's body. Emma was a much better choice than the doxy his father had chosen. If he wasn't so angry, he'd have laughed at the irony.

"Good morning, sir." The waiter in the dining room greeted him with irritating heartiness. "And a Merry Christmas to you."

"Good God," he exclaimed. "Is it really Christmas Day?"

"Yes, sir. Folks who're traveling sometimes lose track of the days." The waiter placed a napkin across Grey's lap. "Will you be staying for our banquet tonight? We're offering roasted goose with apple stuffing and a traditional English plum pudding."

"No." Grey searched the rest of the dining room with his eyes, looking for Emma. Where was the woman? Still sleeping peacefully in her bed? Dreaming, no doubt, of the pleasant life she planned to lead as his wife—no more trudging to work at the schoolhouse, no cooking or housekeeping. She'd have plenty of time to dream up grievances against him and to plan boring entertainments to show off her new status and parade her husband about like a tame monkey. She might even insist they return to England so she could take part in London's Season.

"Sir?"

"What?" He scowled at the waiter still hovering at his side.

"Would you like to order?"

"Coffee," he growled, "and the full English breakfast."

"Very good, sir." The waiter departed, returning in a moment with his coffee. "There is no newspaper today, sir, but I've brought you a selection of the local paper from yesterday and some back issues of the *London Times.*" He set the papers and the coffee on the table and departed once more.

Grey checked the clock on the wall, it was nearly nine in the morning. If Emma didn't come down soon, she'd miss her breakfast altogether. He'd decided during the night that they would have more success finding a justice of the peace in Vancouver than in Gold City. The train left at noon. He'd give her another thirty minutes.

He sipped his coffee and shook out the latest edition

of the *Times*, turning the pages with desultory interest. Most of the headlines concerned preparations for the Queen's golden jubilee, culminating in a grand parade and presentation of the newest crop of girls making their debut. The whole affair bored him, and he scanned the pages without really paying attention until a bold headline with his own name caught his eye.

In stunned disbelief he flattened the paper onto the table and read. Beneath the caption LOST HEIR was a notice issued by the firm of Gossop and Black to the effect that Sir Alexander North had passed away suddenly at the age of fifty-four and the firm of solicitors was trying to trace the heir to his estates, namely, one Greydon North. Anyone having information of said Greydon North was requested to contact said firm of solicitors, forthwith.

For long moments he sat staring at the announcement, his breakfast cooling on the plate. His father hadn't disinherited him after all. He was now Sir Greydon North and in possession of estates and a sizable fortune and the responsibilities that went with it. He checked the date of the paper. It was four weeks old and the announcement indicated his father had died several weeks prior to that. His mother was a widow with, as far as he knew, no means of her own.

He must telegraph the solicitors immediately. She'd need money, and he needed to ascertain if she wished to continue living in the country or if she would prefer a move to London or Bath. Whatever she wanted, he vowed to himself, she would have. Anyone who had spent more than twenty-five years as the browbeaten wife of Sir Alexander North deserved to spend the rest of her life in cosseted luxury.

He folded the paper and signaled to the waiter. "Have

the front desk prepare my account." He pushed aside his uneaten breakfast. "I'll be checking out immediately."

"Very good, sir."

He made a note of the solicitor's address and strode out of the dining room. "Send someone to ask Miss Douglas to come down at once," he ordered the desk clerk. "We need to be on our way."

"The young lady already left, sir." The desk clerk seemed to find the circumstance a personal affront.

"That's ridiculous." Grey was in no mood for further complications. "Where would she go?"

"Can't say, sir, but she asked me to give you this." The clerk reached behind himself to extract a long envelope from one of the pigeonholes that held the room keys.

With an irritated flick of his finger, Grey opened the flap and drew out the single sheet of paper. He opened it up and a few bank notes fluttered out of its folds. He felt an instant foreboding. What had the woman done now? He scanned the lines she'd written, then read them again more slowly. Then he stuffed the letter back into its envelope, scooped up the money from the floor and shoved the whole lot into his pocket.

Blast the woman! The last thing he needed was a runaway bride. If she thought she could just walk away, after all that had passed between them, she was sadly mistaken. His innate sense of honor would not permit him to abandon her, even if she deserved it. And where the hell had she gone! "Did Miss Douglas ask for directions?" He scowled at the desk clerk.

"No, sir."

"Did she ask for help to carry her valise?"

"No, sir."

"Did she say or do anything to indicate where she was going?"

"I believe she was interested in the train, sir."

Of course. He relaxed his scowl. She'd gone ahead to the train station, but why she was in such an almighty rush escaped his understanding. There was only one passenger train a day to Vancouver and it didn't leave for another two hours. He had plenty of time to send his telegram and find her. He hoped she didn't plan to sulk all the way to the coast.

He paid his bill, ran upstairs, taking the steps two at a time, fetched his own case, and was back downstairs and out the door before the clerk could put the money in his cash drawer. The station was only a few steps away.

"Well, well." The doctor who'd tended him stood in his path. "How's the patient today?"

"No lasting damage." Grey was impatient but he owed the doctor his life. "I believe I'm in your debt." He reached into his pocket to extract his billfold. "What do I owe you?"

"Not as much as you owe the young lady." The doctor accepted payment for his services but seemed inclined to chat. "She's the one kept you from freezing out there on the trail, and it was her nursing that brought you through the delirium. Where is she, by the way?" The doctor peered over Grey's shoulder, as though expecting Emma to appear.

"She's gone ahead to the train," Grey replied, furious that Emma had embarrassed him by disappearing but intrigued by the doctor's comments. "I thought it was Paget and Wesley who brought me in."

"They got you into town, but Miss Douglas built the tent and started the fire and kept you warm while she waited for rescue. You owe her your life, Mr. North. I'm sorry I missed her." The doctor buttoned up his coat. "Well, I've another patient to check before I can enjoy my Christmas dinner. Merry Christmas to you." He waved and set off into the snowy street. Grey followed, a thoughtful frown furrowing his face as he crossed the road to the train station.

"Mr. North?"

He turned to face the young constable hovering in the telegraph office. "Constable." He studied the familiar face but couldn't put a name to it. "Aren't you stationed in Prospect? What brings you here on Christmas morning?"

"Duty, sir. Inspector West wanted the information out of San Francisco as soon as possible and I got the short straw."

"What information?" At the mention of San Francisco, he was instantly alert. He didn't believe in coincidences.

"About the bank, sir, and Miss Douglas's father and that Parnell Wilde feller. Inspector West wanted to know if we should charge him with murder."

"Murder!" Grey was thunderstruck. "Who did he kill?"

"Well, I don't know as I should be discussing police business." The constable ran a finger along the tight collar of his tunic. "But seein' as how you're a trustee an' all and Miss Douglas is the schoolmarm, I guess it wouldn't hurt." He then proceeded to fill Grey in on the details of the police investigation.

"So the authorities in San Francisco think Parnell Wilde is involved?"

"Oh, he was there, all right. They just don't know if he pulled the trigger."

"They're sure it wasn't a suicide?"

"That's what they say now. They're wondering if Mr. Douglas was framed for the embezzlement, too. The whole case is being reinvestigated."

With a flash of insight he understood. Emma was going home to try to clear her father's name. That's why she'd given up the security of her position in Prospect and the comforts of Mrs. Royston's home. And put herself in danger! Blast the girl! Didn't she realize her father's killer wouldn't hesitate to murder her as well if she threatened him? On second thought, he realized, it wouldn't matter if she did. If Emma believed she held the key to her father's murder, she wouldn't let fear prevent her from bringing his killer to justice. And yet she had delayed her journey by two days in order to nurse him back to health. He did, indeed, owe Emma, and more than the doctor knew.

"Thank you, officer. I'm much obliged," he nodded to the constable, "and you can tell Inspector West that I'll look after Miss Douglas." He set off to the telegraph window, sent a brief message to the solicitors and a longer one to his mother, then went in search of Emma.

Forty-five minutes later he had to face the fact that she'd stolen a march on him. She was nowhere in the station. She wasn't with Frank Wesley; he'd managed to run that young man to earth at a cheaper hotel on the other side of the tracks. She hadn't made an appearance at the livery stable, and Paget swore he hadn't seen her since he'd carried Grey's unconscious self to the hotel. Even though it galled him to appeal to a stranger for news of Emma, he finally asked the ticket agent if a young woman with red hair had purchased a ticket from him that morning. He hated looking like a fool. He hated it even more when the agent informed him that just such a young woman as he described had boarded the caboose of the freight train at six o'clock that morning.

"Seemed dead set on getting to Vancouver before dinnertime. Wanted to surprise her family and all. I told her we didn't have a passenger car for her to ride in, but the brakeman's a tenderhearted fellow. Said she could ride in back with him if it meant so much to her."

Seething with frustration and a sneaking admiration

for her initiative, Grey paid for his own ticket. Before boarding, he wrote two letters. The first, to his banker, explained that he'd been unexpectedly recalled to England and commissioned that worthy to manage the hotel until his return. A second letter, to the trustees, included Emma's resignation. He posted the letters, then boarded the train and took a seat in the mahogany-lined club car and buried his nose in the newspaper he'd brought with him. Not that month-old news from England engrossed his interest, but the paper discouraged conversation from fellow travelers.

But the newspaper couldn't block out his own bad-tempered brooding. As soon as he caught up with Emma he'd put an end to her foolish heroics. They would be married immediately and the police informed of whatever evidence Emma thought she had. Then they'd set out for England. She could consider the journey their honeymoon. He ground his teeth together. At least his mother would be happy to meet his bride.

Yet, even his foul humor could not block out the spectacular scenery that sped by the window as the train hurtled down steep mountainsides, through long snowsheds, and climbed back up the next slope. Rounding a curve above Spences Bridge, Grey couldn't help but be awed by the engineering feat that brought a train along a network of trestles and tunnels and impossible grades to traverse the Rocky Mountains. He put down the paper, ordered a whiskey, and gave his whole attention to the scene outside his window. His only regret was that Emma wasn't there to share it with him.

Once she'd given Grey the slip, Emma found the trip to Vancouver an interesting experience, if not the most comfortable one. True, the stove kept the caboose cozy and warm, but every time the crew got out to set signals or check the axles, cold air rushed into the little car, along with steam and ash from the engines. As well, she hadn't learned to anticipate the halts and was nearly thrown from her chair each time the train braked. Still, she thought, tucking her feet under her skirt and brushing the soot from her gloves, a few minor inconveniences were a small price to pay if they allowed her to avoid meeting Grey over the breakfast dishes.

It was midday when the freight pulled into the new Vancouver station. Although it wasn't the passenger train, several horse-drawn cabs waited at the station and she was able to hail one of them, despite the brakeman's concern that no family was waiting to meet her.

"It's a surprise, remember?" She shook his kindly hand and thanked him for letting her share his quarters on the train. When he was out of earshot she told the cabbie to take her to the docks. The quicker she set sail to San Francisco, the better. After her reckless gesture in overpaying Grey for her room in Gold City, her purse was alarmingly thin.

"There you go, Miss." The cabbie opened the door of the hack and helped her to alight. "I hear the *Aurora's* set to leave on the four o'clock tide."

"Thank you." She paid him his fare and wished she could tip him more handsomely. "Merry Christmas to you," she said and declined his offer to carry her valise. "I'm sure you want to get home to your Christmas dinner."

"Good luck to you, Miss." The driver tipped his hat and remounted the driver's seat of his cab.

Emma turned and walked purposefully down the pier, determined to board the *Aurora* even if she had to haggle for a ticket. "Good evening, Captain." She set her foot on the gangplank and marched up to the deck of the ship. Fortunately for her pride, she was able to purchase shared accommodation in an inside cabin for a sum her purse would allow.

Five days later, as the *Aurora* slipped through the Golden Gate and into San Francisco's famous harbor, she stood on the deck and watched the city emerge from its shroud of fog. The air felt soft and damp against her skin, a welcome contrast from the harsh, dry cold of Prospect.

A thrill of anticipation ran through her at the sight of the city, rising up from the bustling harbor in a network of streets and avenues along the three large hills. The smell from the fish docks hung on the morning air; church spires pierced the mist pointing into the sky. Past the rotting hulls of abandoned ships, beyond the vice of the Barbary Coast, the city offered music and art and culture and commerce—and danger. She clasped her hands together, pressing her fists into her rib cage, feeling the hard outline of the key, close to her heart. Somewhere in this big, bustling city was the man who had killed her father.

During the long days of her journey she'd decided that Matt Douglas could not have killed himself. He would never do anything so cowardly, nor would he leave his daughter to face scandal and ruin, alone. She'd been wrong ever to have accepted the results of the first investigation. She had betrayed her father's memory. Now she was determined to right that wrong.

The ship bumped alongside the pier and she clutched at the rail to keep from being knocked over. Behind her, a press of passengers surged forward, most returning home, eager to find familiar faces in the crowd on the dock, but a few were newcomers, gazing with awe and apprehension at the beautiful city. Emma wasn't sure where she fit. San Francisco was her birthplace, and since she'd sent him a telegram, she assumed Everett Jergens was in the crowd on the dock, waiting to welcome her back, but was it really her home? So much had happened since she left here. She'd changed. Grey . . .

"Abigail." She recognized Everett's voice and only then realized he was calling to her. She'd become so accustomed to "Emma" that "Abigail" seemed a stranger.

She waved her hand in acknowledgment, then picked up her valise and joined the crowd inching toward the gangway. Ten minutes later she had her feet on the dock and Everett's burly body standing between her and the hubbub on the wharf. "My dear, it's so good to see you." He wrapped her in a bear hug, then took the valise from her hand and steered her along the pier toward the cable car terminus at Union Square. "We'll take the tram," he said. "So much quicker than bringing a carriage. Come, you must be tired." He took her arm and hustled her through the crowd. A cable car was just loading.

"Your telegram came as a shock, Abigail," he said once they'd found seats. "I thought you well settled in your new home, but I'm delighted to have you here, my dear." He patted her knee in a fatherly way. "Now, tell me what brought you on this sudden journey."

"It's a long story, Uncle Everett." She watched the city passing by them, refreshing her memory as the tram passed the impressive buildings of the financial district, the brightly painted Victorian houses that marked the march of wealth up to the heights of Nob Hill, their bay windows jutting out to afford the owners a view of the harbor. It was all so familiar and yet strange. Her two years as a schoolmarm in Prospect had eclipsed her life as a pampered debutante.

"You must be tired."

She smiled up at him, glad to have one dear and faithful friend in a world where hostility waited around every bend. "I am," she admitted. "The shipboard accommodations were meager, to say the least. I'll be glad to stretch out on a proper bed."

"Are you staying for good?" The question sounded anxious, but she put it down to her own overstretched nerves and her friend's concern for her.

"I don't know."

"You're welcome for as long as you like, child, but I wish you would tell me what has happened to bring you here."

The tram car halted and passengers got off; others got on, jostling her as they searched for seats. The bell clanged and the car jerked into movement. Emma glanced about, realizing they could easily be overheard. "I'll tell you all about it after I've had a rest," she murmured. "Suffice to say, Parnell Wilde played a part. Did you know he came to Prospect?"

"Parnell did?" His eyebrows flew up in surprise. "I'd hoped he'd disappeared for good."

"Why?" Everett had never expressed disapproval of Parnell before.

"He's a ne'er-do-well, Abigail. You're well rid of him."

The cable car was reaching the end of its run up California Street. Two more stops and Everett and Emma stepped down from the wood-lined car and into the rarified air of San Francisco's wealthiest neighborhood. From there it was only a short walk to Everett's mansion, modest by the standards of its neighbors, but palatial compared to Mrs. Royston's practical dwelling. A butler opened the door as they climbed the steps to the pillared entrance.

"Thank you, Fergus." Everett handed Emma's valise to

the servant. "Take this to Miss Douglas's room and ask your wife to bring us some refreshments."

The butler bowed and departed while Emma followed her host into a large, high-ceilinged sitting room, flooded with light from tall, rounded windows. Her feet sank silently into the thick carpet as she crossed to a silk-covered settee. Settling herself into its comfortable cushions, she couldn't repress another sigh. She'd missed the creature comforts in Prospect.

While she was still removing her gloves the housekeeper appeared with a pot of tea and a tray of sandwiches and sweets. "Oh, that looks wonderful, Mrs. Fergus."

"Thank you, Miss. It's good to have you home again." The housekeeper set the tray on a low table close to Emma and withdrew.

"Shall I pour?" Emma set her gloves aside and reached for the heavy silver teapot, filling the cups with the tawny brew. She handed the bone china to Everett and suddenly remembered Mrs. Royston's kindness in packing a china cup for her to use on the trail. She hoped Grey would make sure it was returned to her. As soon as she settled matters here, she'd write to her former landlady and make sure. She sipped her tea, closing her eyes and relishing the taste. "Wonderful," she said. "The tea on board the *Aurora* left much to be desired."

"No doubt." Everett reached for one of Mrs. Fergus's sandwiches, then settled back into his winged chair, regarding Emma with an intent look. "Tell me why Parnell Wilde sought you out in Prospect."

"He wanted to renew our engagement." She pulled a face. "I refused." She sipped her tea, then added, "He told me you'd dressed him down—the same day my father died."

"Yes." Everett confirmed Parnell's tale without hesitation.

"There was something fishy about that young man, Abigail. I'm sorry you've been hurt, but I'm not sorry you broke your engagement to him. I always suspected he was using you and his connection with Matt to further his career at the bank."

"Why didn't you tell me?"

"I wanted to, my dear." He put down his teacup and folded his hands, regarding her sadly. "I shared my concerns with Matt, but you were so happy we decided not to interfere. I only wish . . ." He left the sentence incomplete, but she could well imagine the rest. And yet, Parnell had sworn he was innocent, both of her father's murder and of the embezzlement. Oddly, she believed him.

Parnell might have been sly and devious but, as Everett had pointed out, he was also indolent, too lazy to plot and carry out the complex schemes required of an embezzler and much too squeamish to actually kill. But if it wasn't Parnell, who? Unless she could find the answer, her father's memory would always be tinged with disgrace. She pressed her hand against the key, finding reassurance in its hard edges. The answer lay there. Her father had seen to it.

"And was it Parnell's tale that brought you haring back to San Francisco?" Everett broke in on her brooding.

"No." She shook her head to clear her mind. "I came back because he confirmed what you'd told me. The investigation has been reopened." It was the truth, if only part of it. For some reason she couldn't explain, she kept the key a secret. Her father must have known she would be the one to find it. He'd entrusted the key to her and her alone.

"Yes. The police paid a visit to the bank several weeks back. I didn't meet with them myself, but the bank's new president told me there were new questions surrounding your father's case."

"Who is the new president?" It surprised her that Everett hadn't been named to that position. He'd been her father's right-hand man since he'd started the Pioneers Bank with two other partners, neither of whom worked in the day-to-day operations. It would have been natural for them to name Everett to the president's chair.

"Oh, some Eastern upstart, name of Darcy McCue. The board of directors felt it was time for new blood." His bitter tone betrayed his disappointment. "Young whippersnapper. Does things his own way. Too cocksure of himself to take advice from a man of experience."

"Oh, Uncle Everett, I'm sorry." For the first time since she'd set foot on land, she looked hard at her old friend. The lines about his mouth had deepened since she'd seen him in Prospect. His skin was pallid, and the pouches below his eyes hung heavily on his cheeks. "Perhaps you should think of retiring. I'm sure you've earned a rest."

"Perhaps." He stared glumly toward the window, but Emma guessed he wasn't seeing the weak sunlight fighting its way through the damp air or contemplating a life of ease. If anything, his face seemed to have grown even more strained, every year of his age etched into the lines spreading like a spiderweb across his cheeks.

"Well," she attempted a cheerful tone, "if you don't mind, I think I'll go up to my room and lie down for a little. It has been an exhausting journey."

"Of course." Everett's attention snapped back to her. "I shouldn't have detained you here, keeping a lonely old man company."

* * *

Grey North walked out of the Pioneers Bank consumed with frustration, an emotion he'd grown overly familiar with in the days since Emma had given him the slip. A reluctant grin tugged at the corner of his mouth. He had to hand it to her. He never would have thought she'd wangle her way onto a freight train and arrive in Vancouver six hours ahead of him. He'd managed to find the brakeman from the freight, who confirmed a young woman had ridden in the caboose from Gold City to Vancouver. "Going to see her family," he'd said with a benevolent smile. Grey had thanked the man, then gone to check the docks, but no one could tell him anything about a young woman traveling alone to San Francisco.

Finally, he'd headed for the telegraph station and sent off a flurry of telegrams. One to the London solicitors, informing them of a delay in his plans. Another to Frank Wesley in Gold City, telling him to keep an eye on the team he'd left at the livery stable; it was the least the young fool could do, considering all the trouble he'd caused. Lastly, he'd sent a wire to the Pioneers Bank, in San Francisco, requesting an interview with the president.

Then he'd caught the fastest boat in the harbor sailing to Seattle. From there he'd transferred to the Northern Pacific Railroad and was in San Francisco, by his calculations, at least a day ahead of Emma, assuming she'd taken passage by ship the entire distance. It was a calculated gamble, but one he felt justified in taking. A woman traveling alone would find it easier to avoid the problems of changing from ship to train. He scowled and turned his steps toward the harbor. He'd spent a whole day watching the docks without catching sight of Emma. Then he'd interviewed the bank president and learned nothing to ease his worry.

Emma hadn't contacted Mr. McCue but the police

had. The investigation into Matt Douglas's murder—they were calling it a murder now—was picking up steam. The bank had reexamined the books and felt the evidence could implicate another employee as well as Mr. Douglas. And no, they were not at liberty to divulge the name of their second suspect, but they could say he had not been arrested.

Now, he paced along the embarcadero, blind to the sights and sounds of San Francisco's most notorious neighborhood, his eyes searching the crowds milling about on the piers, devising what he would do to Emma when he finally found her.

He'd watched over her like a hawk since the break-ins in Prospect, convinced that her safety was at risk. Nothing that had happened since had eased his mind. In fact, now that she had returned to the scene of the crime, so to speak, he felt even more anxious for her. Why the hell couldn't the woman behave like an ordinary female and let him look after her?

He knew the answer before he'd formed the question. Emma was not an ordinary female. Every other woman he'd met would give her eyeteeth to become Lady North, but even when he'd done the right thing and offered for her, Emma had gone all stiff and starchy and refused him. She was in trouble. He knew it. If she'd had any sense at all, she would have accepted his protection instead of haring off on a freight train—a freight train!—just to avoid him. He kicked at a stone in his path and scowled at the scuff on his boot.

He could just let her go. After all, he'd done the honorable thing. If she was too proud and pigheaded to marry him, he could wash his hands of her. No, he couldn't, damn it. The woman had saved his life. Muddled memories of the "angel" in his bed flashed into his mind, driving out his anger. She'd been soft and beautiful, giving and loving. She was his now. He wouldn't let her go.

A shout went up from the pier before him and he joined the crowd to watch the passengers disembark, his eyes peeled for a slender woman with flashing eyes and rich auburn hair, but he was disappointed. Emma was not among the press of passengers descending the gangplank of the *Idaho.* His gaze drifted down the harborfront. A bevy of ships docked along the many piers. Could he have missed her in the crowd? Unwillingly, he turned his glance toward the brothels and gambling dens that lined the harbor, part of San Francisco's notorious Barbary Coast. Could Matt Douglas's murderer be hiding in that denizen of vice? Could the same man be lying in wait for Emma? He shuddered. He had to find her before her mule-headed obstinacy landed her in even more trouble.

Since the Pioneers Bank hadn't heard from her and neither had the police, his only other lead was Everett Jergens. He supposed he could just go to the man's house and ask for her, but he felt a strange reluctance to reveal himself. Something about Jergens's trip to Prospect just didn't add up. Grey couldn't put his finger on the problem, but he didn't trust Everett Jergens, old family friend or not.

He turned abruptly from the waterfront and strode back the way he had come. He'd gotten Jergens's address from the bank, he might as well use it. He hopped one of the trolley cars that climbed up and down the steep streets. It was a fascinating invention. If he wasn't so preoccupied with Emma, he'd have studied the mechanism dragging the cars up grades that would tax the strongest horses. As it was, he spent his time scanning the faces of the other passengers.

At the top of the hill he descended from the car,

checked the house numbers, and quickly made his way to the address he'd gotten from the bank, just in time to see Emma Douglas descend the steps and come toward him, her brow furrowed, her eyes cast downward, her step hurried and furtive.

Instinctively, he stepped out of sight, shrugging his coat up around his ears and pulling his hat low. She'd given him the slip once, he'd no intention of giving her a second opportunity. She passed quite close by him but was too preoccupied with her own thoughts to notice a tall, broad-shouldered man barely concealed by a Lombardy poplar. He was about to step out and join her, when he saw Everett Jergens dodging along the row of trees that lined the sidewalk while following Emma. Swiftly, he left his hiding place and crossed the street, turned smartly to the left, and walked toward Jergens. When he'd passed the older man he turned again and, keeping to his own side of the street, followed. So long as Jergens kept Emma in his sight, and he kept Jergens in his, he was confident he'd be close enough to protect her should anything happen.

Emma boarded a cable car but Jergens held back, choosing to wait for the next trolley. Grey waited, too, chafing at the delay. Emma would be all the way to Union Square by the time the next car came along. Still, he suspected her danger came from those she knew rather than from a stranger. With Parnell Wilde safely languishing in Inspector West's jail cell, he believed Everett Jergens posed the greatest threat. He slowed his pace, sauntering casually along the street, stopping to admire the imposing houses along the way, keeping one eye on Jergens pacing restlessly about the trolley stop. When the car finally arrived, Jergens was first on; Grey boarded at the last minute, catching the rail and swinging himself onto an outside seat at the back, well away from Jergens, who'd taken a seat at the front, impatiently leaning forward, as though he could somehow hurry the system.

When they stopped at Union Square, Jergens was first off, thrusting his way through the crowd of passengers and setting off down the plank road toward the mission. Mystified, Grey followed, losing himself in the crowds, yet, because of his height, managing to keep Jergens in sight. Did the man intend to walk the two miles to the mission? And where was Emma? He'd been so sure Jergens was following her, now he wondered if he'd been led on another wild-goose chase. But before they'd proceeded very far, he caught sight of Emma, disappearing through a door set into a stone wall. Jergens halted then slouched into the shadows close by the Sisters of Mercy Convent. Grey took up a position across the street, alert to every movement either from Jergens or the convent.

"I need to speak with your Mother Superior," Emma told the nun who answered her knock at the door. Her heart beat heavily against her ribs. Her whale-boned corset pressed tightly against her lungs. She could hardly breathe within its constrictions. Her palms were damp and her reticule, now holding the key unstitched from her corset, weighed heavily on her arm.

"Wait here, please." The sister showed her into a comfortable parlor. "I'll ask Mother Superior if she is free." The nun slipped out of the room with a quiet whisper of skirts. Emma sank onto a small sofa to wait. Once her eyes adjusted to the dim interior, she studied her surroundings. Pictures of saints and biblical scenes adorned the timbered, adobe walls and richly patterned rugs showing the influence of native Indian and early Spanish cultures covered the stone floors. But the details of the room were overlaid by a soothing timelessness and reverence. The tension in her shoulders eased just a little.

"Miss Douglas? This way, please." The nun who had opened the door to her reappeared and ushered her down a long hallway to the Mother Superior's office at the end of the building, overlooking the garden. The friendly sister announced her name and then withdrew.

"Miss Douglas." The Mother Superior stood behind a large desk, her hands folded into the sleeves of her black habit, her face serene but her eyes alight with interest. "I knew your father. Please sit down and tell me how I can help you."

"You knew Papa?" The obvious surprise in her voice embarrassed Emma. "I mean, he never said . . . we're not Catholic."

"I haven't always been a nun." The Mother Superior smiled with such youthful mischief that Emma blinked. "I knew your father when we were children. We went to school together. We were sweet on each other for a little while; but in the end, I chose the Church. We are a cloistered order. I rarely leave the convent, but Matt used to visit me now and again. I knew he had a daughter. I've been expecting you."

"Why?" Emma was too dumbfounded to be polite.

The Mother Superior shook her head and sighed. "The last time I saw your father he was very troubled. He wouldn't tell me what was wrong but he feared for his safety, and yours. He told me he had some important papers which he daren't keep at home or at his bank. He asked me to hold them for him. I urged him to go to the police, but he refused. He said he wouldn't betray a friend." She turned her head and looked out at the lush garden. "That was the last I saw of him." She turned back to Emma, her eyes sorrowful. "When news of his death filtered through to us, I considered going to the police myself but I could not. After much prayer, I believed I must keep his confidence. Now, what have you to tell me?"

"I know so little," Emma's voice trembled, "but I found this." She withdrew the key from her reticule. "It was hidden in the frame of a photograph and the name of your convent was with it."

"Ah, yes." The nun rose from behind the desk and crossed the room to where a large picture hung on the wall. Carefully she removed it and revealed a small safe. She lifted the ring of keys that hung from a chatelaine at her waist and inserted one into the lock. The safe opened and she withdrew the familiar shape of a safety deposit box. "I believe your key will open this." She returned with the box, setting it on the desk before Emma.

For a long moment, Emma only stared at it. Now that the moment had arrived, when she would finally learn the secret of the message her father had left, she felt paralyzed.

"Go ahead, dear," the Mother Superior urged her, a wealth of kindness in her voice. "Your father was a good man. There is nothing to fear."

With a grateful glance at the nun, Emma lifted the key and inserted it into the lock. Then she took a deep breath and turned the key. The catch snicked open. Her hands trembled as she raised the top on the metal box and peered inside. A sheaf of papers covered with her father's distinctive handwriting met her gaze. She drew them out and discovered the missing ledger pages. She spread them over the Mother Superior's desk and studied each one, noting every meticulous entry with growing disbelief. She was no bookkeeper, but the information was so clear it didn't take an expert to realize Matt Douglas had discovered the thief who had defrauded the bank and attempted to frame him for the crime. She'd been prepared for something of the sort. What truly drove the breath from the lungs was the name of the felon.

She pressed her fingers to her temples and closed her eyes, trying to cope with yet another blow to the world she thought she knew. It wasn't possible. She must have misread the documents. She opened her eyes and studied the pages once more, but the numbers danced before her eyes, making rational thought impossible.

"Do you understand figures?" She turned to the Mother Superior who waited at a discreet distance on the other side of the room.

"I keep the accounts for the convent."

"These papers"—Emma waved helplessly at the pages spread atop the desk—"could you tell me what they say?"

With a sympathetic glance at Emma's anxious face, the Reverend Mother crossed to the desk and read quickly through the first several sheets. "This is evidence proving Everett Jergens guilty of embezzlement. These documents should be placed before the police." She looked up at Emma. "Miss Douglas!" She laid a hand to Emma's brow. "You're so pale, child. Are you faint?" She knelt beside Emma, chafing her hand and peering up into her face. "Who is Everett Jergens?" she asked with acute perception.

"My father's oldest friend." Emma stared round-eyed at the crisp white wimple of the nun's habit. "He's like an uncle to me."

"Oh, my dear." Mother Mary Margaret clasped Emma's hands in a comforting grasp. "It is a bitter cup."

"He's always been there." Emma continued to stare at the nun's headpiece although she didn't really see the starched white fabric. "He stood beside me at the grave."

"Betrayal is the hardest to bear," the Mother Superior soothed her, "and all the harder when the traitor is a friend, but you will prevail. Consider Our Lord Jesus in the Garden of Gethsemane when Judas betrayed him with a kiss. Our Savior knows your sorrow, child, and He shares it. You are not alone."

"What will I do?" The magnitude of Everett's treachery seemed to have robbed her of the power to think.

"You must lay the legal matter before the police," the nun replied without hesitation, "and you must lay the grief in your heart at Our Lord's feet." She closed the security box and locked it, then returned the key to Emma. "I think we'd better leave these here for safe keeping until the police have seen them." She replaced the box in the safe. Then she came back to Emma and took her hand. "Come with me, child. We will go to the chapel to pray. When you have recovered your courage, you will go about clearing Matt's name."

Without protest, Emma followed the Reverend Mother back through the long corridor and into a beautiful chapel. While the nun knelt before the altar, Emma slipped into a pew and tried to order her thoughts. No wonder her father hadn't taken the evidence to the police or to his partners at the bank. For the sake of their friendship, he'd given Everett a chance to explain, a chance to repay his debt. But Matt must have suspected Everett might take desperate action, otherwise he wouldn't have hidden the evidence at the convent. For the sake of his friend, Matt had taken a tremendous gamble—and lost.

She should be angry. She wished that fury would rage

through her veins, releasing her from the paralysis that gripped her. Anger would set her free to weep and to hate and to lash out. But though her mind raced in useless circles, her heart remained numb. Dry-eyed, she rose from the pew and slipped silently from the chapel, leaving the Mother Superior to her prayers. There was only one thing she could do for her father and she regretted it with her whole heart.

She walked out of the convent, her face set, her eyes trained straight ahead, only one thought in her mind. She must get to the police station. She would worry about the consequences later.

After that everything happened so fast she could not recall the exact sequence of events but one minute she was walking down the street, her mind filled with troubled thoughts, the next she was careening into the path of a galloping horse. She caught a glimpse of sharp hoofs above her head and put her hands up to shield her face, too late to dodge out of the way. Then, suddenly, she was seized about the waist and yanked to safety. The whisper of wind from the pawing hoofs fanned her cheek.

"Damn it, Emma, you've scared me half to death." Grey North held her in a hard, fast grip that threatened to break her ribs.

"You're squashing me." She struggled briefly against his hard embrace then turned her face to his shoulder as dry sobs wracked her body.

"Aw, Emma, I'm sorry." His hold slackened, losing its rigidity, yet keeping her safe in a more tender embrace. "Hush, love. It's all right now."

"No, it isn't." She hiccupped into the fine wool of his coat. "Nothing is right." The last pillar in her world had crumbled. She'd thought Parnell Wilde's perfidy had destroyed her trust but that was as nothing compared to Everett's. He'd betrayed her and . . . "What happened?" She pushed herself away from Grey's shoulder and looked up into his scowling face.

"You nearly went under the hoofs of this man's horse." He pointed to an ashen-faced stranger leading a fidgeting horse toward them.

"Miss?" The stranger peered at her as though seeking confirmation that she was all in one piece. "Are you all right?"

Emma nodded, although she still felt weak in the knees, but whether from her near brush with death or the nearness of Grey North she couldn't say. "I'm sorry to have caused you distress."

"It wasn't you." The man's color was returning and with it his indignation. "It was that other chap, running through the street like that, pushing and shoving. There ought to be a law."

Emma's blood ran cold. There *had* been a hand on her back just before she'd looked up to see the horse's rearing hooves above her head. "Did you know the man?"

"No, good thing for him I didn't or I'd have him hauled up before a judge." The stranger looked around the square. "Gone now, of course. Older chap, portly. Surprised he could move so quick."

Beside her Emma felt the quick tightening of Grey's arm about her waist, but all he did was thank the horseman for his skill in avoiding what had seemed like the inevitable trampling of an innocent bystander.

"More credit to you than me," the stranger replied. "I couldn't have held him any longer. If you hadn't snatched the lady out from under his feet, I hate to think what might have happened." He shuddered, then ran a hand down his horse's neck. "It's given Maxim the jitters too. If you're all right, Miss, I'll go let him run off his fidgets."

When the horseman had remounted and left them, the small crowd that had gathered dispersed, leaving Emma alone with Grey. "What are you doing here?" She suddenly realized that Grey had no place in San Francisco. She'd become so accustomed to him being part of her life, in the first moments of shock she'd merely accepted his presence as predictable. Now that her mind was functioning again, the circumstances of their last meeting came crowding into her conscience, leaving her red-faced and self-conscious.

"Chasing you, of course. Surely you didn't think I'd just let you disappear."

"As I recall, my disappearance would have suited you very well." She tipped her chin up in her old defiant attitude, but she didn't feel defiant. She felt hurt and lonely and vulnerable, but she wouldn't use her pathetic state to make a play for Grey's sympathy. "You can let go of me now." She put both hands against his chest and pushed. "I'm not going to collapse."

"You do know it was Jergens who pushed you." Despite her protest he did not release her.

"No." Her denial was quick and automatic but came more from loyalty and habit than from conviction. "There are any number of older, stout men in San Francisco. Anyone might have pushed me. It was merely an unfortunate accident."

"It wasn't, you know. I saw it."

This time she was glad for his support as her legs lost their ability to hold her upright. "You saw Uncle Everett deliberately push me into the path of a galloping horse?"

"Yes."

She covered her face with her hands, trying to block out the pain. She no longer had the strength to fight Grey but leaned on him for his strength.

"Come." He signaled a cab. "You need to get warm. The Palace Hotel," he said to the driver.

In no time they were stepping out of the cab before the impressive entrance of one of San Francisco's most elegant establishments. He guided her in through the grand entrance and commanded the doorman to show them to a private parlor.

"Are you a guest here, sir?"

"Yes," Grey snapped, "now hurry up, man. The lady is in some distress."

"Right this way, sir." They were shown into a pleasant sitting room with a comfortable sofa and a warm fire.

"Sherry," Grey ordered, "and tea." When the porter had departed, Grey seated himself on the sofa beside Emma. "I'll let you decide which you want when they arrive." He caught her hands in a comforting grip, then drew off her gloves, tugging at each finger of the fine leather, setting them neatly on the arm of the settee. "You're freezing, Emma." He wrapped his warm hands about her cold ones while she sat, meek and silent. He chafed her fingers and rubbed her arms, trying to bring warmth to her body, but no amount of fussing could crack the ice that surrounded her heart. She didn't want it to. If she thawed, she would feel, and if she felt, she would be overwhelmed with the pain of yet another betrayal, this one perhaps the worst of all.

Only last evening she had dined with Everett, recounting for him her school teaching adventures and then listening to his beloved voice retell the stories of her childhood. Tales she knew by heart but never tired of hearing. Tales she would never hear spoken by another voice again.

A waiter came in with a silver tea service and a decanter of sherry. He set both down on a low table, then waited until Grey had slipped some money into his hand before withdrawing. "Come here by the fire," Grey said, holding out a glass of sherry to her. "Drink this. It'll settle your nerves."

"Stop ordering me about." She lashed out at the only target available.

"That's better." Grey took her hand and curled her fingers about the stem of the glass. "I worry when you're biddable."

For the briefest of seconds she considered sticking out her tongue but she hadn't the spirit to fight with Grey. He watched her, a deep scowl furrowing his brow, even though his eyes burned with emotion. She turned her back on him and tasted the sherry, letting it warm her from the inside as surely as the fire warmed her from without.

"Have something to eat." Grey stood by the sofa and gestured to the plate of small sandwiches that had accompanied the tea. "Then we'll decide what to do next."

"We?" She stoked her anger against him, using it to shut out the greater pain. "My business is none of your affair."

"Of course it is. We're getting married."

"We are not!" She set her empty sherry glass down on the mantel with a small snap.

"We'll talk about it later." He smiled blandly at her and bit into a sandwich. "Sure you don't want one?" He held out the plate to her.

Her stomach rumbled, but she would rather starve

than give him the satisfaction of accepting his offering. "I couldn't possibly."

"Suit yourself." He took another sandwich for himself, then settled comfortably on the sofa, one arm resting along the back. "Now, suppose you tell me all about *Uncle* Everett and why he tried to kill you."

"He didn't . . ."

"He did, you know." Grey hunched forward on the sofa, his elbows on his knees, his gaze never leaving her face. "It was by the merest breath that you escaped. Did he kill your father, too?"

She gasped, caught by the brutality of the truth she'd been trying to avoid. Hearing Grey put it into words made it real. She pressed a hand to her heart, as though she could ease the unbearable ache.

In two strides Grey was at her side, wrapping her in his arms, crooning softly in her ear, offering all the comfort he could give. She gave up fighting him. Tears coursed down her face, sobs shook her body, and she buried her face against his shoulder as all the hurt and sorrow broke through the last of her reserve. Grey held her, rubbed her back, handed her a handkerchief, and let her cry and cry and cry. By the time she was finished her head hurt, her eyes were swollen, her nose was red, and his handkerchief was a sodden mess. When he pushed her away enough to look into her face she turned her head, humiliated. To a man who'd sworn off marriage she couldn't think of a less appealing sight than herself at that moment.

"I'm sorry," she mumbled through the hand she put up to cover her face.

"Why?" Grey's abrupt question brought her glance swinging back to his face. "For loving your father? For mourning his death? For feeling the betrayal of a trusted friend?" He shook his head slightly, then pulled her close again, resting his chin against her hair. "I don't see you've a thing to apologize for, Emma."

"I've ruined your handkerchief."

She felt his chuckle deep in his chest. "I don't mind." He pressed a kiss against her brow, the touch of his lips on her skin driving out the worst of her hurt. "Now, will you have a cup of tea and a sandwich and talk to me like a sensible woman?"

She nodded slightly and then wished she hadn't, for when he released her she felt bereft all over again. Taking herself firmly in hand, she lifted her chin, sniffled once, then balled up the handkerchief and dropped it into her reticule. "I could do with some refreshment." She walked with firm step to the sofa and seated herself at one end. There would be no need for Grey to touch her again.

"Where were you going when you were knocked down?" he asked from his vantage point beside the fireplace.

"To the police."

"Why?" The hard voice demanded an answer.

She glanced toward him, then looked away before giving him an account of her actions. Even as she detailed the evidence that pointed to Everett's guilt, she felt as though she were telling someone else's story. The villain of the piece could not be her beloved friend.

"In that case," Grey said, "we must complete your mission. I'll go with you."

"Yes." She nodded but made no move to stir from the cozy room.

"Emma, you can't hide your head in the sand forever." Grey came to kneel beside her, taking her hands in his. "The man tried to kill you. You can't give him a second chance."

"But he'll hang." She choked on the word. How could she explain to this determined and confident man that she couldn't bear to be the cause of Everett Jergens's execution, no matter how well deserved.

"I expect so, if it can be proved he killed your father. Remember that, Emma. Even if you're willing to forgive the crimes committed against yourself, are you willing to ignore the wrongs done to your father?"

"No." She arose and shook out her skirts. She'd received so many shocks in one day her mind was addled. Before everything else, she was determined to clear her father's memory. She must put that first. She drew a ragged breath and tilted her chin. "I'm ready."

"Good girl." Grey took her arm and escorted her from the hotel, through the bustling, busy streets and on to the police station. He insisted on accompanying her when she was escorted into the captain's office.

"Well, Miss Douglas, that's quite a tale." The captain of police regarded her with a mixture of respect and disbelief after she'd recounted her information. "Of course, my department will have to investigate your story. If it proves out, we'll bring charges."

"And what of the attempt on Miss Douglas's life?" Grey's usual urbane manner was conspicuously absent. "Do you intend to give Jergens another chance to harm her?"

"Now, don't get all het up." The captain favored Grey with a fierce scowl. "I'll have my men be on the lookout for him. In the meantime, Miss Douglas, I'd advise you to take care. Is there a friend you could stay with for a while?"

The best friend she'd had for the past two years was the man who now stood accused of attempting to murder her. She shook her head, helpless.

"I'll see to the lady," Grey growled, "but the sooner Jergens is locked up, the better."

"That's settled, then. Do you want to give me the key to that box or come with me yourself to retrieve its contents?"

"I prefer to keep the key myself." Emma felt for it inside her reticule, a sense of relief passing over her when her fingers closed on its knobbly form, her last connection to her father.

"Let's go, then." The captain walked smartly around his desk and opened the door, waiting while Grey and Emma preceded him. "I'm going out," he barked to the sergeant at the desk. "If you need me, I'll be at the Sisters of Mercy."

Outside on the street while they waited for the captain's buggy, Emma felt her courage waning. She tensed every time an impatient pedestrian jostled her, flinched at the sound of hoof beats, and found herself clinging to Grey's arm with a death grip. She deliberately loosened her fingers. Grateful as she was for his support, she mustn't allow herself to become dependent on him. As soon as Everett was apprehended, Grey would be free to go and she would be alone.

"What will you do now?" Grey asked. They had seen the documents safely into police custody and now stood on the boardwalk in Union Square.

"I don't know." She looked about in bewilderment, as though expecting an answer from the city. "I'll have to go back to Uncle Everett's house to collect my things." She didn't tell him that she was nearly destitute. She'd counted on Everett to support her until she'd found another position.

"I won't let you go back to Jergens's house."

"But I must. I've nowhere else to go."

"I'll take a room for you at the hotel."

"You will not! Do you want to ruin what little reputation I have left?"

"You disappoint me, Emma. I thought we'd gotten beyond worrying about what people say."

She blushed so hotly she felt as though her face were on fire. "Only in the wilderness, Mr. North."

"Then come back to the wilderness—with me."

"No." She turned on her heel and strode toward the cable car, catching hold of the brass rail and swinging herself on board as it passed. To her chagrin, Grey did the same, taking the seat beside her, not one whit abashed by her effort to put him in his place.

"Very well, then, we'll both go. The housekeeper can protect your good name."

"I'm not playing games." She glared at him, attempting outrage but all too conscious that as far as Grey was concerned, her reputation could never be salvaged. In the eyes of society, she'd committed an unpardonable sin, but no one else need know if Grey would just go away.

"Neither am I, Emma." He shot her a hard stare. "We *will* do the right thing."

She turned her face away and they completed the ride to the top of the hill in silence.

When they disembarked from the trolley she set out for Everett's house at a brisk pace, resolutely silent. Grey strode moodily beside her. *Aren't we a fine couple?* She grimaced. They weren't even married and already he treated her like an odious obligation. No matter what Grey considered the "right" thing, she would not marry him on those terms. Much better to put him out of her mind, and out of her heart, and to seek out some other position even more remote than Prospect.

"Oh, Miss," the housekeeper greeted her at the door. "I'm so glad you've come. It's Mr. Jergens."

"What about him?" She felt a knot of fear forming in her stomach.

"He's gone crazy. I sent Fergus to fetch the police."

Chapter Ten

"Where is he?"

"In the study, sir. He's locked himself in and I heard him smashing things. I think he has a gun."

"Wait here." Grey thrust Emma behind him, then looked to the housekeeper. "Show me."

But Emma wasn't about to wait quietly in a corner while the two men she loved best in the world faced each other over a loaded pistol. She pushed past him and dashed down the hall to the room at the back of the house. "Uncle Everett," she shouted, rapping on the door and rattling the handle. "Uncle Everett, let me in."

The door was wrenched open and he stood before her. His clothes in disarray, his face flushed, the smell of whiskey on his breath. He brandished a bottle in one hand and a revolver in the other.

"Abigail!" A deathly pallor replaced the drunken flush. He staggered backward. "I thought you were dead."

She froze, all the life drained from her. "It *was* you?" she whispered. Despite everything, she'd hoped . . . but the guilty look on Everett's face confirmed the truth she'd tried so desperately to avoid.

"Stay back!" Everett raised the gun. His hand wobbled, but the barrel pointed straight at her chest. "Don't come any closer," he shrieked, his eyes blazing with a mad desperation.

"Drop it, Jergens." Grey lunged past her, using his broad shoulders to shield her slighter frame. There was a deafening explosion. A bullet whistled past Emma's ear. She screamed and saw Grey grab his arm, blood seeping out between his fingers. Everett cocked the pistol again, taking a second aim.

"Uncle Everett!" Emma screamed, and plunged toward him, trying to knock the weapon from his hand. "Don't!" But the man was past reason, past logic, and past the reach of love. He grabbed her around the waist and held her between himself and Grey, the gun pressed to her temple.

"Back off!"

"Easy, easy." Grey stepped back, his hands in the air, the blood oozing steadily onto his sleeve. "Let her go, Jergens. You don't want to hurt her."

"Just stay away."

"Okay." Grey moved to lean against the window frame. "See. I can't reach you. Just let Emma go."

"I can't. She's all I have left."

"What do you mean, Uncle Everett?" She forced herself to remain calm, to speak as though they were discussing the latest book in his library rather than debating whether he should shoot her. Surely the years of comradeship and love would break through the insanity she'd glimpsed in his desperate face the instant before he'd fired the gun. "You have everything."

"I don't." His voice rose to a demented shriek. "Matt had everything. Everything I wanted. He had your mother, you, the bank, wealth, position—everything. It should have been mine. I loved your mother first, Abigail. I would have made her happy." He was sobbing; she could feel the shaking of his body, but the pistol remained pressed to her head. "Claire would have married me; but then she met Matt and cast me aside. Oh, she was happy to be my friend, to dance with me at parties and let me escort her when she went riding, but I wanted more. I would have given her everything."

"But she's been gone for years." Everett's fanatical passion after all this time bewildered her.

"Yes! I never had the chance to make her love me." His breath rasped against her neck as his grip on her waist tightened. "But then," his voice took on a cunning tone, "I decided I could still win. I'd gain a fortune to make Matt's look like pocket change. I risked everything with a pair of prospectors who told me they'd discovered the richest deposit in California. But they lied, Abigail!" He was shrieking now, hysteria overcoming reason. "They kept coming back to me, demanding more money. To dig a deeper shaft. To hire more men. To buy more equipment. Their demands were insatiable. What was I to do? I couldn't afford to walk away. And then I knew." His voice dropped to a sly whisper. "I took the funds from the bank." He chuckled with wild glee.

"At first I thought of it as a loan. I'd pay back every cent once we struck gold. I managed for five years." He sounded proud of his accomplishment; then his voice changed again, charged with hate. "I'd have been all right, too, if that reclusive old biddy hadn't decided to pay a surprise visit to the bank. She hadn't used her account in years." He whined now, like a petulant child. "Why did she have to choose the one day I was away? After years and years, she'd decided to change banks and wanted all her money. Selfish bitch!" He jabbed the gun hard against her head. "Of course, the ledger didn't match her passbook, and Matt," he sneered the name, "your precious Papa started an investigation of every account we held. He should have trusted me!"

"You're right," Grey shouted. His face was white, perspiration stood on his lip, but his eyes held cool and steady. "Matt Douglas wronged you." His tone was conversational, as though he could calm the desperation in Everett's mind. "You were right to frame him for the embezzlement. How did you do it?" As he talked he inched his way along the wall, closing the distance between himself and Everett. Emma prayed his ploy wouldn't end in disaster.

Everett's grip relaxed slightly as he turned his attention to Grey. "It was easy," he crowed. "I'm an excellent bookkeeper—not that the partners appreciated me."

"But how did you make it seem like Matt?" Grey was so close she could see the dampness of the blood on his sleeve.

"I made a few false entries over his forged signature. It was child's play." Everett sounded almost indifferent to the details of the theft, but his calm didn't last. His voice rose again to a shrill howl. "But he found me out. He confronted me. Said he had the evidence." He was sobbing now, his breath rasping hot and moist on her neck, but his grip never slackened. The gun never left her head. "I shot him, Abigail. I had to. He was going to expose me. I couldn't let him send me to jail."

"Of course not." Grey's voice was cool and controlled, but she could see the dread in his eyes. "You had no other choice. We understand. But you have a choice now. You don't want to hurt Emma, do you?"

"She'll tell." The gun pressed so hard she nearly cried out in pain.

"No!" Grey's hoarse shout echoed off the walls. Emma stumbled as Everett jerked her backward, making sure she stood directly between him and Grey.

"Get back!"

"Okay, okay." Grey raised his hands in a placating gesture. "Tell me what happened next, after you killed Matt."

"I put the gun in his hand to make it look like suicide," Everett explained, as though it were the most natural thing in the world. "I even faked the note. It really was his writing, you know. I used the letter he'd sent me. I just tore off the bits that mentioned my name. It was perfect. But before I could find the false ledger pages, Parnell Wilde showed up and I had to get away."

"You've been very clever, sir."

Emma fixed her eyes on Grey's agonized face, praying he wouldn't risk his own life for hers. She tried to shake her head at him, to send him away to safety, but even as she made the attempt she knew it was pointless. Grey would never abandon her with a madman.

"If only I could have found the ledger sheets," Everett complained. "For two years I've looked and looked, but I can't find them. I even broke into your old house, Abigail, to search for those pages. It was me who ransacked your room in Prospect, you know. But you didn't have them. Of course, you wouldn't," he crooned, as though talking to himself. "You're like my own daughter. You'd never betray me, would you, Abigail?" She could feel the sweat pouring off his face and soaking into the neck of her gown. He was completely irrational.

"Of course not, Uncle Everett." She twisted slightly, trying to ease away from the gun, give herself a chance to run if Grey got close enough to grab it. "Why don't you let me go now and we'll talk this over. We can help you, Uncle Everett. I'm sure you never meant to hurt anyone."

"I never meant to hurt you, Abigail. But you ran away from me."

"Oh, Uncle Everett." Her voice shook with emotion. "I didn't run away from you. I ran away from the gossips and from my grief. Never you."

"Is that true?" His hold on her slackened, the gun barrel easing away from her head.

"Of course, Uncle Everett. You were my only friend."

"Oh, my dear child. Thank you for throwing a crumb to a grieving old man." The gun moved. There was a horrific explosion close to her ear. She screamed and fell forward as his arm dropped from about her.

"Uncle Everett. Uncle Everett!" She lay on the floor, tangled in her friend's arms, and for the second time in her young life witnessed the results of a bullet to the head. "No. No." She covered her eyes, shaking with horror. "No!"

Before she could do more she was snatched up in a pair of strong arms and carried from the room. "In there." Grey jerked his head toward the study as a policeman and the butler came rushing toward them. "Get a doctor," he barked to the housekeeper and strode up the stairs, shouldering open one door after another until he found the room with Emma's belongings.

He laid her onto the bed, removing her hat, loosening her jacket. "It's all right now, love. I've got you safe."

"Your arm?" she whimpered, mesmerized by the red stain that continued to spread along his sleeve.

"A scratch. That's all." Grey shrugged off her concern. "You're shaking." He yanked the quilt over her. "Where the hell's that doctor?" he growled at Mrs. Fergus as she came bustling into the room with a jug of hot water.

"Right behind me, and I'll thank you to mind your language in front of Miss Douglas." The housekeeper elbowed him aside. "I'll tend to her now, sir. You'd best remove yourself from her bedroom."

After all they'd been through, the housekeeper's concern for propriety struck him as ludicrous. Still, Mrs. Fergus could do more for Emma now than he could. Bowing to the inevitable, he did as he was told and left the room, coming face to face with the doctor in the doorway. "You the patient?" The doctor looked at the blood on his coat sleeve.

"No." He jerked his head toward Emma's room. "Your patient is in there."

"Looks to me like you need bandaging."

"It'll keep." Shock and a fear that gnawed a hole in his stomach made him abrupt. "See to the lady."

"Very well, but you'd best wait for me downstairs."

He nodded and proceeded down the elegant stairway to the main floor of the house. A swarm of policemen buzzed in and out of the study, and he saw a litter arrive to carry Everett Jergens's body away. He turned away, suddenly dizzy, and sought the refuge of the front parlor. It wasn't the loss of blood alone that forced him to seek a chair where he could put his head between his knees and draw deep, revivifying breaths. As long as he lived he doubted he would rid himself of the sight of a madman with a gun pressed to Emma's head. He shuddered and leaned back in the chair, resting his head against the cushion, stretching his legs out in front, and staring at the ceiling, afraid to close his eyes. The sooner he married her the better. For all her independence, Emma needed a protector.

Some time later the doctor found him there. The house had quieted, so he presumed the police had finished their business and departed. "Now, let's have a look at this." The doctor produced a pair of scissors and began to cut away the coat and shirt from Grey's left arm. He would have protested but the effort didn't seem worthwhile. The coat was ruined anyway.

"You're lucky." The doctor squinted at the torn flesh of his upper arm. "Bullet passed right through. No real damage."

"It hurts like hell," Grey growled, irritated that he should be considered lucky after being shot.

"Expect so." The doctor poured out a tincture and pressed it into the wound.

If he thought he'd been in pain before, it was nothing compared with the agony that shot through him now. He had to fight to keep from swooning as the doctor cleaned the wound before wrapping his arm with bandages.

"Fergus," the doctor spoke to the butler who hovered just inside the door, "get this man a whiskey." When the butler appeared a few minutes later with the requested spirits, the doctor had packed up his bag. "Drink this." He took the whiskey and handed it to Grey. "If it's not enough, have another. You'll be in some pain for a day or two, but the big worry is infection. If you become feverish, send for me." He nodded to the butler and departed.

Grey downed the whiskey in one gulp, then held out his empty glass. "I'll have that second." He attempted an insouciant smile but failed miserably.

Fergus poured him another glass of Everett Jergens's best whiskey. "Might I suggest you seek your bed, sir?"

"Good idea." Grey sipped more slowly at the second drink. "Can you call a cab? Don't think I'm up to the trolley car."

The butler coughed slightly. "There are plenty of empty bedrooms here, sir. Mrs. Fergus would be happy to make one up for you. We'd feel better," he added hastily before Grey could protest. "I'll watch for that fever the doctor mentioned."

It was a tempting offer. He'd be close to Emma. Jergens couldn't harm her now, but he'd had the fright of his life watching that gun at her head. "How is Miss Douglas?"

"She's resting now. The doctor gave her something to make her sleep. The poor girl. She was like a daughter in this house." The butler shook his head, a mixture of sorrow and disbelief deepening the lines in his aged face. "I don't know what's to become of us all now. Mrs. Fergus and I, we've worked for Mr. Jergens for over twenty years." He wrung his hands together. "And Miss Douglas? Where will she go?"

Grey gestured to the whiskey bottle. "Get another glass, Fergus, and drink up. You've earned it."

"Yes, sir. I believe I will." The butler poured out a full measure of spirits for himself and downed it in one gulp. Then he placed the glass on the tray, straightened his lean shoulders, and assumed his usual impassive bearing. "And you'll stay with us for a bit, sir?"

Grey nodded and Fergus went off to inform his wife.

After a long and painful night, well fortified by the whiskey bottle, Grey's head ached abominably and his arm throbbed with every beat of his heart, but there was no fever and no blood seeped through the doctor's neat bandages. His physical recovery would be swift, but the nightmare of what might have happened would haunt him to his dying day. Consequently, when he met Emma at the breakfast table, he was unusually sharp with her.

"What are you doing out of bed, woman? Haven't you the sense God gave a donkey?"

"Good morning to you, too." Emma glared at him, then pointedly turned her back.

He closed his eyes briefly and prayed for patience. When he opened them she had left the room. Just like he remembered in his own home. His mother and father could never spend more than five minutes together without his father issuing an ultimatum and his mother shrinking into herself as though trying to be invisible. It seemed the new Lord North was no better than the old one.

He speared ham and eggs onto his fork and put it in his mouth, chewing and swallowing without tasting but determined not to insult the housekeeper as well as his wife. At least, he corrected himself, the woman who would become his wife as soon as he could arrange the legal details. He sighed. Hard to believe the waspish woman who'd walked out of the room was the passionate "angel" who'd shared his bed and shown him a glimpse of Eden.

He pushed away his empty plate and closed his eyes against the ache in his head. How had he been so naive as to let Emma Douglas trap him into marriage? He wasn't a green youth. To be fair, it was he who'd insisted on marriage, not Emma. She'd run away. Run away and nearly gotten herself killed. He shuddered and rubbed a hand across his brow. What had she been thinking, dashing past him like that? She'd no business scaring him that way. He brooded on his grievance, adding layer upon layer, probing the sore spot on his heart as surely as the doctor had probed the wound on his arm. The results were just as painful.

Upstairs a door slammed and the sound of a woman's

feet hurrying down the stairs brought him from his chair and out into the hallway just in time to catch Emma before she sped out the front door. "Where are you going?" He caught her arm before she could put her hand on the doorknob.

"Not that it's any of your affair," she glared at him, "but I've business to attend to."

"It is my affair," he shot back. "You're my fiancée."

Sparks of temper exploded in her eyes and he knew he'd blundered. "It may have escaped your notice, Mr. North, but we are in America now, and females have the right to say whom they will and will not marry. *I* will *not* marry you."

He cast a quick look behind him, checking to see if Fergus or his wife lurked within earshot. "Come into the sitting room," he hissed, "where we can talk in private."

For a moment he feared she would defy him, but in the end, she gave a short nod and led the way into the room where the doctor had bandaged him up only yesterday.

"Very well, then." She didn't sit down but stood in the middle of the room facing him, her chin tipped at a defiant angle. "What do you have to say?"

"I want your agreement to marry me as soon as it can be arranged."

"Why?" She glowered at him as though he were one of her unruly pupils.

"Why?" He was stunned. "For heaven's sake, girl, you know why. I've ruined you, and now I must do my duty and make an honest woman of you."

Emma's face had paled alarmingly during his speech and he wondered if she were about to swoon, but when he would have offered her his arm, she brushed him aside. Her voice was faint but steady when she replied,

"You've done your duty and I've refused you. There is nothing more to say. You are free to go."

"You can't be serious." He took a step toward her, lowering his voice. "Have you considered that you might be carrying my child?"

It didn't seem possible that she could pale further, but her skin took on the waxen hue of death; still she would not yield. "If I am, it is none of your concern."

"Don't be ridiculous. How will you support yourself, let alone a child as well?"

"I'll manage."

"Emma," he tried a coaxing tone, "you're overwrought. When you've had time to consider, you'll realize that I'm right." He ran a hand around the back of his neck and looked at the floor. "I've something to tell you."

"Yes?" she prompted when he fell silent. He looked at her face and saw some of the color had returned to her cheeks and a glimmer of something like hope shone in her eyes.

"My father has died." He made the bald statement. "I am now Lord North. As my wife, you will be a titled lady."

The hope he thought he'd glimpsed died in an instant, replaced with a cold fury. "And you think that matters to me? That I'll be persuaded to marry a bully, because he holds a title?" She made an exclamation of disgust. "Well, I thank you for your *gracious,*" she leaned on the word, "your gracious offer, but I decline the privilege of being Lady North. You see, I've too much of the revolutionary spirit to be swayed by arguments of rank and title."

"I didn't mean . . ." He tried to salvage what little regard she had for him.

"Please"—she held up her hand—"no more. I've listened while you stated your case. Despite all your persuasions,

I remain firm. I will not marry you, Lord North. Now, please, if you are sufficiently recovered from your wound, leave these premises."

"Very well." He yanked a card from his pocket and scribbled the address of his father's solicitors on the back. "I must return to England. You can contact me here when you come to your senses, and I'll make arrangements for you to join me." When she refused to take the card he dropped it on a table, along with the money she'd left to pay for her room in Gold City, and stormed out.

Out of the room and out of the house, he strode down the street in only his shirtsleeves. Mrs. Fergus had managed to launder and mend his shirt but had declared his coat past saving. He barely felt the cold. Temper warmed him all the way to the Palace Hotel and on to the booking offices of the Union Pacific Railroad.

By evening he was on the train to New York, his passage booked on a steamer to London. Before the month was out he'd be home. He slumped in his seat and stared out the window at the darkened country speeding by. He couldn't really apply the word home to the cheerless pile where he'd lived the formative years of his life and where his mother still resided, but it was the place where duty bound him.

When Grey left her, Emma stood frozen in the middle of the sitting room waiting for the hurt just under her heart to ease. She played the scene over and over in her head, searching for some small solace in Grey's words but finding none. Not once had he said he loved her. Not once had he touched her with affection. Not once had he apologized for calling her a liar and a cheat. His proposal, she could hardly call it that, his order that she marry him was based solely on his warped idea of chivalry and the notion that he had despoiled her virtue.

Well, she gave herself a mental shake, she was no longer a virgin but she was still a whole and capable woman. She would not enter into a union with a man who despised her, merely to assuage his conscience. Even if it broke her heart.

"Excuse me, Miss," the butler tapped on the door, "there's a gentleman here to see you."

"What sort of gentleman?" She was in no mood to deal with newspaper reporters or curious opportunists.

"I believe it's a lawyer."

Emma sighed and stripped off her gloves. She really hadn't anything urgent to do. She'd invented the excuse of business in order to flee from Grey. His departure saved her the trouble. "Show him in here, Fergus, and ask Mrs. Fergus to bring in a tea tray."

When the butler withdrew, she seated herself in a high-backed chair with her back to the window. The light wouldn't shine on her face and she could disguise from her visitor the ravages of the past twenty-four hours.

"Miss Douglas?" Fergus opened the door and a small gray-haired man in a starched collar and tight coat stood before her.

"Yes?"

"I'm Joseph Ainsworth, Miss Douglas. I've handled Mr. Jergens's legal affairs for the past number of years. I wish to read his will to you."

"But I'm not related," she protested. "I believe there is a cousin still living in Minnesota."

"You are the only person named in the will." The lawyer sat down on the settee and opened his briefcase, taking out a folded legal document. "The opening paragraphs deal with the usual preamble attesting to Mr. Jergens's place of residence and his state of mind at the time of the writing of the will." Mr. Ainsworth flipped over the first page and ran a finger down the second until he came to the pertinent sections. "Yes, here is the significant portion." He cleared his throat and began to read, " 'To my dearest Abigail Emma Douglas, I bequeath all my property, wherever situate. It is my wish that she should enjoy the full privileges of my wealth without encumbrance.' " The lawyer flipped through another couple of pages and frowned.

"Of course, this will was written some years ago, when Mr. Jergens's estate was considerably greater. However, I can assure you that this house is yours, although it is heavily mortgaged. There is an insurance policy that will pay off the outstanding debt and leave you some small sum for investment."

"But Uncle Everett committed suicide." She gazed blankly at the earnest little lawyer.

"The policy is of long standing. I believe your claim will be accepted."

For a long moment she merely stared at him, unable to process the stunning information that her financial troubles were at an end. She could resume her former life—shop in the mornings, take tea in the afternoons, and attend parties in the evenings. No need to search for another teaching position. No need to shiver in a cold schoolroom while she waited for the fire to catch. No more Bessie Smith. No more trustees. No more wilderness.

"Miss Douglas?"

"Oh! Yes, of course. I don't know what . . ." She made an effort to stop babbling. "I'm sorry, I've received several shocks in the past two days."

"I understand, Miss Douglas. If I may offer my services, I would be happy to execute the will for you and to attend to any other matters you may care to entrust to me."

"Thank you, Mr. Ainsworth, I would count it a great favor."

"Of course, Miss Douglas." He folded up the will and returned it to his briefcase. "It will be my pleasure. I can meet with you at my office, or call on you here when I have matters to discuss."

"Thank you, Mr. Ainsworth. If you send me word, I can come to your office." She rose, signaling an end to the interview, and the lawyer took his leave.

Immediately she went in search of Fergus and his wife to relate the latest startling turn of events. "Oh, Miss, I'm so pleased." Mrs. Fergus reached out her arms to hug her the same as she had when Emma was a child. The butler was more circumspect but his smile was no less broad.

"That's that, then." He rubbed his hands together. "Will you be wanting to make any changes, Miss?"

She started to shake her head, then remembered the gory scene in the study and changed her mind. "Only Uncle Everett's study. Once the police have finished, we'll do it over as a sewing room for you, Mrs. Fergus."

"Very wise, Miss." Fergus left them.

"What would you like for dinner, Miss?" The housekeeper began a lengthy account of the contents of the larder and the possible dishes she could prepare for the evening meal. Such a mundane topic after all the traumatic events of the past twenty-four hours gave Emma an insane desire to laugh. Instead, she listened politely to Mrs. Fergus's ramblings, agreed to all her suggestions, and left the topic of menus in her hands.

"I'm sure whatever you decide will be perfect." She left the kitchen and went to the sitting room to retrieve her gloves. She had to get outside, away from the stifling atmosphere of the house, out into the fresh air, where there was no smell of blood or hate or madness.

For lack of a better alternative, she took the cable car down the hill and made her way to the Woodward Gardens. The flower beds were bare at this time of year, so she wandered through the conservatory, seeking peace for her soul among the exotic blooms. By the time she returned home for dinner, she had achieved a measure of outward calm. Inwardly, she struggled with an aching heart. In time she supposed she'd grow used to the loneliness. In time Grey North would become a distant memory, their night of passion a foolish escapade best forgotten.

"The table is set in the dining room, Miss," Fergus informed her as he took her coat. "Mrs. Fergus says she will serve up in twenty minutes."

"Thank you, Fergus." She walked slowly up the stairs to her room, removed her gloves and hat, and brushed the droplets of moisture from her hair. In Prospect it would be snowing, the trees covered with a sparkling mantle that caught the sun and dazzled the eye. Here, winter was merely drab and damp. She put the unhappy comparison from her mind and went downstairs to dine in solitary splendor. The dining room table was far too large for one person. The china, crystal, and silver far too elaborate, and the five-course dinner far too lavish. In the midst of luxury she longed for Mrs. Royston's simple kitchen and hearty shepherd's pie.

When dinner was over, she turned reluctant feet toward the study. She forced herself to walk through the room, touching the familiar objects, trying to recall the happy times she'd spent there. Times when Everett fed her candies from a secret store in his desk drawer, or when she was a little older, produced trinkets of jewelry from that same drawer, while he told her stories of her mother. Stories her father didn't know. If she concentrated on the good times, perhaps she could blot out the sight of her beloved "uncle" waving a gun and threatening her life while his eyes glazed with madness.

Fergus had removed the blood-soaked rug and replaced it with another from the attic, but a stain on the wall served as a stark reminder of her last, violent meeting with her old friend. She touched the tall window frame and shuddered. She would never forget the sight of Grey standing there, blood oozing from his arm.

She moved to the big, heavy desk and sat down in the worn leather chair, catching the scent of shaving cream and cigar smoke that permeated its depths. She ran her fingers along the leather blotter, then opened the top drawer and looked inside. There was nothing there but a welter of bills. No candies, no trinkets. She pulled out the papers and smoothed them, noting that most were marked past due. She settled herself to sort the contents of the desk and discover the true sum of his debts.

When she reached the bottom of the last drawer, it was late and her eyes ached with fatigue. The pile of unpaid bills was stacked on her left, a sheaf of legal papers on her right. The usual flotsam that accumulates in a desk she'd thrown into the fire. She bent down and peered into the back of the bottom drawer and saw one more bundle of papers. She reached in and drew them out, catching her breath when she recognized a photo of her mother on top of a packet of letters. With shaking hands, she untied the ribbon that held them all together. She opened the first envelope, took out the thick sheet of paper, and began to read.

It was a love letter, written by her mother to Everett Jergens, full of passion and promises and the overly romantic gushing of a very young woman. She folded up the page and put it back in its envelope. Then she took up the second, but her hand faltered as she opened the flap. These were private. Whatever had happened between her mother and Everett had happened before she was born. She turned the bundle over and picked up the last letter. This one was a note of farewell. Her mother had met Matt Douglas. Matt was loyal, dependable, and steadfast, her mother had written. She did not share a grand passion with him as she had with Everett, but she was looking to the future. Grand passions tended to burn out, leaving the lovers bereft and bitter. Better to choose wisely and for the long term. Matt was devoted to her and would make an excellent husband. She was sorry, but better that she and Everett should part now than wait until they had exhausted themselves with the power of their infatuation and grown weary and cold toward each other. Claire concluded by saying she would always treasure his friendship.

Emma folded the letter and tucked it back into its envelope. She retied the bundle and sat staring at it for long moments before picking it up and carrying it to the fireplace. No doubt there were more secrets contained in the thick vellum pages, but she didn't want to know them. Everett had loved her mother with a white-hot passion and been badly let down. He had a right to his privacy. She would pry no further. As the flames caught the dry paper, flaring upward in bright tongues of fire, she pondered Claire Douglas's view of marriage. Was friendship and trust and dependability more necessary than passion? Having loved Grey North, could she ever settle for something as lukewarm as friendship?

Far off she heard the ringing of a church bell and then another and another. Startled she opened the window to look out and listen. In the distance, down by the harbor, she could see flares exploding in the night sky. A crowd of revelers passed under her window singing and shouting, some of them dressed in fanciful costumes. With a start, she realized it was New Year's night. The stragglers in the street had been part of the parade. She waited until the last bell stopped chiming, then closed the window. "Happy New Year." She offered her reflection an ironic salute.

Grey watched the English landscape flash by the train windows, the tension in his shoulders growing tighter with each passing mile. Every rotation of the wheels that brought him closer to Northmount estate tightened the noose of responsibility about his neck. He felt as though it would choke him. The green English countryside, so beloved of the poets, left him unmoved. He much preferred the dark forests and soaring peaks of Canada. When the train pulled into the station, the jostling crowds irritated him, making him long for the wide open spaces of his new country.

"Sir?" His gaze swung around to the coachman who'd accosted him.

"John?" He grinned as he recognized the accomplice of the youthful escapades that had so enraged his father. He clapped the other man on the back and shook his hand. "It's good to see you, John."

"And you Mr. Greydon, or, I should say, Lord North." The coachman returned his handshake and then seemed to remember himself. He stepped back, drawing an impassive mask over his friendly face.

"Never mind that," Grey growled. "How's my mother?"

His gaze roved up and down the platform looking for his luggage.

"Eager to see you, sir." John moved past him and Grey followed, headed for a pile of luggage being unloaded at the far end of the station.

The coachman and one of the trainmen loaded the trunk into the boot of the coach and tied it in place. Then John hoisted himself onto the driver's seat while Grey stepped reluctantly into the coach. The conveyance made him feel claustrophobic, and he much preferred to handle the horses himself. At least the journey to Northmount was only a few miles long. He leaned back against the plush cushions. His father's carriage was well-sprung and well-appointed, confirming the solicitor's opinion that he was now responsible for a considerable fortune.

The carriage swayed as they turned in the short drive that led to the house his father had dubbed with the wildly inappropriate title of Northmount Castle. The only topography resembling a mountain was a faint rise behind the house, and in Grey's opinion, a turret stuck onto a plain square house didn't make it a castle. Perhaps that's why he'd disliked Mrs. Allen on sight. Her pretensions reminded him of his father.

When the carriage stopped, he opened the door and jumped to the ground before John could descend from his perch. "Drive on," he shouted, and watched the carriage lumber on toward the stables. He was here now. Might as well get on with it. He paced toward the front entrance with long strides. Benton must have been on the watch for him, for the door opened before he'd set foot on the bottom step.

"Welcome home, Lord North." The butler bowed and

pretended he'd never scolded Grey as a boy for tracking dirt from the barnyard into the front parlor.

"Thank you, Benton. Good to see you." He removed his long coat and handed it to the butler, together with his hat and gloves.

"It has been some time, my lord." The old eyes raked him from head to foot. From old habit, Grey straightened his shoulders and hoped the dust on his boots could be overlooked by token of his long journey.

"Where is my mother?"

"In the library, my lord, but perhaps you would like to change before going in to her."

Apparently his dust could not be ignored. He shrugged and turned toward the stairs. If Benton wanted him to wash and change his shirt he'd no objection.

"I'll have your trunk sent up immediately, my lord. Dodson," he named his father's valet, "is waiting for you in the master bedroom."

Halfway up the stairs, Grey halted and looked back. "Then send him to my room."

"But, my lord."

"And stop calling me 'my lord' with every breath." The tension that had been building since he'd left San Francisco boiled over.

"Yes, sir." The butler was as impassive as stone.

"Bah!" Grey took the rest of the stairs two at a time. He'd hoped that with his father gone he could come home with good grace, but even without his father's harping presence, the house itself oppressed him.

A half hour later, properly groomed and dressed, he went to greet his mother in the library. It had been five years since he'd last seen her, but he remembered that, as a wife, she'd been nearly invisible. No doubt, as a widow, she'd hidden herself away in even deeper seclusion. He prepared himself for a dismal meeting. He was considerably surprised, therefore, when a youthful, vibrant woman looked up from a map of the estate spread out on his father's desk, her face breaking into a wide smile.

"Greydon!" She rushed toward him, her arms outstretched. "At last!" She launched herself into his embrace with all the enthusiasm of a child.

"Hello, mother." Grey submitted to her hug, surprised by the strength of her arms as she tugged at his shoulders, bringing his cheek down to her level. She kissed him, then leaned back holding his hands in hers and spreading her arms.

"Let me look at you." She let her gaze run over him, her eyes lighting with pleasure. "Handsome as ever," she declared, "but surely you didn't manage to travel all the way from Portsmouth in those clothes."

"No, Dodson took me in hand. Made sure I was presentable before showing myself to you."

"For shame! Don't tell me you came home after all these years and didn't come to me the instant you arrived."

"Benton seemed to think I needed cleaning up." A rueful grin pulled at the corner of his mouth.

"Yes, Benton." His mother scowled and dropped his hands. "Your father's servants are determined to keep me in my place. You'll have to dismiss them."

"I beg your pardon?" He watched in amazement as she perched on the edge of the desk, crossing her legs and swinging one foot in irritation.

"I'd do it myself," she explained, "but your father's solicitor says I can't. Something about the terms of the will. However, you're the new lord. I expect you can get rid of them for me. Oh, don't look so bemused," she laughed as he gaped at her. "Did you think to come home to a weeping widow set to fasten herself about your neck and drag you into her welter of grief?"

The picture she described was so accurate of his anticipation he had to wonder if she'd become psychic. Again she seemed to read his mind and chuckled. "Come"—she slid off the desk and took his hand—"let's take a walk about the garden and talk."

"Walk in the garden?" He raised one eyebrow and pointed his chin to the steady drizzle outside the window.

"Oh, a little rain won't hurt us." His mother marched to the door calling for Benton to bring her coat and umbrella. "I can't stand being cooped up inside for hours on end."

Bemused, he shrugged and followed her into the front hall, wondering if some alien spirit had come to inhabit his mother's body. The notion was no more bizarre than the reality of the cheerful, robust woman shrugging into an oversize macintosh. "Thank you, Benton." She took the umbrella from the butler's hand.

"Might I say, ma'am, that I strongly advise against venturing out in this weather."

"No, you may not." She turned on her heel. "Hurry up, Greydon," she tossed the words over her shoulder and strode outside without waiting for him. He caught up to her before she'd reached the gravel path leading down into the dreary looking garden. "You see what I mean?" she said. "They insist on treating me like a not-too-bright invalid, and I won't have it. You'll have to get rid of them, Greydon."

"Perhaps I could instruct them to treat you like a very bright invalid instead."

She giggled and slid her arm through his. "It's so good to have you here. Tell me all about Canada. Your letters were far too brief."

As he talked, they paced along the paths between the barren flower beds. She listened with her head cocked to one side, watching his face, as he recounted tales of adventure in the wilderness and sketched a picture of the Rockingham and Prospect.

"You're going back, aren't you?" she asked as they rounded the last bit of shrubbery and found themselves facing the drive.

"What makes you say that?" He avoided a direct answer.

"It's in your face and your voice. When you speak of your new country you fairly glow with enthusiasm."

The drizzle was turning to a steady downpour. "Let's go indoors." He avoided her too-perceptive gaze. "I've only just got here. Plenty of time to talk about what comes next."

"Yes," she agreed, then tapped her finger against his chest, "but I'm counting on you to protect me from the clucking hens inside."

"I promise." He grinned and caught her elbow to hurry her through the rain. They burst through the front door, laughing and shaking the water from their clothes.

"Madam, you'll catch your death!" Benton hurried forward to take their wet things. "If you'd care to retire for a little while before dinner, I'll send Martha to you with a hot posset."

Seeing his mother's glower, Grey stepped between her and the hovering servant. "It's all right, Benton. We'll just build up the fire in the library and dry ourselves out."

"Of course, my lord." Benton spoke through stiff lips, and for a moment Grey was tempted to give in to his mother's request and sack him on the spot. Instead, he caught her eye and grinned, inviting her to share his amusement.

But Lady North was in no mood for mirth and stalked off to the library muttering under her breath. Grey caught up to her there just in time to take the fireplace poker from her hand before she stabbed the embers into ashes. "You'll put it out altogether." He carefully stoked the fire and laid a new log onto the coals, then seated himself in one of the capacious armchairs and enjoyed the sight of his mother striding up and down the room holding a muttered conversation with herself. "You must be warm enough now," he said when she had traversed the carpet several times. "Why don't you sit down and talk to me?"

"Oh dear!" She hurried toward him, her face stricken with chagrin. "Here you are, barely in the house after years away, and I'm treating you to a show of bad temper." She perched on the arm of his chair and touched her fingers to his hair, smoothing it back from his brow as she had when he was a child. Unerringly she found the small scar at his hairline, the relic of a rock-climbing adventure. His father had thundered at him for the better part of an hour when he'd been brought home with blood streaming down his face. Not because of the injury, he was rather proud of his son's venturesome spirit, but because the accident had occurred while Grey was in the company of the coachman's son.

His mood darkened and he pulled away from his mother's caress, a scowl pulling at his features. "What happened to him?" He slouched lower in the chair, folding his hands across his chest and staring hard at the toe of his boot.

His mother didn't pretend to misunderstand. She rose from her perch on the chair arm and moved to a seat on a small sofa. "He took a stroke, dear. You remember, his was a driven personality. If he wasn't in a temper about something, he was just as worked up over his latest enthusiasm. His doctor often urged him to take a holiday, but he never did, not even to go grouse shooting with his friends."

"Or to take you on a trip to the continent." He didn't try to hide his bitterness.

"Well, that was a foolish wish." His mother smiled sadly. "What I really wanted was for him to share his life with me. But . . ." She paused for a long moment, twisting the ring on her finger. "You're very like him, you know."

"Never!" The word exploded from the depths of his soul.

"Oh, you're not bullying or loud"—she gave her head a tiny shake— "but you are passionate and single-minded . . . and stubborn."

"I am not." His denial was hot and instant.

"See?" She smiled at him, a gentle, mocking curve to her lips that made him feel foolish.

"At least I'm not loud," he muttered.

"There's nothing wrong with passion if it's tempered by reason, and a single-minded approach is necessary to worldly success. Even a modicum of stubbornness can be useful, but not when it drives a man and his son apart."

"It was his fault." He sounded like a petulant ten-year old and he knew it, but he'd nursed his grievances against Alexander North for so long he couldn't give them up.

"Yes, it was." His mother surprised him by agreeing. "He was old enough to know better. You were only a boy." She caught his gaze and held it with an unrelent ing scrutiny of her own. "But you're older now. You should be wiser."

"How so?"

"You could be a little forgiving. Try to see things from his point of view."

"How can you say that?" He waved a hand toward her, indicating her appearance. "You seem happier now, as a widow, than I've ever known you. Don't tell me he didn't make your life miserable." Her cheeks whitened and he was instantly contrite, coming out of his chair to kneel by her side, clasping her hands in his. "I'm sorry. I had no right to say that."

"Why not?" She patted his hand. "It's the truth." She took a deep breath and smiled fondly into his face. "Marriage is a very complicated business, my dear. If you stay for a while, I'll tell you about mine."

Benton entered, looked down his nose at mother and son huddled together in an undignified embrace, and announced that dinner would be served in twenty minutes. His tone strongly implied that they should clean themselves up before coming to the dining room.

Chapter Eleven

Emma paced restlessly through the rooms of the house that was now hers. It was only a month since Everett's death and she felt as though her world had turned inside out for a third time in two years. First, the police had revised their verdict on her father's death, so it was now officially listed as a murder. Then, thanks to Mr. Ainsworth's diligence, the will had been processed in record time, giving her possession of Everett's house, and a settlement from the insurance company that paid off his debts. Finally, the lawyer had pressed the bank to restore the funds they'd wrongfully seized from her father's accounts, with the result that she was now a wealthy woman. As far as society was concerned, it was as though she had never been away. Doors which had been closed to her now opened wide. She was free to resume her old life.

But she wasn't the same Abigail Douglas who'd fled the city in sorrow and disgrace. She was Emma now, a woman tested and tempered by life. In Prospect, she had known harsh reality, but she had also tasted purpose and independence. For all the comfort and convenience of

San Francisco, she found herself bored. She missed Mrs. Royston's cheerful gossip, missed the satisfaction of useful work, missed the challenge of surviving on the edge of the wilderness. She even missed Bessie Smith.

She left the ornately furnished sitting room and wandered into the kitchen, to find Mrs. Fergus baking bread. The homey smell, reminiscent of Mrs. Royston's house, brought Prospect sharply to mind. Did Bella still bake cakes for Jed Barclay? Was Mrs. Allen still looking down her nose at her husband's parishioners? Had Rose learned to make toast? Had Grey . . . She clamped her mind shut on the thought. She would *not* think about him.

"Was there something you wanted, Miss?" The housekeeper brushed butter over the newly baked loaves. "You seem a bit distracted."

"Oh, it's nothing, Mrs. Fergus. I'm just not used to being idle all day."

"Well, it's time you did." Mrs. Fergus scowled and swatted at the flour on her apron. "It wasn't right that you should have gone off into the wild to teach a bunch of unruly brats. You're a lady, Miss, and don't you forget it. Why don't you go calling on your friends?"

"I'm meeting Janie Baxter later." She trailed a finger across the floured tabletop. "We're going shopping, and then we'll have tea at the St. Francis Hotel. I'll be back in time for dinner."

"That's fine, Miss." The housekeeper's face was wreathed in smiles. "I hear there's to be a ball at the Mortimer house."

"Yes." She didn't seem as excited about the prospect of the ball as Mrs. Fergus, even though her new wardrobe included several ball gowns. She'd spent hours yesterday trying them on and studying her image in the mirror. The dresses fit perfectly. The fine fabrics felt wonderful against her skin. The colors and styles showed off the elegance of her figure and enhanced the creaminess of her skin. She'd tried her best to be thrilled, but mostly she was bored.

"If you'd like to go into the morning room," Mrs. Fergus suggested when Emma picked up the kettle and set it down again, "I'll bring you a cup of tea."

"Thank you, Mrs. Fergus." Emma accepted her dismissal and meekly did as she was bid. She might be mistress of the house, but the kitchen belonged to Mrs. Fergus. Shaking her head at the ridiculousness of her situation, she went to the small desk set into the bay window of the morning room and took out paper and pen. When Mrs. Fergus brought the tea she was deep into a long letter to Mrs. Royston.

She finished her letter, drank her tea, then pulled on her gloves, waved a final farewell to Mrs. Fergus, and took herself off, determined to enjoy her outing. It was only the strangeness of returning to her former life that made her feel discontent, she assured herself. It had nothing whatever to do with missing Grey North.

She caught the cable car at the end of the street and told herself how happy she was to be living in a city with such a modern convenience. As she wandered through dozens of shops, she deliberately contrasted their luxury with the sparse offerings of Jed Barclay's Mercantile and Miss Watson's millinery. Over tea with Janie she tried not to compare the St. Francis with the Rockingham.

"Did you know Todd Rivers is coming to the Mortimer ball?" Janie asked with a sly glance at Emma's bare left hand.

"Really?"

"Wasn't Todd an old flame of yours? Before Parnell Wilde came on the scene?"

"It was so long ago." Emma sipped her tea, then placed the cup onto its saucer. "Isn't he married?"

"No." Janie's eyes practically snapped with excitement. "Everyone thought he was going to pop the question to Amy Roch on New Year's Day, but he didn't." Janie slanted a sideways glance at Emma. "Haven't you heard from him?"

"He did pay a condolence call," Emma admitted.

"Condolences for your father's murderer?" Janie's eyebrows rose in a sharp vee.

"Perhaps condolence was the wrong word. He'd heard about the shooting and came to be sure I hadn't been injured."

"Of course." Janie grinned broadly and helped herself to another dainty sandwich. "So what are you wearing to the ball? I believe Todd always liked you in blue."

"I haven't decided yet if I'm going."

"I'm sure Todd would be happy to call for you if you're worried about going alone." Janie cocked her head to study her friend from under lowered lashes.

"Don't be ridiculous. The Mortimer house is only three blocks away." To a woman who'd built the morning fire in Prospect's schoolhouse for two winters, the journey was a mere stroll in the park.

"Then what are you dithering about?" Janie moved on from the sandwiches to the sweets.

"Nothing." Emma made up her mind and snatched a tiny cake before Janie could eat them all. It was foolish of her to spend evening after evening shut up in Everett's house trying to fill her hours with reading and needlework. A ball was just what she needed to get her back into the swing of things. "What's your dress like?" she asked, then listened with only half an ear as Janie described the creation of tulle and silk she hoped would captivate James Stockley and force him to realize he couldn't live without her.

"I wish he'd hurry up and ask me," Janie concluded. "It's so embarrassing to be twenty-two and still not married, but James has always said a man can't ask a woman to be his wife until he's well launched on his career."

"And is he?"

"Yes," Janie breathed, "at last. He's been promoted to news editor at the paper. The job comes with a raise."

"Do you really intend to live on a newsman's salary?" Emma looked at the expensive walking dress Janie wore and the stylish arrangement of her hat. "Wouldn't your father make you an allowance?"

"Of course, he would." Janie clicked her tongue in annoyance. "I told James so, two years ago, but he insisted that if he couldn't support a wife, he wouldn't have one. Where do men get these ideas?"

"Goodness only knows." Emma pinned a bright smile on her face to cover the pang in her heart. Grey North had some foolish ideas about marriage too, but she wasn't about to share that information with anyone, not even Janie.

"Men!" Janie pulled a face and giggled. "What would they do without us?" She reached across the table and clasped Emma's hand in both of hers. "It's so good to have you home. I've missed you. Don't go away again."

The night of the ball Emma dressed with care, spending far longer than necessary twisting her hair into a fashionable arrangement on top of her head, pulling loose a few tendrils to curl down her neck. The sapphire-blue gown was a dream of silk and velvet, the style emphasizing the slenderness of her figure. Thank goodness the huge bustles of previous years had fallen out of fashion. She touched the bare skin at her throat, then opened the top drawer of her dresser and took out a flat, velvet-lined box, flipped up the lid, and drew out a cameo pendant on a silver chain. She fastened it about her neck, then stood back to inspect herself in the long mirror. The cameo was lovely, but she'd bought it for herself. There was no love from an adoring father or indulgent uncle to warm its cool ivory.

She studied her image again and saw the perfect picture of a fashionable young lady dressed for a ball. So, why weren't her eyes sparkling? Why did her cheeks seem too pale? She pinched them to bring in the color and chewed on her lips for the same reason. Then she abruptly whirled away. Grey had said she bit her bottom lip when she was nervous. She wasn't the least bit nervous.

She tossed a heavy cloak around her shoulders, tying the strings tightly, picked up her evening bag, and left her room in a small rush. She would not spoil her evening thinking about Grey North.

"You look lovely, dear." Mrs. Fergus stood at the bottom of the stairs, watching her headlong descent.

Emma paused, then placed her foot on the next step with delicate precision, descending the rest of the stairs in a graceful glide. "Thank you, Mrs. Fergus. I believe I'm in the latest style."

"You should have an escort." Mrs. Fergus frowned.

"Fergus will accompany me to the door," Emma dismissed the housekeeper's concern, "and come back for me later. I'll be quite safe."

"You should go in a carriage."

"It would take more time to harness the horses than it will take for us to walk." Emma moved toward the front door where the butler awaited her. "Don't fuss, Mrs. Fergus."

"I wish that nice Mr. North hadn't left so suddenly." The housekeeper refused to be quelled.

"Well, he did," Emma said shortly. "Good night, Mrs. Fergus." She stepped outside. It was a clear night with a hint of frost in the air. Stars twinkled from a velvet sky, drawing her eye unerringly to the largest, the north star. She dropped her gaze, focusing her attention on the walkway. "Come along, Fergus." She stepped out briskly. "It's too cold to stand about."

The butler regarded her with silent disapproval, apparently sharing his wife's views on the proper way to attend a ball, but he did step smartly along at her side. In barely more than ten minutes they'd arrived at the Mortimer mansion. Lit torches lined the driveway leading to the imposing entrance. Marble steps fronted a wide porch, its roof supported by fluted Corinthian columns. Every window gleamed with light. The sound of music spilled out into the courtyard. It was a scene she knew well, one where she should feel at home, and yet tonight she was a stranger.

The last time she'd attended a ball she'd been engaged to Parnell Wilde and her father had been among the most respected men in the city. The people she would meet here tonight she'd once considered her closest friends. They had invited her back into their circle. She should be happy. She straightened her shoulders and set her foot on the bottom step. The door was flung open onto a huge hall filled with light and music and color.

"Thank you, Fergus. I can manage on my own from here." The butler grumbled something unintelligible but stood aside. Chin high, she mounted the stairs, alone, and swept through the front entrance.

"Good evening, Miss." The butler glanced at her invitation, then gestured for a maid to relieve her of her heavy cloak. When she was ready, he announced her name, Miss Emma Douglas, and she moved forward to be received by her host and hostess.

"Abigail Douglas! Well, I declare!"

"I'm called Emma now."

"Oh, well . . ." Mrs. Mortimer stuttered and looked to her husband for guidance.

"Emma, is it?" Mr. Mortimer took her gloved fingers between his hands and studied her face a moment. He seemed to like what he saw for he nodded approvingly. "Welcome to Mortimer House . . . Emma."

She passed on into the ballroom, a huge rotunda in the center of the house, rising to the second story and surrounded by a gallery. She let her gaze follow the line of the curving stairs and ornamented balustrade to discover a small orchestra. She couldn't help but smile as she compared the Mortimer ball with Prospect's entertainments where Les Smith and his fiddle provided the music and the schoolroom provided the floor for the dancers. She wondered if the Mortimer guests would have as good a time.

"You're here." Janie grasped her arm and dragged her behind one of the pillars where they could watch the whirl of dancers without being trampled by them. "What took you so long?"

"Don't you know it's fashionable to arrive late?"

"Pshaw! I never want to miss a minute of the fun. Oh, look!" She pointed to some place across the ballroom but pulled Emma even farther into the shadow of the pillar before she could determine the object of Janie's interest.

"What? I can't see anything with you pushing me into the wall." Despite her grumbling, Emma was glad for

Janie's enthusiasm and girlish pleasure. She needed someone to brighten her mood.

"It's Todd." Janie hissed in her ear. "He's looking this way." She whirled about, sending her skirts flaring. "Get out there." From hiding Emma in a corner she now pushed her forward with such strength she jostled a pair of dancers and had to apologize.

"Janie!" she protested, but swallowed whatever else she'd intended to say when Todd Rivers bowed before her.

He beamed with pleasure. "Welcome home."

"Thank you, Todd. It's good to be here." She made the polite rejoinder automatically.

"Hello, Todd." Janie bobbed at her elbow.

"Good evening, Janie," Todd replied without taking his eyes from Emma's face.

"Aren't you going to admire my dress?" Janie pouted.

"No." He continued to gaze into Emma's face, a warm smile creasing his cheeks.

"Todd Rivers, you're a horrible person." Janie wrinkled her nose but her attention was diverted when James Stockley was announced.

"May I have this dance?" Todd held out his arm as Janie dashed toward the end of the receiving line.

Emma nodded and stepped lightly into his arms. They circled the room to the strains of a Strauss waltz. "I've missed you." Todd guided her expertly between the other couples.

Now was the moment when she should simper and produce an arch reply; that's how the game of flirtation was played. But life had changed for Emma, and she no longer indulged in silly games. "It's kind of you to say so," she replied instead.

Todd's extraordinarily handsome face darkened slightly. "Do you have any plans, now that you're home?"

"Not yet. It's so soon after Uncle . . ." She missed a step and would have tripped if Todd hadn't tightened his arm about her waist, holding her up while she regained her balance.

"I understand." He looked down into her face, pity and outrage warring in his eyes. "You shouldn't have had to endure all that. No woman should be exposed to such ugliness." He smiled again. "Tell you what, I'd like to make you forget the bad times. We could start by going riding tomorrow. What do you say?"

The music ended but he still held her loosely in the circle of his arm waiting for her answer.

"Come after lunch," she said, and watched his eyes light up.

"My turn." Janie's older brother tapped Todd on the shoulder as the orchestra struck up a lively polka.

"All right, but I take her to supper." Todd relinquished her only after he'd written his name on her dance card.

The rest of the evening passed in a whirl of color and sound and laughter as old friends took the opportunity to greet her, acting as though the horrific events of the past two years had never happened. Emma smiled and joked and accepted invitations to teas and concerts and a bridal shower, but all the time she felt like an outsider watching someone else perform her part. When Todd took her into the dining room for the midnight supper, her shoes pinched, her face ached from smiling, and her eyes burned from too much heat and light.

"Are you feeling ill?" Todd asked as he brought her a glass of lemonade. "You look pale."

"I'm not used to such late nights." She took a grateful sip of the cool drink. "A schoolmarm in Prospect has an eight o'clock curfew."

"I've never understood why you disappeared like

that." Todd sat down beside her. "You had friends here who could have helped you."

"Not really." She glanced at him from under upraised eyebrows.

He looked discomfitted for a moment, apparently conceding the truth of her statement. "I would have helped you," he said finally, his eyes dark and intent, a ruddy flush tinging his cheeks. They sat in silence for a few moments before Todd spoke again. "Parnell Wilde seems to have disappeared, too."

It was a statement, but she could hear the question behind it. "Yes," she replied and chewed on a dainty sandwich while she considered how much she wanted to tell Todd. "I believe he has left the country," she said finally. "I doubt we'll see him again."

Instantly Todd's face brightened. "Do you want more?" He gestured to the empty lemonade glass in her hand. "Or would you rather have tea?"

"Neither, thank you. What I would really like," she glanced at him apologetically, "is to go home."

"Of course." She could hear disappointment in his voice but he recovered almost at once. "May I escort you?"

"I'd like that," she said, thinking it would save her the trouble of sending for Fergus; but the brilliant smile that wreathed Todd's face told her she might have given a false impression. "I'm really very tired." She tried to emphasize the reason for her decision.

"I'll send for my carriage."

"Couldn't we just walk? It's only a step and the fresh air will do me good."

"If you wish." He looked doubtful. Young ladies in San Francisco did not go out walking at midnight. Society imposed rules as harsh as any the Prospect school board could dream up. Only Grey North had encouraged her to ignore the rules and live life to suit herself—until she'd stepped on one of his rules. Then he'd gone all righteous, making that preposterous offer of marriage. For all his fine words, he was just as hidebound as Mrs. Allen.

She turned a determined smile on Todd and got to her feet. "I wish," she said firmly. Their exit from the supper room was slowed by the press of people, but eventually they gained the relative quiet of the front hall. A maid produced Emma's cloak and Todd's coat and, at last, they were outside in the crisp darkness.

"That's better." Emma drew a deep breath, hugged her cloak tight to her body, and set off at a vigorous pace.

"Hey, what's the hurry? Todd ran a couple of steps to catch up with her.

"It's too cold for a stroll."

"But the moon is shining." He pointed to a full moon directly overhead. "Isn't that romantic?"

It was, she admitted privately, but she wasn't ready for romance with Todd Rivers. She glanced upward, again seeking the north star, then pulled her attention back to the street under her feet. *Drat Grey North.* She would not waste her time remembering moonlight and magic with him. "Here we are." She pointed to the lamp shining in the window of Everett's house. She didn't yet think of it as her own. "Fergus will be waiting up for me. Thank you for seeing me home." She held out her hand to him.

"Until tomorrow." He raised her hand to his lips, his eyes never leaving hers. He kissed the back of her hand, then turned it over and pressed his lips to her palm before closing her fingers over it. "Dream of me," he said, then stood watching until she'd mounted the steps to her front door and been admitted. "Tomorrow," he called softly as the door closed behind her.

"You're home early, Miss." Fergus took her cloak. "Did you not enjoy the ball?"

"The ball was lovely." She headed toward the stairs. "I'm just not used to late nights. Thank you for waiting up, Fergus. I don't need anything more." She hastened into her bedroom and lit the lamp beside her bed, its soft glow a relief from the harsh brilliance of the new electric lights at the Mortimer mansion.

She kicked off her shoes and pulled the pins from her hair, letting it fall about her shoulders. By the time she was ready for bed her headache had disappeared but, perversely, she was no longer tired. She blew out the lamp, then moved to the window, drew the curtains aside, and looked up into the sky, compelled to gaze, not at the romantic moon Todd had pointed to, but at the constant light of the north star.

"There's a letter from Prospect for you," Fergus announced, a few weeks later, as he brought her breakfast. After a week of sitting alone at the dining room table, she'd felt so lonely and absurd, she'd stopped using the formal rooms of the house and now took most of her meals on a tray in the cozy morning room.

"Thank you, Fergus." She set aside her book, *The History of Woman Suffrage,* and reached eagerly for the envelope he proffered. Susan B. Anthony and her colleagues were engaged in important work but, for the moment, news from home took precedence. She broke the seal and pulled out the closely written pages, wondering when she had begun to think of Prospect, instead of San Francisco, as home. Then she began to read.

My dear Miss Douglas (Emma),

Thank you for your letter. I send you my sincere cond lences on the loss of your old friend. You have suffered so many losses in so short a time, my heart aches for you. If you'll take my advice, you'll leave that terrible city and return to Prospect. A new life, Emma. That's what you need.

Now, to our news. The school trustees have found another teacher to finish out the term. Louisa Graham has come out from Toronto for an extended visit to her sister, the new Mrs. Sean O'Connor, and has agreed to fill in at the school until you return or a permanent replacement is found. Do come back, Emma. Our plans for the First Annual Victoria Day Concert are well under way and I'm counting on you to play for us. The new piano is supposed to arrive as soon as the ice is out of the river. Mr. North made all the arrangements before he left for England. It'll be shipped by rail to Gold City, but not even Mr. Paget felt ready to haul it overland on a snow road. And speaking of Mr. North—isn't it exciting? We may have a true English lord living in Prospect! Mrs. Allen is telling everyone he won't return here, now that he has inherited his estate in England, but I hope she's wrong. I've put his name forward to open the ceremonies for the Victoria Day Concert. Mrs. Allen thinks it should be her husband and Mrs. Carlton thinks it should be her husband, the mayor, but I hold that Lord North is practically royalty and deserves the honor. I've sent a letter to him via his solicitor. Jed, you remember Mr. Barclay . . .

Emma could practically hear the simper in Mrs. Royston's voice.

. . . he says I mustn't set too much store by Lord North. Jed says an English nobleman has too many responsibili-

ties. He'll not be returning to Prospect. It's the first time I've disagreed with Jed, but we've agreed not to argue.

Oh, I must tell you about Rose. That girl! She's gone and got herself a job at the Rockingham. Seems the cook there took a shine to her when she helped with my dinner, so now she's helping out in the kitchen—I pity the patrons who have to eat her cooking—but she's getting a regular pay packet and that's a great boon to her parents. I've let her keep her room here, with me. It wouldn't do for her to live alone at the hotel. She's an irritating little snip, but I won't let her ruin her reputation. Pay packet or not, she'll be properly chaperoned until she has a wedding ring on her finger.

The weather has been most severe. The snow is five feet deep in my front yard. . . .

The letter went on to describe Bella's struggles to find a replacement for Rose, her gratitude to Jed Barclay for keeping her walkway cleared and for shoveling a path to her chicken house so she could gather the eggs and feed the hens, and ended with another admonition for Emma to return to Prospect.

Work will heal your sorrow, Emma, and the frontier needs women like you.

Yours most sincerely, Bella Royston.

Emma read the letter through twice, while her coffee cooled in its cup, then folded the page and tucked it back into the envelope. For a long time she sat, tapping the letter against her fingers while she stared into nothing. Finally, she picked up her breakfast tray and carried it to the kitchen, the breakfast largely uneaten. Work and the frontier, Bella claimed, would heal a person, heart and mind. She glanced out the window at the leaden February sky and felt a sudden longing for clear mountain air and brilliant sunshine. Even five feet of snow seemed preferable to the constant drizzle of San Francisco in winter. She shook her head to clear her thoughts. Surely she could find meaningful occupation without returning to Prospect and risking a meeting with Grey North.

But Grey was in England and unlikely to return. She pushed open the door to the kitchen with a jab of her elbow. She didn't care. If she wanted to stay in San Francisco, she would, and if she decided to return to Prospect, she'd do that, too, no matter what Grey North might do. "I'm going out for a walk." She handed the tray to Mrs. Fergus. "I need some fresh air."

The Mortimer ball was merely the beginning of the social season. Every day Emma received callers and invitations. It was as though, having wronged her once, San Francisco society was determined to take her to its heart as never before. She attended concerts and plays, went riding, took walks along the plank street to the mission, and attended an endless round of parties. In all of these excursions, Todd Rivers was her constant companion.

Todd stood beside her when Janie and James announced their long-awaited engagement at an afternoon reception in the Baxter home. Amid the general hubbub of congratulations and good wishes, he held her hand and refused to let go when she would have freed herself. "People will talk," she whispered and tugged at her fingers.

"I hope so." Todd looked intently at their clasped fingers. "Emma, I'd like to call on you tomorrow. May I?"

"You've called on me nearly every day for weeks." She tried to divert the serious intent in his voice with a flippant rejoinder.

"Only to escort you to some affair with dozens of other people. We need to talk, Emma, just you and I."

There could be no mistaking the subject Todd wished to discuss, and she reluctantly agreed to expect him at three o'clock the following afternoon. After all the time they'd spent together, it was only natural, and, she supposed, he had every right to expect her to return his feelings. Todd was everything she could wish for, handsome, wealthy, and charming. He was attentive and obliging. He would make a good husband. She'd be a fool to dither and risk losing his affection. And yet . . .

"I must go and give Janie my best wishes." She finally withdrew her hand from his and escaped into the crowd of laughing young women who surrounded the bride-to-be.

"Emma!" Janie caught her in a tight hug and whispered in her ear. "You'll be next. I'm so happy for you."

"I wish you all the best," Emma replied, masking her disquiet. "You and James deserve your happiness."

When the party began to break up, Emma was one of the first to take her leave. "Come tomorrow and talk wedding plans," Janie invited.

"Not tomorrow. I've another engagement."

"Oh, I see." Janie raised her eyebrows and looked significantly toward Todd, then giggled and squeezed Emma's arm. "In that case, you're excused."

Feeling as though the world were closing in on her, Emma escaped into the late afternoon sunshine, rejecting Todd's offer to see her home. She wanted time alone. "I'll see you tomorrow," she said by way of excuse when she saw the hurt look on his face.

It was a relief to spend an evening at home. She had

a quiet dinner served on a tray while she read before the fire. The food was tasty and the book one of her favorites, but she couldn't settle. She carried her used dishes into the kitchen and would have lingered to help clean up except that Mrs. Fergus chased her away. She wandered back to the sitting room and tried to lose herself in the book, but her mind kept jumping away from the words. At last, she closed the pages and sat brooding until the fire had died down to mere embers.

At ten o'clock she climbed the stairs and prepared for bed but couldn't sleep. A long time after she'd blown out the lamp she lay wide awake, staring into the darkness. Finally, she left the warmth of her bed to kneel by the window. With her gaze fixed on the north star, she searched her heart, seeking the answers to her restlessness, forcing herself to confront the raw truth of her desires. Much later, she crept back to bed, at peace with herself, and fell into a deep and contented sleep.

In the morning she was up betimes, had her breakfast, and left the house early. She caught the cable car down to the business district and presented herself at Mr. Ainsworth's office mere minutes after it opened for business. Despite having no appointment, the lawyer met with her immediately. An hour later she departed, well pleased with the outcome of their discussion.

She spent another hour strolling the shops, hunting for a wedding present for Janie, and finally caught the tram back to the top of the hill in time to eat luncheon and prepare for her interview with Todd. By two-thirty she was waiting for him in the sitting room, a decanter of sherry at the ready. At three o'clock precisely Fergus admitted him to the house.

"You look beautiful." He came to clasp her hand. "I've always thought so."

"You've never seen me clinging to the gunnels of a canoe at the edge of a rapids." She gestured to the tray with a decanter of sherry. "Please, help yourself."

"I don't know how you managed in such primitive conditions." He ignored her offer of refreshment. "If I have my way, I promise you'll never know hardship again."

"Actually, you can't make that promise." She moved away, going to stand in the long window, gazing out at the street but not seeing it. "You see"—she turned her head to look over her shoulder—"I'm going back."

"What!" He stood motionless in the center of the room. "Emma, you can't. I've come to ask you to marry me. I thought you understood." He came toward her and would have embraced her if she hadn't put up a hand to stop him.

"I'm sorry, Todd, truly I am." She flinched when she saw the hurt bewilderment on his face. She hated causing him pain, but to marry him would be worse. Todd was too fine a man to be saddled with a wife who loved another man.

"But all these weeks, we've been together constantly." He took her hand again, holding it against his heart. "What's happened? Have I offended you? If I have, I apologize. I wouldn't hurt you for the world. Darling Emma, just tell me what's wrong and I promise you, I'll set it right."

"It's not you, Todd." She stared at the floor and wished he didn't look so abject. "It's me and it's this"—she waved her free hand to indicate the luxurious room—"and the frivolous life we lead. I thought I wanted it," she begged him to understand, "but I don't. I've realized that. I want work and purpose in my life. I've been infected with the frontier spirit." She attempted a small smile. "I don't belong here anymore."

"But you don't need to work. I can provide for you, Emma. Anything you want."

"No, you can't, Todd, because what I want can't be bought. I want to feel needed. I want to feel I'm contributing. Being a schoolteacher can be frustrating work, but it also has extraordinary rewards. When I teach a child to read, I've opened the world to him. When one of my girls passes her senior matriculation, I've set her on a path to independence. No amount of wealth can give me that, Todd."

"There's another man, isn't there?" He shoved his hands into his pockets and turned his back to her. He hadn't listened at all. A hint of irritation pulled her brows together.

"There was," she admitted, determined to be honest both with Todd and with herself, "but he's gone. Back to England to take up his title. I'm going back to Prospect to be useful, not to take a husband." She moved away from the window to stand beside the sofa, feeling just the slightest bit impatient that he continued to press his suit.

"There's charity work you could do here. Give me a little more time, Emma. I know I can make you love me." She heard the thread of desperation in his tone. Her irritation vanished under a wave of guilt.

"I'm sorry, Todd. It was wrong of me to accept your escort all these weeks. I didn't mean to lead you on, but I won't compound my error by offering you false hope."

"My mother has formed a ladies musical club. They organize recitals for young performers and contribute to a scholarship fund for gifted pianists. You can be useful here, Emma." Once again he hadn't listened.

"It's not the same, Todd. There are other people to do

the work here. In Prospect, I'm truly needed." She tried to soften her refusal. "I'm so sorry, Todd. You've been a wonderful friend. I wish I could return your affection, but believe me, I'm not the right wife for you."

For a long moment he stared at her, his eyes dark with disappointment; then he shook his head, as though coming out of a daze. "It has nothing to do with Prospect, Emma. You're still in love with him. You should have told me sooner." He spun on his heel and stalked from the room. A few seconds later the front door slammed and she was alone. She sank onto the sofa and touched her fingers to her forehead, rubbing at the tension that knotted her brow. She had now refused five offers of marriage—six if she counted Grey's, although his was more a command than a proposal—she should be better at it.

She left the sofa and poured herself a glass of sherry, then held it high. "To old maids," she said aloud, then tipped the spirits down her throat.

Grey drew his horse to a halt on the small rise from which his father had drawn the grandiose name for his estate. He turned in the saddle to face the woman who held her mount easily beside him. Since the day he'd arrived home, his mother had been a source of constant amazement. Today she'd taken him on a tour of the estate, pointing out where she'd had fences repaired, improved water supply to the cattle, and experimented with a new strain of wheat.

"It's a hybrid," she explained. "We're using the methods pioneered by Gregor Mendel in Austria. I'm hoping to get a strain that resists mildew."

"What do you know of science?" He didn't mean to

sound insulting but astonishment drove him to blurt out the question without regard to good manners.

To his relief, his mother threw back her head and laughed. "Oh, Greydon," she chortled, "you are so like your father. He thought a woman should be empty-headed too."

"I admire intelligent females," he protested as a picture of Emma Douglas's shrewd green eyes flashed into his mind.

"Intelligent females!" his mother scoffed. "You mean you like to dally with women who can amuse you with clever words, but in your wife or your mother or your daughter you expect banal inanities and no threats to your exalted male position."

"Mother!" he expostulated. His father had been known to entertain ladies of the *demi-monde* on occasion, but Grey had believed his mother knew nothing about such matters.

"Because a woman is willing to tolerate certain situations in her life doesn't mean she's deaf and blind."

"You knew?"

"Of course, I knew." She dismounted and walked toward a small outcropping of rock. Grey followed, leaving the horses to crop at the grass.

"I'm sorry." He braced one foot against a boulder and leaned his elbow on his knee while she found a seat on a flat, smooth rock.

"At first I was so angry," she looked sadly into his face, then sighed and turned her head to gaze over the meadows below them. "I wanted so badly to share every part of your father's life, to be important to him, to be, as our wedding vows demanded, his helpmeet. But he wouldn't let me. He took a wife to produce an heir, to act as hostess to his friends, and to keep a comfortable house. He did not look to me for companionship." Her mouth turned down at the corners, deepening the lines from nose to lip. For the first time since he'd come home she looked her age.

But the moment passed quickly. She turned her gaze back to him and smiled, banishing the gloomy moment. "That was then," she said, "and this is now. Don't be sad for me." She stood up and brushed the dust from the skirt of her riding habit.

"Forgive me," he said as they strolled back to the horses, "I don't mean to be rude, but you are so different now."

"Now I'm myself." She let him boost her into the saddle, then drew the reins into her hands and looked down on his puzzled face. "This is who I am, Greydon. Alexander wanted me to be someone else. Come on," she flashed him an impish grin, "I'll race you to the stables."

"No fair," he shouted as she sent her horse flying down the slope before he'd remounted. He bent low over the stallion's neck and urged him on, catching the slower mare as they shot into the stableyard.

"Good girl!" His mother patted her horse's neck and walked her around the paddock for a moment before dismounting and handing her over to the stable hand. "You had the advantage of me in your mount." She cast a calculating eye over the stallion. "I've a notion to try Storm myself." She cocked her head and watched the horse being led into the stable.

"No! He's too much for you." Grey's answer was quick and definite, but when he caught the defiant gleam in his mother's eye he hastily changed tactics. "I wish you'd reconsider. Storm requires a strong hand. Are you sure you have sufficient strength to manage him?"

"Well done." Lady North grinned and slipped her arm through his. "You see, son, a woman is a perfectly rational being when you treat her with respect instead of issuing orders. I shall reconsider my wish to ride Storm."

They chatted amiably as they walked toward the house; then they parted in the front hall, Lady North to seek out the housekeeper and Grey to the library to meet with the solicitor. They didn't meet again until dinnertime, a meal that was served in the breakfast room, much to Benton's disapproval and Grey's delight. The huge formal dining room was cold and unfriendly, not designed for the exchange of confidences, and he needed to have a heart-to-heart talk with his mother.

"Have you made any plans for the future?" Grey asked after the servants had left them alone.

"You mean, do I intend to hang on your coattails?" Lady North fixed him with a keen glance as she sipped her wine.

"You've a right." He scowled at the excellent roast beef on his plate. "It is my duty."

"Greydon North, don't ever speak to me like that again." She slapped a hand against the table, setting the candles teetering in their holders. Startled, he looked up to find her shaking a finger in his face, her eyes stormy. "After all I've shown you, told you. You disappoint me, son. I thought you understood."

"I understand that you're happier as a widow than you were as a wife."

"But do you understand why?"

He shrugged and took a deep swallow of wine. "I presume because my father was a bad husband."

"By his own lights, he was a very good husband." His mother wouldn't let him off with an easy answer. "I had a home, servants, horses—anything money could buy. I had ease and leisure, was free to entertain my friends, his conjugal demands," she blushed but continued in a defiant tone while Grey squirmed in his chair, "his conjugal demands were minimal, especially once you were born. Everyone would say I had no cause to complain of my husband."

"Then, if he was such a satisfactory husband, why weren't you happy?" She'd succeeded in catching his full attention and he leaned forward across the table, genuinely trying to understand.

"Because he shut me out of the important things and because I was bored."

"Bored! With the running of this place? You had, what?"—he counted them off on his fingers—"a dozen household staff to manage, not to mention the extras hired when you had people to stay. You always had embroidery in your hands, a grand piano to play on, books to read . . ." He ran out of breath.

"The household staff pretended to consult me but they knew their jobs very well. Embroidery is considered a suitable occupation for a woman, no matter if she pricks her fingers twenty times an hour, and you should thank your lucky stars that I did not avail myself of the piano. As to the books"—she stabbed a morsel of beef onto her fork as ferociously as a soldier might ply his bayonet—"your father thought only books of sermons and insipid essays on country life were suitable reading for me. Heaven forbid I should read a novel, or study Shakespeare's plays, or indulge myself with poetry. Have you read Keats and Byron?" She waited expectantly for his reply.

"In school."

"And what did you think of them?"

"Overly moody for my taste. Why would anyone write an ode to melancholy?"

She chuckled. "Perhaps he was a bit preoccupied with

death—the poor man had consumption, after all—but he admitted to his feelings, Greydon, expressed sorrow and longing and joy and love." Her eyes were bright, her face lifted in a smile, and she leaned toward him with the eagerness of a young girl. But the brightness faded almost at once. "That's why your father forbade me to read them." She sat back in her chair, her mouth pulled into a tight line. "He thought it was unseemly for a woman of my station to experience strong emotions, let alone read of them."

She sighed and pushed her plate away. "But that's not what's important. The problem in our marriage was that your father didn't respect me. He had a fixed idea of what a proper wife should be, and he was determined to force me into that mold, regardless of my own inclinations."

"And if you'd been allowed to follow your own course? What sort of marriage would you have had, then?" Despite having already made up his mind that marriage was a trap designed to deprive men of their freedom, he found himself hanging on her words.

"We'd have had a partnership, a true and loving union of two complete people. Your father hated farming and left all the decisions about land management and stock breeding to his steward. To him the estate was a necessary appurtenance to denote his place in society, whereas I love the land. He wanted me to do a little genteel dabbling in the garden, but roses bore me. I wanted to oversee the cultivation of acres of crops. As far as the cattle were concerned," she made a small moue, "even after I'd borne a child I wasn't supposed to know about reproduction. No matter how many times I begged him to let me take a more active part in the estate, he refused. *A woman's place . . .*" she imitated her late husband's ranting tone of voice and thumped her fist on the table.

Despite himself, Grey chuckled. "And in this ideal partnership of yours," he asked, "how would his life have improved?"

"Are you playing devil's advocate, or do you really want to know?"

Emma's voice calling him a bully and refusing to marry him echoed in his mind. "I really want to know."

"He'd have had someone to share the burdens of responsibility, someone who could talk to him as an equal, bolster him up when troubles came, and someone to rejoice with when fortune smiled. He'd have had a loving, articulate, fascinating woman to share his life. He might have had more sons or a daughter." A deep sadness filled her eyes, a reflection of the loneliness of her life. "And he wouldn't have had to seek consolation from a whiskey bottle, or a London tart, or a fit of temper." She finished her litany with a sharp edge to her tongue.

"If you were so ill-suited, why did you marry in the first place?"

"My father, your grandfather, was even more adamant about a woman's place. When Alexander North came calling, he couldn't wait to hustle me to the altar. I didn't object"—she twisted the heavy ring on her left hand and sighed—"I thought, hoped, that as a wife I would have some influence. As a daughter I had none."

The door opened and Benton, accompanied by two serving girls, entered. He watched with an eagle eye as they cleared away the remains of the meal. "Will you take tea here, madam?" The butler looked as though he'd just encountered a nasty smell.

"No, Benton. Bring it to the library." Lady North

scowled at him and pushed her chair back before anyone could hold it for her.

"Yes, madam."

He really was an annoying fusspot, Grey thought as he escorted his mother into the cozy library. He looked forward to telling Benton and the rest of the staff that, as a consequence of his meeting with the solicitor that afternoon, they were now directly employed by Lady North and not by himself. He was grinning broadly when his mother poured him a cup of tea and demanded to know what was so funny.

When he told her she howled with laughter. "Oh, thank you, Greydon. I shall have such fun. I don't think I'll sack them, after all. It will be more amusing to watch them squirm when I give outrageous orders. Now, tell me," she said when their mirth had subsided, "why are you so interested in my views on marriage?"

"You seem to hold strong opinions on the subject." He leaned back in his chair, stretching his legs out before him and contemplating the scuffed toe of his boot, unwilling to meet her direct gaze.

"Tell me about her."

"She's beautiful and intelligent and unafraid and contrary and stubborn." He'd described Emma before he realized he'd never mentioned her to Lady North. "How did you know?"

"Mother's intuition?" She patted his hand. "So, what's the problem?"

"She won't marry me."

"You told your father you'd never wed."

"And I meant it. But I've compromised Emma. It's my duty to give her my name."

A small pillow struck the side of his head once and then again. His mother stood over him, the cushion in her hand and her eyes snapping with fury. "You stupid boy!"

"I know," he admitted his guilt. "She led me on, but that's no excuse."

"No, you obdurate oaf. Did you tell this Emma she had to marry you?"

"Of course." He looked in amazement at her blazing eyes. His father had always been the one to storm at him about respectable behavior, not his mother.

"Did you *ask* her to marry you?"

"Well, not in so many words." He tugged at his suddenly too-tight collar.

"No, you stamped around with big, clumsy feet and declared *you* would do *her* the honor of bestowing your title on her poor, unworthy head."

"It wasn't exactly like that." But it was close enough to make him feel like a fool. He stood up and walked to the fireplace, leaning his shoulder against the mantel.

"Do you want to marry her?" His mother pinned him with an uncompromising gaze, demanding an honest answer. "Do you love her?"

He hadn't thought of it that way before. He'd been so fixed on his obligation to Emma, he had never considered the state of his heart. Now, half a world away from her, he knew with blinding clarity that he did love her. His offer to marry her was more than mere duty. It was his fondest wish. "I do," he said in the dazed voice of one newly awakening from a deep sleep. "I love her."

"Truly? As someone you want to share the rest of your life with, not merely a pleasant interlude?"

"Yes." He was nodding now, his eyes widening as understanding grew. He turned toward his mother and caught her hands, tugging her into an exuberant hug. "But she won't have me." He suddenly remembered and strode about the room, his hands clasped behind his back, in perfect imitation of his father. "I've asked her, twice. The first time she ran away. The second time she ordered me from her house."

"I can't wait to meet her."

He looked over his shoulder, wondering if his mother hadn't understood that he'd been refused. She sat in the center of the sofa, her eyes as bright as stars. "No, I haven't lost my mind," she said, and patted the cushion beside her. "Come, sit down and tell me more about Emma."

"She's like no one I've ever met before." He tugged a hand through his hair and came to sit beside her. "She's the schoolmarm in Prospect." For twenty minutes he talked of Emma, of her spirit, her courage, her sharp tongue, and the way she made him laugh and how he hated being away from her.

When he finished his mother nodded, seemingly well pleased with the unhappy state of his heart. "I'm so happy for you, Greydon."

"Did I not explain that I'm miserable?"

"Yes, dear. That's what makes me so happy. If you weren't, then you're not truly in love."

"Did I also explain that she refused me?"

"How could she refuse when you never asked?" She held up her hand to silence his protest. "You told her. Now go back and get down on your knees and ask her, beg her to make you happy. Tell her you love her, promise to share all of your life with her. Promise you'll never shut her out. Tell her you need her. Then see if you don't get a different reply."

Hope sent his spirit soaring. He could be in Halifax within the month. He could . . . His elation evaporated.

"But what about you?" He gazed fondly at the mother he'd just begun to know. "I can't leave you here alone."

"You won't." She patted his knee, just as she had when he was a small boy who'd received a scolding and needed cheering up. "I've got the running of the estate to keep me busy and I've invited my old governess to come and keep me company. It was she who taught me my revolutionary ideas. We'll have great fun together, upsetting Benton and behaving as we please. When you've married your Emma, bring her to visit me, or maybe I'll visit you." Her eyes grew round and earnest. "Are there wild Indians in Prospect, Greydon? I've never seen a wild Indian."

He kissed her hand. She was determined to set him free, but he heard the sadness behind her teasing "You're wonderful, Mama." He used the childhoo name and hugged her hard. "If you come to Prospect, promise to introduce you to an Indian chief."

"And you'll write to me." She swallowed hard.

"Every week. And I think you should ask Keenan," h named a distant cousin, "to come and act as your facto Not that you aren't capable of dealing with the estat yourself," he added hastily as the storm clouds gathere in her eyes, "but to set my mind at rest. Besides, if yo come visiting me, you'll need someone here to manag things in your absence."

"Very well," she conceded, "for your sake."

Once her decision was made, Emma found the da flew by. The house that had been home to Everett Je gens but never felt like hers was sold. Mr. and Mr Fergus were provided with a pension. She placed h funds with the new federal bank, who promised her very comfortable return on her investments, and boug a ticket on a steamer to Victoria, then went shopping and came home with enough books to fill two trunks. Prospect needed a lending library. If she couldn't have her old job, she'd run a library. And she'd make Mrs. Allen take out a subscription. She might have left Prospect under a cloud, but she would return with her head high.

She knew a moment's sadness when she bid farewell to Janie, but it was more for a past friendship than for a present one. Janie had been a friend of her youth, but their lives were taking different directions. Even if she stayed in San Francisco, they'd grow apart. Janie would be the happiest of wives and mothers, but that would never be enough for Emma. The frontier was in her blood and she was going home.

At last she boarded ship, the same ship she'd sailed on the first time she'd left San Francisco, but this time was different. This time she left with no regrets and no guilt. This time she knew where her future lay. She watched the hills behind the harbor disappear into the mist, then set her face to the north, eager to join the builders and dreamers opening up the wilderness.

Storms slowed her passage from San Francisco to Victoria, but when she stepped onto a paddle wheeler in Gold City, bound for Prospect, the sun shone from a cloudless April sky. The streams and rivers ran full with spring runoff, and the earth was waking from its long winter sleep. The bright green of new growth tipped the dark evergreens that climbed the mountain slopes. The damp earth sprouted fresh grasses and tiny wildflowers. Birdsong flitted from treetop to treetop, filling the valley with the joy of spring.

Emma's spirits rose in answer, her excitement growing as the stern-wheeler neared the Prospect landing. This time she would start her new life filled with energy and enthusiasm. Her room with Bella Royston was assured, but as soon as possible she planned to have a house built for herself, a house that included a room for her library. She'd enlist Lottie O'Connor's aid in the project. She almost laughed aloud when she thought of Mrs. Allen's reaction to two disgraced schoolmarms setting up a public library and inviting the ladies of the town to subscribe. She might even start a discussion group, a monthly meeting where the housewives of Prospect could leave their chores and their domestic concerns to discuss literature and history and suffrage for women. Mrs. Allen wouldn't dare stay away.

The more she thought of it, the more her enthusiasm for the idea grew. She couldn't help wondering what Grey North would make of her project, but dismissed the thought. Grey was out of her life. She couldn't help loving him, but she wouldn't spend her life brooding on the "might-have-been." Nor would she settle for a marriage without love. A vision of the Hodders made her shudder. She set her mouth in a determined line. It seemed she was destined to spend her life as a spinster, far too exacting in her demands to make a comfortable wife. Hers would be a life filled with useful work, amply more satisfying than being harnessed in an unhappy marriage.

The ship's whistle roused her from her reverie. The had arrived. The time for dreaming had passed: the tim for action begun. The boat bumped against the pier an she went to supervise the disposition of her trunks. A well as the seeds of a public library, she'd brought bun dles of sheet music and the whole of her new wardrob including a fur coat. For a time, she would be the mo stylish woman in Prospect.

"You're going to need a team to haul all this up th

bank." The boatman scowled at the mountain of luggage waiting to be unloaded.

"You get it onto the dock. I'll see about delivering it to Miss Douglas's lodgings."

She whirled about so quickly she nearly lost her balance and had to clutch at the rail to keep from falling in the water. Grey North, broad-shouldered, handsome, and brimming with vitality, stood on the pier, eyeing her welter of luggage and grinning from ear to ear. He extended a hand to help her alight. Dazed, she put her fingers in his, felt the jolt of electricity that flowed between them at the slightest contact, and saw all her newfound resolve for independence explode in a shower of sparks as her eyes rested on his beloved face.

"I thought you'd gone back to Britain," she whispered when he'd consigned her luggage to the care of a freight wagon and escorted her to his shiny buggy.

"I did." He placed both hands on her waist and swung her up onto the seat before she could object. He stood looking up at her, squinting into the sunshine. "But I couldn't stay away. Not from the wilderness and not from you."

Her heart pounded with longing. More than anything she wanted to spend her life with this man. Wanted to see the sunlight glinting on his hair as it turned from gold to silver. Wanted to share her dreams with him. Wanted to grow old, secure in his love. She turned her face away. He didn't love her. "Nothing has changed, Grey." She clasped her fingers tightly together in her lap. "I appreciate your consideration, but I won't marry you."

"Ah, Emma, everything has changed." He leaped up onto the seat beside her and picked up the reins, easily turning his horses and heading them up the steep road that led from the dock to the town laid out along the embankment above. "I've changed and so have you." He cocked his head to admire her traveling outfit. "Most fetching." He let his eyes run over her from the tip of the feather curling around the brim of her hat to the fashionable heels on her buttoned boots.

She blushed and couldn't help sending him a coy look from under her lashes, but quickly took herself in hand. "Compliments won't change my mind. I've means of my own now. I'm going to have my own house and open a library."

"Really!" Grey seemed more delighted than disturbed by her announcement. "I hope your house has plenty of bedrooms. My mother plans to come for a long visit and we'll need space for the children."

"There is no child." She blushed so hotly she felt her face was on fire. "As you can see"—she sat up very straight and placed a hand on her slim waist—"there is no need for you to continue pressing your suit." She folded her hands together and sat primly silent and erect for several seconds before exclaiming, "Where are we going? Mrs. Royston lives over there." She pointed back at the street they had just passed. "She's expecting me."

"I told her you would be delayed."

"Of all the arrogant, high-handed, presumptuous men in the world, Grey North, you are the worst! Take me to Mrs. Royston's at once."

Grey chuckled and kept the horses moving forward. "It's good to have you back, Emma. Apart from my mother, you're the only woman I know who puts me in my place." He turned the horses down a narrow, grassy track overarched with newly leafed birches. A few minutes later he drew the team to a halt. "Look." He looped the reins around the brake and pointed to a carpet of pink fairy-slipper that spread under the trees and trailed down to a tiny stream.

"Oh!" She caught her breath in delight, overlooking, for the moment, that Grey had brought her here without her permission. "It's beautiful."

"Not as beautiful as you." He took her chin in his fingers and turned her face to his. "Your sea-green eyes are more lovely than the new grass, your face is finer to look upon than the spring flowers. You are dearer to me, Emma, than even the wilderness in April. Don't look so befuddled," he laughed as she stared in open-mouthed amazement. "My mother told me if I wanted to win your heart, I'd study the poets. And I do want to win your heart, my dearest love." The humor still twinkled in his eyes, but behind the laughter lurked a yearning that lifted her heart to sing with the birds.

"I am presumptuous and high-handed, Emma. I can't promise never to annoy you. But I do promise to respect you, to listen to you, and to share my whole life with you, if you'll let me. I love you, dearest Emma. I humbly beg you to do me the very great honor of becoming my wife."

"You love me?" she breathed. "You're not just bowing to some code of honor?"

"I love you with a love as broad as this land, as untamed as the frontier. I loved you since first we met, but I was too puffed up in my own conceit to realize it. I'd convinced myself that marriage was only for fools. I was the fool, Emma. I ask for no greater happiness than to have you for my wife. I'll spend the rest of my days adoring you, and I promise to find you as fascinating on our fiftieth anniversary as I do today." He held her face between his hands, his mouth a mere breath away from hers.

"I'm still going to start a library." Her voice was choked with emotion. She wanted to say yes, she wanted him to kiss her, she wanted to pour out her love for him, but she needed to assert her independence as well.

"I'll help you."

"And I'll organize a women's study group."

"I'll convince the Miners Association to make a donation."

"Even if I use it to buy Mrs. Hartley's *Ladies' Book on Etiquette and Deportment*?"

He winced but answered fair. "I'll leave it to your best judgment." He brushed his lips lightly over hers. "You haven't given me an answer, Emma. Surely that violates one of Mrs. Hartley's precepts."

Her heart lifted with joy. She floated as light and free as the birds. "I don't give a fig for Mrs. Hartley." She threw her arms about his neck. "Kiss me, Grey."

He did. Their embrace was long and thorough, and when at last they broke apart, they were both breathless and her smart new hat had been knocked sideways to hang over one ear. "Is that a yes?" Grey tucked an escaping tendril of hair behind her ear.

"Oh, yes," said Emma.